About the Authors

Jane Porter loves central California's golden foothills and miles of farmland, rich with the sweet and heady fragrance of orange blossoms. Her parents fed her imagination by taking Jane to Europe for a year where she became passionate about Italy and those gorgeous Italian men! Jane never minds a rainy day – that's when she sits at her desk and writes stories about far-away places, fascinating people, and most important of all, love. Visit her website at: www.janeporter.com

Clare Connelly was raised in small-town Australia among a family of avid readers. She spent much of her childhood up a tree, Mills & Boon book in hand. Clare is married to her own real-life hero, and they live in a bungalow near the sea with their two children. She is frequently found staring into space – a surefire sign she is in the world of her characters. She has a penchant for French food and ice-cold champagne, and Mills & Boon novels continue to be her favourite-ever books. Writing for Mills & Boon is a long-held dream. Clare can be contacted via clareconnelly.com or on her Facebook page.

Annie West has devoted her life to an intensive study of charismatic heroes who cause the best kind of trouble in the lives of their heroines. As a sideline she researches locations for romance, from vibrant cities to desert encampments and fairytale castles. Annie lives in eastern Australia with her hero husband, between sandy beaches and gorgeous wine country. She finds writing the perfect excuse to postp~~~~ ~~~~ ~~~~ ~~~~ her or join her newsl~~~~ ~~~~

Greek Playboys

December 2021
A Price to Pay

January 2022
A League of Their Own

February 2022
Hidden Heirs

March 2022
Unbending Demands

April 2022
The Ultimate Game

May 2022
A Deal in Passion

Greek Playboys:
A League of their Own

JANE PORTER

CLARE CONNELLY

ANNIE WEST

MILLS & BOON

First Published in Great Britain 2022
By Mills & Boon, an imprint of HarperCollins*Publishers,* Ltd
1 London Bridge Street, London, SE1 9GF

www.harpercollins.co.uk

HarperCollins*Publishers*
1st Floor, Watermarque Building,
Ringsend Road, Dublin 4, Ireland

GREEK PLAYBOYS: A LEAGUE OF THEIR OWN
© 2022 Harlequin Books S.A.

The Prince's Scandalous Wedding Vow © 2019 Jane Porter
Bought for the Billionaire's Revenge © 2017 Clare Connelly
The Greek's Forbidden Princess © 2017 Annie West

ISBN: 978-0-263-30406-0

MIX
Paper from
responsible sources
FSC™ C007454

This book is produced from independently certified FSC™ paper
to ensure responsible forest management.

For more information visit: www.harpercollins.co.uk/green

Printed and Bound in Spain using 100% Renewable electricity at
CPI Black Print, Barcelona

THE PRINCE'S
SCANDALOUS
WEDDING VOW

JANE PORTER

For Lee Hyat.

Thank you for being my first reader, my friend,
and my cheerleader.

This one is for you!

PROLOGUE

PRINCE ALEXANDER JULIUS ALBERICI had known change was coming. His June 27 wedding to Princess Danielle would require a return to his Mediterranean island kingdom, Aargau, for prewedding festivities. After the ceremony and reception, a two-week honeymoon had been planned, and then he'd finally be free to return to Paris with his bride, where he oversaw an international environmentalist group focused on improving sustainability in fragile ecosystems.

His work was his passion, and Danielle had expressed support for his work—a positive in an arranged marriage. She'd also agreed at the time of their betrothal to live wherever he chose, understanding that ultimately they'd end up in Aargau as soon as Alexander needed to step into his father's shoes and ascend the throne.

But that day—replacing his father—was supposed to have been years away, decades away, as his father was a strong, athletic man and a vigorous, powerful king. Or he had been, until his winter cold lingered into early spring, a nagging cough that wouldn't clear even with antibiotics. And then in mid-April came the diagnosis of lung cancer and now King Bruno Titus Alberici had been given months to live. *Months.*

It was unthinkable, unfathomable. Alexander had never been close to his father—King Bruno might be beloved by the people, but he was cold and unforgiving behind closed doors—yet Alexander couldn't imagine the world without his fierce, unapologetic father. Now his father was determined to manage his death, just as he'd managed his life—without emotion or weakness. To that end, there would be no changes in palace life or protocol. Alexander's late-

June wedding would not be moved forward. Bruno's illness would not be made public. There would be no changes in wedding date or venue. There would be no acknowledgment of ill health. There would be nothing to alarm the people until an announcement had to be made, which in King Alberici's mind was notice of his death.

His mother, the queen, agreed with the plan because that was what she did—supported her husband. It had been her role from day one of their marriage, and she'd fulfilled her responsibilities. Now it was time for Alexander to fulfill his, which was to marry and have an heir so the monarchy would live on.

Alexander stirred restlessly, feeling trapped in his cabin, even though it was by far the largest on the ship. He pushed open the sliding door and stepped out onto the balcony, leaning on the railing to stare blindly out at the sea.

This trip, organized by his closest friends, had been a mistake. He couldn't relax. He felt guilty being on a pleasure cruise when his father was growing weaker at home, and yet both his parents had insisted he go, determined that he keep up appearances.

The trip was to have been a last hurrah before the wedding preparations began in earnest. Princes didn't do bachelor or stag parties, so instead, Prince Alexander Alberici's best friend, Gerard, had organized a week cruising the Aegean and Ionian Seas. Troubled by his father's swift decline, Alexander had left the details to his friends, knowing they were far more excited about this last adventure—concerned that it might indeed be their last adventure—but now wished he'd been part of the planning, at least when it came to approving the guest list.

The yacht itself was impressive. Large, new, and the very definition of luxurious, with two different pools, a hot tub, a sports court, a disco, and a movie theater. But the luxurious appointments couldn't make up for the fact that it was a boat, and they were all trapped together—not a problem if everyone was on good terms, but inexplicably Gerard had permitted Alexander's cousin, Damian Anton Alberici, to bring his girlfriend, Claudia, along.

It wouldn't have been an issue if Claudia didn't also happen to be Alexander's ex-girlfriend, and their breakup six months earlier had been acrimonious at best. He'd been stunned and uncomfortable when he discovered Damian was now dating Claudia, but to bring her on this trip? Why make it awkward for everyone?

Alexander's jaw tightened, his gaze narrowed on the pale rocky island ahead, each island so like the last.

The tension on the yacht just made him eager to return home, which was saying something as home wasn't exactly pleasant, either. His mother was struggling to come to terms with his father's terminal diagnosis. Virtually overnight his father had wasted away, his strong frame increasingly frail. The palace staff, sworn to secrecy, were incredibly anxious, tiptoeing around, walking on eggshells. And yet no one discussed what was happening. But that was because they didn't talk in his family, not about personal things. There was no sharing of feelings and certainly no acknowledgment of emotions. There was only duty, and he understood that all too well.

The sooner the wedding took place, the better, and Princess Danielle Roulet would be a good match. She was lovely and well-bred, and fluent in numerous languages, which was essential in Aargau's next queen. She was also sophisticated and would be a stylish princess, something he knew his people would appreciate. It was not a love match, but it would be a successful marriage because they both understood their duties and responsibilities, and best of all, the wedding would give the people of Aargau something to celebrate, which was sorely needed when the crown would soon change hands.

Now, if he could only get off this yacht and get back to his family—who did need him, despite what his parents might say, or not say—because Alexander was finding nothing pleasurable in this last bachelor getaway.

CHAPTER ONE

JOSEPHINE JUST WANTED the yacht to leave.

Why was it still here? The Mediterranean was huge. Greece alone had hundreds of islands. Couldn't the yacht go somewhere else? The luxury pleasure boat had been anchored outside the cove of her tiny island, Khronos, for two days, and after forty-eight hours of endless partying, blaring music, and shrill laughter, she'd had enough.

The revelers had even come onto the island earlier in the day, their testosterone-fueled speedboat racing them to shore. Jo had hidden behind the cliffs and trees above, watching as the dozen hedonists descended on her beach.

The young women were stunning—tan, lithe, and beautiful in tiny, barely-there bikinis—and the men were lean, chiseled, and handsome. While the women splashed in the surf and then lounged on the beach, the men sprawled on chairs and towels in the sun, looking like indolent princes. They were there to party, too, and there was plenty of alcohol and other things that made Josephine wrinkle her nose in disgust. Only one of them didn't drink, or smoke, or make love on the beach. Sometimes he sat on his own, but other times, people surrounded him. He was clearly the center of the group, the one with the wealth, the sun around which all the others orbited.

She watched the revelers out of curiosity and with a sprinkling of disdain, telling herself not to judge, but the interlopers on her beach clearly enjoyed a pampered, decadent lifestyle, a lifestyle for those born of privilege, or those lucky enough to be invited into the elite circle. Her dad used to say she was critical of such people because she'd never be one of them, and maybe there was some truth in that.

But she liked to use her brain, and she enjoyed her work assisting her father, who was one of the world's leading volcanologists, which was why they lived in the middle of the Aegean Sea, taking advantage of Greece's volcanic arc.

Her work included documenting her father's findings, and she'd proved indispensable to his research. He was the first to admit that he wouldn't have his enormous body of work without her assistance. But late in the day, she'd turn to her passion—drawing, sketching, painting. She had run low on paper and canvas again, but her father would be returning in ten days, and he always brought back fresh supplies for her.

This afternoon she carried her sketch pad with her to the rocks overlooking the sheltered beach cove, thinking she'd draw the scene below—well, not everyone, but the one who'd caught her attention. The one man she thought was by far the most fascinating. He appeared otherworldly with his thick dark hair and straight black brows over light-colored eyes—blue or gray she didn't know. But even from a distance the lines of his face appealed to the artist in her: his jaw was square, cheekbones high, his mouth full, firm, unsmiling.

Her charcoal pencil hovered over the page as she studied the face she'd drawn. His features were almost too perfect, his lower lip slightly fuller than his upper lip, and she just wished she was closer so she could see the color of his eyes.

Even more intriguing was the way he sat in his chair, broad shoulders level, chin up, body still, exuding power and control. Josephine glanced up from the sketch to compare her work to the real man, and yes, she'd captured the sinewy, muscular frame as well as the hard set of his jaw and chin, but his expression wasn't quite right. It was his expression that intrigued her and made her want to keep looking at him and trying to understand him. Was he bored, or unhappy? Why did he look as if he wanted to be anywhere but on that beach, with these people?

He was a mystery, and she enjoyed a good puzzle. It gave her mind something to focus on, but now he was rising, and everyone else was rising, gathering their things and heading to the boat.

Good, she told herself, closing her sketchbook, and yet she couldn't help feeling a stab of disappointment as the speedboat whisked her mystery man back to the massive yacht anchored outside her cove, because he was, without a doubt, the most interesting man she'd ever seen, and now he was gone.

Later that evening, Josephine was returning from doing her last check of the equipment in the cottage when she heard loud voices, as if in argument, from just outside the cove. She crossed to the beach, listening intently, but this time she heard nothing, just the sound of the yacht engine humming. Was the yacht finally leaving?

As usual, it was brightly lit and pulsing with music. On the top deck she could see couples lounging and drinking. There were others on a deck below and then others at the far end of the yacht, in the shadows.

The yacht was moving. She could see the moonlight reflecting off the white wake. She was sorry to see her mystery man leave, but glad the noise would be gone. The music was terrible. She was still standing there when she heard a muffled shout and then saw someone go overboard. It was at the back of the yacht, where people had been on a lower deck in the shadows.

She rushed closer to the water's edge, attention fixed on the point where the person had gone into the water, but no one resurfaced. Sick, panicked, Josephine worried that someone could be drowning. She couldn't just stand idle while someone died.

She yanked off her sundress and dived between the

waves to swim out to where the yacht had been anchored
for the past two and a half days. Diving beneath the surface
of the water, she struggled to see in the gloom, but all was
dark, so dark, and the reef dropped off dramatically not
far from her, the coral giving way to deep water. Josephine
swam with her hands in front of her, searching, reaching,
lungs burning, bursting, and just when she was going to
push back to the surface, she felt fabric, and then heat. A
chest. Shoulders. Big, thick shoulders. A man.

She prayed for help as she circled his neck with her
arm, hoping for divine strength because she needed su-
perpowers in that moment, her own lungs seizing, desperate for air.

With a groan, she pulled up and he rose with her. Not
quickly, but he was floating as she swam, his huge body
heavy, but she'd never swum with such resolve. She'd grown
up in the ocean. She'd spent her life swimming, deep, exploring caves and the reef, and even though spots danced
before her eyes she told herself she could do this because
she wasn't alone. She had faith that she was meant to be
there when the body fell overboard, and she was meant to
find him, and she was meant to save him.

And she did.

She surfaced and, gasping for air, towed him to shore.
Once she'd dragged him out of the waves, she kept pulling,
hoping she wasn't hurting him as she wrestled him onto the
firm damp sand. Once she knew they were out of the surf,
she rolled him onto his side, allowing water to drain from
his mouth and nose, before settling him onto his back. It
was only then she realized it was him.

The beautiful brooding man.

The one who'd barely seemed to tolerate the others.

The one who suffered no fools.

She'd never had to resuscitate anyone before, but her
father had taught her years ago, and she remembered the

basics, although guidelines kept changing every year or two. She pinched his nose closed and then breathed into his mouth with five strong breaths, followed by thirty chest compressions. She put her ear near his mouth and listened. Nothing. She heard nothing. She repeated the cycle with two strong breaths into his mouth and another thirty compressions. After each cycle, she listened and watched his chest, checking for signs of life.

She wouldn't give up. *Breathe, breathe, breathe*, she chanted in her head, repeating the cycle, praying as she did, asking for divine help, not at all prepared to lose him.

Breathe, breathe, breathe.

Live, live, live.

Just when she was sure her efforts were pointless, his chest lifted—not much, but it moved, and it was enough to give her hope. Determined, Jo breathed into his mouth, those two strong breaths, and this time she felt air exhale from his lips and saw a definite rise and fall of his chest. His breath was rough and raspy, but it was a breath. It wasn't her imagination. He was alive.

Her eyes stung with tears. Her hands began to shake as she shoved her long, wet hair behind her ears, overwhelmed and exhausted. The sheer enormity of it all hit her, and she sat back on her heels, shoulders sagging. She'd saved him. But now what? What was she to do with him?

Her adrenaline faded, and she began trembling in earnest, wiped out. She didn't know how she'd managed any of it. She was a good swimmer, a strong swimmer, but it was a miracle she'd been able to find him and pull him to the shore. He needed medical help, and she had no way to call for assistance. Her radio was broken. Her dad would be bringing a new one when he returned, but that wasn't for days. Ordinarily, she wouldn't mind being cut off— she'd gone weeks before without communication—but this was different.

Her brow creased as she glanced out toward the sea, the mouth of the cove empty, the moonlight reflecting brightly on the water, the only sign of the yacht a distant glow of yellow light on the horizon.

How did no one notice that he'd gone overboard? How could they go without him?

Gently, she stroked his hair back from his brow, only then noting the blood matting the thick hair at his temple. He was injured, and from the nasty gash on his forehead, he'd been injured before he'd fallen—or been pushed— overboard.

She'd heard raised voices. She'd heard a fight. It was what had drawn her attention—that and the hum of the yacht engine. From the mark on his brow it looked as if someone had struck him. Why?

He blinked, trying to focus. His head hurt. Pain radiated through him. He struggled to sit but the world tilted and swam around him. He blinked again, not understanding why everything was so blurry. It was almost as if he was underwater and yet, through the haze, he saw a woman leaning over him, her face above his, her expression worried.

He struggled to place her. How did he know her? Did he know her?

The effort to think was too much. He gave up trying to focus and closed his eyes, sinking back into oblivion.

Pain woke him again.

A heavy, brutal pounding in his head made him stir, his eyes slowly, carefully opening, trying to minimize the ache in his head.

It was day, either early or late he didn't know because the light was soft, diffused.

A woman was moving around the room. She wore a loose white dress, the gauzy fabric fluttering around her bare legs. She paused at the small square window, her brow creasing as she gazed out. Her hair was long and straight, falling almost to her waist.

For a moment he wondered if she was an angel. For a moment he wondered if he had died and gone to heaven. Not that he deserved to go to heaven. Strange thought, but true. He struggled to rise but immediately felt nauseous.

Biting back a curse, he slowly sank back against the pillow, realizing he wasn't dead—or at least, he wasn't in heaven. He couldn't be, not if he hurt this much.

His muffled groan must have reached the angel girl, as she turned in her white dress, the delicate fabric floating behind her as she moved toward him, so young, so beautiful he was certain she wasn't real.

Perhaps he was feverish. Perhaps he was hallucinating, because as she knelt next to him, the sun's rays seemed to narrow and cast a glow around her, highlighting her long golden-brown hair, her smooth brow, and the high, elegant cheekbones above her full lips.

Maybe hell was filled with angelic beauties.

He was finally coming to. Josephine moved forward, crouching at his side. "Hello," she said in English, before it struck her that it was unlikely English was his native language. Most of the conversation she'd heard on the beach had been French, while others had spoken Italian. "How are you?" she asked in French.

He blinked and struggled to focus, his eyes a brilliant blue, contrasting with his long, dense black lashes.

She tried Italian next. "How do you feel?"

His brow tightened. He grimaced, responding in Italian. *"Tu chei sei?"* Who are you?

"Josephine," she answered, as he slowly reached up to touch his head, where a crust had formed on his cut. "Careful," she added in Italian. "You've been injured. It's finally stopped bleeding."

"What happened?"

"You went over the side of your yacht."

"A yacht?" he repeated in Italian.

"Yes. You were with friends."

"Dove sono?" he murmured, his voice a deep rasp. *Where am I?*

"Khronos. A small island off Anafi," she answered.

"I don't know it."

"Anafi is very small. No one knows Anafi, and Khronos is even smaller. It's privately held, a research site for the International Volcanic Research Foundation—" She broke off as she realized he wasn't listening, or at least, he wasn't processing what she was saying, his features tight with pain. "Do you hurt right now?"

He nodded once. "My head," he gritted.

She reached out to place a palm against his brow. He was cooler now, thank goodness. "You were running a fever last night, but I think it's gone now." She drew her hand back, studying him. "I'd like to see if you can manage some water, and if you can, then we'll try some soup—"

"I'm not hungry. I just want something for the pain."

"I have tablets that should help with the headache, but I think you should eat first. Otherwise I'm worried it'll upset your stomach."

He looked at her as if he didn't understand, or perhaps he didn't believe her, because his blue eyes were narrowing and his mouth firmed, emphasizing his strong jaw, now shadowed with a dark stubble.

He'd been striking from afar, but up close he was absolutely devastating, his black hair and brows such a contrast to his startlingly blue eyes. His features were mature and chiseled. Faint creases fanned from his eyes.

As his gaze met hers and held, her pulse jumped. "It's been almost a full day since I pulled you out of the sea—"

"How?" he interrupted.

"How?" she repeated.

"How did I get here?"

"Your boat. Your yacht—"

"I don't understand this yacht." The wrinkles in his forehead deepened. He struggled into a sitting position, wincing and cursing under his breath. His hand lifted to his temple, where the wound was beginning to bleed again. "When was I on one?"

"The past few days. Probably the past week or more." She sat back on her haunches, studying him. "Do you not remember?"

He shook his head.

"What do you remember?"

He thought for a moment, and then his broad, sunbronzed shoulders shifted irritably, impatiently. "Nothing." His voice was hard, his diction crisp. Authority and tension crackled around him.

Her jaw dropped ever so slightly. "You don't remember who you are? Your name? Your age?"

"No. But I do know I need to find a bathroom. Can you show me the way?"

He had questions for her later, many questions, and Josephine fought to hide her anxiety over his complete loss of memory. She prepared them a simple dinner, talking to him as she plated the grilled vegetables and lemon-garlic chicken. "I think you must be Italian," she said, carrying the plates to the small rustic table in the center of the room. The table divided the room, creating the illusion of two spaces, the sitting area and then the kitchen. "It was the first language you responded to."

"I don't feel Italian." He grimaced. "Although I'm not

sure what that even means. Can a person feel their nationality?"

"I don't know," she answered, sitting down across from him. "But I suppose if I woke up somewhere else I'd be puzzled by the different cultural norms."

"Tell me about the people I was with."

"They were all about your age. Although some of the girls seemed younger. They all looked…polished. Affluent." She hesitated. "Privileged."

He said nothing.

"Everyone seemed to be having a good time," she added. "Except for you."

He glanced at her swiftly, gaze narrowing.

"I don't know if you were bored, or troubled by something," she added, "but you tended to be off on your own more than the others. And they gave you your space, which made me think you were perhaps the leader."

"The leader?" he repeated mockingly. "The leader of what? A band of thieves? Pirates? Schoolboys on holiday?"

"You don't need to be rude," she said slowly, starting to rise, wanting to move away, but he reached out and caught her, his fingers circling her narrow wrist, holding her in place.

"Don't go."

She looked down to where his hand wrapped her wrist, his skin so very warm against hers. She suppressed a shudder, feeling undone. She was exhausted from watching over him, exhausted from worrying. It had been a long night and day, and now it was night again and she felt stretched to the breaking point. "I'm just trying to help you," she said quietly, tugging free.

He released her. "I'm sorry." His deep voice dropped. "Please sit. Stay."

His words were kind, but his tone was commanding. Clearly he was accustomed to being obeyed.

Her brow furrowed. She didn't want to create friction, and so she slowly sat back down and picked up her fork, but she felt too fatigued to actually eat.

Silence stretched. She could feel him watching her. His scrutiny wasn't making things easier, and she knew his eye color now. Blue, light, bright aquamarine blue. Blue like her sea. Reluctantly, she looked up, her stomach in knots. "I thought you were hungry," she said, aware that he hadn't yet taken a bite, either.

"I'm waiting for you."

"I've lost my appetite."

"The company you're keeping?"

She cracked a small smile. "The company's fine. I think I'm unusually tired tonight."

"I suspect you were up all night worrying about me."

It was true. She hadn't been sure he'd survive. There were complications for those who'd nearly drowned. "But you made it through, and here you are."

"Without a memory, or a name."

"I suppose we should call you something."

"Perhaps," he said, but it was clear from his tone that he didn't agree and wasn't enthusiastic about being called by a name that was probably not his.

"We could try names out, see if anything resonates."

He gave her a long, hard look that made her stomach do a funny little flip. "I'll say names and you tell me if anything feels right," she pressed on.

"Fine."

"Matthew. Mark. Luke. John."

"I'm fairly certain I'm not an apostle."

Her lips twitched. "You know your Bible stories, then."

"Yes, but I don't like this approach. I want my own name, or no name." He stabbed his fork into his dinner but made no attempt to eat. "Tell me about you," he said, turning the tables. "Why are you here on what appears to be a deserted island?"

"Well, it's not deserted—it's an island that serves a scientific purpose, housing one of the five research stations for the International Volcano Foundation. My father is a professor, a volcanologist. We were supposed to be here for a year but it's been almost eight."

"Where is he now?"

"Hawaii." She saw his expression and added, "He is a professor at the University of Hawaii. He juggles the teaching and the fieldwork. Right now he's back in Honolulu, lecturing, but he'll return end of the month, which is now just nine days away."

"And he has left you alone here?"

She hesitated. "Does it seem strange to you?"

"Yes."

Her shoulders shifted. "It's actually normal for me, and I don't mind. I like the solitude. I'm not much of a people person. And the quiet allows me a chance to do my own work, because when Papa is here, it's always about him."

"What about your mother?"

"She died just before I turned five."

"I'm sorry."

She shrugged again, uncomfortable with the sympathy. "I don't remember her."

"Would she approve of your lifestyle here?"

"She was a volcanologist like my father. They worked together for ten years, doing exactly what he's doing now, but in Hawaii, so yes, I think she'd approve. Perhaps her only disappointment would be that I haven't gone off to college or earned all the degrees that she did. I've been home-schooled my entire life, even with the university courses. My father says I'm more advanced than even his graduate students, but it's not the same. I've never had to be in the real world or compete with others for work. I just work."

"What is your field of study?"

"I'm a volcanologist, too, although personally I prefer the point where archaeology intersects with volcanology."

"Vesuvius?"

She nodded. "Exactly. I've been lucky to work with my father on the volcanology of the southwestern sector of Vesuvius, where archaeological and historical data have allowed scientists to map the lava emitted in the last several thousand years. I'm fascinated by not just the lost civilizations, but the power of these volcanoes to reshape the landscape and rewrite the history of man."

"It doesn't sound as if you've missed anything by being homeschooled."

She smiled faintly. "I haven't been properly socialized— my father said as much. I'm not comfortable in cities and crowds. But fortunately, we don't have that problem here."

"Your mother was American, too?"

"French-Canadian, from Quebec. That's how I ended up Josephine." Her smile faded as she saw how his expression changed, his jaw tightening and lips compressing. "You *will* remember your name," she said quietly. "It's just going to be a matter of time."

"You spoke to me in French, didn't you?"

"I tried a number of languages. You responded in Italian, so I've stuck with Italian. *Est-ce que tu parles français?*"

"*Oui.*"

"And English?" she asked, switching languages again. "Do you understand me?"

He nodded. "I do."

"How fluent are you?" she asked, continuing in English, testing him. "Is it difficult to follow me?"

"No. It doesn't seem any different from Italian."

He had almost no accent, his English was easy, his diction relaxed, making him sound American, not British. She suspected he'd been educated at one point in the United States. "Would you mind speaking English then?"

"No."

"But should it give you a headache, or if it creates any stress—"

"No need to fuss over me. I'm fine."

She opened her mouth to protest but thought better of it. He was a man used to having the final word. So who was he? And why did he, even now, ooze power?

"Tell me again about the people I was with on the yacht," he said. "Tell me everything you know."

"I will after you eat something."

"I'm not hungry anymore."

"That's strange, because my memory seems to be fading, as well."

He gave her a hard look. "I'm not amused."

"Neither am I. You've been through a great deal, and we need to get you strong. And as I am your primary caregiver here—"

"I don't like being coddled."

"And I'm not known to coddle, so eat, and I'll tell you everything. Don't eat, and you can fret by yourself because I have things to do besides argue with you."

His eyes narrowed and his jaw hardened, making a small muscle in his jaw pop. For a long moment he just looked at her, clearly not happy with the situation, but then he reached for the plate of chicken and took a bite, and then another, and did a pretty impressive job of devouring the rest. He lifted his head at one point and met her gaze. "This is good, by the way. Very good."

"Thank you."

"You made this?"

"Yes."

"Here?"

"Yes."

"How?"

"I have a freezer, and I use the kiln outside for roasting the potatoes and baking. The rest I prepare on the stove."

"A kiln?"

"It makes excellent flatbreads, and pizzas, too. I learned how to cook in a kiln when we lived in Peru. That was before here. I loved Peru. My father loved the stratovolcano." She smiled faintly, remembering his excitement and obsession as Sabancaya roared to life, spewing ash and rumbling the mountain. If it weren't for the village women, Josephine would have been forgotten. Instead they took her and her father in and helped teach Josephine to cook, and as a thank-you, Josephine would look after the children, giving the hardworking mothers a break.

"Where else have you lived?"

"Washington State, Hawaii, Peru, and Italy, but that was brief, before here. We've been here the longest."

"Was every place this isolated?"

"No, this is definitely the most remote, but I'm truly happy here."

"Is that why you just watched us on the beach and didn't come introduce yourself?"

She laughed as she reached for his plate. "I think we come from different worlds. I am quite sure I'd be an oddity in your world."

His brow creased. "You think so?"

"Absolutely. I wouldn't know how to drape myself over and around handsome men." Her lips twitched. "I can't for the life of me just lie on a beach. I need to be active, and instead of sunbathing I'd be catching fish, and examining the water table, and trying to figure out the volcanic history of the exposed rocks—" she broke off. "Not your kind of girl at all."

"What is my kind?"

"The kind that looks like a swimsuit model. The kind

that doesn't lift anything, not even her own swim bag. The kind that pouts when you don't feel like talking."

"Interesting," he drawled, blue eyes glinting.

"How so?"

"You didn't like my friends. You never said that earlier. This is new information."

"I shouldn't have said anything. It's not factual and not important—"

"But revealing about you."

"Exactly. There is no reason to share my feelings on anything. I should be focused on assisting you. Who I am and what I feel isn't relevant in any way."

"You're allowed to have opinions."

"I'll voice them if they'll be helpful. Me judging your female friends isn't helpful. It's just me being petty and unkind and unnecessary."

"Why do I feel like you are a rare breed?"

"Because I am strange. I don't fit in. I never have."

"Sounds a bit defeatist, don't you think?"

"I would agree with you if I were here licking my wounds. But I'm here by choice, because I'm happy here. I sleep well here. I can breathe here. I don't feel odd or different, and on Khronos I don't second-guess myself, and that's a good thing."

"You're saying society makes you uncomfortable."

"Absolutely." She carried his plate and fork to the small sink in her very small kitchen and felt his gaze bore into her back as she filled the small plastic dish tub with water to let them soak. "But I've been raised outside society so it's to be expected."

"Have you ever lived in a city?"

"Honolulu."

"Is that a proper city?"

She turned and shot him a disapproving look. "Yes. Honolulu has some beautiful architecture and it has a fascinating history. Hawaii isn't just beaches and surfing." She didn't tell him, though, that she didn't enjoy going back to Oahu anymore because it was too urban for her now. There were far too many cars and people and it had been overwhelming, which was why she'd elected to remain behind on Khronos while her father went to teach.

She turned away from the sink, wiped her hands dry on a dish towel and carried the water carafe to the table. "There were maybe twelve of you that came onto the beach," she said, taking her seat again. "Seven men, including you, and five women. The yacht was huge. One of the biggest, most luxurious yachts I've ever seen. Your group would come onto the beach during the day and everyone would swim and sunbathe, eat and drink." She shot him a long look. "There was lots of drinking. Everyone seemed to be having a good time."

"And the night I went overboard?"

"There was music playing—as always—and a party. As always. Your friends were on the top two decks—the top deck you all used as a disco, so the music and dancing were there, but there were others on the second deck, and I wasn't sure if they were in a hot tub or a pool, but people there were just hanging out, talking and laughing. But what got my attention on that last night was the arguing at the back of the yacht. I heard voices, or thought I heard voices, and things sounded like they were getting a little heated. It was what caught my attention and what drew me to the edge of the water."

"*I* was arguing?" he asked quietly.

She hesitated, frowning. "Yes. No. I don't actually know that it was you. I just heard arguing, and then there was a shout and a splash. I couldn't see that well and for a second wondered if someone had maybe jumped overboard, but when the person went under and didn't resurface, I panicked and raced out."

"Saving me."

She tapped her fingers on the table, suddenly uncomfortable. "I didn't know it was you. I just knew someone was in trouble."

"That couldn't have been an easy swim."

"No, but I was terrified you were going to drown. I couldn't let it happen."

"You risked your life for a stranger."

"What is the point of being a strong swimmer if I can't save someone now and then?"

She'd deliberately kept her tone light, wanting to ease the tension.

He didn't smile. "I would have died without you."

"But you didn't. Now we just need to get your memory back, and all will be well." She gave him a bright smile and then rose, moving around the room, adjusting the shutters to give them more of the evening's breeze, and then taking her broom and sweeping out some sand that had found its way inside.

She could feel his gaze on her the entire time and it made her skin prickle and heat. She felt herself flush and her pulse quicken. He watched her the way surfers watched the waves—with focus and quiet intensity. It was unnerving and she suddenly wanted to adjust her skirt and gather her hair. She wanted to be pretty and worth the attention—

Josephine gave her head a shake.

She couldn't try to be someone she wasn't. She'd done that in the past, in Honolulu, for example, and it had been disastrous. "Judging from your accent," she said crisply, giving the threshold one last hard sweep of the broom, "you could be from Belgium, Luxembourg, France, Italy, Switzerland, Monaco, Sicily, Malta, Aargau—maybe even America. You've certainly managed to nail the American drawl."

He grimaced. "I don't feel American."

She returned the broom to the corner. "Then we can cross the States off the list." She did a quick count in her head. "Leaving nine possible cultures or nationalities."

"We're whittling down the list."

She laughed, and then her laughter faded as she studied the huge bruise still darkening his brow. "I just wish I knew how that happened," she said, nodding at his temple. "Were you injured in the fall? Did it happen before you went over the side?"

"I've wondered the same."

She studied his expression, debating if she should reveal her worries, but then he said what she'd been thinking, his voice deep, his delivery slow and thoughtful, "Because if it wasn't accidental—that would change everything, wouldn't it?"

CHAPTER TWO

HE DIDN'T KNOW his name. He didn't know where he was from. He didn't know what he did, or where he lived, or why he'd even be on a yacht "with friends." He didn't know if someone had meant him harm or if he'd simply had an accident and fallen overboard.

But there was one thing he did know, and it was this: he wanted her.

He woke thinking about Josephine and fell asleep thinking about her and it was all he could do to hide the physical evidence of his desire. He wasn't a boy. It shouldn't be difficult to control his hunger, but the fierceness of his desire made him wonder if he'd ever felt like this about anyone before or if this was typical of him. Desire. Hunger. Impatience.

Perhaps the intensity of the need was due to all the other unknowns.

He tried to distract himself with reading the books on the shelves in the house. When he was tired of reading, he swam or lay on the warm sand, soaking in the heat of the sun. But inevitably, as time passed, his thoughts turned to Josephine. He wanted to see her. He just wanted to be near her, so he'd pull a shirt on, one of the shirts from her father's closet that she'd lent him, and assist her with her work. He'd help with her notes, or he'd water the garden— anything if it meant he could be at her side, as he'd come to crave her shape, her scent, her smile.

She was beautiful and brilliant as well as innocent and earnest. He was certain she was a rare gem, a jewel among even the world's most beautiful women, and he said that to her one day, after they'd emerged from the sea following a swim.

She smiled at him, amused but also shy. "Thank you for the compliment, but seeing as you don't remember anything of your world, I'm not sure it's valid."

"I don't have to compare you to know that you're smart and kind. You're also cheerful and optimistic, and you make me happy. I have a feeling I'm not always easy to please."

"You certainly weren't cheerful on the beach with your friends. In fact, you were often quite aloof, sitting off on your own, staring out at the ocean. I would watch you and sketch you—"

"Sketch me?"

She nodded, blushing. "It's what I like to do when I have free time."

"I haven't seen you draw since I've been here."

"I do when you're not around, or late at night when you're sleeping."

"What do you draw?"

"This and that." Her blush deepened. "Mostly you."

He loved how her pink cheeks made her eyes look even more green. She was so fresh and pretty. She reminded him of a mermaid...a siren from the sea. "Why draw me?"

"You fascinate me."

"Why?"

"You have to know." Her lips pressed, her expression suddenly reminding him of a prim schoolteacher. "Don't make me spell it out."

He was enchanted by the line her full lips made and the firmness of her chin. His fingers itched to reach out and trace her pink cheek and the shape of her mouth. And just like that, his body hardened, the desire hot and insistent. "Apparently, my head injury has made me a little slow. Be kind and explain to me why someone like me would fascinate you?"

Her chin lifted higher. "I'll only tell you this one time."

"I'm listening."

"You're unbearably attractive—"

"Unbearably?"

"You're very intelligent."

"Can we get back to the unbearably attractive part? Is it possible to be *unbearably* attractive?"

"Yes. You've proven it. Let me continue." She tapped her fingers as if counting her points. "You have a sense of humor—when you want to."

"I suppose that is a drawback, being unpredictable."

Her lips twitched. "You have rich friends. That yacht was enormous. But that's really more of a negative then a plus."

"Why a negative?"

"From an environmental standpoint, it's terrible."

"I agree."

Her brows arched. "You do?"

"I do. I'm always worried about the environment."

"You are?"

He nodded.

She frowned, a faint link forming between her eyebrows. "That's interesting," she murmured.

"Is it?"

Josephine nodded. "You're starting to have a clearer sense of self. I think some of your memories are returning. This is a good thing."

He felt a sudden wash of unease, and he didn't understand it. The return of his memory should be a great thing, and yet all he felt was a pervasive dread. "Let's talk about you instead."

"Why? I'm a boring academic—"

"Not boring, and academics are exciting."

She laughed. "Are they?"

"I went to school with brilliant women. There is nothing sexier than a smart woman—" he broke off as he realized what he'd said. He'd gone to school with brilliant women. And he knew he hadn't meant high school or grammar school. He'd meant university, and the words had been so comfortable, so natural. He also knew that calling university *school* was very American. Had he gone to school—college—in America?

He could see from Josephine's expression that she'd heard the reference, too, and understood it, as well.

"Your memory *is* returning," she said softly, breathlessly.

"You're healing me," he said. "All this sun and swimming."

She smiled back at him. "It's not as if there's a lot to do here. No TV or video games."

"But even if you had those, I don't think it's something you'd do. You love being outside. You're at home in the sea."

Her cheeks were pink, and her eyes were bright as she tucked a long strand of sun-streaked hair behind her ear. "I've always grown up next to the sea. First in Hawaii and then here. I can't imagine not swimming. If I go too many days without getting wet, I feel off. The sea always restores me."

"You are a fish."

She laughed. "My father says the same thing. He says that I have scales and they dry out if I'm out of the water too long. Thus my close proximity to the beach."

"So maybe not a fish but a mermaid."

"Maybe," she answered, smiling, feeling strangely shy and sensitive because everything inside her seemed to be shifting and lurching. Changing.

She'd noticed it before, and she'd tried to suppress the feelings, but she couldn't pretend it wasn't happening, or real, any longer. She couldn't pretend that he wasn't aware of her. She couldn't pretend that there wasn't something taut and electric between them, because there was something about the way he looked at her, something in the intensity of his expression that made the air catch in her throat, making her heart gallop. The way he looked at her terrified her and yet, at the same time, thrilled her. Being near him was wonderful, confusing, exhilarating. No one had ever looked at her as if she were so important. No one had ever made her feel so beautiful. Every conversation made her feel alive, and she didn't know why because there was nothing terribly revealing said. And yet he fascinated her. He'd fascinated her on the beach when he'd been just a mysterious stranger, and her fascination only grew with every day because how could he—this gorgeous, handsome stranger—want her?

And yet, being wanted was doing something to her, seducing her, making her question everything she believed. She'd always thought that she'd never have sex with someone, not unless he was her forever love, the man who would marry her, the man who would share a life with her. Looking into his eyes, she figured she was losing out on something beautiful. This felt special. It felt like a once-in-a-lifetime opportunity, something she wasn't prepared to miss.

It helped that she knew the attraction wasn't one-sided.

It was clear from the heat in his gaze that he desired her, and the knowledge was a heady power. An aphrodisiac that made her restless and curious. He could make her feel so much with just a look. How would she feel if he touched her? *Kissed her?*

She didn't let herself think further than that. She'd never experienced more than a couple kisses, kisses that hadn't inspired her in any way, making her think there was no need to repeat the experience. Until now. Somehow she sensed that kissing her mysterious stranger would be entirely different. Maybe even life-changing.

But did she want that?

She looked hard at her stranger, who truthfully was no

longer a stranger, but someone who was quickly becoming very important to her.

She'd spent so much of her life alone, or alone with her father—which was virtually alone since he rarely spoke, his head always down, buried in his work. She understood her father's fascination with his work and his commitment to research, but every now and then she wanted…more.

She wanted to be seen.

She wanted to be known.

She wanted to be…loved.

Growing up as she had had taught her tremendous self-reliance, but there were times she felt that her life had also left her empty and aching for more. More connection. More expression. More emotion.

Usually these thoughts and feelings happened late at night, and she'd blame fatigue and the need to sleep.

But she was feeling these things almost constantly lately. The arrival of her mystery man had changed something within her.

His arrival had made her aware of the world out there and that there was more to the world than she knew. But even with that knowledge, she also knew she was happy on Khronos. Most of the time she wanted nothing but her work and the sun and the sea. Most of the time she was utterly content.

She needed to be content again.

Abruptly, Josephine rose, moving away, trying to escape the heat suffusing her skin and ache filling her chest. Her father had left her here to manage the foundation's station. She needed to stay focused on her responsibilities. "I'd better get back to work," she said huskily.

"Can I help?" he asked.

She shook her head. "I'm just going to check the solar panels. You relax—"

"That's all I've done the past few days. Show me what

you're doing, or what needs to be done, so I can help while I'm here."

She smiled tightly. "Okay, follow me."

The old Greek cottage had been constructed of stones, without the charm of whitewash, and while it looked ancient and almost abandoned from the front, there were clean, well-maintained stairs behind—stairs that rose up to a clearing filled with a mass of solar panels and equipment, and another smaller stone house.

"That's where the foundation keeps all the seismic monitoring equipment. The equipment is connected to portable seismometers along the edge of the island, as well as some in the water. You see, we're sitting practically on top of a volcano. Khronos is just the tip, which is why we have the seismometers to detect rock movement in the earth's crust. Some movements may be the result of rising magma beneath the surface, which could mean an awakening volcano. We also have equipment here that monitors gases like sulfur dioxide, as an increase in sulfur dioxide could be an indication of magma near the earth's surface."

"And if that should happen? What do you do?"

"It hasn't happened in the past ten years, so I think I'm safe. Odds are, I'm safe."

"You're pretty nonchalant about something potentially catastrophic."

"Some people are terrified of volcanoes, particularly supervolcanoes, but there has never been such an eruption in human memory, and did you know there are actually quite a few people who choose to live near a volcano because they're drawn to the geothermal energy, the minerals and the fertile soil? I'm a fan of geothermal energy because it's very clean, and the resource is nearly inexhaustible.

"Speaking of energy, come see," she said, walking farther back along a compact dirt path that cut deeply through the rough, rocky terrain dotted with a few gnarled olive trees. "Twenty years ago the foundation was powered by those wind turbines before us. Unfortunately, they were prone to breaking down and the repairs were costly, and then new, improved solar technology became a better answer, so eventually no one bothered to repair or replace the turbines."

"They do look forlorn," he said, taking in the line of tall wind turbines that covered the top of the island.

"Luckily for us, solar works incredibly well, allowing the foundation to live completely off the grid. We use solar energy for almost everything. Light, heating, cooking, powering the radio—when the radio actually works—and now for desalination."

He'd been studying the solar panels, but she noted how his interest was piqued by the mention of their desalination system.

She walked him back to another frame, this one with its own set of panels, plus tubes, dials and black rectangular features, and motioned for him to crouch down beside her. "This is our baby and my personal favorite because this one gives us all our fresh water. In the beginning, we had to bring everything in, including gallons and gallons of water. We'd collect rainwater when we could, but if we had no rain, we'd begin to panic. Now, thanks to a partnership with my father's university, we're able to turn salt water into drinking water using only solar energy. Although there are over eighteen thousand desalination plants across the world, this one is unique in that it combines solar energy with brand-new technology allowing a family to generate enough clean water for individual use."

"How is it different from traditional desalination?"

"You're familiar with the desalination process?"

"Salt water is brought to a boil, creating steam. The steam is run through a condensing coil."

"Right. The traditional method is very energy inefficient and requires expensive, complex infrastructure. Over half of the cost of a distillation plant is spent on energy."

"So this is membrane distillation?"

She was impressed he knew that much. Perhaps he'd studied science in school, or something environment related. "Yes and no. The university took conventional membrane distillation, where hot salt water flows across one side of the porous membrane and cold freshwater flows across the other, and added in a layer of carbon-black nanoparticles. The carbon-black nanoparticles attract light, heating the entire surface of the membrane, converting as much as eighty percent of sunlight energy into heat, giving us more water with less energy. It's ideal for us with a compact footprint, but it will also revolutionize the way the world desalinates water because the nanoparticles are low-cost and commercially available."

"Fascinating," he murmured, studying the section with the nanoparticles and then the tubing where water dripped into a clear canister. "By integrating photothermal heating with membrane distillation you've created more productive and efficient technology."

"I haven't. The university program did. We're lucky the scientists and engineers agreed to let us work with it here. We've had it eighteen months now and it's transformed our lives." She nodded toward the small garden off to the side. "Tomatoes, cucumbers, lettuce, carrots, and more. All possible now due to a never-ending supply of clean, drinkable water."

"I'd heard about an American university developing something like this, but it's amazing to see it in use here on Khronos and to know it's not just theoretical."

"It's a game changer for the world."

"Indeed," he murmured, and yet he wasn't looking at the system but rather at her; his gaze locked on her lips and she felt his scrutiny all the way through her.

Heat bloomed in her cheeks. She felt overly warm, her skin exquisitely sensitive, and she looked away, trying to hide how flustered she felt. She wanted his kiss and yet she feared it, too.

She wasn't experienced, and she knew most women her age would have had a number of significant relationships by now. She suddenly wished she'd had a more conventional life, a life where she'd had dates and boyfriends so she'd know what to do and how to respond.

She wanted to respond. Could he tell?

"You're bored," she said huskily, rising and brushing the coarse dirt from her hands.

"I'm not," he answered, rising, as well. "I'm fascinated by everything here. Not just by how you're managing to survive in the middle of nowhere but by you and this father of yours. I can't imagine any other father leaving his only daughter defenseless in such a remote spot."

"I'm not defenseless. I have the radio——" she broke off, lips tightening. Her heart was racing and her stomach churned and she felt close to tears and didn't know why. Nothing had happened, and yet somehow everything was happening and she seemed to be losing control. "Normally it works. I've never dropped it before. I've never broken it before. That accident was a fluke, just like you being here is a fluke. I've spent four years on Khronos and we've seen plenty of yachts, but none have ever stopped here before. And we've certainly never had any castaways, either——"

"Why are you afraid?" he asked, interrupting her torrent of words.

"I'm not." And yet her voice was high and thin, breathless.

For a long moment he was silent, studying her, and then he reached out and lightly traced her eyebrows, the right and then the left. Her breath caught in her throat as the touch sent sparks of hot sensation shooting through her veins. She stared at him, deep into his eyes, as he continued to explore her face, his fingertips light as they caressed the length of her nose, and then her cheekbone, and finally down along the line of her jaw.

"You are so beautiful," he murmured, his voice deep and rough.

She felt his voice and his touch all the way through her, an erotic rasp that teased her senses, making her skin flush and her body ache.

"No makeup, no designer clothes, no expensive blow-outs. Just beautiful you," he added. "I didn't know women like you even existed."

"You say that now, but if you put me next to your lovely ladies from the yacht, you'd see how I'd pale in comparison."

"I don't think there is any comparison. You're extraordinary. Your mind. Your passion for your work. Your beauty. You're perfect."

"You're going to give me quite an ego."

"Good. You should know you're special. One in a million."

She drew back to look him in the face. He didn't turn away, letting her look, allowing her to see the flare of heat in his eyes.

"If you really feel that way, would you kiss me?" she whispered. "Unless that's not how you feel—"

"I've wanted to kiss you from the moment I opened my eyes and saw you in the room looking like an angel."

She swallowed hard. "I'm no angel," she murmured, even as her pulse beat double time, and her gaze drank him in, lingering on the hard, clean line of cheekbone and the shadow of a beard darkening his strong jaw. He shaved every morning, using her father's kit, but by late afternoon he had that shadow again. And then there was that mouth, his wide, firm mouth, his lips lovely. She'd loved drawing his face and loved his mouth most of all, wondering what it would feel like against her own. Wondering what he'd taste like. Wondering if kissing him would be different from kissing alcohol-fueled Ethan in Honolulu two years ago. That kiss had been so awful and sloppy that it had killed all desire to date.

He closed the distance between them, his hands circling her upper arms, bringing her in against him. His blue eyes glowed bright, the heat in the depths holding her, trapping her. Life seemed to slow, and the world shrank to just them.

Josephine could feel the thudding of her heart, and his hands wrapping around her arms, his skin so warm. She shivered at his heat and the way his hard chest pressed against her breasts, making her conscious that she was braless, and her nipples were tight and yet tender, and so sensitive to every breath he took.

This was what she wanted. This was all she wanted. Just to feel his mouth on hers...

His dark head dropped and very slowly his lovely, sensual mouth captured hers, sending sharp hot sparks of sensation through her. She heard a whimper and prayed it wasn't her. His hand rose to cup the back of her head, holding her still while his lips traveled over hers, teasing, tasting, discovering. She shuddered as more sparks of feeling shot through her, the heat making her melt on the inside, her brain flooded with wildly contradictory signals. She wanted more, so much more, even as another part whispered that she was out of his league.

"Second thoughts?" he murmured, lifting his head, his blue gaze meeting and holding hers.

"Um, yes. No. No." Because truly, she'd never felt so alive and so full of yearning about anything, but this was crazy. Her feelings were crazy. Excitement filled her veins, making her feel daring and wild…two things Josephine was not, nor ever had been.

And yet, it felt so good to feel excited and alive.

It felt so good to be touched and kissed.

"Tell me what you're thinking," he said, stroking her cheek, sending rivulets of fire through her, fire that she could feel in the tips of her breasts and deep between her thighs.

"Because it's obvious you're thinking."

"I know, and I'm sorry for it—"

"Don't be. Talk to me."

She drew a quick, shallow breath before blurting, "Do you think you could be married?"

"No."

"So you don't think you have a…a wife…somewhere?"

"No."

"How can you be so sure?"

His broad shoulders shifted. "Just the way I know I'm not American. It doesn't feel right. It doesn't sound right. It doesn't sound like…me."

He released her and she took a step back, and then another, not because she wanted to be apart from him but because she couldn't think when she was close to him and this conversation was important. "Your memory is returning."

"It must be."

"What sounds like you? Could you describe yourself? Who do you think you might be?"

"European. Wealthy." He grimaced. "Mediterranean, most likely. I think I run a company, or own my own company, and I'm good at it. I feel like I have quite a few employees, so my company can't be small. And I have a nagging suspicion that I'm a perfectionist, and, quite possibly, not easily pleased." He looked chagrined. "And if that is all true, I've just described a man that sounds like a pompous ass, which makes me despise myself, even though I don't yet know myself."

She laughed. "Considering that you don't know yourself, I think you're being a little hard on yourself. After spending the past few days with you, I think you're a better person than you described. My gut says you're a very good person, as well as something of a loner, because even when you were with your friends, you were still a bit distant, and rather alone."

"Probably because I'm an unlikable prat—"

"No!" She interrupted with a throaty gurgle of laughter, and the sheer joy in the sound stopped her. Was that really her giggling? Sounding so impossibly girlish and happy? Josephine went through life very seriously. She was committed to facts, not feelings, and her life revolved around work and being useful and practical.

"What are you thinking now?" he asked.

"Is it that obvious I have a tendency to overthink everything?"

"I like it. I like you. Don't ever apologize for being you, Josephine."

The commanding gruffness in his voice made her throat swell closed. She felt a ridiculous need to cry. It had been such a strange and wonderful few days with him here, and everything inside her felt full and tender and new.

"We should head back to the house so I can focus on dinner," she said.

He caught her by the wrist to stop her from escaping. "You never answered my question. What were you thinking just a moment ago?"

She suppressed a shiver as he stroked the inside of her wrist with the pad of his thumb, setting her alight. "That I'm happy," she said unsteadily, trying not to look at his mouth, trying not to remember their kiss earlier, because it had been perfect, and he made her feel beautiful and perfect, and standing close to him made her shockingly aware of how much she wanted to feel more. "And…" She gulped a breath and then lifted her chin, determined to finish her thought. "I'm happy you're here."

CHAPTER THREE

THE SKY WAS putting on a show tonight, the sunset a stunning orange on top of red, while waves crashed onto the beach—but the beauty was lost on him. Tension rolled through him. He didn't yet know himself, but he sensed parts of himself. It was strange and disorienting as well as infuriating. He didn't like not knowing himself, and he didn't want to be called by a name that wasn't his.

He wanted his name, and his identity.

He wanted to be himself, whoever that was, good or bad. He'd take the good and bad, fully embracing both because it was beyond frustrating to feel and think without a foundation of self, never mind self-knowledge.

Every time he heard himself say *I think*...a little voice inside him stopped him, questioning him. *Are you sure? How do you know?*

So, hurrah, his memory was returning, but it wasn't fast enough. He was impatient with the process. He didn't want pieces of himself; he wanted *all* his memory back. He wanted his life back. It wasn't enough to sense things about himself. He needed to *know*. He needed the truth.

The darkness inside him threatened to engulf him tonight and it crossed his mind that this life of hers was not him, which just made him want to know what his life was. He was by no means bored on Khronos, and he was enjoying being with Josephine, but this quiet island of hers wasn't his life.

He knew with certainty that his life wasn't quiet.

His work wasn't calm.

His world had stress and chaos and deadlines and people.

"Here," Josephine said, emerging at his side on the

beach, a glass of wine in her hand. "I think you could use it."

He arched a brow.

"It's good wine," she said, smiling, her full lips curving, the sweet lift of her lips reminding him of their kiss earlier, and how soft her mouth had been beneath his, and how good she'd felt in his arms. Hunger stirred and he imagined doing all sorts of things to her that weren't innocent and would probably shock her.

But she'd enjoy it, and he'd enjoy her pleasure.

"And I need it because…?" he asked, smashing his hunger, not needing one more torment tonight.

"You're pacing this poor beach like a caged tiger. I'm hoping a couple glasses of Father Epi's merlot might help you relax."

He took the glass from her. "We've never had wine before."

"I don't normally drink, but this is a special occasion."

"Is it?"

She nodded, color suffusing her lovely cheekbones. "I thought we should do something different tonight. Make tonight special. Hopefully it will provide some diversion and distract you from whatever is bothering you."

"You don't need to worry about me."

"But I do."

"Why?"

"I care about you." Her shoulders lifted and fell. "Which is why we're having dinner alfresco tonight. I've set a table for us and we will enjoy dinner outside and watch the sun set, and you'll be my first real date. Unless that is too awkward?" She bit into her lush lower lip for a moment, struggling with her confidence. "Am I horribly awkward? I'm afraid I am."

"There is nothing awkward about you," he answered huskily, reaching for her and drawing her close. "I would enjoy a dinner date with you very much, *bella*," he murmured, his head dropping to kiss her soft, warm mouth. For a moment she stiffened, and then in the next, she leaned into him, giving herself up to him. He traced the seam of her lips with his tongue and when her lips parted, he claimed her mouth, too, his tongue teasing hers, tasting her, wanting her. She shivered against him, and he kissed her jaw and then the side of her neck, feeling her shiver again as he kissed his way down to her collarbone, the air catching in her throat. She was so sensitive. He battled his desire, keeping his need in check.

She wanted a date. She wanted romance. He could do that.

"You don't have to do anything," she said quickly, breathlessly. "I'm taking care of the dinner and I've already set the table. Want to come see?"

He nodded because he did want to see, very much so. He offered her his arm, and she shyly tucked her hand through the crook of his elbow. They left the beach, returning to the little house, which looked altogether different with the glowing fire outside in a fire pit and a small round table covered with a vivid tablecloth with bright birds and butterflies against a black wool background. There were two place settings on the table, and tall tapered candles glimmered in the center. It was charming and rustic and he was touched that she had gone to such pains for him.

"That's not a Greek tablecloth," he said.

"No, it's from Peru. My dear Azucena made it for me before we left. I was supposed to save it for my hope chest—" She broke off when she saw his confusion. "Do girls not have hope chests where you're from?"

"I'm not sure. What is that?"

"It's where you save things for your wedding. Linens and quilts and other things to help you begin your new home once you're married."

He noticed she wouldn't look at him as she talked, and color darkened her cheeks.

"I'm not planning on getting married," she added, moving around the table, adjusting the plates and glasses, "and it seems like such a waste to leave this lovely tablecloth in a chest forever, so I brought it out tonight. It's pretty, though, isn't it?"

"It is." But he wasn't looking at the cloth. He was looking at Josephine as the candlelight illuminated her profile. She'd changed at some point from her casual sundress into a long blue skirt that she'd paired with a white peasant-style blouse. Her long hair had been pulled into a loose knot that she'd attempted to secure with what looked like wooden sticks, but long tendrils of hair were slipping out and curling loosely at her neck and around her face.

Her cheeks were flushed and her eyes bright as she glanced at him, and her expression was nervous and shy, sweet and hopeful, and it was the hopefulness in her green gaze that made his chest tighten and ache.

He had a feeling his life was full of beautiful women, but none were like her. How could they be? Who could possibly be as smart and beautiful and yet also so capable? He marveled at her ability to make do with so little. She complained about nothing.

"Why won't you marry?" he asked, wanting to touch one of those long, loose tendrils that had slipped free from her chignon to rest on her smooth, tanned shoulder.

"It's just unlikely," she answered, giving him a smile. "It's not as if men wash up on my beach often."

"I did."

"Yes, but it took me eight years to rescue my first prince."

His brow creased. "Prince?"

She smiled, and a small dimple appeared near the corner of her mouth. "Like the story 'The Little Mermaid,' except I don't intend to give up my soul in order to marry or in order to make him—or anyone—happy."

"I confess, I don't know the story."

"How can you not know it?"

"I was an—" he stopped and looked away, perplexed. He'd come so close to saying *I was an only child.*

But was he?

And was that why he didn't know the story?

"It's not an American story," she added, "although Disney did a version of it. It's Hans Christian Andersen, and his stories are invariably really sad and depressing. I think they were meant to scare children into good behavior, but they gave me nightmares so my dad told my mom not to read them to me anymore, but of course I remember the ones that upset me most."

She glanced at him. "But no depressing conversation. Dinner is ready. Shall we eat?"

Josephine plated their dinner—roasted lamb fragrant with garlic, oregano, thyme, rosemary, and lemon juice. She loved cooking Greek food and tonight's lamb paired perfectly with the merlot and the sky, the stunning sunset fading to just a wisp of red and purple on the horizon.

He held her chair for her as she sat down, a chivalrous gesture that made her feel safe and protected. "Thank you," she murmured, watching as he took the seat opposite her, the candlelight reflecting off the bronze of his cheekbones and his inky-black hair. She felt a sizzle race through her as his blue gaze met hers and held. It was hard to think clearly when he made her feel so much, her pulse racing, her body humming with nerves and excitement.

She wanted him to kiss her again.

She wanted him to hold her and make her feel all the things she'd felt earlier, because this magic wouldn't last. He'd be gone before she knew it and this time here, together, would be just a memory. A memory she'd cherish forever.

"I can't imagine a more inviting table setting, or a more beautiful dinner companion," he said, lifting his wineglass. "To you, Josephine. Thank you for everything."

"It's my pleasure," she said, lightly clinking the rim of her goblet to his.

He sipped the wine and nodded. "This is really good wine."

"It's Greek, made by Father Epi in the monastic community Mount Athos. It's my father's favorite and what he always brings back with him."

"I'll have to remember it."

She felt her lips curve. "I'd rather you remember your name and those important things like where you live and what you do." Her smile faded. "Your family must be frantic. If you were mine, I'd be beside myself."

"It'd be nice to know who they are."

"I'm sure they are heartsick, as are your friends."

"Hmm."

She shot him a speculative look. "You don't think so?"

His jaw hardened, his gaze narrowing. "They didn't come back."

She'd thought the same thing many times. Carefully, she added, "Maybe they didn't know where you disappeared. It is a huge sea."

"Whoever I fought with knew I went overboard. Why didn't he sound the alarm?"

"If that person did know…you're still in trouble. That person is dangerous. He or she meant to do you harm. Otherwise the yacht would have circled back. Your friends, the rest of them, would never have left you."

"That's the first time, you said *he or she*." His gaze met hers and held. "Until now, you've always said *he*. Do you think it was a woman?"

"I don't know. I shouldn't have said anything. And I shouldn't speculate. I was never close enough to your group to hear conversations. I only watched from afar, and to be honest, I only really watched you." She felt her face go hot once again. Her shoulders twisted. She didn't know where to look. "You were the most interesting."

His gaze locked with hers and held, and what she saw in his eyes made the air bottle in her lungs and her skin heat. He wanted her, desired her, and it struck her for the first time that it wasn't because he was grateful she'd saved him—which was what she'd always told herself until now—but because he liked *her*, Josephine Robb, social misfit. It shouldn't matter that she could speak a half-dozen different languages but didn't know anything about popular American culture, but it did whenever she returned to the States. While women her age discussed fashion and the current social-media sensation, she felt foolish and exposed, a fish out of water.

It was all she could do to eat her dinner, and it was one of her favorite meals. Chewing, swallowing, talking, smiling became a challenge because she could feel him from across the table; she could feel his energy and it was dizzying. Her breasts peaked, her body felt hot, like liquid, and she pressed her knees together, trying to deny the sensitivity between her thighs.

"You've become very quiet," he said, as they finished their meal.

The candlelight flickered, casting a dancing shadow across his face. Her gaze followed the shadow and light as it moved over the slash of cheekbones, the strong forehead, the line of his nose, and the utterly masculine jaw. He was handsome and virile but also hard, with a toughness, a fierceness, at his center that made her think she wouldn't ever want to be his adversary. Far better to have him in her corner, on her side.

"I should clear the table," she said huskily.

"No, you shouldn't," he answered, his gaze focused intently on her.

She felt her mouth tingle beneath his scrutiny, and her face warmed, the skin feeling taut and sensitive. The heat in his blue eyes took her breath away, making her heart pound. Awareness rippled through her, desire coiling low in her belly with a need and a desperation she'd never felt until now. He'd awakened something within her that made her restless, even frantic.

She didn't just want him; she needed him.

There might never be another who made her feel this way. Beautiful and valuable. Excited and alive.

"Come here," he said, leaning back in his chair.

He didn't extend a hand, nor were the words sharp or frightening, but the command was undeniable. He expected her to go to him. He knew she'd obey.

And she knew it, too.

She rose on shaky legs and walked around the small table to his side.

His dark head tipped, and his gaze slowly traveled over her, from her hot flushed cheeks to her full mouth and down over her shoulders. His attention riveted on the tips of her breasts pressing against the thin gauze of her blouse, and then finally moved down over her waist and hips.

The hunger in his eyes made her tremble. She wasn't frightened, and yet the heat in her body now seemed to center low, pooling in secret places that made her damp. She felt as if he was slowly turning her to wine and honey.

"I want you," he said, and his deep voice had a rasp in it that made her nipples tighten. "But I'm trying to be respectful," he added. "I'm aware of how much I owe you—"

"No."

"I do. I owe you my life."

"Then don't want me. Not if it's because you're grateful. I don't want to be wanted out of some misguided gratitude—"

She broke off as he reached out and pulled her down onto his lap, his hands locking around her waist.

"I don't want you out of gratitude. I want you because I can't sleep at night anymore because my body aches for you. I want to touch you and taste you and be in you. The only reason I've held back is because you're innocent. I'm hoping to God you're not, because then I wouldn't feel like such a bastard for wanting to take you and make you mine."

Her thighs clenched as heat ricocheted through her, the desire as sharp as a razor's edge.

"Tell me you're not a virgin. Tell me this wouldn't be your first time." His gaze, so hot, blistered her, while his deep voice scratched her senses, gravel-rough.

"It would be my first time," she answered unsteadily, "but everyone has to have a first time. Why can't it be with you?"

"Because I don't think I'm good for you. I don't think I'm what you need."

"How do you know that?"

"I don't."

"*Exactly*. We don't know very much of anything except that I'm as attracted to you as you are to me, and I like how you make me feel. I like this, whatever this is, between us and I want more of it, not less."

His jaw flexed, hardened, just as she could feel him harden beneath her bottom in undeniable proof of his desire. His erection made her feel even more sensitive and she exhaled in a rush, overwhelmed by the sensation coursing through her. "I want you," she said thickly, sliding her hands up his chest, exploring the hard, warm plane of muscle. "I want you to be my first."

Her words were like gasoline on an open flame.

He wanted to strip her bare right there and feast on her. He wanted his mouth on every inch of her. He wanted her, oh, so very wet and writhing beneath him.

He could make her squirm and shudder and cry out his name.

If he were a gentleman, he'd release her, push her off his lap and tell her to go to bed.

He'd go for a swim to cool off and he'd swim until he burned off this terrible need.

If he were a gentleman, he'd wait for her to fall asleep before he returned to her father's room where he slept every night.

But he wasn't a gentleman. He didn't know very much about himself, but he knew that much.

Head dropping, his lips brushed hers, not because he was being careful with her but because he was feeling cruel.

He wanted her to ache for him.

He wanted her to crave him the way he craved her, and so he teased her lips and teased her with touches that were light and unsatisfying, his caress brushing her shoulders, the sides of her breasts, the outside of her hip, every touch designed to make her arch and flex, her slim back a bow drawn taut.

She was breathing harder now, short gasps, and her mouth lifted, trying to find his. She wanted his kiss. She wanted him.

He grazed the pebbled nipple of one breast with the back of his knuckles, a fleeting touch that made her whimper and her body gyrate on his lap. Her eyes were cloudy, the pupils so dilated her eyes looked almost black now.

He brushed the other just to make her dance again, and she did.

He nearly growled with pleasure. She was his.

Finally he took her mouth, his lips claiming her, his hunger barely leashed. As he took her mouth, he drank in her groan of pleasure. Her mouth was both hot and cool. She tasted fresh and impossibly sweet, and as his tongue traced the seam of her lips, her mouth opened to him. His tongue plunged in, sweeping, stabbing, punishing.

He didn't know why he wanted to punish her. She was nothing short of heaven, an angel here on earth.

Maybe that was why he was angry—and not with her, but with himself.

He didn't deserve her.

He shouldn't take her.

He shouldn't be the one to steal her innocence.

For God's sake, she'd kept a hope chest, filled with desires and dreams and hopes, and tonight she'd brought out a special tablecloth, and now he was going to take her virginity?

He shouldn't do this, he shouldn't. He didn't even know if there were other claims on him. He didn't think he was married—he wore no ring; there was no tan line—but could he have a significant other waiting for him somewhere? Worrying about him?

Missing him?

He broke off the kiss and lifted her, putting her on her feet before walking away, putting distance between them so he couldn't reach her easily.

For a moment the only sound was the crackle of the fire and the hum of the ocean as waves broke on the shore.

The rising moon cast a pale glow and he knew if he turned, he'd see her where he'd put her. She hadn't moved. She stood frozen, staring at him, waiting.

Wondering.

"I can't do this," he ground out. "I can't just take your innocence because I want to. It's wrong, at every level."

"Not even if I give you permission?" she said.

He heard the wobble of hurt in her voice and he glanced over his shoulder to see that yes, she was exactly where he'd left her. She looked rooted to the spot, except she no longer glowed. Her lips were pressed together and she looked pinched. Wounded.

And he'd done that to her, as well.

Pain twisted within him and he hated himself for putting her through this. He ought to know better. He was a man, not a boy.

"You should be protected," he said roughly. "It's what your father would want for you, and what you need. I can't just wash up on your beach and claim you—"

"Why not? Why not if it's what I want?" The bruised tone was gone, replaced by something stronger, fiercer. "I'm twenty-three, almost twenty-four. This isn't the Middle Ages. I am not a ward, and I do not belong to a man. I can decide for myself what is best for me."

He laughed, the sound mocking and unkind. "And you think I'm best for you?"

Her chin notched up. "I think you can teach me what I want to know."

He lifted a brow. "Teach you?"

"As you can tell, I haven't had a lot of experience. I've actually had almost no experience. There have been kisses," she added flatly, "and some uncomfortable groping, but that is all. As you can see there are not a lot of men here, and I'm happy here, so I'm relatively…untutored…when it comes to sex. Which is why I want you to be my first so I won't feel so…foolish…the next time."

The next time.

Her words flamed his temper. Primal emotion flooded him, making his blood boil and his shaft throb and ache.

He hated the idea of her with anyone else. He hated to think of any man touching her.

"You say you owe me your life," she added, her winged brows arching higher, as imperious as a queen. "Well, I don't want your life. I just want you to bed me. I want you to show me how it is between a man and a woman so that

I can be confident in the future. It would help me feel less awkward when I have sex in the future."

"You keep calling it sex. Why not lovemaking?"

"Because I'm a scientist and haven't been raised with euphemisms."

"But when you're with someone you truly desire, it's not just sex—it's bigger and more powerful. Transformative, if you will."

"Would it be that way with us?"

"If it's right."

"And if it's not?"

"It would feel like two bodies touching, rubbing, with hopefully a release in there somewhere."

"Sex can be bad, then?"

"With the wrong person, yes. With the wrong person it can be disconcerting."

"Even for a man?"

"It's a profoundly intimate act. I always enjoy it best in the context of a relationship."

"Ah." Her head nodded once, a thoughtful movement. "That's why you don't want to do it with me. We have no relationship. It wouldn't satisfy you."

"On the contrary, we have a very unique relationship, and making love to you is all I've thought about these past few days. But if I were to take you to my bed, I'm not sure I could, or would, let you go."

"Then don't," she answered simply.

For a moment they stood where they were, just looking at each other, the crackle of the fire mimicking the crackle of heat in his veins, making his shaft longer and harder, making him ache for her.

She patted the chair he'd left. "Come back here," she said coolly.

It wasn't a plea but a command, just as he'd commanded her earlier.

"Come sit down again and let me sit with you, like we were," she added. "Let us see how this goes without your conscience telling you things. I have a conscience of my own. I don't need yours deciding what I want or need. I can and will do that for myself."

He'd found her innocence seductive, but this version of Josephine was far sexier and even more compelling.

He sauntered toward her, aware of how her gaze boldly moved over him, giving him the same thorough examination he'd given her earlier, before her attention focused on his hips and the rigid length of him thrusting against the fabric of his trousers.

The tip of her tongue touched her lips and he wanted to roar with need and lust. She might be innocent and yet she had a sensual nature which called to him, stirring him. He took his seat and leaned back in the wooden chair, his brow lifting, challenging her. "Your Highness?" he taunted lowly.

She sat down on his lap, legs together, facing him. "Now what?" she whispered.

He didn't answer her with words. Instead he drew her arms behind her back and wrapped one hand around both of her wrists, holding her captive and still. He liked her like this—helpless and his. He liked how her breasts jutted and her lips parted, her breath coming fast.

He kissed the corner of her mouth, and then her mouth, feeling how her lips quivered against his.

He licked at her lower lip, his tongue finding all the nerve endings inside. She wriggled on his lap, hips rocking, and he longed to reach down and rub her between her thighs. Part of him wanted to shock her, while another part wanted to soothe her. She was passionate and responsive and utterly gorgeous…and right now she was his, all his.

"Can you feel me?" he growled, kissing the side of her neck, his teeth scraping across her skin. "Can you feel me between your thighs?"

She nodded her head, a jerky nod, even as his tongue flicked her tender earlobe and then swirled inside the shell of her ear, making her groan.

"I can feel you," he murmured, tugging on her hands, drawing them lower so that he held her hands against her butt, making her back arch even more. Her white cotton blouse clung to her small, high breasts, the thin fabric outlining her nipples. His head dropped and he sucked on one nipple, drawing on it hard.

She gasped, and whimpered, grinding down against him. He could feel her through his trousers, her body hot, wet.

With his free hand he worked the blouse off one shoulder, revealing the simple white cotton bralette, the thin fabric cup damp from his mouth. He stroked the pebbled nipple, making her squirm again.

"I can feel your heat and your need," he said, his lips just below her ear. "You are so wet, and it's so sexy."

She shuddered at his words.

"What I want to do with you is very hot and rather indecent. I'm afraid it would shock you."

She was finding it increasingly hard to breathe. "How so?"

"I would like to touch you, everywhere, and discover with my hands and my mouth what you enjoy. I'd like to kiss you between your thighs and use my tongue to make you come—"

"Would you enjoy that?" she asked, interrupting him.

He laughed softly at her wrinkled nose, her expression indicating disbelief.

"I would like it very much."

"You're telling me the truth?"

"I will always tell you the truth. No lies between us. It would ruin everything."

She stared deep into his eyes. "I do trust you," she said quietly, firmly, as if giving him reassurance. "Which is why I want you to be my first. You're supposed to be my first. I've been waiting for you."

"As much as I like the sound of that, I'm afraid it doesn't make sense."

"But it does. It's science," she said, "the laws of some-thing or other. Nature or physics. If I could think clearly, I could tell you why it's meant to be, but I can't think clearly, not with you kissing my neck and everywhere else. You're clouding my rational brain."

"I should stop."

"No. You should most definitely not stop." She drew her head back down to his, kissing him sweetly, persuasively. "Promise me?"

"Promise," he answered, rising with her in his arms. As he walked, he kissed the side of her neck, making her breath catch in her throat. He was already hard and hun-gry, but that faint hitch in her breath made his body burn and throb.

She was gorgeous and sensitive and she made him feel so many good things. He wondered if he'd ever felt like this before. He couldn't imagine desiring anyone as much as he desired her.

He headed to the stone house, hesitating in the center room, not sure which way to go. Josephine pointed to her room. Her bed was small, considerably smaller than her father's, but it would still be plenty big enough for the two of them.

In her room, he sat down on the edge of the low bed and drew her between his thighs. His hands ran up and down her sides, stroking the length of her, savoring the feel of her. She was slim and toned and yet she had lovely curves, perfect breasts and generous hips, and a firm backside that was meant to be touched.

"What do I do?" she whispered as he reached for the hem of her blouse.

"Nothing. Let me," he answered, lifting her blouse up and then untying her sarong so that the fabric fell to the ground. Next to go was the plain white bralette and matching white panties, and once they were off, she was his, and beautifully bare. He smothered his groan of appreciation. "You are so beautiful," he said, drawing her even closer to kiss one pink-tipped breast. Her nipple puckered, tightening as his lips brushed the sensitive tip.

His body throbbed all over again, his erection straining against the zipper of his trousers. His tongue swept the peak lightly before his mouth closed over the damp tip. She shuddered as he drew on the nipple, her slim back arching. His hands settled on her hips, holding them firmly, thumbs stroking her hip bones.

She practically danced in place, making soft little whimpering sounds. She was so sweet, so innocent, and he battled to keep his desire in check, not wanting to rush.

The first time was special. The first time should make her feel good and beautiful.

He kissed his way to her other breast, giving the dark pink nipple the same attention and then some, pulling harder on the tip, working it and feeling how her body responded, hips rocking harder, her legs now trembling.

He stroked down her hips and then to her outer thighs and back again. He stroked lightly, awakening every nerve he could as her breath became increasingly shallow. She was practically panting as he caressed up the inside of her knee, up her smooth taut thigh to tease the curls between her legs. But instead of touching her then, he caressed back down her thigh and then up so that his knuckles grazed her. She bucked a little against his hand as he trailed a finger where she was most sensitive.

She was trembling against him now, her hands on his shoulders, holding her up. He slipped a hand between her thighs, finding her slick folds. She was so tender, so warm, so wet. He desperately wanted to put her on the bed and part her thighs and lick her, and taste her, but he didn't want to overwhelm her. This was clearly all so new to her, and so he contented himself with stirring her and heightening her senses and her pleasure. He wanted her fully aroused to make sure her first time was as comfortable as possible.

She shuddered again when his fingertips traced her delicate lips and then her nub. Her breath even shuddered as he stroked her, oh, so lightly there.

"I can't stand anymore," she said lowly, hoarsely.

"Sit. Switch places with me," he said.

Her expression was uncertain and yet she did as he asked, and he used the moment to strip off his clothes before kneeling in front of her, his hands circling her ankles. He stroked the fine bones in her ankles and then up over her shins and calves to her knees, and then down again, working the backs of her calves. He could feel her relax, her breath grow deeper and slower. Gradually, he shifted his attention higher on her legs, stroking up her thighs and down again, and with each stroke he pressed her legs back, opening them gradually to him. She stared at him, fascinated, her husky breath the only sound in the dark room.

The moon wasn't yet high enough to see her well, but he could see enough to be painfully aroused—pale skin, her thick honey-brown hair tumbling over one shoulder and breast, and the triangle of curls at her thighs. She gleamed in the dim light, her long limbs exquisite, her small, full breasts perfect. He felt beyond hungry; he was ravenous and he wanted to feast on her. Instead he was careful, and he leaned between her thighs to press a tender kiss in the hollow where her thigh connected to her pelvis. She groaned softly as he blew lightly on her inner thighs, focusing the air on her curls. She jerked against his hold, her breath hitching again.

"This is a kind of torture," she murmured.

"The best foreplay always is," he answered, parting her there to slip his fingers across her. She was hot and so tender, her soft flesh like liquid velvet. He kissed her on her nub, then used the tip of his tongue across her.

She shivered and cried out.

His body went rock hard, so hard he felt as if he'd pop out of his skin. He wanted her, wanted to be buried in her sweet wet heat, buried so deeply that they were one, forever one, making her his, and only his. He kissed his way back to the junction of her thighs, kissing her lightly, soothing her before rising up and shifting her back on the bed and slowly extending his body over hers, covering her.

Her arms wound around his neck, her fingers at his nape.

"Kiss me," she whispered.

And he did.

Josephine closed her eyes at the hunger in his kiss. His lips were firm and the pressure of his mouth parted her lips. She shuddered at the feel of his hand under her breast and then on her breast, fingers stroking the tight, peaked nipple, sending rivulets of feeling throughout her body. Her hips pressed up against his, his thick shaft extended across her belly. She'd always wondered what this would be like, and he was right; she'd imagined it as a clinical sort of thing, but there was nothing clinical in the heat and texture and sensation.

He made her feel so wonderfully alive. She couldn't imagine this moment with anyone else, just him.

He lifted his head to gaze down at her. There was something in his expression that made her chest tighten and her heart thump with pain.

"You promised," she whispered. "You promised you wouldn't stop. And I won't regret this, I swear to you." She caressed his neck and then her hands went to his shoulders. "Don't be afraid."

He laughed low, as though amused. "I'm not afraid, and

I'm glad you're not afraid, either. The first time isn't always comfortable, but it'll get better."

"I've heard that, too."

He kissed her, smiling against her mouth, and then his smile faded as the kiss turned hot and electric. She opened her legs for him, allowing his hips to settle between her thighs. He entered her slowly, taking his time, and Josephine had to draw a deep breath and tell herself to relax when it began to pinch and then burn, and then there was all that fullness and that pressure inside her, so different from anything she'd ever felt before. He was right. It wasn't comfortable and she wondered how anybody enjoyed this.

He must have sensed her panic, because he held still and kissed her, biting and then sucking on her lower lip, distracting her from everything but his teeth and tongue. Gradually the sting eased and the pressure was less overwhelming. He rocked his hips a little, shifting inside her, and as he eased out and then in, she found herself holding her breath again, but this time because it was a strange fluttery sensation that felt new but good.

"Do that again," she urged.

He laughed softly. "Many, many times," he answered, withdrawing again to thrust in more deeply. The fluttery good feeling happened again and continued with every thrust, and the pleasure built, the sensation erotic, making her arch and dig her heels into the mattress of the bed.

He met the lifting of her hips with a deeper, harder thrust, and the pleasure continued to rise, pressure and pleasure swirling, tightening so that she felt almost dizzy from it. She didn't know what she was waiting for, or reaching for. She just knew he couldn't stop, and she wanted whatever it was that he was doing and making her feel. Emotion and sensation joined together, hot and intense, as she tried to grip him with her body, wanting to keep him inside her where he felt so good, but he wouldn't be stopped and her skin grew hot and damp, and she felt the heat sweep through her, her skin prickly and tingling all over.

She panted with the need and tension, her body wound up, too wound up, and she didn't know what to do or where to go with the tension, and then he reached down, between them, and touched her where she was so very sensitive, circling her nub even as he drove into her, and his touch there, as he thrust deep inside her, made her shatter. She stifled her cry by pressing her mouth to his chest, but the waves of pleasure didn't stop. The climax continued, hard and intense, breaking her into a million shimmering pieces. She felt like stardust strewn across the sky and it was earth-shattering, heart-stopping.

Even as she was still floating like stardust, her mind so scattered, she felt him groan and stiffen, his hoarse guttural cry not so different from her own.

Josephine's arms tightened around him and she held him fiercely, desperately thinking her life would never be the same.

It could never be the same.

He would forever be a part of her now because she had just given him a piece of her heart.

He woke up in the night and glanced around, wondering what had woken him, and then he realized it was the moonlight streaming through the window, falling across the bed in white streaks of light.

The moonlight illuminated Josephine's elegant profile. Her features were delicate and refined, reminding him of a fairy-tale princess. Every day he discovered something new about her, and tonight he'd discovered her passion. Part of him felt guilty for taking her virginity, and yet another part of him agreed with her—they were meant to be. Destined to be together. She was beautiful and brilliant, innocent and earnest, and temptingly sweet.

His head dipped and he pressed a light kiss to her temple and then another to her cheek.

She stirred and moved closer to him, her slim warm body pressed to his. "What's wrong?" she murmured sleepily.

He stroked her long silky hair back from her cheek. "Nothing."

"You're awake."

"The moon woke me."

"I'll close the curtain."

"No, don't. Then I couldn't see you, and I want to see you."

Her lips curved, her cheeks rising with her soft smile.

He dropped another light kiss on her lips. "You're a jewel, Josephine. A rare jewel."

Still smiling, she nestled even closer so that her cheek rested on his chest. "Thank you for the compliment, but seeing as you don't remember anything of your world, I'm not sure it's valid."

"Let me be the judge of that."

"Yes, my lord," she said with a faint laugh, her breath a light caress against his bare chest, and then she fell back asleep, and he lay awake for another hour, just holding her and watching the big full moon high in the sky.

This wasn't his life, or his world, but in some ways he was quite certain it was the best life he'd lived, as well as the best world.

Josephine woke the next morning and stretched and smiled as she felt his arm tighten around her. He was here. It wasn't a dream. She was so glad because it had been the best night of her life.

She slipped from bed and pulled on her bikini and then headed outside for an early-morning swim. As she swam she heard the buzz of a helicopter. It was far from the beach, but the hum grew louder. She stood up in the water, hands over her head, waving frantically as the helicopter moved toward her and then headed in a different direction, flying away.

She ran back toward the house. He was just leaving her bed, pulling on the pair of her father's shorts she'd given him along with the other clothes. The shorts were huge and so he anchored them with a belt as he raced back outside with her.

"It came so close," she said, running toward the beach. "And I waved, and I thought it must have seen me but then it went away."

"Maybe it did see you. Maybe it's gone for help."

"Maybe."

They spent the rest of the day on tenterhooks waiting for the helicopter to return or a glimpse of a boat, but the morning turned into afternoon, and then dusk fell. "I'm sorry," she said to him where they sat side by side on the sand.

"I'm not," he answered, turning his head to look at her. "I'm glad. This gives me more time with you. It gives me more time to discover you and all the different ways I want to know you."

"But we made love."

"There are so many ways to make love."

She chewed her lip, hiding her smile. He made her feel so excited and nervous and shy and hopeful and all those emotions kept rising in her, bubbling up, making it impossible not to smile.

"You like that," he said, his voice dropping, growing husky.

She blushed, even as her smile stretched wider. She shouldn't smile. She shouldn't encourage him, and yet she loved how he made her feel and how amazing it had been to be his last night. His weight, his scent, his heat…the friction and the pleasure.

"I did," she said unsteadily. "I loved it. I loved being with you. It was...perfect."

"And that was just the beginning," he answered, drawing her toward him, pulling her on top of him as he lay back. She felt him beneath her, hard and warm, his chest crushing her breasts, and his erection pressed to the apex of her thighs, the heavy rigid length making her impossibly aware of his desire. His hands shifted from her waist to her hips and then lower, to cup her butt, his hands so warm on her that she felt as if she was melting.

He cupped the back of her head, kissing her deeply, making her whimper with need. She wiggled against him, her hips dancing over him, encouraging him, practically begging him to take her.

She wanted him to fill her and stretch her. She wanted the maddening pressure and then the explosive release. She wanted everything he'd shown her last night, and even more wild and fierce tonight.

Passion—she wanted the passion he'd awoken within her.

And then he was lifting her and he was sliding lower, holding her thighs apart until he settled beneath her, his face under her most private place.

She pressed against his shoulders, trying to escape, but he held her knees firmly, keeping them wide-open so that he could her kiss there, between her thighs. She shuddered and swallowed a cry.

"Take your bikini bottoms off," he told her. "Now."

It was a definite command but also unbelievably sexy, and she peeled them off, trying not to panic. This was what she wanted—him. Them. Earlier today she'd wanted him to want her like this; she'd wanted him to show her all the things she didn't know, and he could, she thought. He could teach her and share with her, helping her discover the world that lay beyond Khronos's beach.

"Come here," he growled. "Kneel over me."

She'd wanted to be daring; she'd wanted to take risks but this was terrifying. "I'm not sure—"

"I am. I want you. I want to taste you again. Last night was not enough."

Heat rushed through her, heat and need and fear that perhaps this was all a dream and once she opened her eyes, he'd be gone.

And then his mouth touched her there, and his tongue found her between the slick folds, and she cried out as he stroked her and sucked on her, drawing the sensitive nub between his lips and then his teeth, tugging and licking until she felt as if she'd explode out of her skin.

He slipped a finger inside her, finding more sensitive spots as he sucked on her, and she couldn't fight the intense waves of pressure and pleasure building. She screamed as she climaxed, and the orgasm shuddered through her, making her body writhe and bend.

He lifted her up and turned her around so that she lay in the sand, and he stretched out over her. She stared up at him, so dazed she could barely focus.

"You liked that," he murmured, pushing her hair back from her face.

"You could say that," she whispered, reaching up to tug on his shirt. "But I'm feeling greedy. I want you. I want what we did last night. That was heaven. Please take this off. Your shorts, too."

"We have to be careful," he said. "I wasn't careful enough last night. I didn't pull out fast enough."

She struggled to follow what he was saying and then she understood. Careful as in careful not to get her pregnant. Careful as in birth control. "Oh. Right. Smart." Why hadn't she thought of any of that?

But then, there was no time for thinking about anything, not when he was settling over her, handsome and naked and beautiful. She'd never met anyone half so beautiful. And then he was kissing her again and lowering himself to cover her before he entered her, his thick shaft stretching her and filling her so that her breath caught and she had to relax to accommodate him.

But then when he began to move, slowly, the uncomfortable sensation eased, and the pressure became a good pressure as he found the spot inside her that liked being touched. "Again," she said, lifting her hips. "Do that again and again."

He laughed softly against her neck. "My pleasure."

And then she didn't want to talk anymore, not when she was feeling so much heat and sensation and emotion.

With him, like this, she felt beautiful. Together with him, like this, everything was perfect.

The days passed, one after another. The sun shone brightly every day, long hot days that only cooled in the late afternoon as the wind blew. They spent most of their time together. He felt guilty that she wasn't working very much, but he knew that it was just a matter of time, too, before her father would return and everything would change. Maybe that was why he couldn't get enough of Josephine, craving her body and warmth. Or maybe he couldn't get enough because she felt like sunshine and life—so open and warm and affectionate. Her smile did something to him, creating strange pain and pressure in his chest. He feared what he didn't know, and yet it only served to make the present even more important. It made *her* more important. He wasn't going to lose her, either. She was his. She belonged with him. He knew that much.

"My father should be back very soon now," she said, curling up against him late one afternoon, her hand on his chest, her fingers lightly caressing his skin. He loved the way she touched him. It felt right. She felt right in his arms, in his bed. "Just three days, and when he returns, he will know who to contact," she added, "and what to do."

The news should please him. Obviously, he knew they could not remain like this forever. But he dreaded reality, unable to fathom the future or the truth of it all when he was so removed from it here with her.

She misinterpreted his silence, because she looked up at him, giving him one of her radiant, reassuring smiles, which never failed to put an ache in his chest. "My father will like you. Very much."

He couldn't answer her smile, not when there was so much heaviness within him. "There is a whole world out there that we don't know."

"But we will discover it together, yes?"

He kissed her brow and then the tip of her small, straight nose and then, finally, the lushness of her lips. Almost immediately desire flared, the warmth of the kiss sparking hot cravings. He pulled her closer, wanting to lose himself in her rather than at the edge of the unknown. The unknown wasn't his friend. But she was. Here on Khronos, she was his world. She was his everything.

"I love you," she whispered, as he entered her, thrusting deep.

He didn't say it back, but then, he didn't think she expected him to.

Later that night, he woke up and glanced toward the windows, looking to see if it was light. But there wasn't a wall of windows where he expected glass to be. The window was on a different side of the room, and it was a simple square window with a simple grid in the middle.

He frowned. This wasn't his room. This wasn't his home.

He swung his legs out of bed. The ground was very close. It jarred his knees. His bare feet arched against the

roughly cobbled floor. Why was he here? He didn't belong
here. He lived somewhere grand. He lived somewhere…

His throat worked. He swallowed as the past returned,
colliding with the present, because he *knew*.

He knew his name. Alexander.

He knew who he was. He knew what he was.

Alexander glanced around the room, understanding
where he was. Not in Aargau but in Greece, on this island
with Josephine who'd rescued him.

He looked over and there she was, still sleeping in the
bed. Her bed. Her cottage. Her island, not his.

Her long honey hair spilled across her bare shoulder. Her
thick lashes rested on her cheek. She was stunning even in
her sleep. His very own mermaid.

She'd saved him. He would have died—drowned—if not
for her, and then when he was still weak, she'd taken care
of him. And then last night she'd told him she loved him,
and he hadn't answered her with words, but he'd shown her
how much her faith in him mattered to him by making love
to her for hours, worshipping her body since something inside him kept him from giving her his heart.

He'd thought that maybe he couldn't give himself to
her fully because he didn't know who he was. It was what
she'd said, and he'd hoped maybe it was true, but now he
knew why he couldn't love her. Because she wasn't his,
and he wasn't free.

He was Prince Alexander Julius Alberici of Aargau, and
he was betrothed to another.

CHAPTER FOUR

HE NEEDED TO tell her.

Alexander needed to tell her that his memory had returned, that he knew who he was.

But he also knew that once he did, everything would change. Forever.

He wasn't ready to lose her. He wasn't ready to lose the warmth of what they had. He'd never felt like this with anyone, and he'd never been wanted like this by anyone. She didn't even know who he was, or what he was, and yet she wanted him.

And so that day, all day, he watched her, paying attention to everything, committing to memory the sunlight on her hair and how it illuminated her stunning profile. He watched her walk and that way she'd almost skip because of the joyous bounce in her step. She was so buoyant, so happy, she radiated light and goodness.

Hope and strength.

He hadn't been raised with women like her. He hadn't ever known that women like her existed. His mother had been born a princess and had been raised strictly, taught to be conscious and vigilant about the image she presented, conscious of her elevated place in society. Lovely Josephine was nothing like his mother. She was free and lacked conceit and arrogance. She was humble and practical and so quick to smile and laugh.

He'd dated many women over the years but there had never been anyone like Josephine.

And his fiancée, Princess Danielle, was nothing like Josephine, either.

The heavy rock returned to his stomach, the weight re-

minding him that his past and future were about to collide
and it would be painful and ugly.

No, he couldn't think of the future now—it wasn't here.
And he couldn't dwell on Princess Danielle, either.

He didn't want to think of anything but Josephine,
acutely aware that they were on borrowed time and that
the real world would intrude soon, and once it did nothing
would ever be the same.

"What's wrong?" Josephine asked, coming up behind
him to wrap her arms around his neck. She leaned against
him, kissing his cheek, her body so warm against his back.
She smelled of sunshine and lavender and the honey-va-
nilla-scented shampoo she used on her hair. "Is your head
hurting again?"

Not his head, he thought, but his conscience.

He'd spent the past week making love to her, promising her the future, even as another woman counted down
the weeks, anticipating their wedding in the Roche Cathedral across from the Alberici palace. He was going to end
up hurting one if not both of them. He reached up to cover
one of Josephine's hands. "My head is fine," he answered
quietly. "I just keep thinking about the future."

"It won't be so bad," she said, her voice gentle.

She was always so gentle with him, so patient. As if he
deserved tenderness and patience when he was anything
but tender and kind himself.

She wouldn't like who he was, he thought.

She wouldn't like Prince Alexander Julius at all.

The emotion was intense and uncomfortable, so uncomfortable that he couldn't allow himself to go there. Instead,
he pulled her down onto his lap and kissed her, his hand
fisting in her thick hair, warm from the sun.

But kissing her only made the emotion hotter and fiercer.
He didn't want to let her go. There was no way in hell he
wanted to lose her—she was the first woman he'd ever

needed, ever craved—but at the same time, Alexander didn't know how he'd reconcile his duty and responsibility to his kingdom and Princess Danielle with his feelings, and Alexander knew too well that in his world feelings didn't matter. Feelings, in fact, were inconsequential. What mattered was fulfilling one's duty.

He'd tell her tomorrow, he vowed, breaking off the kiss. Her green gaze met his and held. She looked at him with such trust, such love. His chest tightened, guilt pummeling him. He'd never been dishonest with anyone before. How could he hurt her? How could he do this to her?

She wouldn't stand in the way of his wedding to Danielle, either. She'd tell him to do the honorable thing. She wouldn't ask for anything for herself.

Her hand rose to lightly skim his cheekbone and then his mouth and finally his jaw. "What's wrong? Tell me."

He wanted to. God, how he wanted to, because there were still things he didn't remember and things that weren't clear. Like the trip on the yacht with his friends. He wasn't even sure which friends had been there. Shouldn't he remember that? And he didn't remember the beach, and he didn't remember a fight, and he didn't remember going overboard.

If his memory had returned, why were those details still blank?

"I just want to remember the yacht," he said after a moment, hating the turmoil within him. He'd always known himself. He'd always been confident. No, he didn't like this new version of himself. "I want to remember my friends and the circumstances that brought me to you."

She rubbed the line of his jaw and then lightly dragged her fingernails across the stubble of his beard. "I do, too. And then when I know what happened, I will find your friends and give them a piece of my mind because how dare they treat you so shabbily! How dare—"

He stopped her words with a kiss, and as he kissed her he felt a shaft of pain through his chest. She was, without a doubt, the very best thing he'd ever known, and soon he'd break her heart. And just maybe break his, too.

Josephine woke with a start, a familiar sound puncturing her dreams. It was a boat.

Her father's motorboat. She flung back the covers and practically jumped out of bed, trying to absorb the fact that her father was home two days earlier than expected.

A strong muscular arm reached for her. "Where are you going?" he murmured sleepily.

"My father's home," she answered, heart hammering, trying to imagine her father's reaction if he walked into the cottage and found her in bed with a strange man. Her father was tolerant but it would have been too much for him. She dragged her hair into a ponytail. "You stay here. I'll go speak with him."

"I'll go with you."

He stood unashamed before her, tall, muscular, tanned, *naked*. Heat rushed through her, and her hands shook as she pulled on a sundress, covering her nudity, suddenly aware that she wasn't at all prepared for this moment. She'd convinced herself that her father would like him, but would he?

"Let me talk to him first, and then I'll bring him inside and introduce you two. I think it'd be better if I tell him what's happened—"

"Why are you upset? Will he be angry to find me here?"

"Not if you're dressed. But he's a father. I'm his little girl."

"Understood."

She pulled up the covers and then, glancing at the bed, realized how it would look. She took one of the pillows and a quilt and carried them to the living room, where she made a second bed on the ground.

He'd followed her into the living room, brow lifting quizzically. "My bed, I take it?"

"Yes." She shot him a desperate look. "Do you mind?"

"Am I really to sleep there?"

"If you'd prefer, *I* can sleep there—"

"Don't be foolish. I love sleeping on the floor."

"You don't mean that."

"True. But for you, I'd do anything." And then he pulled her into his arms and kissed her hard, the kiss hot and possessive. When he lifted his head, his blue gaze scorched her with its heat. "And I do mean that."

He released her and Josephine slipped out of the cottage and ran down to the beach where her father was anchoring the boat. He was just reaching for the second line when he saw her. "Perfect timing," her father called.

She took the line from him and attached it to the mooring buried deep in the sand. He jumped out to give her a hand.

"You're back early," she said as he finished attaching the heavy chain through the iron loop.

"I was worried about you. I couldn't reach you on the radio."

"It broke a few days after you left."

"And you couldn't fix it?"

"I dropped it, smashing too many parts."

"I bought a new one, just in case."

"Smart thinking." She pushed her hair back from her face, feeling ridiculously nervous. She wasn't used to feeling this way, not around her father. "How was your trip? Everything go all right?"

"Everything went well. Had some good news while at the university. Picked up some more grant money, which is always nice."

"Money pays bills."

"Also necessary when restocking supplies." He waded

back into the water and climbed into the boat and began dragging boxes and crates forward. "How have things been here? Anything exciting?"

She darted a glance toward the stone house. "Actually, yes. Far more exciting than usual." She took a quick breath. "We have a visitor."

Her dad stopped in his tracks, slowly straightening. "A what?"

"A visitor." She smiled brightly. "It's quite the story, too. You see, he went overboard and I saved him." She gulped more air, needing courage. "He was injured in the accident. He's lost his memory. Can't remember anything, not his name or where he's from."

"He's been alone with you this entire time?"

"Not the entire time. Just a week or so."

"A week or so." He paused, his weathered forehead creasing even more deeply. "Here? On the island?"

"Yes."

"Where is he now?"

"Inside the house. I asked him to stay there while I told you about him. I knew it'd be a shock. It was a shock to me—" she broke off as her dad jumped over the side of the boat and started for the house. "What are you doing?"

"Going to tell this fellow to pack up—"

"Pack what?" she cried, running to catch up with him. "He went overboard. He has nothing!"

"Great. It'll make it that much easier to ferry him to Antreas and hand him over to officials there."

"What are you talking about?"

"You know nothing about this man. He could be dangerous."

"If he was dangerous, wouldn't I know it by now?"

"I'll be the judge of that."

"Dad, stop. Listen." She grabbed his coat sleeve, tugged on it hard, stopping him. "He has *amnesia*."

"Which would make him all the more unpredictable. You're lucky he hasn't hurt you—"

"Why would I hurt her when she saved my life?" Alexander said, his deep voice catching them both by surprise. He approached her father and extended a hand. "I'm grateful for your daughter's bravery, Professor Robb."

Her father warily shook his hand. "I understand you've had an accident."

"I did."

Her father stepped back, still studying him, his expression shuttered. His closed expression worried her. Her father was a professor—his career had been filled with young people, students—and he was usually affable, friendly. He wasn't now. What was wrong?

"Let's get the supplies in," her father said, turning to her. "While you put away the food, I'll set up the radio."

"Can I help?" Alexander asked.

"No, but thank you," her father said.

"Then I'll give you some time to catch up."

In the cottage, Josephine kept glancing at her father as she unpacked the groceries and various supplies needed for life on Khronos. Her father worked on the radio, attaching it to the solar panels that would maintain a constant charge. Normally he'd talk to her while he worked. This morning he was silent.

She folded her arms and faced him. "You're upset."

"Do you know who he is?" he asked. "This shipwrecked man of yours?"

"No. But he's obviously European, and wealthy. It was a huge yacht, incredibly luxurious."

Finished with the radio, her father went to his backpack and retrieved his computer and a pile of newspapers. "He's a prince from the kingdom of Aargau. And he's been missing for over a week."

She laughed. "A prince?"

Her father didn't smile. His expression was stony.

"A *prince*?" she repeated, her throat suddenly scratchy.

"Yes."

"You're sure?"

Her father flung down the stack of newspapers. "It's in all the news, in papers from all over the world. Everyone is looking for him. It's been in the headlines daily. At first he was merely missing, but they have now begun to worry he's not going to be found—at least not found alive. All the more tragic as he's supposed to be getting married in just a few weeks."

He was getting married?

No…

No.

"Maybe it's a different person. Maybe—" she broke off as her gaze fell on the top newspaper, the headline paired with a photo. The bold headline read "Prince Alexander Feared Dead," and while she didn't recognize the name, she recognized the face in the photo.

It *was* him.

And his name was Alexander.

Alexander. She said the name silently, rolling it over in her mind, before looking back down at the photo. Her mystery man, her beloved stranger, wasn't a rich Italian but a Mediterranean prince. Thirty-four-year-old Prince Alexander Julius Alberici, who was engaged to marry Princess Danielle Roulet at the end of this month.

Her father returned to the radio, adjusting the signal. "I'm going to call the Greek authorities," he said. "They'll in turn alert the authorities in Aargau. I imagine they'll send help right away, probably a helicopter."

She crossed the floor to the open window, where she stood facing the sea. She couldn't see Alexander, not from where she stood, but she knew he was out there, probably in the sheltered cove.

"Do you have to call today?" she asked quietly, her back to her father, her gaze still on the bay. "Can you wait until the morning? Give us this last day."

"That would be cruel. His family thinks he's dead."

She nodded, swallowing hard around the lump filling her throat. She didn't want to be cruel, but she would miss him. Terribly.

"Can you at least wait until I'm gone?" she asked, glancing over her shoulder to where her father sat at the table with the radio.

"I'm going to call soon," her father answered.

She fought the salty sting of tears and forced back the lump making it difficult to swallow.

It was ending so quickly. She'd thought she'd have at least two more days before her father returned, but instead he was here and taking control, and she was grateful he was doing the right thing, the proper thing, but she wasn't ready to say goodbye to Alexander.

She didn't want to be here when they came for him. She couldn't imagine parting, never mind surrounded by strangers who didn't understand what the past week had been like.

It had been heaven on earth.

She'd never been so happy in her entire life.

And yet he wasn't hers. He was never meant to be hers. What they'd shared here on Khronos was a mistake—no, she wouldn't call it that, but a fluke, something that hadn't been meant to be. And while the time they'd shared couldn't be taken from them, there was no future for them. It was unlikely their paths would ever cross again.

"I don't want to be here when they come for him," she said quietly, her gaze meeting her father's before shifting away. "May I have your permission to take the boat to Antreas? I haven't been off Khronos in ages. It'll be good for me to get out and do something."

"You don't want to see him off?"

"You know how I am about goodbyes. I find them painful."

"Won't the prince be offended?"

"It will be better for him if people don't know he was here alone with me. It will be better if help comes and they find you."

"The truth will get out. It always does."

"But that won't be my problem then. He'll be home in Aargau with his family and his fiancée." The words stuck in her throat. She managed a tight smile. "And at least this way I'll have some dignity. Goodbyes always hurt too much."

"You've been this way ever since you lost your mom—"

"I don't want to talk about her. Let me gather a few things quickly as I'd like to leave soon. I'll take the boat to Antreas for the night and return by noon tomorrow."

"It's too far on your own."

"It's a straight shot north. I'll be fine, and I've done it before." She managed another small, brittle smile. "And when I return tomorrow, all will be well, and life will return to normal."

CHAPTER FIVE

ALEXANDER RETURNED FROM his swim to discover Josephine had left, and she'd gone without a word to him. She'd gone without a goodbye.

Her father attempted a weak explanation, which only made Alexander grit his teeth. It was a battle to hide his shock and disappointment.

"She didn't know how to say goodbye," Professor Robb added. "She doesn't like to cry."

"And why would she cry?" Alexander retorted stiffly.

The professor pushed a set of newspapers across the rough-hewn table, giving him a glimpse of headline after headline.

"Aargau's Prince Alex Missing"
"Tragedy on Yacht in Aegean Sea"
"Royal Prince Feared Dead"

"She knows who I am," Alexander said.

Professor Robb nodded. "But so do you, don't you?"

"I started remembering pieces a few days ago, but it wasn't until yesterday that I remembered my name and who I was."

"You didn't tell her."

Alexander didn't reply. "When will she return?"

"After you're gone."

"And when will that be?"

"I suspect help will be arriving later this afternoon."

The professor was right.

A helicopter from Aargau's Royal Navy arrived within hours, a medic on board in case Alexander needed care, but after a quick exam, he was cleared to fly, and they left Khronos.

Alexander didn't speak the entire flight to Aargau, nor did he speak as the Mercedes whisked him from the helipad to the palace. It was just a fifteen-minute drive and he stared out the window seeing, but not seeing, the streets of Roche, Aargau's capital city, home for the past one hundred sixty-five years to the royal Alberici family.

His family.

As the chauffeur drove him, with cars driven by security ahead and behind him, he wondered why he didn't feel relief that he was home.

He wondered why sights that were familiar didn't fill him with any comfort or pleasure.

Instead he felt only an oppressive sense of dread. He knew his father was ill—he remembered that clearly—but there was something missing in his memories, something that didn't explain the dread that felt like a lead weight in his gut.

Perhaps it was because he didn't remember his time on the yacht. Perhaps it was because he feared questions about the trip and his injury and his questionable memory. He didn't want to alarm his mother by letting her know that there were things he didn't remember. He needed to protect her from more stress. The past nine days couldn't have been easy for her.

Arriving at the palace, the gates opened for the parade of black Mercedes and then closed behind them. The palace was surrounded by thick walls dating back to the fifteenth century, and portions of that early fortress remained: a chapel, a tower, a prison dungeon. Newer buildings had risen around the medieval architecture, sometimes incorporating them, sometimes ignoring them. The Alberici family lived in the eighteenth-century palace, and guards and staff filled some of the other buildings. Years ago Alexander had claimed the tower as his own, converting each floor into rooms of his own. He had a private gym on the ground floor and an office one floor above that. His private library was on the third floor, with access to a guest suite on the fourth. The stairwell between the fourth and fifth floors led to the roof and the parapet where antique cannons remained.

When he needed to be home for long periods, he'd retreat to the tower guest suite, sleeping there to give himself some much-needed privacy. No one entered the tower without his permission, and he limited access when he was in residence to his own butler and valet.

His butler and valet were on the palace front steps as the motorcade drew to a stop, and they ushered him to his suite of rooms in the palace, where he showered, shaved and dressed.

"Are you well, Your Highness?" his valet asked after giving Alexander's coat a tug, adjusting the fit over his shoulders.

"Yes, thank you," Alexander answered.

"You have quite a cut on your head, sir."

"It's nothing."

"The doctor has seen you?"

"A navy doctor checked me out on the way here."

"Very good, sir."

And then Alexander was off, leaving his suite for that of his parents' rooms.

The meeting with his mother and father was brief. His father was in a chair, his eyes closed, when Alexander entered the room. His mother, Serena, was sitting in a chair nearby, embroidering. She'd taken up embroidery a few years ago and now it was rare to see her in private without a needle and thread in her hands.

Seeing that his father was sleeping, he paused at his mother's chair, stooping to kiss her forehead. At fifty-five she was slim and elegant and until recently had looked far younger than her years, but his father's change of health had unfairly aged her. "Hello, Mother."

She reached up to pat his cheek and tears filled her eyes. "Alexander," she said, the quiver in her voice betraying the stress of the past few weeks.

He glanced to his father's chair. His father looked shockingly thin, his complexion gray. "How is he?"

Her shoulders shrugged. "He's—"

"Tired of worrying about you, you thankless scoundrel," his father answered, his voice hoarse and thin.

Alexander smiled faintly. His father wasn't joking, either. He'd been a disappointment to his father ever since he was a boy and had refused to hunt and shoot animals and whip his horse and do any number of things that a male should do to prove his dominance. "You can stop worrying then. I'm back, safe and sound," Alexander said lightly.

"It crossed my mind that you were deliberately staying away, enjoying our discomfort."

"No, never." He glanced down at his mother, his expression softening. "I'd never want to distress Mother. Now, you, you're a different matter." His lips were curved, his tone dry and slightly mocking because that was how he and his father communicated. With biting sarcasm and stinging disdain.

"Ha, I knew it." His father struggled to sit up in his chair and Alexander went to his aid but his father brushed him away. "I'm not so frail that I can't sit up in my own chair."

"Never doubted your strength, sir."

His father cleared his throat and then coughed and coughed. And coughed some more. It was a long time before he could speak. "Your cousin," he rasped, eyes watering, voice quavering. "He's been quite anxious about your return. Damian's been checking in a half-dozen times a day."

"Hoping to inherit, I'm sure."

His father looked at him hard from beneath dark brows. "He has always respected the crown, unlike you."

"I was a boy when I said those things. Don't you think it's time to forgive?"

"I forgave you, but I won't forget."

Alexander held back the words he wanted to say. There was no point in defending himself, no point in arguing his case. It would change nothing. "I would have it no other way, Father."

"Princess Danielle's family has also been in touch daily. Have you spoken yet with her?" His mother asked, diverting the attention. "She's been frantic."

"Does she do *frantic*? I've only ever known her to be the epitome of calm."

"Not frantic as in frenzied, but concerned," his mother conceded. "Which is why we like her so much. She won't embarrass you. She won't embarrass us."

"A perfect wife," he murmured.

And yet his mother heard, her dark blond eyebrows rising. "I thought you liked her."

"And I do," Alexander answered. "She's a perfectly lovely princess."

"Faultless," Serena added.

"Right." He gave her a slight bow and then another in the direction of his father, and he was off. The great homecoming was over.

Alexander's close friends were warmer in their greetings. They descended on him, gathering in his large suite in Alberici Palace, exclaiming over his tan, offering fierce hugs and pats on the back. These were men who'd grown up with him and gone to university with him and served in the Royal Navy with him, and they were damn glad to see him home.

"We were desperate," Gerard said as they all took seats

in Alexander's living room. "Once we discovered you were gone, we notified the palace immediately, and they sent planes and helicopters, and the Greek Air Force and Navy joined in the search, but there was no sign of you. We honestly feared the worst."

"When did you realize I was missing?" Alexander asked, the only one not to sit.

Gerard grimaced. "When you didn't come out for breakfast, and then lunch, I knew something was wrong. I ended up breaking your door down."

"Well, I broke it down," Rocco corrected. "Gerard was trying but not very successfully."

Everyone laughed, but the laughter died to an uncomfortable silence.

"Have you talked to her yet?" Marc asked after a moment. "She's been really upset."

"Danielle?"

"No, Claudia," Marc answered. "I hate playing the big-brother card, but it seems that you owe her an apology."

"Not now," Gerard murmured. "He's only just returned. This isn't the time."

"Why not now?" Marc retorted. "Better to handle this now without Damian here, don't you think?"

Alexander glanced from Marc to Gerard to Rocco. There were undercurrents he couldn't read. Things had happened that he didn't understand. He still had no memory of the trip and yet clearly he needed his memories. "What is this about Damian? And where is he?"

His three friends all glanced at each other before Gerard, the diplomat, answered. "It's been a difficult ten days for him. You and he had that...falling-out...on the ship. And then you went missing. He's been juggling shock and grief—"

"About what?" Alexander interrupted, frustration sharpening his voice.

"Damian said you'd consumed more liquor than we knew. Maybe it was true," Rocco said bluntly.

"And not to play big brother again, but Claudia wasn't yours anymore, Alberici," Marc added. "You broke up with her, not the other way around. You should have left her alone."

The gathering abruptly ended. Alexander asked Gerard to remain behind. He and Gerard had been roommates at the Naval Academy and then had served together all three years in the Royal Navy, and there was no one Alexander trusted more. Gerard was a vault. The man knew how to serve, protect, and keep a secret.

"I need you to tell me what you remember of that last night," Alexander said after the other two had gone.

"What's happened?" Gerard asked quietly. "Something has, hasn't it?"

"Other than the fact that I'm being accused of hitting on my ex-girlfriend and fueling a feud with my cousin?"

"None of that took place?"

"I don't believe so."

"But you don't know."

"I'd like to look at the footage from the yacht's security camera."

"I already requested it."

"And?"

"There is none."

"What?"

"There is no footage, that end of the ship was never equipped with security cameras."

Unbelievable. Alexander closed his eyes and held his breath, containing his disappointment. He'd been counting on footage helping him piece together the mystery of what happened on the boat, and why.

"So what do you remember of that last night?" Alexander said, when he could trust himself to speak calmly.

"You were having a drink with us and said you'd be right back, but you never returned."

"What time did I excuse myself?"

"It was after dinner, so maybe ten. Annaliese said it might have been a little earlier. Gigi thought it was a bit later. But ten is a safe bet." Gerard watched Alexander pace the length of the room and the tense silence stretched. After several minutes passed, he said, "You're worrying me, Alex. You are the most detail-oriented person I know. Nothing escapes your attention. Why all the questions? What's happened?"

"I don't know," Alexander said simply, facing his friend. "I've told no one this, but I trust you, and I need your help. I have no memory of that night at all. It's all a blank, and I was hoping you could help me clear up some of the mystery."

Gerard's jaw dropped. "So you don't know how you ended up in the water?"

"I don't remember anything from the trip." He hesitated. "But it's worse than that. For an entire week, I had no memory at all. For a week I didn't know who I was. I didn't know my name."

"How did you manage?"

"I was rescued by a girl on an island. She saved my life and took care of me."

"That's a story."

"It was like a story," he agreed. "The Prince and the Mermaid."

"There is a story like that by Hans Christian Andersen."

"Does it end happily?"

"For the prince."

"And the mermaid?"

"She sacrifices herself for him and turns to sea foam."

"I don't think I'd like that story."

Gerard's brow creased. "I'm worried about you, Alex. If Damian knew this, it could be quite bad for you."

"I know." Alexander sighed and dragged a hand through his hair. "I need the missing pieces. I need my memory. And I definitely need the security footage from the yacht."

Josephine was sure that once she returned to Khronos, life would be fine. Prince Alexander would be gone and she'd be able to focus on her work again.

She expected some sadness and knew she'd miss his company, but she'd lost her mother and lived, and so she'd survive Alexander's departure just fine. The tears she cried at night into her pillow were just part of the process of letting him go. And she would let him go. The intense memories would eventually fade, and over time she'd think of him less and less until one day she could remember him with something other than pain.

It was a good plan, and it might have worked out that way if she hadn't discovered she was pregnant two weeks after his departure for Aargau.

Josephine had suspected within days of Alexander leaving Khronos that she *could* be pregnant, but she'd told herself she was being dramatic, letting her imagination run away with her, which was why she waited almost two weeks to take an over-the-counter pregnancy test that she bought in Athens when she was there with her father for a foundation meeting.

She'd waited until she was alone to buy the test, and then in her hotel room she followed the steps and told herself everything would be fine, that she didn't need to panic or worry—

And then came the immediate positive result.

She *was* pregnant.

And Josephine sat on the side of the bathtub, holding the stick, thinking that she'd known. She'd known because her body felt different. Her breasts were fuller and more sensitive, and she felt nauseous and fatigued.

She couldn't even pretend to be shocked. They'd made love a half-dozen times and they hadn't taken precautions. Yes, he'd withdrawn, but it wasn't true birth control. It was far from foolproof. She didn't know why they hadn't discussed it more. She didn't know why it hadn't been a more urgent issue. It was stupid. She'd behaved irrationally. She'd behaved as if she was the one with amnesia, not he.

And she wasn't just pregnant, but pregnant with the child of one of the most fascinating, wealthy royal families in the world.

Josephine felt sick. Heartsick. Disgusted with herself, disgusted by her lapse in judgment.

If she went to her father she knew what he would say. He would say she had three options: terminate the pregnancy and tell no one, keep the child and tell no one, or keep the child but tell Alexander because he had a right to know.

It took little or no thought to eliminate option one: she wasn't going to end the pregnancy. That wasn't an option, not for her. She tried to imagine raising Alexander's child in secret, and that wasn't a viable option, either. It wasn't right or fair, not to him or their child. But how could she just show up at the Alberici palace in Roche and demand an audience? Never mind just a week before Alexander's wedding to Princess Danielle?

Stomach churning, she waited for her father to return from his meeting. "I need to reach Prince Alexander," she told him. "I need to speak with him about a matter of some…urgency."

Her father eyed her in silence for a long minute. "You're pregnant, aren't you?"

She nodded.

"Well, that explains the food poisoning. It wasn't food poisoning at all."

"I had hoped."

"So had I." He sighed and shook his head. "This is going to change your life. It will never be the same."

"You don't think I'll be a good mother?"

"It's not that simple. I'm not a monarchist, and I don't know all the laws in Aargau, but this isn't just any baby. You're carrying the future king's heir."

"Maybe I shouldn't tell him."

"You are as honest as they come, Josephine. You'd never keep the truth from him, or a child from his father. You wouldn't be able to live with yourself. So contact the palace security—I have a number, they left it with me when they came for him—but don't expect this meeting of yours to be easy. Your news could change everything."

The return to Khronos was so different from his departure two and a half weeks earlier. When he left, he hadn't thought he'd see Josephine again and he'd been livid with her, seething the entire trip to Roche. At the time, he didn't know what had upset him more—the fact that she'd left Khronos without telling him, or that she'd left the island without him telling her who he was.

He'd known that day, and every day since, that he should have told her his memory had returned. He'd been painfully aware that he should have handled things differently.

And now he was to see her again. She'd sent word through his security that there was an urgent private matter, and she'd asked his security how she should best deliver this urgent, sensitive information.

He'd known at once why she was reaching out. It was the only reason she would reach out.

Alexander requested the helicopter and flight crew for the following morning and now they were traveling above the blue-green water. Soon they'd be touching down on Khronos. He wondered if she had any idea he was on his way or that if her news was as he expected, then he'd be taking her back to Aargau with him. Today.

Helicopters were impossibly noisy, their turning blades impossibly distinctive. Josephine emerged from the small house, her pen still in her hand as she shielded her eyes to look up into the sky. The huge helicopter was flying low and coming directly toward her.

Her heart fell even as her stomach lurched, not a good combination when she was already nauseous.

Her father stepped out from the house, as well. His brow creased as he took in the helicopter dropping even lower. "He must have gotten your message," her father said.

She swallowed hard, her legs suddenly weak. "Maybe it's someone else."

"It's the same helicopter that came before. If he is any man at all, he'll be inside it and eager to speak with you."

Josephine wanted to throw up. She put a hand to her middle to slow the churning sensation that made her feel so sick. "You sound pleased."

"I'll be pleased if he comes in person to sort this out with you." He glanced at her, his expression suddenly critical. "Perhaps you'd like to change and comb your hair."

"Why? Because he's a prince?"

"No, because he's the man you love."

Josephine refused to change out of her yellow checked sundress, but she did run a brush through her hair and then pulled it back into a smooth ponytail, and then she took a seat at the table in the house and waited.

It wasn't long before she heard his footsteps outside and then his rap on the door that was already open.

She rose, hating how nervous she felt. "*Prince* Alexander Alberici," she said, accenting the word *Prince*. It wasn't polite, but then, she didn't feel polite. How could she when she was suddenly blisteringly angry?

"May I come in?" he said formally, still standing on her threshold.

"You know the house. You know your way around."

He entered, stooping slightly to clear the low doorway and then straightening once he was inside. His gaze swept the stone walls and rugged beams running across the ceiling. "Nothing's changed," he said.

"It's been this way for a hundred years. I expect it'll remain this way for another hundred."

He crossed the floor, glancing right and then left. "Your father?"

"Is at his desk in the foundation office." She struggled to contain her temper. "So no, there is no one here. It's just you and me. We won't be overheard."

"I wasn't worried about that. I wanted to be polite and pay my respects."

"How kind of you."

"You are angry."

"I am." She hadn't even realized just how deeply upset she was until he stepped through her door looking even more handsome than she remembered. He'd been beautiful to her in her father's faded chambray work shirts and linen shorts, but now in elegant trousers, dark shirt, and dark tailored blazer, he looked powerful. Magnetic. He was a man of position and wealth. And he knew it, too.

"You didn't have to reach out to me," he said, slowly walking around the central room, studying everything as if he'd never seen it before.

She hated his slow, lazy perusal because she was sure it wasn't lazy at all. He was doing his best to remember details. Or perhaps he was checking details against his memory. Either way, he had no right to be so relaxed, so indolent, in her home.

Her arms crossed over her chest, fingers curling into

small, tight fists. "Does Princess Danielle know you're here?"

"We're not married yet."

"What does that even mean?"

"She doesn't get access to my personal schedule."

"Does she even know about me?"

"The palace hasn't released any information about you." He gave her a considering glance. "Unless you'd like the palace to release information?"

She shot him a furious look, giving him the full measure of her wrath. "When did your memory return?" She asked, her voice flat, hard. "At what point on Khronos did you know who you were?"

"The day before your father returned."

She stared at him, clearly struggling. "You should have told me."

"Yes."

"Why didn't you?"

"Because at that point I wasn't ready to lose you."

Her mouth tightened; her jaws ground together. She was not going to cry. She would not allow herself to show any weakness or emotion at all. "You mean you weren't ready to stop having sex."

His black eyebrow lifted. "Is that what we were doing? Having sex?"

"Unprotected sex. And there were…are…consequences."

"I suspected that was why you reached out to the palace."

"You're not shocked?"

"As you said, there are consequences."

"You sound so cavalier," she gritted out. "You must have a plan in mind. A suggestion for managing this *complication*."

"Are you enjoying yourself?"

"No. I'm sick and heartsick and I should have heard

the truth from you. I should have heard the truth, if you knew it."

"Agreed. I was wrong. I am truly sorry."

His apology caught her off guard and she felt herself sag, so she sat down in the chair at the table, her hands balling in her lap.

He crossed the floor, approaching her, so tall that she had to tip her head back to look him in the eye.

"I didn't tell you," he added, "because I was determined to find a way to save us."

"Save us?" She made a soft, hoarse sound of protest. "How? You were engaged to someone else. Your wedding was weeks away. You weren't free to be with me. You weren't free to make love to me."

He crouched in front of her, his hands on her knees. "I can't change what happened when I didn't have my memory—"

"No, but that doesn't mean I don't regret it." She pushed his hands off her knees, feeling burned. "All of it."

"No."

"*Yes*. I hate that week we spent together. I hate that I fe—" She broke off, swallowing hard, smashing the words that had nearly escaped her lips. *I fell in love with you*. But she couldn't love him. Not anymore. She'd smash her feelings now, just as she'd suppressed the words. What had happened was history. The past was behind them. The only thing to do now was move forward without him. Somehow.

"Have you seen a doctor?" he asked.

She shook her head.

"Then how do you know?"

"I took a test in Athens yesterday, and I took it because I've never been late, and my body is different. Everything feels different. I'm violently ill, sometimes in the morning, sometimes at night. The only time I seem to be okay is in the afternoon and early evening." She fell silent for a moment before drawing a breath for courage. "I wouldn't have reached out to you if I wasn't certain. I am pregnant. And I intend to keep the baby. I don't need anything from you—"

"Of course you do. It's my child, too."

"I'm not asking for support. I'm not asking for—"

"Anything, yes, I know. But it doesn't work that way, *cara*. You are carrying my child, my heir. You might not ask for anything, but that doesn't mean you don't get everything."

She blinked, not understanding. "I'm sorry. I don't follow. What is everything?"

"Marriage. My home. My kingdom."

"But I don't want any of those—"

"I knew you'd say that. I was actually counting on you saying that. You didn't sleep with me to become pregnant. You didn't make love to me for any ulterior motive. You are not one of those women that try to entrap a man."

"Maybe it's time for you to go. You know the truth. I've kept nothing from you—"

"We need you to see a doctor. We need to be sure."

"I am sure."

"Yes, but I can't end my engagement to Danielle without proof. It wouldn't be fair to her."

"I don't want you to end your engagement to her. You're engaged to her. You must marry her—"

"I can't, not if you're carrying my child."

Her lips parted but no sound came out.

"The babe you're carrying is Aargau's future king or queen." Alexander rose. "I shall go look for your father and let him know you'll be returning to Roche with me."

He was so very different from her Alexander. But then, on the other hand, he wasn't. He'd always been rather imperious, if not downright commanding. She'd known from the moment he'd first spoken to her that he was a man familiar with authority and accustomed to being obeyed. But that didn't mean she had to fall in with his plans. She'd fallen in love with a man, not a prince, and she wanted the man, not the prince. "No, I'm not going."

His mouth tightened. Creases fanned from his eyes. He looked as if he was hanging on to his patience by a thread. "I'll explain to your father—"

"No need to look for me, I'm here." Her father stepped through the doorway. "I've heard most of what's been said. And I agree with Prince Alexander. You should see a doctor. You should be certain. Feelings are not facts, and what you both need now are facts. Having clear facts will help you make the right decisions."

CHAPTER SIX

SUNLIGHT PIERCED THE TALL, narrow windows of the tower suite. Holding her breath, Josephine watched the light pattern the smooth stone floor, focusing on where the blue-gray fieldstone disappeared beneath the pale ivory-knotted fringe of the burgundy and peach antique carpet.

If she stayed very still and very calm, she could lose herself in the streaks of golden light.

If she stayed very still and very calm, she could almost believe she hadn't been locked for days in a high tower without any connection to the outside world.

And then, since she *was* pretending, she could pretend her room, with its high vaulted ceiling, lovely, narrow leaded windows, and imposing four-poster bed in the middle of the floor, was a luxurious historic hotel room, and she was a guest at this stunning five-hundred-year-old castle, making her much envied by those who loved luxury travel. She would also pretend that the man who'd locked her here, the man she'd fallen in love with, was a handsome, kind prince instead of a cold, heartless one.

Unfortunately, Josephine wasn't good at sustaining the pretend game. It wasn't that she didn't have an imagination, but being the daughter of two scientists, she was more practical than impractical and loathed everything about her tower, and the man who'd locked her here.

Jo sat up straighter as she heard the scrape of the key turning in the lock. She fought a momentary panic because once the door opened, she couldn't play her games of pretend. It was so much harder to manage her emotions with Alexander in the room.

Four weeks ago Josephine wouldn't have believed any

of this was possible. But then, four weeks ago she hadn't known who Alexander was.

Four weeks ago, neither had he.

Now she wished she'd never told him she was pregnant. She'd thought she was doing the right thing, the honest and fair thing. But Josephine regretted her decisions with her whole heart as Alexander was neither honest nor fair, as it was his decision to put her here in this tower suite. It was his decision to lock the door. It was his decision to cut her off from communication with the world, but locking her away wouldn't help his cause. If he imagined that a few days of solitary confinement would weaken her resolve, he was painfully mistaken. She'd spent weeks, *months*, alone on Khronos while her father was off teaching. She wasn't afraid to be alone, and she wasn't easily intimidated.

But she was beginning to realize that her upbringing, so isolated from society, had not prepared her for dealing with complex relationships, and she suddenly doubted herself. She'd always thought she was a good judge of character, but apparently she wasn't. It seemed that she knew too much about science and too little about human beings. Which was why she'd told Alexander on arriving in Aargau that she'd include him in their child's life, even share parental responsibilities with him—because that was the fair thing to do—but he'd refused to even consider co-parenting. Their baby would live with him in the palace. Their baby required both mother and father, and they'd do it together. Married. And that would never ever happen. She'd never agree to marrying him, not after he'd revealed his true colors.

The door swung open and Prince Alexander Julius Alberici stood on the threshold, tall, broad shouldered, and impeccably groomed. His thick black hair was ruthlessly combed back, hiding the fact that it had an inclination to curl. His blue eyes focused on her with that laser focus that always made her feel as if he could see straight through her.

She sat up taller, her own shoulders squaring, chin lifting defiantly. She'd been told on first arriving in Roche that she should curtsy before him, and she'd laughed. *Laughed.* "I'd sooner have a lobotomy," she'd snapped.

Prince Alexander had heard and his lips had tightened.

His mouth—which she'd once thought so lovely—tightened now, but she no longer cared. Right now she didn't care what he thought, and right now she didn't care what he did, as long as he let her return to Khronos. It felt as if every good and tender feeling had been smashed, and it was his fault. He'd done this to her. To *them*.

"Can I help you?" she asked coolly.

Alexander entered the tower bedroom, unsurprised to find her where he'd last seen her, in the middle of her bed with a pile of books around her, her expression hard and shuttered. Her sketchbook was open next to her, a charcoal pencil against white paper, but the page was blank.

"How are you this morning?" he asked, stepping into the room, the door closing and locking behind him.

He saw her head turn, her honey hair scraped back from her face, pulled into a severe knot at her nape. Her green gaze focused on the door, her lips compressing with displeasure as the lock scraped closed. He knew she hated being locked in, and he hated locking her in. But he wasn't about to run the risk of her leaving Aargau in the dark of night, not when she was pregnant with his child.

"I am as tired of this as you," he said flatly, approaching the bed. "I just want a resolution. I want us to move forward."

Her head jerked up, eyes flashing with contempt. Even with her hair drawn back and not a bit of makeup to enhance her features, she was strikingly beautiful. He'd wondered when he first returned from Greece if he'd imagined her and her breathtaking beauty. He hadn't. If anything, she was more ethereal, and even lovelier than he'd remembered.

But her delicate beauty belied her strength. Josephine was livid, and she was not about to be strong-armed into marriage. "I don't like this any more than you," he added. "Marry me so we can be done with this. We were friends once—"

"*Not* friends."

"On Khronos you told me you loved me, Josephine. You said the words."

Color flooded her cheeks, making her eyes brighter. "I had no idea you weren't free. I had no idea you were...*you*."

"Neither did I."

"For your information, I liked the other you better, the one with amnesia. The one that didn't know his name, because at least he knew how to be kind. What you're doing now is unforgivable. You can't lock women in towers. It's medieval. Machiavellian." Her chin lifted, her gaze locking with his. "Even *you* must know that it's not done."

"I'm not happy about this, *bella*. I would prefer you to have a normal guest suite. I would prefer to be able to introduce you to my family and friends—"

"And your fiancée, Princess Danielle Roulet? What about her? Or have you not given her any thought or consideration?"

"You know I ended my engagement to her the moment we had confirmation of your pregnancy." He leaned against one of the enormous wooden posters on the antique bed. "There is nothing standing in the way of our marriage now."

"Nothing but my objections, but apparently that doesn't signify in your world. You're a prince, and I'm just an ordinary American girl."

"Who will one day be queen."

"I don't want to be queen. I'm not marrying you."

"Josephine, I'm trying to make this work—"

"Locking me in a tower is not making it work, Alexander!"

"You shouldn't have tried to run away."

"I wasn't running away. I was simply leaving the castle."

"With the intention to take a ferry to Italy and then disappear into Europe." He gave her a sympathetic look. "Next time, don't admit so much to a taxi driver, especially when he's a member of palace security."

"I did think it strange that you had a taxi just waiting outside."

"He wasn't there for you, if that's any consolation."

"It's not."

"Can we agree that you're not going to run away anymore? Because if you can give me your word—"

"I'm not sure I can, Alexander. I'm sorry."

"I am, too, because the baby you carry is my heir and thus the heir to the Aargau throne, which gives you two choices—marry me, or grant me sole custody of our child."

He saw her lips press and pain shadow her eyes. "You know I'd never give up my child. You're not giving me a choice."

"Most women would jump at the opportunity to become Aargau's queen."

"I'm not one of them."

"You're offended because it's not a romantic proposal."

"I'm offended because you're arrogant and rude, and baffled by what you call a proposal. You've flung the word *marriage* at me as if I'm a dog being dangled a bone. But the bone, Your Highness, isn't remotely appealing."

Alexander was torn between amusement and outrage. He wondered what his old self would have thought of her response. He'd been told by his friends that his old self lacked a sense of humor. That was interesting because sometimes Josephine made him want to laugh. Or shake her. Or make fierce, hot love to her.

"I'm phrasing things badly," he said. "But we have a wedding to plan, *cara*. We can't keep arguing and wasting time. We have to marry soon. It's essential we avoid scandal."

"You mean it's essential to *you*. I don't care about the scandal."

"That's because you live on an uninhabited rock, apart from society. The rest of us, I'm afraid, are not so lucky."

"You're not serious."

"About the marriage, or being determined to avoid scandal?"

"Both."

"We don't do scandals in Aargau. There has never been a divorce in the Alberici family."

"Just unhappily married, is that it?"

"My parents and grandparents and great-grandparents all knew better then to air dirty laundry. If there is strife, it's dealt with privately, behind closed doors. As we are doing now."

"So women are routinely locked in chambers and towers here?"

"You failed to mention the dungeons."

"I suppose if you have a historic castle, one should use all the rooms."

His lips twisted faintly. She amused him, and yet their current situation was anything but laughable. The palace was in an uproar. His father wasn't speaking to him. His mother was quietly frantic. The public couldn't understand what had happened to their prince.

"I want out of this room," Josephine said clearly, firmly.

"And I want you out of this room. I'd like it to become my retreat again. It used to be one of my favorite rooms, but holding you hostage here has diminished my pleasure in it."

"Poor Prince Alexander. How you suffer!"

He had to smash the laughter. "You are in such a foul mood. Perhaps I should kiss you—"

"No!" She scooted back on the bed. "You come near me and I'll throw every book I have at your head. And I've a good arm. Believe me."

"I do. That's why I want to move forward. It's why I want to introduce you to my kingdom and my people, but I can't do that until we've come to an understanding."

"We can raise our child together without being married." She paused, her winged eyebrows arching even higher. "Or resorting to locking me away as if I'm a dangerous criminal. You must know your strong-arm tactics only make me dislike you and mistrust you more."

"Trust goes both ways."

"Absolutely, and when have I ever let you down? Or betrayed you in any way?"

"You left me on Khronos. You disappeared without a word. And then you tried to run away from here after we saw the doctor. Josephine, I accept that I haven't been the model prince, but you have a poor track record when it comes to staying in place."

"Fine. Next time I'll put up a few signs to advertise that I'm leaving so there won't be any mixed signals," she flashed, hiding how much he continued to hurt her. She told herself she didn't care about him anymore, but if that was true, why did his every word wound? Why did he have such power over her? Worse, how could this be the man she'd loved so passionately on Khronos? He was nothing but cold and hard and calculating. How had she not seen his true nature before?

"Give me your word that you will not run, and I'll move you from the tower to a proper suite in the palace. Better yet, accept my proposal and let us plan the wedding together so that our baby will be born without any shame or scandal surrounding his or her birth."

If only it were that easy, she thought, drawing her knees to her chest and wrapping her arms around her legs, trying to anchor herself, craving safety and stability. Ever since she'd arrived in Roche, she'd felt rootless. Lost. She desperately missed her life on Khronos, needing her work to give her days structure and purpose. "I want to return to Khronos," she whispered. "I want to go home."

"Not until after the baby is born, but then yes, you could go for a visit."

"A visit," she said, her voice trembling.

He said nothing and she glanced around the room, taking in the thick stone walls, the narrow windows, the heavy beamed ceiling. "You're punishing me."

"That's not fair."

"I was a virgin when I met you and now I'm pregnant. Doesn't seem fair at all."

"You wanted to be with me."

"Because I thought you were free. I thought you cared about me."

"I do care about you, which is why I'm marrying *you*, not Danielle."

"You're only marrying me because I'm pregnant!"

"Do you want me to deny it? No, it's true. I'm marrying you because you're carrying my child, but that doesn't invalidate my offer—"

"Oh, it does. It most certainly does, *Your Highness*."

He sighed. "You're being childish."

"You're being hideous."

"We can't go back, Josephine. We can only go forward."

"And we will," she agreed huskily, "but not together. We might have created a baby together, but that doesn't mean we must punish ourselves for eternity—"

"Marriage is not hell."

"So says the man who had a girlfriend *and* a fiancée."

"I broke up with my girlfriend months before my engagement was announced."

"But you were privately engaged to the princess, weren't you?"

"We've had an understanding for years, yes, but Danielle also dated. She had relationships—"

"That still changes nothing. I'm not about to have my heart broken by a man who only cares for himself."

"But why would it be broken if you don't care for me? This isn't a love marriage, Josephine. It's a business deal, an arrangement to protect our child, who will inherit the Alberici wealth and title."

She blinked, hard. "So I don't matter."

His sigh was deep, heavy. "Of course you matter."

Her head dipped, her gaze dropped. "Please leave."

"It's time to put our child first. Stop with the selfishness—"

"*Me?* Selfish? Clearly, you don't remember Khronos or what happened there. But I do. And I was never selfish, never unkind, not toward you."

He left her then, and as the door closed behind him, she put her head down on her knees and fought tears.

She was exhausted and nauseous and sick of emotion. She wasn't used to feeling this much, and certainly not used to so little physical activity. For a girl who'd grown up outside, so close to nature that she felt she was an extension of the mountains and sea, being cooped up in a tower, in a castle, in a city, was a terrible punishment indeed.

Alexander descended the tower staircase to his office on the second floor, aware that Josephine wasn't wrong. He was different here. He had to be different here. On Khronos he'd been just a man. In Aargau he was the future king. He'd rather enjoyed being just a man. There had been freedom, and an ease he didn't know in his world here.

Aimee, his secretary, was at her desk when he entered the room and she glanced up at him, a troubled crease between her brows. "Her Highness has requested you join her in her rooms immediately." Aimee glanced at her watch. "That was nearly an hour ago. Her staff has followed up with me twice since, worried I haven't passed on the message."

"You knew where I was."

She gave a faint smile. "Yes, but you said not to bother you, and so I didn't."

Alexander crossed the Alberici castle grounds, heading for the pale yellow eighteenth-century palace that travel guidebooks always falsely claimed had been inspired by the architecture of Versailles but in reality drew its inspiration from the Royal Palace at Caserta, which was just fifty years older and much closer geographically.

Alexander climbed the grand pink and yellow marble staircase to the second floor and headed back down the long corridor to the set of rooms that were his mother's. There was no need for him to knock as her butler opened the door, announcing him.

Queen Serena waved him to a chair near hers. "You kept me waiting long enough," she said as he sat down and stretched out his legs.

"I came to you the moment I was free."

"I'm hearing things, worrying things." She gave him a long look. "Do you have any news for me? News that would ease some of my anxiety, because your father grows weaker. He slept most of today. We're running short on time, particularly if you hope to have him present at your wedding. Or perhaps you intend to marry after he's gone?" His mother's tone was cool and distant. But then, it was the tone he knew best. She was beautiful and regal, elegant and refined, always cognizant of her power and responsibility as the queen of Aargau.

"Of course I want him there."

"Then the wedding needs to be sooner, not later."

"I understand."

"Then what is the problem, Alexander?"

"Josephine isn't…ready…to marry."

"Excuse me? She's carrying your child, the heir to the kingdom."

"I understand."

"The longer you wait, the more difficult it becomes from a PR standpoint. You understand that, don't you? We're trying to do damage control, Alexander, and all we need is a small, private service in the palace chapel—"

"Unless she wants the formal service in the cathedral."

"We don't have time to plan a formal wedding, and she doesn't need a big, formal wedding. Your father is very unhappy that she's trapped you."

"*I* trapped *her*, not the other way around."

"You're a prince. She is no one."

He knew his mother well enough to know that she wasn't trying to be cruel or rude, just honest. "She didn't care that I was a prince, and she is most definitely someone."

The queen sat back in her chair, her jaw dropping slightly. "You *love* her."

"I want her, yes. But love? I don't know about that. I was once teased for being so emotional. Now I'm criticized for not having feelings. Having feelings would make all of this easier."

"I didn't have…feelings when I married your father. But they developed over time. Yours will develop, too." Her head tilted. She studied him intently. "Are you completely recovered from your accident?"

"Why do you ask?"

"You haven't been the same since you returned home. You are less…you."

He gave her a half bow. "Apologies. I shall try to be more…me."

"I don't appreciate the sarcasm, Alexander. It's very tense here, not simply because your father slips away from us a little more every day, but King Marcel Roulet is livid that his daughter has been profoundly embarrassed just a week before her wedding. And I've just been informed that you are keeping your American locked in your tower—"

"I did lock her in the first night. But she hasn't been locked in since."

"But she believes she's locked in."

He shrugged. "She has a tendency to run away. I need her to remain."

Her eyebrow lifted. "This is not how we conduct our affairs, nor is this how an Alberici royal handles his fiancée. Less drama, more efficiency, please. Put the ring on her finger. Give me a wedding date. We'll have a party this weekend—"

"Too soon."

"She could be *showing* by the next, Alexander."

"Then make it a week from now."

"An engagement party on a Wednesday?"

"Or Tuesday. We'll keep it small and intimate, for our closest friends and family only."

"Fine. But we'll need a portrait of the two of you to give the media." Her glance narrowed. "I don't suppose we can take your official engagement portrait and photoshop Danielle out and put your new girl in her place?"

"Was that a joke, Mother?"

Her lips curved faintly. "I was not always Queen Serena, Alexander. I, too, was once a young girl with a sense of humor and a hunger for adventure."

Josephine crossed to the window of her tower room, stepping up on the footstool she'd positioned beneath it, needing the extra height to look out the leaded glass. It was late afternoon, but due to the summer solstice a week ago, the sun was still high in the sky, shining brightly on the thick, gray slate roofs of the various castle buildings and then, farther out, the high, majestic stone walls that surrounded the castle itself.

She rested her chin on her fist, staring out, taking in Roche, Aargau's capital city famous for its medieval architecture and charming, narrow cobbled streets. She might have liked Roche, but after days of confinement she felt suffocated by all the walls and slate and cobbled stone. Her jaw tensed as her gaze went to the glimpse of sea beyond the city streets, the dark blue water calling to her, reminding her of Khronos.

A scrape sounded at the door, and the lock turned. She nearly fell off the stool as the door swung open and she took a sudden step back, misjudging the distance to the floor and needing to grab the wall to keep from falling down.

"Careful," a crisp, low feminine voice said from the doorway. "That's a good way to hurt yourself."

Josephine stiffened, surprised that it wasn't Alexander as he was the only one who'd been to visit her since she arrived, and yet she knew immediately who had come, having seen photos of her in magazines. "Queen Serena," she said faintly, letting go of the wall.

The slender blonde queen approached. "I haven't thwarted your escape plans, have I?"

Josephine thought she heard a hint of amusement in the older woman's voice. "I don't have Rapunzel's hair," she answered. "And even if I did, the window is a little narrow."

Serena stopped before her, her back straight, her bearing regal. In her icy-blue dress with the ropes of pearls, she looked every inch a queen. "I'm sorry I haven't been to see you sooner. I'm afraid our hospitality isn't what it should be."

"Does your son routinely lock his women up?"

"No, you're the first." She grimaced. "I'd like to say that it's a sign of his affection but you and I both know his behavior is inexcusable. One doesn't lock up beautiful young women in towers anymore. It's positively medieval."

"That's what I told him."

"Machiavellian."

"I said the very same thing."

"What are you going to do?"

"I don't know."

"What do you want to do?"

"Leave."

"What is keeping you here then?"

"Besides the locked door? The need to protect the baby." Josephine's chin lifted. "And not because he or she is an heir, but because he or she is my child."

"And Alexander's."

"I don't want Alexander, though. I realize he's your son, and you love him—"

"He's a man. Men are notoriously thickheaded and thin-skinned, but they have their uses and virtues."

Josephine wasn't sure how to take that last bit. She felt her shoulders tense, and she clasped her hands tightly. "I used to care for him very much, before he was—" she glanced around the room, and her hand followed in a sweeping gesture "—this."

"He's afraid of losing you."

"No, he's afraid of losing his heir, not me."

"If you truly believe that, you don't know my son."

Josephine's lips compressed and she held her tongue, not wanting to argue with the queen, because of course she'd take Alexander's side. She was his mother.

"But he won't lose his heir," Serena added after a moment. "You're not a woman who'd keep a child from his father, so there is something else driving him and making him act like a Neanderthal. Men usually only resort to caveman tactics when cornered and desperate." She glanced from Josephine to the bed, still piled high with books. "You're a scientist. Don't let your emotions cloud your brain. I understand you have a very good brain, so use it. Put my son on notice. Make him earn your favor."

"That will never happen."

"Fine. Then make him earn your trust, but do *something* so that you feel properly empowered and can respect yourself, if not him."

Josephine frowned. "You don't think I respect myself?"

"I think you know what you need to do, but your pride is keeping you from making the right decisions."

"Your solution is for me to marry Alexander."

"I have no solutions, but I do have a preference, and that is for my grandchild to grow up in a stable, loving home."

Josephine looked at the queen for a long, tense moment. "What happens now? When you leave, do you just lock me back in?"

"No. I have no patience for locked doors, secrets, or games."

"So I could leave now with you if I wanted."

Serena's fair head tipped. "Is that what you truly want? To leave here now?"

"I want Alexander to stop intimidating me."

"Then isn't it time to stand your ground?"

The queen walked out, and true to her word, after she left the door remained open, wide-open. Josephine waited a minute, and then another, and another, wondering when one of the palace security would come and close the door, locking it.

But no one came.

Josephine hesitated a long moment and then crossed the threshold, leaving her suite for the tower stairs. For another minute she stood at the top of the circular staircase listening. She heard voices coming from below, and then something was being moved or dragged, something heavy.

Josephine carefully went down the stairs to the next floor. The door was wide-open and it looked like a library, a very handsome library with vast bookshelves that rose all the way to the ceiling. Two men in uniform were carrying chairs while a woman ironed the creases from a heavy brocade cloth covering a table that had been placed in the center of the room.

She didn't know if she made a sound or if one of them felt her there, because suddenly they were all nodding and murmuring polite greetings while continuing with their work.

As if she hadn't just been locked away upstairs for days.

As if it was perfectly acceptable for her to wander around the tower.

She continued down the next flight of stairs, wondering if she'd now be stopped, wondering when she'd be told to return to her room, but she passed staff and no one said anything to her or expressed surprise that she was roaming the tower. She peeked into the room on the second floor and discovered an office suite. It was surprisingly sleek and modern, with computers and big screens and stylish leather chairs and lots of steel and plates of glass set into the wall, filling the spaces where a cannon or some other weapon must have once been.

A pretty young woman sat at one of the sleek ebony desks in the corner typing away on a computer. She looked up and nodded at Josephine before continuing with her work.

Everything seemed so ordinary and yet at the same time, everything was extraordinary.

Josephine cleared her throat. "His Highness, Prince Alexander," she said, her voice not entirely steady.

The young woman looked up again, smiling politely,

professionally. "His Highness has arranged for dinner at nine in the library. That is on the third floor, one level up."

"Thank you." And yet still she hesitated, chewing on her lip, trying to process what she was hearing and seeing. It seemed she'd been given freedom. Was this the queen's doing? Or had Alexander changed his mind?

Josephine walked down the last set of stairs to the first floor. She pushed open the cloudy glass door and entered a huge private gym. There were free weights and weight machines, a treadmill, a stationary bike, and another piece of equipment she'd never seen before, and behind all that was a stone wall covered with brown, gray, and dark green bumps.

She looked at the wall hard, trying to understand what the bumps were before walking toward it, letting her fingers trail over a light gray wedge jutting out from the tower wall at her shoulder height.

"It's a climbing wall," Alexander said, behind her.

She turned around to find him standing not far behind her. He was wearing charcoal-colored shorts and a white T-shirt, and his bronzed skin was flushed, his black hair damp. She couldn't help noticing the way his thin T-shirt clung to the planes of his broad chest and the curve of his sinewy biceps.

"I didn't realize you were here. I'm sorry I interrupted your workout," she said.

"I'd stepped out for a moment to take a call," he answered, lifting the hem of his T-shirt to wipe his jaw, revealing his hard, flat abdomen with his chiseled abs. "But you're not interrupting. I'm just about finished."

She heard the words but couldn't focus on them, suddenly transfixed by the glimpse of his chest, reminded of how that lean, hard torso had felt against her. Her gaze dropped to his hips just before he dropped his shirt, covering himself, but she remembered him there, too, and how his body had given her such pleasure.

Josephine swallowed hard and averted her gaze, but it was too late. Heat rushed through her and she felt tingly and exposed, even as a deep craving hit her, making her ache for the feel and weight of him. "It's an impressive gym," she said hoarsely.

"You're welcome to use it anytime."

She didn't want the gym, though. She wanted him. And the unbidden thought made her loathe herself because she shouldn't be so weak. She shouldn't still want him, not after everything that had transpired. "Your mother came to see me just a little bit ago," she said, struggling to distract herself. "Was that how my door was left unlocked?"

"It's been unlocked for the past two days."

"It hasn't."

"It has."

"But that scraping sound—the lock turning…"

"It's just the hardware. It's old. It should be replaced."

"You let me think I was locked in."

"I did."

"That's horrible. You should be ashamed."

"I am."

"You don't sound it. If anything, you seem rather pleased with yourself."

"I'm pleased to see you."

Her lip compressed and she glanced away, but not before her gaze swept over him, focusing on his midsection, seeing yet again that lovely hard torso in her mind's eye.

She'd been fascinated by him before they'd ever met. She'd watched him on the beach, interested in only him. She'd filled her sketchbook with his likeness.

He was her weakness.

And yet she felt increasingly vulnerable, and not at all safe. "I'm afraid this isn't going to work," she said, her voice low and husky. "And I don't know how to make it work since I no longer trust you."

"I'll earn your trust back."

"I don't think—"

"You have to give it a chance, Josephine."

"It will take time."

"Yes, it will. Unfortunately, it's the one thing we're short on, and so I ask you to trust me that the trust will grow."

"Alexander."

"We need to marry soon—as in right away. As it is the baby will be born early, and we can fudge a few weeks, but every day it will become harder to hide the facts of his or her conception. I can handle gossip. I'm accustomed to slights and insults, but I don't want there to be excessive speculation about our child's birth. Nothing should mar his or her future. Life is hard enough without being born under a cloud of doubt."

Finally, he'd said something she agreed with. Life was hard, and no child should have to grow up with any stigma or gossip surrounding him or her. "Do you even like children?" she asked.

"What a strange question."

"I think it's a fair question. You had never mentioned them before."

"Before? You mean on Khronos when I didn't know my name or where I came from or even my native tongue?"

She squirmed inwardly, thinking he'd made a fair point. "You never asked me how I felt about becoming a mother. You never asked me my feelings on anything."

"I'm sorry."

She shot him a narrowed glance. "So my bedroom door will remain unlocked?"

"Yes."

"You're giving me my freedom back?"

"Freedom to explore the palace grounds, yes."

"But not beyond?"

"You may leave to explore Roche provided you have ample security. But I warn you, it won't be the same as before. The people know you're here—"

"How?"

"I'm followed constantly, *cara*. When I leave these castle walls, I'm followed and photographed and everything I do and eat and buy is documented. Which is why I've kept you here, on the inside. I'm trying to buy you time, giving you a chance to mentally adjust to the changes taking place."

She was silent a long moment. "I don't have very much control anymore, do I?"

"No."

"Or very many options."

"Unfortunately, no."

"What options do I have? What am I allowed to decide?"

"The time of day you'd like to be married. The choice of venue for the ceremony—the chapel here, within the palace grounds, or the Gothic cathedral on Roche's historic square."

He added in the same flat, unemotional voice, "You can choose the type of reception we will have. You have absolute control over the wedding details, large and small. You can decide where we will honeymoon—"

"I don't want a honeymoon."

"You don't think it would be good for us to get away and have some time alone?"

"I've had time alone with you. And look at me now."

A possessive heat flickered in his blue gaze and the edge of his mouth lifted in a sensual curl. "I'd like a week with you where you don't have to cook or wait on me. I'd like to do nothing but keep you in bed all day."

She felt the curl of his lip as darts of sensation raced from the tips of her breasts through her belly to between her thighs. "I think we did that, too."

"There are so many things I want to do with you—"

"No, thank you."

"You'd enjoy it."

"Just like I enjoyed being locked in your tower?"

He considered her words. "Bondage is a form of foreplay. I find the idea of tying you up, or maybe handcuffing you to the bed, very erotic. I think you would, too."

Her pulse leaped. Heat stormed her cheeks. "You clearly don't know me, not if you think I'd enjoy being handcuffed or tied up."

"You don't know that until we try."

She'd never imagined such a thing, and yet she could see herself naked, tied to her bed, waiting for him. Waiting on him. It was shocking and yet thrilling. A frisson of raw desire, spiked by nervous excitement, shivered up and down her spine. "You are being blatantly sexual," she murmured huskily.

His gaze slowly roved her face, lingering on her lips. "You like me blatantly sexual."

"You made me sexual."

His broad shoulders shrugged. "Chemistry has never been our problem. We work. We make sense. Why? I don't know. You're the scientist. You tell me."

Her breath caught in her throat as heat and awareness surged through her. It had been almost three weeks since they'd been intimate and yet her body remembered him and ached for him to hold her down and make her his again. She could remember his lips at her neck and the roughness of his chest against her breasts and the thickness of his hard, hot shaft entering and filling her. When he was with her, in her, she felt unbearably good... She felt complete.

And part of her desperately wanted him again. She wanted his warmth and the sensation of being his, and only his, but another part of her knew he wasn't good for her. Her desire made her dependent. Her desire clouded her thinking. She struggled to remember why they were at odds, needing to create distance, needing a form of defense. "But it's changed," she said breathlessly. "We did have chemistry, but that was before, back when we were on Khronos. When I felt safe with you. I don't anymore."

"You will again."

"So I can go out? I can resume normal living?"

He took so long to answer that she dreaded the answer. "It won't ever be the normal you knew before," he said at length, "but yes, you can go out, and yes, you can go shopping, or out for a meal. But it will be choreographed at our end. Palace security will want to know the details so they can have a plan, create a route, and ensure your outing will be as stress free as they can make it."

"My normal isn't shopping and restaurants. My normal is home. My work. The beach."

"You will have work. It will just be different—"

"Is that supposed to appease me?"

"No. I'm being honest. I think it's better if we lay all the cards on the table. The truth is you will have a new life here, and you will have a new normal, and I promise that I will do everything in my power to help you settle in so that you can be happy, eventually."

A new life here.

A new normal.

Be happy...eventually.

The words echoed in her head. She raised a hand to her face, fingertips pressing against her forehead where pain throbbed. She didn't want a new normal, and she didn't want a new home, but none of that seemed to matter, and honestly, she had no one to blame but herself. She'd lost her head on Khronos. She'd thrown caution to the wind. They'd made love a dozen times. Risks had consequences and the consequence was that they'd created a new life.

She dropped her hand, looked up at him. "Does anyone even know about me?"

"They know you rescued me after my...accident. They know you saved my life, and they believe you're here to be thanked by my parents."

She frowned as a troubling thought came to her. "What about the pregnancy? Does anyone know about that?"

"No. It's a closely guarded secret. Only four people know you are pregnant: our parents and the doctor who performed the ultrasound, and I'm determined that no one else know, not until we choose to make an announcement, most likely once you are well into your second trimester."

"Who is *we*? The palace, or you and me?"

"It will be up to us, I promise."

Up to us. *Us.*

"Don't you think I should meet both of your parents before I say yes?" she asked, taking a deep breath. "I realize your father is the king, but he will be the grandfather of my child. I want to be sure he approves of...me." *Us.*

Alexander hesitated. "My father can be difficult."

"Is that your way of saying I should lower my expectations?"

He smiled crookedly. "You're quite good at subtext."

CHAPTER SEVEN

THEY WERE TO have dinner in his tower library that night. Alexander had given his staff instructions to set a proper table and provide a proper meal with a proper dessert, and since he had a few minutes before dinner, he stopped by his father's room.

The king's butler opened the door to Alexander. "He's awake," the butler said. "But he's not in the best of tempers."

"Thank you," Alexander replied, grateful, as forewarned was forearmed.

King Bruno was in bed already, and he watched Alexander approach his bed from beneath heavy lids. "You've cleaned up. Who are you trying to impress tonight?"

"I'm having dinner with Josephine."

The king's jaw tightened, his expression closing. When his father said nothing else, Alexander added, "I intend to present her to you tomorrow, Father."

"I'd prefer not."

"I'm aware of that, but she doesn't need to be, and then after I introduce you, I'm moving her into the palace. It will be a short meeting. You won't have to do much—just nod and I'll whisk her out and it will be over."

"I heard that you and Damian had a falling-out. I hope it's not true."

His father had always been more interested in Damian than him. "We're fine."

"Why hasn't he come around, then?"

"I wondered the same thing."

"He's always been very loyal to me."

"Just as I have, Father."

But Bruno had no response to that, choosing to close his eyes, ending the conversation.

In the tower library, iron-and-glass wall sconces had been lit so that the room glowed with red and gold light. A ruby brocade cloth covered the round dining table and the stemware had ruby-colored crystal stems. The walls of books added to the richness, and Josephine found herself relaxing as they were presented with their second course.

"You will meet my father tomorrow before lunch," Alexander said. "I cannot predict how he will behave."

"You have a difficult relationship?"

"It's been tense since I was a very young boy."

"Is he that hard to please?"

"He's quite pleased with my mother."

"How have you disappointed him?"

"I'm too cerebral. He would have preferred a son more like my cousin, Damian. Damian is physical, shrewd, and aggressive. My father admires a man who will lay down the law and command."

"How are you not commanding?"

Alexander smiled, and then his smile faded. "Josephine, we might never be who we were on Khronos, but that doesn't mean we can't be happy and that we can't create a strong and loving family for this child and any others we choose to have."

"Would you want more?"

"I would like more."

"Because you need an heir and a spare?"

"Because I was an only child and was often lonely. I would love my son or daughter to have siblings, brothers and sisters to play with. Why grow up in a castle if you have no one to chase you up and down stairwells, or play hide-and-seek with in the dungeon?"

She swallowed hard, unaccountably moved by his words. "Your nannies didn't play with you?"

"How can a nanny ever be a substitute for a brother? Nannies don't whisper secrets and share dreams."

Josephine hated the lump filling her throat. She didn't want to care for him; she didn't want to feel connected, and yet his words made her heart ache. She understood better than he knew. She had grown up alone and lonely. She had grown up wishing for a playmate, someone to talk to late at night, someone to wake up with in the morning, someone who would go on an adventure with her. Instead, she'd spent her life entertaining herself. She'd spent her childhood trying to pretend she didn't need anyone.

"You want our child but you don't want me," she said after a moment. "I think that is the most difficult part for me. And maybe it sounds selfish—"

"But I do want you. I want you very much. I locked you here, trapping you in my home, to keep you from leaving."

"To keep your unborn child here."

"To keep *you* here, Josephine." He signaled for the table steward to leave, and once the door closed, leaving the two of them alone, he said, "I still don't have all of my memory. It hasn't completely returned," he added. "It's incomplete, and there are areas of my life that still have…blanks. I know things because people have told me things, but I have no memory of them."

"Such as?"

"The trip with my friends on the yacht."

"Is that all?"

"The first day or two on Khronos."

"You were recovering from an injury. I'm not surprised you're having difficulty with those memories."

"But I was on the yacht for a week before the accident. That's essentially nine days I don't remember, plus the week where I had amnesia."

"What do the doctors say?"

"I haven't told them."

"Why not?"

"Because I'm worried it would get back to my mother, and she has enough to deal with at the moment."

"Is there more I don't know?"

"My father is dying," he said bluntly. "He has lung cancer. It's stage four now. The radiation and chemotherapy have stopped. There is no more prolonging his life. The only thing that can be done is to try to make him as comfortable as possible—and that's not working."

"And this is why you keep saying we're running out of time. Because you literally are running out of time."

He nodded. "I want my father there when we marry... if humanly possible."

"But why didn't you just tell me? I would have better understood the pressure and urgency."

"Because this is how families like mine operate. We're royals. We maintain facades. We keep up appearances. We're not supposed to have problems. We're not supposed to struggle. And to accomplish that, we suppress anything that is remotely problematic—"

"Like emotions?"

His lips curved wryly. "Indeed, emotions are terribly dangerous."

"I think living without emotions is dangerous."

"Says the woman who loves volcanoes and lava."

"Don't forget plumes of ash."

"How could I?" He hesitated, gathering his thoughts. "We don't do *dramatic* here. And we don't have volatility in the palace. It's all very contained and controlled."

"That's dreadful."

He hesitated. "It can be."

"So who knows about your father?"

"Just a handful of us. Those who must know."

"Rather like my pregnancy."

"But that will be good news, just as our wedding will be good news. I know my mother is hoping our happy news will help soften the public's grief when they learn of my father's cancer."

Josephine swallowed hard, her mouth going dry. "That's a lot of pressure."

"I've grown up in a fishbowl. You're being thrown into it. But I have faith in you. You're a strong swimmer."

His gaze held hers, and there was something in his eyes, as well as the gruffness in his tone, that made her feel tender. She pressed her hand to her chest, pushing against her heart. "Thank goodness I like the water."

He rose and left his chair, and once standing next to her, he reached into his coat and withdrew a small velvet box. As he lifted the lid, he knelt at her side. "Josephine, would you do me the honor of marrying me and becoming my wife and future queen?"

She looked from the huge ring in the box—a massive square-cut emerald surrounded by layers of diamonds—up into his face. He was so very handsome and yet so very aloof. In Khronos he'd been relaxed and physical, and she suspected that in bed he'd be just as sensual here, but she worried that there was no room for emotion. She wondered if he'd ever loved a woman. She wondered if he'd ever love her.

His mouth tugged into a reluctant smile. "I'd hope you would say yes."

She flushed. "Yes, it is a yes. I'm sorry."

"Don't be sorry. Just give me your hand."

Mortified, she held her hand out to him and he slid the ornate ring on her fourth finger. It was loose and slid sideways. She shifted it around, struck by the weight of it.

"We'll get it sized tomorrow," he said, rising.

Josephine couldn't look away from the immense emerald. "It's beautiful."

"It's an Alberici family heirloom, from the early nineteenth century."

She balled her hand to keep the ring from slipping sideways again. "Your world is overwhelming."

"Trust me, I understand."

"I never wanted to be a princess...not ever, not even as a young girl playing make-believe. I loved fables, not fairy tales. I identified with animals, not villagers."

"I never wanted to be a prince," he said, taking his seat at the table again. "As a boy I rebelled against my birth. I didn't want to be nobility. I didn't want to be privileged. My father thrashed me for being ungrateful and undeserving of my position, and I learned never to voice my concerns or objections again."

"It must have been quite a thrashing to have permanently silenced you."

"The thrashing wasn't that bad, but being sent away from home was. Although I imagine it would have happened sooner or later."

"Do you remember it still?"

"The conversation with my father, or the punishment?"

"Both, I suppose."

Alexander leaned back in his chair. "I remember the conversation because I felt very pleased with myself. Rather righteous, if you will. You see, from a young age I'd been uncomfortable with royal protocol, almost cringing when government officials and the public bowed to me, thinking I'd done nothing to earn their loyalty and deference. I didn't think it fair that I was simply born with advantages. It wasn't egalitarian."

"Oh, dear, I can see that being problematic if your father was as old-fashioned as you say."

"Mmm. How dare I be a populist?"

"And you, his only child."

"An embarrassment to the Alberici name." Alexander smiled wryly. "I'm sure I didn't help things by pointing out to my father that the monarchy was a huge expense for the people of Aargau, costing over two hundred million euros a year to support the monarchy here, and yes, a portion comes from the Alberici estate, but didn't an equal portion come from the Aargau government, which was really from the taxes the people pay?"

"You didn't."

"I did."

"And then what happened?"

"Thrashed, sent to my room without food or water for the night, and then the very next day I was packed up and shipped off to a military academy where the staff was told to turn me into a proper man."

"I would think that was an invitation for abuse."

"For someone raised outside society, you understand it very well."

"I read a lot."

He reached across the table to fill her glass with more sparkling water. "I remained at the academy until I was seventeen, then served three years in the Royal Navy and was finally allowed to attend university at twenty. I escaped Europe for four years in New Haven, Connecticut, where I studied philosophy, economics, and environmental science before returning to Europe to earn a graduate degree from Cambridge in land economy, a field that combined environment, law, and economics."

"That's why your English is so good."

"I confess, I liked living overseas and loved my time in America. You have a freedom we don't have here. It's probably why I took a job in Paris after my graduate degree. I wasn't ready to come back to Aargau and be Prince Alexander. I liked being one of the people."

"You don't think you can be one of the people as your country's king?"

"Not the way I was raised."

"Then when it's your turn, do it differently so that our son or daughter can embrace a future in which he or she has the opportunity to be happy."

"I would encourage a career, then."

"Your father didn't have one?"

"From the age of eighteen he has been king."

"He has done his duty, then."

"Yes."

"And when it is your turn, you will do your duty, too."

The meeting with his father was short and rather brusque, but Alexander admired Josephine's calm and gracious manner even under fire. His father spoke barely a dozen words to her, but at least those words included curt approval granting them permission to marry.

Queen Serena didn't speak until the end, but once her husband had given his blessing for the marriage, she rose and gave both Alexander and Josephine a kiss on the cheek. "Congratulations," she murmured. "And welcome to the family," she added to Josephine.

The meeting lasted barely five minutes and they were done, exiting the room with Josephine's hand tucked into the crook of his arm. Her hand was trembling. He'd had no idea she was nervous until then.

He glanced down at her bent head as the doors to his father's room closed behind them. Her thick, light brown hair with the streaks of blond had been pulled back in a stylish twist. She was wearing a simple navy dress paired with navy heels. Small pearl drop earrings dangled from her earlobes. "You look very elegant," he said quietly, trying to distract her from the hollow ring of their footsteps on the marble floor. "Have I seen this dress before?"

She reached up and touched the matching strand of pearls at her neck. "No." Worry darkened her green eyes. "Your mother sent the dress, shoes, and jewelry to me this morning. She said I was probably wishing I had something chic for my presentation and hoped the dress and shoes would help me feel suitably prepared."

He was surprised, but then again not. His mother excelled at soothing and smoothing tension. And yet she was no pushover. His mother was probably the strongest woman he knew. "I wish I had thought of that. You do need a new wardrobe. And an assistant. I will have a team meet with you after lunch."

"I don't need an assistant or a new wardrobe, and I have this dress now in case I need to see your father again."

He stopped on the bottom marble stair. "I don't think you realize what is about to happen. Our engagement is being announced this afternoon. We will soon become the focus of the press and a great deal of speculation, particularly when we announce the wedding is just a week from Saturday."

"Nine days from now?"

"It's not a lot of time, no, which is why we'll have a little preparty next week, either Tuesday or Wednesday, to celebrate our good news—"

"Is that really necessary?"

"We must do something or people will find it odd that I've kept you locked away—"

He broke off as she arched a brow. He laughed softly. "You will never let me forget I locked you up, will you?"

"Absolutely not. You're terrifying. I should call you Bluebeard."

He smiled and kissed her, and then again, his lips lingering against her mouth. She shivered against him, her hands pressed to his chest. "You're too good at this," she murmured. "You make me almost want to be locked up with you."

"I knew it," he said. "Now, where are my handcuffs?"

"Easy does it, Your Highness. We're not even married yet."

"True, and speaking of marriage, I think it'd be wise to make some decisions so my mother won't worry."

"Can't we just make some decisions now and tell her?"

"Do you know what you want?"

"Small wedding, only our immediate family—yours, and my father. I'd like it to be a quick service, if possible, so that it's not too much for King Bruno. Afterward cake and a toast with our parents and then, later, a private romantic dinner for just you and me."

"That's not a very proper royal wedding."

"We both know I'm not a proper royal bride."

CHAPTER EIGHT

WHEN ALEXANDER HAD said that the palace would begin the wedding preparations immediately and that Josephine's days would quickly become tightly scheduled, he hadn't been exaggerating. She'd expected some appointments and anticipated some meetings, but her entire life was taken over. She also quickly discovered that future princesses lived anything but private lives.

Within an hour of the engagement being announced, she was surrounded by staff. There were women at her side who were assistants managing her schedule, with others managing her wardrobe, while others had tasks she didn't yet understand.

It only took a few days of constant companionship to make her miss her tower bedroom, which was far from the bustle of the palace. She missed her view of the sea, which reminded her of Khronos, her father, and the work that had been such a passion for so many years.

She also struggled with the sheer number of women who surrounded her now, women who all had corrections for her. They coached her on how to walk, how to carry herself, how to speak. How to hold her knife and fork. How to lift a glass. How to place a teacup. How to sit. How to rise. How not to cross her legs. How to hold her head. How to smile. How not to smile. And how never, ever to laugh.

The hours of daily instruction were meant to help her. The instruction was meant to help shape her into a proper princess. But all the lessons in etiquette and deportment, all the correction of her grammar, all the jabs at her posture simply made her feel pathetically inadequate. Every moment of her life had become a teachable moment, and for someone who'd been homeschooled and who had done her learning through stacks of books, the very vocal, critical coaching was an excruciating reminder that she was a problem. A *mistake*.

More than once she overheard her ladies murmuring about the difficulty in shaping her into a lady before the party on Tuesday, where she'd be presented to various members of the aristocracy, family friends, and a selection of Aargau's Parliament.

In addition to the lessons, there were fittings and more fittings, and she was tired of standing still, being measured and draped and discussed as if she were a headless mannequin.

In the last four days she'd been pricked with more pins than she cared to remember. She noticed there were no trousers for her and nothing remotely slouchy or comfortable being made. Everything was expertly tailored: scooped necklines, snug belts, skirts with demure hemlines. But the fabrics were gorgeous and every finished item was beyond luxurious.

Alexander appeared at her room one afternoon, interrupting a meeting with Lady Adina, who was again going over the guest list for Tuesday's party with her, ensuring that Josephine was indeed familiar with all the names and the correct titles.

No one had heard him enter, and Josephine didn't know how long he'd been standing there, observing them at her writing table. "Hello," she said breathlessly, happy to see him and grateful for the interruption. "Do you need me?"

"No. Not if you're busy."

"We're not that busy," she said, rising, thinking he looked ridiculously handsome in crisp olive trousers and a starched white shirt, the sleeves rolled up on his bronzed forearms. His shirt hugged his shoulders and molded to his chest and narrow waist. Just looking at him she could see why she'd thrown caution to the wind and fallen for him so hard. "And I feel like I haven't seen you in ages."

"I know, and now I'm heading to Paris but I should be back tomorrow."

She looked up quickly, hopeful. "Could I go with you? I've never been to Paris and I'd love to see something new—"

"I wish you could, but last-minute trips are expensive, even without the additional rooms and security we'd need since we're not yet married." He reached for her hand. "Come, walk with me in the picture gallery. I don't think I've taken you there yet, have I?"

"No," she said quietly, feeling flattened.

His fingers laced more fully with hers. He gave her hand a slight squeeze. They walked silently from the room and down the hall. It wasn't until they'd reached the staircase and gone up a floor and then entered a long corridor filled with enormous oil paintings that Alexander stopped walking and faced her.

"I am going to Paris to see one of my friends, Phillipe," he said quietly. "Phillipe was on the yacht with me, and he's leaving for an extended trip to Buenos Aires and I want to catch him before he goes."

"He hasn't tried to see you or reach out to you?"

"He's close with Damian, my cousin. And the fight on the yacht, it was between Damian and me. I think Phillipe has avoided me to avoid having to take sides."

She was silent a moment in order to process what he was saying. "The fight on the yacht... It was between you and your cousin?"

"Yes."

His expression was so grim that she was almost afraid to ask anything else. But she'd been there, on the beach, when he'd gone overboard, and she'd been the one to rescue him. She'd seen the wound on his head. She knew firsthand the damage inflicted. "This is the cousin your father wanted you to be more like."

"We were raised almost like brothers."

"But he was the one that hit you?"

"Apparently in self-defense."

"What? How?"

"I don't know. That's the problem. I only know what I've been told. If only I could remember, but I can't, and so I'm dependent on the memories of those who were there."

"Have you asked to see the footage from the security cameras? The ship must have them. Everyone has them—"

"It was the first thing I asked for on returning home. But it seems there were no cameras at that end of the ship. It was one of the few places that lacked surveillance."

"Strange, don't you think?"

"From what I've learned, I was the aggressor that night. If what is being said is true, my behavior is inexcusable."

"What are they saying you did?"

He shook his head. "I'd rather not."

"And I'd rather hear it from you than from someone else."

"Fair enough." Alexander moved away from her toward the wall of framed portraits, but he didn't seem to be looking at any of the canvases. "It's all rather complicated, as I'm telling you what Gerard told me took place."

"So Gerard was there? He saw it happen?"

"No, this is what Damian told Gerard."

"I don't find that very reassuring."

Alexander shot her a pensive glance. "According to Damian, he noticed I was missing, and then he noticed Claudia—"

"Who is Claudia?"

"His girlfriend." Alexander swallowed. "And my ex-girlfriend."

Josephine's eyebrows arched but she held her tongue.

"So he went looking for us," Alexander continued, "and found us on the deck off her room. We were having an argument." His jaw tightened. "I had my hands on her. I was threatening her, shaking her, choking her. Damian intervened and rescued her, taking Claudia to get medical care and leaving me alone on her deck."

"How did you go overboard?"

"I don't know."

"No one came to confront you? No one came to kick you out of her room?"

"Gerard came to find me. He said her room was empty."

"Did he then go to your room?"

"Yes, and the door was locked, so he left me alone." Alexander fell silent. "Everyone assumed I'd gone to bed to sleep it off. But when I didn't emerge from the cabin by early afternoon the next day, my friends forced open my door to check and discovered I was gone."

"That's why they never sounded the alarm."

"And why no one knew where to look for me. By early afternoon the yacht had covered a great distance." He drew a breath and forced himself to continue. "What worries me is the fight. The fact that I was shaking her or angry with her. I don't know why I'd be upset. I've never been bothered by her seeing Damian. How could I be? I was the one who ended it with her."

"You think Damian is making all of this up?"

"But why? What purpose would it serve?"

"So you believe him, then? You shook Claudia and choked her, and then you somehow, all on your own, fell off the yacht?"

"People do stupid things when they drink, and I have been told I was drinking heavily that night."

"I'm sorry but none of this makes sense. I've never seen you drink to excess."

"I did, when I was younger, back in my university days. And I had a reputation for being a bit of a hothead when I drank, but that was years ago. Ten years ago. I don't drink like that anymore."

"Tell me about Claudia."

He shot Josephine a sharp glance. "Why?"

"I've never heard you mention her until now and I find it interesting that your ex-girlfriend was on your bachelor trip."

"As my cousin's girlfriend."

"But wasn't that awkward?"

"Claudia is also the younger sister of Marc, one of my best friends. She's been part of my circle forever, which was why I began dating her in the beginning. She knew my world. She understood the rules of my world. She was… convenient."

Josephine didn't know whether she was more shocked, angered, or puzzled. Worse, Alexander's story didn't line up. It wasn't logical. "What were Claudia's injuries?" she asked. "Did the medic on board take photographs? Did she have bruises? Have you spoken to her?"

"Marc, her brother, has told me to stay away from her."

"Is Marc close friends with Damian, too?"

"We met Marc our first year in the military academy. We've been friends with him ever since."

"And Phillipe?" she asked, suppressing a heavy sigh. "How does he fit in?"

"He was another friend from the academy."

"You trust them all? Every last one of them?"

Alexander looked away. He said nothing. His silence ate at her.

She pressed her hands together, fingers interlacing. She was afraid for him. Afraid for both of them. "I'm not trying to play Devil's advocate, Alexander, but something isn't right. I'm worried you've been set up."

He glanced at her, his expression almost bleak. "But what if I did do it?"

She'd been hurt and angry when she'd first arrived in Aargau and locked in the tower, but deep down, she'd always known who he was and what he was. And that was honorable. "I don't believe it. And neither should you."

Alexander's trip to Paris was a waste of time and money. When Alexander arrived at Phillipe's apartment, he discovered Damian was already there. The three of them had dinner together, and on the surface everything was cordial, but conversation was superficial at best. During the meal, they all avoided speaking of the trip. They avoided discussing Alexander's wedding. They actually only spoke of football and the new exclusive VIP club that had just opened up in Paris.

Alexander regretted the trip. He wished he'd remained in Roche with Josephine, and then it crossed his mind that he didn't have to stay. He could leave now and return home tonight. He could return now.

Alexander acted on impulse and rose. "Thank you for dinner, but I should get back. Phillipe, enjoy Buenos Aires. It's a favorite city of mine." He nodded at Damian. "I expect I'll see you back in Roche soon."

"I've been waiting for an invitation to the wedding."

"We're keeping it small and private."

"And the party Tuesday? No invitation for that one, either?"

"I was going to give it to you in person when you came to see me at the palace. You haven't come by. You haven't phoned."

"I was waiting on an apology."

"Ah, I see. Good to know." Alexander tipped his head and started for the door.

Damian was on his feet and he followed. "You need to

get help, Alex, and if you won't do it on your own, I'll make sure you do. I'll speak to your father. I'll go to Parliament. I'll take it to the media."

Alexander turned around. "Why make it public? What do you hope to accomplish?"

"You'll no longer be able to avoid the truth—that you're not well, and potentially unfit to rule in your current condition."

Alexander regarded his cousin a long moment and then nodded. "Good to know." And then he walked out, grateful for the car waiting for him downstairs and the private jet that could fly him home tonight.

Josephine hated being at the palace without Alexander. She felt trapped and bullied, although she suspected Alexander wouldn't understand because he'd grown up here and he'd been raised to conform. But it wasn't just the constant critical company that wore on her; it was her boring, uninspiring routine. She could only hope that once the wedding was over she'd be given more space, as well as more control over her day. Until then, she'd have to stand at windows, looking out, waiting for Alexander to find her and make her feel safe and wanted again. He was the only reason she was here in Aargau. Her hand went to her belly and she cradled it protectively. Well, Alexander and this one. Her baby.

In the beginning she'd been nervous about the pregnancy, but now she was excited, and determined to be a great mother. Josephine had been raised by a single father, and while he'd loved her, he'd never quite managed to be both mother and father. As a little girl, she'd desperately missed her mother, and that ache for a mother had never gone away. Even now, maybe particularly now due to the pregnancy, Josephine longed for a mother to talk to her, give her advice, and reassure her. Fathers were good at many things, but they didn't carry the baby, and they didn't deliver the baby, or nurse, or do any of those other things, and what Jo needed now was a strong maternal figure to help her adjust...or even some knowledgeable girlfriends would do. She hoped that later Queen Serena could maybe become that figure, but until then, Josephine would continue being her own best friend.

On Sunday afternoon, Alexander walked the castle parapet with the stunning views of Roche's medieval walled town against the brilliant blue of the sea. Damian's words haunted him. He'd returned from Paris in the middle of the night, and it had taken him hours to fall asleep, deeply troubled by the tense meal as well as perplexed by Damian's threats.

This wasn't the Damian Alexander knew. This Damian was bitter, with a score to settle.

Was it really about Claudia? Or was there something else that had happened, something that Alexander couldn't remember?

He closed his eyes and drew a deep breath, and in his mind's eye he saw Josephine, lovely, warm, smiling.

He was glad she wasn't Danielle—sleekly sophisticated and coolly polished—and he didn't want anyone to try to make her into something she wasn't, because he liked her the way she was. He liked everything about her. She was the woman he wanted, and she'd be a good queen even if she hadn't been raised in his world. Maybe she'd be a better queen because she hadn't.

He wished he'd taken her to Paris yesterday. He wished they had more time together, just the two of them. Maybe he should steal her from the palace and take her for a drive. They could run away for a couple of hours, just the two of them. They could escape in one of his cars, perhaps one of the convertibles, and drive, the wind in their hair, the open road before them.

Alexander stopped pacing, the idea cementing. He knew where he'd take her, too. It would be an hour drive, but it was a beautiful one, across the middle of the country, through picturesque villages, all the way to the country's highest point, Mount Bravura. But if they were to do it, he'd need to put the plan in motion now.

Alexander made a call to Julio Costa, the owner of the restaurant, and then went in search of Josephine. His valet was the one who told him to look in the tower guest suite.

When his valet saw his surprise, he smiled faintly. "Miss Robb likes it there," he said. "Everyone knows it's her favorite place to go when she needs a break from her ladies."

This drew Alexander short. "Are her ladies difficult?"

"I think they're excessively preoccupied with rules and protocol."

Alexander left the palace for the tower and climbed to the fourth floor. When he entered the tower bedroom he found Josephine standing on a stool before the tall, narrow window. She was barefoot and her chin was propped in her hand, her elbow resting on the thick stone ledge.

"What are you thinking about?" he asked.

Alexander's voice caught her by surprise. She jumped a little as she glanced over her shoulder at him. "Nothing much," she answered.

"Your *nothing much* is always something."

The corners of her lips lifted. She turned back to the window and gestured to the horizon. "I was thinking the ocean from here looks more green than blue, and those puffy white clouds, cumulus clouds, are casting moving shadows on the water, making the sea look as if it's filled with a fleet of ships, all at full sail. I was imagining the adventures those brave voyagers would have."

"You make me want to be one of those brave voyagers."

"But then who'd be king? This kingdom has but one heir, which is you."

A half-dozen different responses came to mind and in the end he chose none of them. "I should have taken you with me last night. I didn't enjoy Paris without you."

"How did it go with Phillipe?"

"Not well." He hesitated. "Damian was there."

One of her winged eyebrows arched higher. "You didn't expect to see him, did you?"

"No. And it was an awkward meal. I left early."

"And your cousin? How was he?"

"Baffling," Alexander said after a long moment. "I don't understand it. I don't understand him." And then he shrugged impatiently. "Let's not discuss him anymore. He ruined my night. I won't allow him to ruin today, and I'm organizing something fun for us for dinner tonight. It will be just the two of us. We'll leave here at six. Our reservation is for seven."

Josephine studied him a long moment, trying to read his expression because he wasn't smiling and yet there was this curious light in his eyes. He looked tired but also eager, and she suddenly pictured him as a boy and thought how lovely he must have been. He wouldn't have been one of those who hurt things and broke things. No, he would have been smart and thoughtful and kind. "I'm looking forward to it," she said, and she meant it.

"Good."

"How should I dress? Do I need one of my formal dresses that require the spandex girdle beneath?"

"That sounds horrendous."

"It feels horrendous."

"Then no, please don't wear one. Be comfortable. Choose a dress that makes you happy."

Josephine went through her wardrobe and in the end chose a ruby-red silk dress that was sleeveless, fitted through the waist, and featured a stunning bright pink flower on the full skirt. The neckline plunged, showing off her tan and her curves, making her feel gorgeous and feminine.

After saying good-night to her staff, she hurried downstairs, where Alexander was waiting by the front door for her. He smiled as she came down the steps. "You look stunning."

Pleasure filled her. She felt stunning tonight. "And you're very dashing in your…um…trousers and…shirt."

He laughed, the sound low and husky and unbearably sexy as the butler opened the front door for them. "I'm rather boring—is that it?"

"Actually, no. You're anything but boring," she said as they stepped outside. Her attention was immediately drawn to the hunter green convertible sports car parked in the drive. It was low and sleek with a handsome cream interior. It was also a two-seater, which meant no room for a driver. "Is that for us?"

"It is. Do you approve?"

"Very much so. But where will your security go?"

"Security will be behind us, but they're to be discreet and give us some room."

"I love it, but I think I might need a shawl for the way home. Let me run back up. I won't be long."

"I can have someone fetch you something—"

"No need. I won't be but a moment." Josephine went back inside and up the marble staircase.

She'd just opened the door to the suite when she heard one of her ladies say, "They said Damian found them together on the yacht, in her room, in her bed. He confronted them and things turned ugly. It's why Damian has been forbidden from coming here."

Josephine froze, unable to make herself move.

"Not surprised about the love triangle. There has always been some friction between those two," someone said.

"It doesn't help that the king has always favored Damian over his own son."

"And Claudia? Where is Claudia now?"

"Paris, I believe."

Josephine felt sick. Her legs shook. She put a hand to the wall, trying to steady herself. Was it true, what her ladies-in-waiting were saying? Had Alexander gone to Paris not to see Phillipe but to see Claudia?

Was it possible that Alexander wasn't who she thought he was?

Closing her eyes, she pictured him downstairs waiting for her next to the sleek sports car, handsome, smiling.

She pictured him as he was when he came to her in the tower...

She remembered how he'd pulled her aside to talk to her in the picture gallery...

Had he been lying to her all those times? Had he been twisting the truth, pretending to be someone he wasn't?

She didn't think so. Maybe she was crazy, but she trusted him. She did.

Josephine drew a breath and pushed the door all the way open, silencing the conversation as she stepped into her sitting room. She ignored the startled glances—as well as the fact that the ladies were sitting in her sitting room—and continued on to her bedroom.

Adina jumped up. "Did you forget something?" she asked, following Josephine into the bedroom.

Josephine counted to ten as she went through her wraps and then selected a charcoal-gray pashmina and draped it over her arm. "I have it now," she said, turning around and heading back out. She didn't pause until she reached the door to the corridor, and then she glanced back at the three women. "If you're going to gossip, please do not do it in my rooms. Good night."

For the first twenty minutes of the drive, Josephine was

quiet, replaying the conversation she'd heard in her room, wondering if she should tell him. She didn't want to spoil the night, and it would certainly spoil the night. She chewed on the inside of her lip, wishing she hadn't gone back to her room, thinking she would be so much happier right now if she'd never heard any of that.

Alexander shifted and glanced at her. "Is my driving making you nervous?"

"No. Just thinking about something I heard earlier. It was disturbing."

"Want to tell me?"

"No." She swallowed around the lump in her throat. "I'm just upset on your behalf."

He shifted again and braked, pulling off on the side of the road. Alexander faced her. "Tell me, *cara*. We're in this together. Let's do this together."

"People are talking," she said quietly after a moment. "Staff. They're saying you…" She closed her eyes, shook her head. "I can't say it. I can't. And I don't believe it, so it doesn't matter."

"But it does matter because clearly it's upset you."

She opened her eyes. "They're saying on the yacht, Damian found you…in bed…with Claudia."

"What?"

"And that's why Damian is angry."

"No."

"And Claudia is in… Paris." She looked at him. "Tell me it's just a coincidence. Tell me you didn't go to Paris to see her—"

"Absolutely not. I didn't even know she was in Paris. Furthermore, we weren't in bed together. I can promise you that. And yes, I know I have memory issues, but there has been nothing between Claudia and me since I ended the relationship, and I haven't wanted to be with her. I might not remember the trip, but I know me, and I wouldn't start something with her again, not when she's involved with my cousin. I hate even discussing Claudia with you, but you must believe me—"

"I do." She reached out, her fingers light on his cheekbone and then his jaw. "I do. I'm just disgusted by the gossip. I'm disgusted that people in the palace would speak that way about you."

"Damian grew up in the palace. His father, Aldo, was my father's twin. I think Damian has always struggled with the fact that my father was born two minutes before his father, making my father the future king and me the heir instead of the other way around."

"Damian resents you."

"I think Damian is envious, yes."

"That explains a great deal," she murmured, leaning forward to kiss him. "But let's not let Damian and his green-eyed jealousy ruin our evening, because I'm so happy being out with you. Let's just savor our night."

"I couldn't agree more."

Now outside the city, they turned off the main highway onto a narrower rural road, and for the next half hour they threaded their way through the countryside filled with farms and little stone houses with charming shutters and window boxes.

Josephine thought it looked like a blend of Provence and Tuscany. "It's so picturesque," she said as they slowed for a shepherd and his flock of sheep, the fluffy creatures slowly crossing the road just ahead of them and then deciding they no longer wanted to cross the road but instead mill about, taking over the road.

"We might be a while," Alexander said, shifting into Neutral.

"I'm enjoying myself immensely," she replied, delighted by the herd's inability to decide if they'd all cross together or one at a time. She entertained Alexander with a sheep-by-sheep accounting, describing the wayward members of the flock, giving them all personalities, including the shepherd, whose quiet resignation coupled with his inability to direct his flock only served to make the sheep more ambivalent about crossing the road in the first place.

"He is not a very good shepherd," Alexander muttered, as five minutes turned to ten.

"Not terribly passionate about his work," she agreed, "but he's giving me the best show."

"He's also going to make us late for dinner."

She glanced at him. "Is that going to be a problem?"

"No. It's Sunday, and Julio is opening the restaurant specially for us."

"I've never had anyone open anything for me."

"Well, you will now. In just five days you'll be Princess Josephine Alberici."

The sun was just setting by the time they pulled in front of the restaurant, with its exterior of local wood and stone. The restaurant owner, Julio, warmly welcomed them before escorting them inside to a table in an alcove with windows all around. The view from the restaurant, which happened to be perched on the edge of a cliff, was nothing short of glorious.

"We're up so high," Josephine said.

"It's Mount Bravura, the highest peak in Aargau and Aargau's only volcano, although extinct now."

"No wonder I like it so much!"

They drifted into easy conversation, interrupted only by the waiter when he took their order and then returned later with their first course. Time passed quickly, and Josephine was surprised when she sat back and glanced out the window and found it was pitch-dark and that the restaurant itself was empty save them and the owner. "It must be late," she said. "All the staff has gone."

"Even Julio?"

"No, he's still here. He's setting the tables for tomorrow."

"I'm sure he'd have no problem kicking me out when he's ready to go home."

She frowned, skeptical. "Even though you are Prince Alexander Alberici?"

He laughed lowly. "Okay, Julio would probably never kick me out, but he's thrilled we're here. Tomorrow he'll share the news with everyone and he'll get a great deal of press out of this. His bookings will double, triple overnight."

"Well, that does make me feel a little better, but I still wouldn't mind stepping out for fresh air."

"Because you're tired or because you want Julio to be able to close his restaurant and go home for the night?"

"You know me so well," she murmured, thinking Alexander had the loveliest blue eyes and his smile created these grooves on either side of his lips. Lightly she brushed a fingertip across his mouth, wanting more than a light kiss. She missed the heat between them. She missed the tension and electric sensation.

He rose and held her chair for her. They left the restaurant for the patio with its breathtaking view. It was only up here, so high, that Josephine got a sense of the island and its size. Lights twinkled far away—the capital of Roche, Josephine thought—with other lights dotting the coast. Waves crested with white reflected the moonlight.

"This was just what I needed," she said with a sigh. "It almost feels like we're on Khronos. It's just you and me."

"You miss Khronos."

"I think I always will. I had so much freedom, and I miss the water everywhere." She darted a look up at him. "And I miss having it be just you and me."

He leaned against the railing and drew her to him, his hands low on her back. "You have no idea how much I've missed you. I want to feel you and love you. It's been too long."

Love her, Josephine repeated silently, even as her heart did a painful double beat. She knew he didn't mean love, *real* love, but still, it was heady hearing the words and knowing he desired her—and at least desire was something. Maybe desire could be enough. Maybe she could be satisfied with being wanted. Maybe she didn't need to be loved. Or maybe her love for him would be enough for both of them.

She stared deep into his eyes, flooded with so many intense emotions, emotions that were stronger than she'd ever felt before, and then, sure of her feelings, she leaned closer, leaning into him, and pressed her lips to his. "It has been too long," she whispered against his mouth. "I need you to love me."

He kissed her back, his hand cupping the back of her head, drawing her against him so that her breasts pressed against his hard chest and her mouth was his for the taking.

The kiss was fierce and hot, his tongue parting her lips, sweeping her mouth before tangling with her tongue, teasing it, teasing her.

She felt as if the kiss was just the beginning of something huge and wonderful and she mimicked the way he kissed her, sucking on the tip of his tongue, drawing on it hard. He groaned against her mouth, his hands sliding down her back to grip her hips and grind her against his hard length.

Her arms wrapped around his neck, her fingers twining in the dark strands of hair at his nape. She tugged at them even as he shifted her hips, drawing her over him again, making her feel his heat and hunger. Sensation flooded her. Emotion flooded her. She'd desired him on Khronos, but it was so much more intense now, her feelings making the need and sensation so much more powerful.

His tongue played her mouth in a rhythmic stabbing that mimicked how the thick head of his shaft pressed up between her thighs. He'd found her breast with one hand and was kneading the peaked nipple, making her whimper and shudder, and if it weren't for the fact that security was just around the corner and Julio was somewhere inside the restaurant, she would have begged him to take her here and now, as the delicate silk of her dress gave her little protection. But then, she wanted no protection. She wanted him, all of him, forever.

He lifted his head. "I'd have my way with you right here if I didn't think it'd make Julio feel awkward."

She laughed and blushed. "I was just thinking the same thing. Can we go back home and be together?"

"Absolutely."

They returned to the palace and he led her to his room. They made love twice, and she spent the rest of the night barely sleeping because she didn't want to forget how good she felt in his arms, in his bed.

CHAPTER NINE

TUESDAY, WITH ITS cocktail party of important people and influential guests, had finally arrived, and Josephine's team spent hours preparing her, giving her a complete makeover. The hairdresser, makeup artist, and stylist fussed over her for nearly two hours but now she was dressed and waiting for Alexander to collect her.

Josephine did a little twirl before her mirror, absolutely thrilled with her dress. The sleeveless gown featured a dramatic V neckline, with a soft cloud of a skirt shimmering with gorgeous gold embroidery. The skirt floated around her legs as she walked and she was wearing glittering chandelier earrings from the Alberici vault. With her hair pinned up, she definitely looked older and more sophisticated.

Alexander arrived exactly on time to escort her to the ballroom, and when he entered her room she expected him to smile and compliment her because it's what he usually did, but tonight he kept his distance and stared at her, jaw flexed, gaze shuttered. Her ladies-in-waiting noticed, too, and they fell silent. The silence grew, making Josephine uncomfortable.

"Something's wrong," Josephine said quietly. "Is it the dress? Would you like me to change?"

"The dress is beautiful."

"Then what is it?"

"I'm having a difficult time understanding why you look so different. I don't understand what has been done to you. You don't look like you."

She remembered the hours of tortured hairstyling and makeup application and lifted a hand self-consciously to her nape, which was exposed tonight, with all her hair coiled and pinned tightly on top. "It might be this style," she said. "It's structured."

"Too structured. It doesn't suit you. You are too pretty to look like an old lady." He approached her and reached out to tip up her chin, examining her makeup. "You're wearing quite a lot, aren't you?"

"The eyeliner is rather heavy, and the lipstick is dark," she said faintly.

"Why didn't you stop them?"

"I was told they'd been instructed to polish me, remove the hard edges."

"There were no hard edges. You're lovely as you are."

His words made her eyes sting and it was all she could do to keep tears from welling up. She glanced at the women in the corner who were hanging on every word and she gave them a faint smile before looking up at Alexander. "Please don't be disappointed. They've been working very hard to prepare me for tonight—"

"You are not a rock," he gritted out, interrupting her. "You do not require polishing or refinement, and if this is what they're telling you, then I will throw them all out, every last one of them, because I like you, and I want you to look like you. I want your mouth to look like your mouth. I want to be able to kiss your lips—" And then suddenly his head dropped and his mouth slanted over hers, and he was kissing her with hunger and passion, as if they were alone.

By the time he lifted his head, ending the kiss, her head was spinning and her senses swam with the erotic pleasure of his kiss. She loved his mouth on hers. She loved the feel of him and the smell of him and the way he made her feel every single time he touched her.

For a moment she just stared up at him, dazed, and then he reached up and began tugging the pins out of her hair one by one. "The public will like you," he growled, his deep voice humming through her. "The public will love you. You don't need to be someone you're not, and you most definitely do not need to be a puppet on a string." He kept pulling out pins until her thick hair fell over her shoulders in long, loose waves. "This is better," he said, combing his fingers through the waves. "This is you, and how I like to see you."

He turned and faced the ladies in the corner. "Do not put her hair up unless Josephine asks for it to be up. Do not apply more makeup than she is comfortable with. Ask her what she wants—do not tell her. Am I clear?"

Josephine was simultaneously awed and horrified. "They will not like me better for that," she whispered, trying not to smile as she wiped away the lipstick staining his mouth.

He turned his head and kissed her palm. "Maybe not, *bella*, but I will."

They were only a few minutes late arriving for the party in the ballroom, and while Alexander had assured her it was an intimate gathering, the fact that they were going to the ballroom spoke volumes.

As the doors opened to admit them, Josephine's breath caught in her throat, and her fingers tightened on his arm as she was immediately dazzled by the splendor of the grand ballroom. Her appreciative gaze swept the space, trying to process everything she was seeing even as people began bowing to Alexander. Immense chandeliers ran the length of the high ceiling, each dripping with glittering crystals, reflecting shimmering light across the elegant baroque ballroom, enhancing the gold and white scheme where gilt-framed mirrors lined the walls.

"Confidence," Alexander murmured at her side.

She eased her grip on his arm and forced a smile, trying to block out the sheer number of people filling the room. There were so many people here, and they were all staring. "This is not a small party," she whispered as his hand slipped to her lower back.

"It's fewer than three hundred," he answered under his breath. "Larger than I hoped but small compared to the usual number we host for formal gatherings." He began introducing her to people, a couple here and a couple there.

She nodded, smiled, and spoke when required, but the entire time she was most conscious of *him*. His warmth filled her and his fragrance teased her nose. Even though she was uneasy with the sheer number of people present, she felt safe with him, reassured by him at her side. There was something in his touch that made her skin come alive. She loved it. She hated it. He was never supposed to be hers, and yet here she was, being introduced to his court as his bride-to-be.

"You're doing well," he murmured when they had a moment to themselves. "You're quite impressive actually. You'll be the princess they adore, and before long their queen."

She glanced up, her gaze meeting his, his irises almost lavender blue in the glittering light. She wanted to tell him she loved him. She wanted him to know how much she cared about him and that she didn't need the public to love her, as long as he did.

Later, as they mingled, she found herself watching him, and she knew he was also watching her. She could feel his gaze on her, and he made her feel so many things—taut, edgy, physical, desirable.

Tonight, everything in her felt sensitive and alive, especially when he looked at her, as he did just now, his lids lowered and his lovely mouth lifted just so, and she felt that half smile all the way through her, the awareness making her skin warm and her body tingle and ache.

Tonight she felt unbearably feminine, all curves and softness. Her breasts. Her waist. Her hips. Her thighs.

She loved everything about him. She loved the way he moved, she loved watching his hands, loved the width of his shoulders. She watched his eyes, the focus, the intensity, the hint of amusement lurking there in the light blue gaze.

Perhaps she wasn't a mistake.

Perhaps she was the right bride.

The party was a success. Photographs of Prince Alexander and his beautiful young fiancée, Josephine Robb, filled the papers, and Josephine could tell from the smiles of the staff that everyone was pleased.

Josephine was pleased, not because the party was a success but because the party was over. She couldn't wait to escape the palace the next afternoon, retreating almost immediately after lunch for the tower bedroom where she could be alone with her favorite view of the water.

She waved at Alexander's secretary, Aimee, on the second floor as she hurried up the stairwell, and then she peeked through the open door to the library and saw Alexander there in a chair reading a thick sheath of papers. She nearly spoke to him but then thought better of it because he was lost in thought, and she raced on up, feeling immeasurably lighter and happier.

The formal party was over. The wedding was coming on Saturday, and then soon the spotlight should be off her, and she and Alexander could develop their own routine and their own life together.

She couldn't wait for them to be a proper family, and she wondered where they'd raise the baby. She was trying to imagine the nursery when she moved too quickly, misjudging the distance between the stone steps. Josephine flung her arm out to brace her fall but it was too late to stop herself, and she screamed as she fell, crying out again as she slammed onto the stairs, the impact knocking the air out of her.

For a moment she lay dazed, and then she pushed herself up into a sitting position. She flexed her hands, tested her legs. Nothing seemed broken. She ached though, with pain in her torso and a wrenched back.

"What happened?" Alexander demanded, charging up the stairs, coming to her side.

"I fell," she answered, trying not to wince, not wanting to alarm him. "I was distracted and lost in thought and my feet ended up going faster than the rest of me."

"You could have been seriously hurt," he said.

"I know. But I wasn't." She allowed him to help her to her feet but she frowned at the twinge in her belly.

"What's wrong?" he asked.

She forced a smile, hiding her pain, thinking now wasn't the time to be melodramatic. She'd just taken a fall, and by most standards it was a very small fall. She hadn't even gone down more than five or so stairs. Everything was fine. She was certain everything was fine. "Just a bit stiff from falling. Your stairs are hard," she added lightly, trying to tease him to ease the tension.

"You shouldn't be coming up here. It's a very old staircase, the steps far too narrow and steep. My mother mentioned they were dangerous years ago—"

"I've never fallen before, and next time I'll go more slowly. I promise."

"There won't be a next time. The tower is off-limits."

"Stop it! You're being ridiculous. I'm fine. Look at me—" She broke off to wiggle her fingers and flex an ankle. "No cuts. Nothing is broken."

"I'm taking you back to your suite in the palace."

"You don't need to take me anywhere, Alexander. I can walk just fine."

"I'll feel better if I see you there."

"Fine."

He held her hand as they started down, and she could tell by the firm clasp of his fingers that he was trying hard not to lift her up and carry her the rest of the way. She was touched by his concern. It was a little heavy-handed, but he'd always been protective.

She was just about to thank him for his assistance when she felt another twinge in her abdomen, sharper, much sharper than before. Startled, she paused on the step and suddenly she had to look at Alexander. Suddenly she needed to hear from him that everything was okay.

"Something is wrong," he said roughly. "Don't tell me everything is fine."

"It's pinching on the inside. It's getting stronger."

"Where?"

She put her hand on her still-flat belly. "Here," she whispered, cupping her womb. "Where the baby is."

He muttered an oath and swung her into his arms. "Let's get you to your room and we'll call the doctor from there."

She was in bed when the doctor arrived, but she'd been to the bathroom twice because she'd noticed she'd begun spotting. She was trying to contain her panic as she added pads to her panties, trying to tell herself that this was just a little blip and everything would be fine.

But as the doctor drew out the fetal Doppler to listen for a heartbeat, her eyes burned and then filled with tears because she could see from Alexander's tense expression just how concerned he was.

They were all quiet as the doctor listened. An hour ago she'd been so happy, almost elated that everything she wanted was finally coming together. But now Alexander stood just behind the doctor, silent, watching and waiting.

When the doctor put the Doppler away and made a call for someone at the hospital to bring over an ultrasound, her heart fell.

"You don't hear anything, do you?" she said, her throat constricting.

"You're still quite early. It can be difficult listening for a heartbeat with a Doppler. The ultrasound will allow me to have a better view, and we'll be able to see the heart beat."

Alexander was thanking him but Josephine closed her eyes and turned her face away, unable to let them see her fear because something was wrong. She felt it. She knew it. From the cramping to the bleeding to the doctor's non-expression, the professional kindness intended to mask concern.

The nurse arrived with the equipment in just thirty minutes but the doctor's silence as he studied the ultrasound image crushed her. She knew.

She knew.

"There is no heartbeat," he said quietly. "I am so sorry."

For a moment she couldn't breathe. For a moment she felt as if she'd just vanish into thin air.

There was no heartbeat.

The little life inside her was gone.

She shook her head, and then again, unable to look at the doctor or Alexander. This time when she turned to face the wall, she stayed that way, even after the doctor and his nurse had gone.

She gripped her hands into fists, trying to keep from screaming. This was her fault. All her fault.

"Josephine," Alexander said, putting a hand on her shoulder.

She shrugged him off. "Don't say anything."

"I know what you're thinking," he said. "I know what you're saying to yourself, and it was such a little mistake, such a simple thing."

"Please go. Please leave." She squeezed her eyes shut, fighting the scalding tears.

"The doctor wants us to go into his office for the procedure he mentioned—"

"I don't want to do it."

"I know, and I don't want you to be put through it, either, but he believes it will be better for you, less risk of an infection."

"Alexander, no."

"I hate this, too, *cara*, but we need to keep you well. We need to do what's best for you now."

The procedure on Wednesday night was horrendous, and Josephine slept in on Thursday, having cried herself to sleep the night before.

She didn't want breakfast Thursday morning, and she didn't want to get up, too spent, worn-out, wrung out, cried out. Queen Serena came by her room just before noon to tell her how deeply sorry she was, and shared that she understood Josephine's grief because she had miscarried, too, and that Josephine should feel free to come to her anytime, for anything.

Josephine got through the short visit without breaking down, but once Serena had gone, she curled into a ball and cried again. The last six weeks had been a gigantic roller coaster and this last drop was too much, too frightening, too heartbreaking.

Worse, there was no reason for Alexander to marry her anymore. He was only marrying her because of the baby, but now that there was no baby he was free.

She'd freed him. That was good, right? Still crying, she threw back her covers and got out of bed. She should go. That's what she should do. She should just go and put this whole nightmare behind her.

Josephine was in the middle of packing the few things she'd brought with her when Alexander entered her room. From his expression, she knew that someone from her staff had alerted him that Josephine was preparing to leave.

"What are you doing?" he asked quietly, taking in the clothes she'd put in the pile to leave at the palace and the sarong and blouse and swimsuit she would take back to Greece with her.

She wiped tears away. "I want to see my father. I want to be in my house again."

"Your father is on his way here for the wedding."

"We're not getting married now," she said, folding another simple blouse. "There is no reason for him to come."

He crossed the room and closed the door that divided the bedroom from the sitting room where her staff had collected. "You can't run away every time there is a problem," he said tersely, facing her. "You have to be stronger than your fear."

"I think there is some confusion here. I'm not afraid. I'm just no longer necessary, which is why I'm choosing to return home."

"Not necessary? You're my fiancée. My intended. My betrothed. We've announced it to the world. We've celebrated it in style. We have a wedding in two days."

"It's a small wedding, a very private wedding. It's not going to be difficult to cancel it."

"I don't understand. I know you're upset about the miscarriage, but why are you doing this to us?"

"Because there is no *us*!" she cried, balling up a T-shirt and smashing it against her knees. "There has never been an *us*. This—" she gestured to him, and then herself "—this has never been about you and me. It's only been about the baby, and the baby is no more."

"You are my fiancée. We're marrying in two days."

"Why? You don't need me. You don't want me. You were only marrying me because I was pregnant, and I'm not pregnant anymore. You're free. Go! Find Danielle. Or find a new princess. Find someone who wants to be your princess. I never wanted the job." She rose and stepped over the clothes, wishing she could fling the doors open and escape, but there was no escape here, and there would be no escape, not until she was on her own island, in her own world.

"I am not going to break off our engagement." His voice was hard, every word sharp and brittle. "I cannot put my father through the humiliation of another broken engagement. It would kill him—"

"He's going to die anyway!"

"How dare you?" He took an enraged step toward her and then stopped himself. "How dare you disrespect him—"

"I'm not trying to disrespect him, Alexander." Her voice broke. "I'm trying to save us from disaster. You don't love me. You desire me. You've sexualized me. But there is nothing else for me… There is no real relationship. I'm to be in your bed, and at your side for important appearances, but what else is there for me? Why should I stay? Give me one good reason to stay!" She was almost trembling with emotion, trembling with the need to hear him say he loved her and wanted her above all else—not because she was pregnant and not because this was duty but because he couldn't live without her. He didn't want to live without her.

"Because you made a promise," he ground out, jaw flexed, blue gaze icy. "My father has given us permission, and we have announced our wedding, and I will not disappoint my father again. I refuse to disappoint my father. I will not."

They weren't the words she needed. Her eyes burned, filling with tears. "So you'll trap me and disappoint me."

"You benefit, *cara*, you benefit beautifully from this arrangement."

"No."

"And there will be children. You will be pregnant again soon—"

"I knew you were not a terribly sensitive man, but your lack of empathy at the moment is astonishing."

"My lack of empathy? My father is dying—"

"And my child just died." Her voice broke and she reached up to knock away the tears, hating them and hating him. He had no idea how much he was hurting her. He had no idea how every word he said wounded. "And I appreciate that your father is a king and I am but an ordinary woman, an American at that, but can you please allow me to grieve for what I have lost? Or are you too self-absorbed with duty and your tortured relationship with your father to allow me time to mourn and heal?"

She'd finally effectively silenced him.

He stood there stiffly, features granite hard, no emotion anywhere on his handsome face.

She should have felt a thrill of victory because she knew that finally something she'd said had penetrated his thick skull and the even thicker wall he kept around his emotions. But she hated that it was the miscarriage that should do it. How much better if he'd actually loved her. How much better if he'd been willing to fight for her.

Alexander saw the pain in Josephine's eyes and her pain unnerved him. She was so open and so vulnerable and he could see what she was feeling—even feel what she was feeling—but the sheer intensity of so much emotion made him shut down and pull even further away.

Emotions had always been problematic for him, but his father's death was even more challenging because this was his last chance to get it right. This was Alexander's last chance to try to make amends with a father who had never wanted or needed him. If there ever was a time to be the son Bruno had wanted and needed, it was now. "I am not indifferent," he said lowly, his voice rough to his own ears. "I am more disappointed than I can say—"

"I don't believe you."

He gave her a slight bow. "I'm sorry."

Her eyes welled with tears. "Let me go."

"No." *Never.*

"You don't need me—"

"But I do." *Always.*

"Those are just words!"

But words didn't come easily to him, either.

What he longed to do was take her in his arms. He wanted to hold her and comfort her, but his own control was being tested. He was battling to keep it all together. He hated what was happening to them, and yet there were bigger things than their own personal drama.

"We will get through this," he added quietly. "I promise."

"You disappoint me," she whispered, averting her face.

He flinched but said nothing.

She blinked hard, adding, "I kept thinking we had a shot at making a marriage work. I thought that there was something real between us. But I was wrong. There is no *us* in your world—there is just you. It's your world, your title, your future...not mine. It was never mine."

She was wrong. There was an *us*, but he didn't have the energy to argue, and so he stopped focusing on Josephine's words, unable to take them in. He'd been mocked for his feelings as a boy. He'd been brutalized in the boarding school by other boys because he'd dared to care...to hurt.

In the navy, he'd been drilled to be tough. Feelings, once again, had been shameful. They made a man weak when he needed to be clearheaded and logical and strong.

So no, he wouldn't feel her pain, and no, he wouldn't let her words register because it would do no good. Her pain and disappointment would change nothing.

His father was dying.

The country would need a new king.

His mother would be widowed and displaced.

Alexander needed to do now what he'd been raised to do. Shoulder the weight of Aargau. Do right by the crown. Honor his father's memory and name.

He didn't know why he'd been on the yacht near Khronos, and he didn't know what had happened on that yacht or why she'd been there to save him, but it had happened and they were now here, and everything was about to change.

Josephine might not like what was happening, but she'd rise to the occasion. He knew she would. Just as he'd known she'd do the right thing by their child.

Josephine understood honor. And in her own way, she understood responsibility and duty. She'd be an excellent queen one day. He just wished the path could be less painful.

"You can return to Khronos after the wedding," he said. "You can take some time once we're married. I will speak with the security—"

"No. Not after. There is no after—"

"Josephine, stop for a moment. Think carefully, please. Look at the bigger picture, if you can."

"You mean you and what you want?" she flashed bitterly.

He ground his teeth together. She didn't understand that he was trying to do the right thing now, which was give his father peace of mind so King Bruno could let go of this life and the pain racking his body. Because his father wouldn't let go, not if he believed the family was in crisis.

His gut hurt. His throat felt thick. Alexander forced the words out because they were not easy to speak. "My father is a fighter. My father has lived his life for his country and his duty. But he's in constant pain, terrible pain, and he's ready to go. The only thing he lives for now is seeing us married. But if that doesn't happen, he'll try to cling to life, which will only increase his suffering. We must protect him from pain. He mustn't think we are in crisis. He needs us to be strong, *cara*. I need you to be strong. I am sorry I've hurt you, and I'm sorry to have disappointed you, but consider him. Consider my mother. They need us to show courage and leadership now. They need to know the monarchy isn't in crisis and that you and I are unified and committed to Aargau."

She stood utterly still, chin lifted, eyes shimmering with tears. She stared at him so long he could see the pulse beating at her throat and the faint quiver of her lips.

Anger blazed in her eyes. Hurt created shadows, too.

"I wish you'd never come to Khronos," she said at last, her voice hoarse. "I wish I'd never seen your yacht anchored in the cove or watched you and your friends on my beach. I wish I had amnesia. I wish I could blank out the entire thing so I didn't have to remember it, either."

He winced inwardly. They were sharp words and they pricked, like shards of glass scraping across his skin.

"I thank God every day because you are what I woke to," he answered gruffly. "I thank God that you were there, grateful that you are here. We will get through this. We are a strong family, and you are part of us now. There is no crisis here. You are hurt and upset, but you belong here. You belong with me. There is no running away. We are out of options and out of time. We will do what needs to be done. You and me, together."

She looked away, her pale throat working, her eyes blinking as she tried to contain her emotions. She'd been through a great deal in the past twenty-four hours, but they couldn't give up now. His father needed peace. The wedding would go ahead as planned, and eventually all would be well. Storms passed, skies cleared. Josephine would get pregnant again, and there would be a royal heir; Alexander didn't doubt it, which was why he could walk out of her room and go to his father's side and assure him all was well and they were looking forward to the wedding on Saturday.

CHAPTER TEN

HE DIDN'T WANT the truth, and he didn't want her emotions. He didn't want her to feel.

So she wouldn't feel. And she wouldn't care about him any longer. She'd do her duty. She'd marry him and stand at his side and fulfill the obligation, and then she'd leave.

She'd return to Khronos and stay there, not for a visit but until her father took a new position with the foundation and was sent elsewhere. She'd go where he went and continue assisting his work. She'd lose herself in the work, and the idea of going somewhere pleased her. She imagined a return to Washington State, or possibly Peru, or maybe even to Mount Etna in Sicily because she'd never feel the same about Khronos. Alexander had ruined it for her.

On Saturday morning Josephine was numb as her staff dressed her. The wedding was a late-morning service, designed to accommodate King Bruno as he was at his best in the morning and wouldn't be too groggy from the heavy-duty pain medicines he took at noon.

Josephine's gown looked like something from a fairy tale. She was reminded of Cinderella at the ball, except her dress was white, with a big tulle skirt, a sweetheart neckline, and an impossibly long train. Her long sleeves were sheer and her lace veil was attached to a delicate tiara, the veil as long as her dramatic train.

The hairstylist curled her hair and left it down in long, loose curls, and the makeup artist took forty minutes trying to cover Josephine's pallor and make her look fresh and dewy instead of heartbroken.

Her ladies escorted her down the stairs to the palace front steps where a special carriage waited. Her father stood next to the carriage in his formal wear looking nervous, and yet his expression cleared as he caught sight of her. "You look so lovely, Josephine," he said, reaching for her hands and giving them a squeeze. "And so very much like your mother. I wish she could be here to see you. She'd be so proud."

Josephine was glad now she hadn't told him about losing the baby, or her anger, or the fact that she'd soon be returning to Khronos. She'd give him this moment. He deserved the moment. "I think Mama is here," Josephine whispered.

Her father wasn't a sentimental man, but his eyes glistened. "She wanted the best for you, but I'm sure she never imagined you here, about to become a princess."

Josephine couldn't answer and was grateful when the royal page opened the carriage door, and her father assisted her up the steps. Her ladies lifted her skirt and long lace veil, and then they were seated together and the door closed. The carriage was off.

The ride to the cathedral on the square should have been short but crowds had lined the sides of the street, hundreds of people, no, thousands, coming out to witness Josephine dressed to marry their prince. They cheered for her, time and again, and she blinked repeatedly, fighting tears, touched by the cheers and the shouts of *Princess Josephine! Princess Josephine!* not expecting such a welcome.

The cheers and nerves all became a blur once she reached the cathedral. Her ladies were there again, somehow making it to the square before the carriage, and once again they straightened her dress and veil and handed her flowers from the carriage, flowers she had somehow missed before.

The walk down the cathedral aisle was endless. Sunlight poured through the tall, arched stained glass windows. The soaring ceiling provided the perfect acoustics for the organ. She knew the classical piece being played. It was Mozart. Her mother loved classical music. The thought gave her comfort as she approached the altar. She spotted Alexander there at the very front, standing next to the robed priest. He was dressed in his Royal Navy uniform, the jacket black, the thick shoulders covered with ropes of gold. He had medals across his chest, and with his black hair combed severely back, he looked tall and powerful, virile and handsome.

Part of her thrilled that he was hers, and another part couldn't forgive him for not loving her. Today should have been joyous, not a duty to be borne.

Reaching his side, her father placed her hand in Alexander's and then stepped back to take his place in the front pew.

She felt Alexander's gaze bore into her but she wouldn't look at him. She just wanted to get the service over and the formalities completed so she could take this gorgeous fairy-tale dress off and remove the delicate, sparkling diamond tiara—a tiara she'd been told was worth millions of euros—because although she was marrying Alexander, she hadn't grown up on fairy tales and she no longer wanted to be his princess.

The drive back to the palace was stiff but not quiet as the crowd chanted their approval, the cheers like thunder as Alexander traveled in the carriage with Josephine.

She lifted her hand and waved to the crowds, smiling when she spotted a sign with her name, but she never once looked at him.

He told himself he didn't mind, but he did. He actually minded a great deal. And so he focused on other things, turning from Josephine's elegant profile, and how beautiful she looked in her lovely gown, to nod and wave to the crowd.

He'd done what he needed to do today. He'd married,

and one day in the future there would be another baby, the heir, and his father could return to his room and his bed, and take his medicine, and escape his pain.

"I think we will save the cake and champagne for later this afternoon," he said as the coach passed through the palace gates. "Let my father rest and my mother relax, and then we'll meet before dinner and have a toast before your father goes home."

She turned her head then and looked him in the eye. "Yes, Your Highness."

"Josephine."

"You got what you wanted, Alexander. Your father can rest easy now. But please don't expect me to celebrate."

Josephine had just finished changing into a slim skirt and elegant blouse—her new official royal uniform, it seemed—when a knock sounded on her door. It was one of her ladies, and she was in tears.

"He's gone," she choked. "King Bruno is dead."

That day there was no celebratory cake or champagne. Indeed, the entire wedding was eclipsed by the death of Aargau's beloved king. The shocked public immediately went into mourning.

Josephine herself didn't know what to feel. On one hand, she was glad the king was no longer suffering, but she felt for Serena and for Alexander. They had been expecting his death but not quite so soon.

Perhaps it was better it had happened so suddenly.

Perhaps it was best that it had happened today as it shifted the focus from the newlywed couple to the funeral for the late king.

Josephine's father returned to Khronos and Josephine kept to her rooms, or when she did go out, she walked the safe paths on the castle grounds, going from the rose garden to the orangery and then through the vegetable garden and the orchard.

Alexander did not come to her, and she did not seek him out.

His mother, though, was another matter, and Josephine took to spending a half hour in the queen's chamber every afternoon after her garden walk, either reading or attempting to do some needlework. She was terrible at needlework but her efforts seemed to please Serena, and so she tried. Serena would have tea served and the two of them would pretend to eat one of the cakes that accompanied the tea tray. During their time together, Serena did not mention her son and Josephine did not bring him up. Sometimes Serena would say something about the funeral plans—the funeral now just days away—and Josephine would nod and listen, because Serena seemed to need that.

Josephine needed someone to talk to as well, but the ladies surrounding her were employees, staff members, not friends. It would have helped to have a friend in the palace. Someone Josephine trusted, someone Josephine could ask for advice, because clearly Alexander had no need of her, not anymore. He was much in demand, busy planning funerals and coronations. Why did he need her now? He didn't. She resolved that the day after the funeral, she'd go. She wouldn't make a fuss. She'd slip away. It was the best way to handle the goodbye since they weren't exactly her strength and Alexander wouldn't pursue her. Alexander no longer needed her.

Alexander was in his tower office at his desk when his secretary approached, letting him know that he had a visitor.

"It's Claudia," his secretary said. "I've taken her upstairs to the library. I thought it better than in the palace."

"Thank you," he said, rising and heading for the stairs.

Claudia was pacing the library when he entered. "I wasn't sure you'd see me."

"Why wouldn't I?"

"You've avoided all of us since the trip."

"Gerard told me you'd left Roche for a while." He hesitated. "Someone else said you've been in Paris."

"I've been in Zurich, not Paris." She looked at him hard. "I thought I'd hear from you, though. I was sure I would. I even left my number with your secretary in case you wanted to speak to me. But when you didn't, I began to worry."

He arched a brow. "Worry about what?"

Her relief gave way to wariness. "You don't remember the fight on the trip, do you?"

"Why would you say that?"

Claudia sat down in one of the winged chairs. "Because I keep thinking, if you remembered what happened, you would have taken action. But you've done nothing, at least not as far as I can see, and I've been on tenterhooks waiting for you to reach out to me."

When he said nothing, she added, "I'm not trying to cause a problem, but I keep thinking, something's not right. This just isn't like you."

He drew a slow breath, telling himself not to react. "What should I have done?"

Her brow creased. "Then? Or now?"

Alexander hated not remembering; he hated the blank spots in his memory. "Both."

"I think this is the wrong place to start the conversation. I think we need to back up and I need to say that you weren't rough with me. You were never rough with me in any way, at any time. You do know that, don't you?"

He clasped his hands tightly behind his back, not trusting himself to speak. Why was Claudia here? What did she want? Was this a trick? Was she going to ask for money?

"I don't know what game Damian is playing with you,

Alex, but you weren't drinking that night, and you didn't hurt me." Her voice broke. "*He* did. You saved me. You found us on my balcony and you tried to help me and he clubbed you with the lantern." She gasped for air. "I ran away terrified, and I've been terrified every day since."

Alexander didn't even realize he'd been holding his breath until little spots danced before his eyes. He exhaled roughly. "Why?" he ground out.

"Because I thought he'd killed you, and I was so afraid he'd kill me. And then when you were found, I was afraid he'd try to silence me. I've been hiding from him. Hiding from everyone, but I can't live like this. I can't avoid him forever."

"Why were you two fighting that night?"

"He thought I was flirting with you. He can't stand it if I speak to you or look at you. He's so jealous of you. You must know that. You have everything he ever wanted—"

"He was always like a brother to me. Growing up, he was always saving me from the worst fights."

"That's not true, either. He was behind those fights and behind those beatings. He always arrived after you were beat up and bloody, didn't he?" Her voice quavered. "Did you ever wonder how he always just happened to be there when you were getting the snot kicked out of you? It was because he paid the other boys to beat you up. He paid them so that he could come and look like the hero when actually all they'd done was what he longed to do—hurt you."

"What do you want from me? Money? A couple hundred thousand euros? What is it, Claudia?"

"I just want to be safe. That's why I'm leaving. I have my own money, and friends in Vancouver, but I needed you to know the truth. I couldn't just go and have you think that you are any way responsible for what happened on that trip."

"I'm not a monster, then," he said under his breath, but Claudia had heard him.

"A monster, Alex? Never. You've always been my hero!"

Aimee saw Claudia out and Alexander paced his room for a moment, trying to process everything he'd just learned.

He hadn't hurt Claudia. He hadn't betrayed anyone. He hadn't failed anyone—with the exception of Josephine, then.

He swallowed hard at that thought because he had failed her, and she was the one who deserved his love and loyalty the most.

Alexander returned to the palace to find Josephine, but when he reached her room, she was gone. One of her ladies said that Josephine might be in the garden as she liked the garden, especially in the latter part of the afternoon. He hadn't known that. He thought he should have known it.

He walked through the rose garden and then the orangery, ending up in the kitchen garden where he found her sitting on a bench beneath a peach tree.

She looked up at him without a smile. She looked at him as if he were a stranger. His gut tightened. They'd become strangers since the wedding.

"Can I help you with something?" she asked coolly, formally.

He wanted to kiss her, touch her, love her, make her his again. Instead he stood there stiffly, aware of the staff probably watching, aware of the security cameras in every corner. He wanted her desperately, but life in the palace was not for intimacy. It was a stifling world, filled with rules and formalities and never-ending protocol.

"I wanted to tell you," he said gruffly, "that Claudia came to see me this afternoon." He frowned, uncertain how to explain everything Claudia had told him. "She said she suspected I didn't remember what happened on the yacht and thought I should know."

"What happened on the yacht?"

"There was a fight, but it was between Damian and Claudia."

"So why were you the one in the water?"

"Claudia said I intervened, saving her from Damian when he became physical." He felt Josephine's gaze bore through him. Did she doubt him? Or did she doubt Claudia? He wished he knew. "Damian grabbed a lantern and struck me with it. Claudia ran away, afraid, and she's said nothing about the incident because she's afraid Damian might turn on her."

"That must be a relief for you to know."

Alexander hesitated, flashing back to how they were on Khronos. How simple life had been and how happy he'd felt with her. Happy and free. She'd been happy, too.

He struggled with the words. "I also just want to tell you I'm sorry. I'm sorry for dragging you into all of this. I'm sorry for forcing you into a marriage you clearly didn't want—"

"Good. You should be sorry," she said, rising. "You did force me into this marriage, and yes, you can be incredibly selfish, but I'm not surprised you went to Claudia's aid. It's what you would do. You understand responsibility. You never fail to do your duty." And then she walked past him, her skirt brushing him as she headed back to her suite.

Josephine entered her bedroom and carefully closed the bedroom door. She lay on her bed trembling. She had no fight left in her, no fight at all. It was time for her to go. Time to leave. Thank goodness King Bruno's funeral was in the morning. She'd pack tonight and be ready to go as soon as they returned from the service.

The funeral was held in the same cathedral as their wedding. The cathedral was packed with kings and princes, and political leaders from all over the world. The service was long, with prayers and songs from the choir, and two speakers—Alexander and his cousin Damian.

Alexander spoke first and was eloquent about his father's virtues and his passion for his country, while Damian spoke of his uncle Bruno's vigor and strength and reminisced about the trips they'd taken, the sporting matches they'd played, and how close they'd been, more like father and son than uncle and nephew.

Josephine could see Alexander's jaw tighten and his fist clench as Damian spoke. She found herself watching Alexander's hand and the way his fingers curled and then unfurled. She kept her gaze fixed on Alexander's hand because it was far better than seeing the pain in his face.

Two hours later, Josephine gave her suite of rooms a last glance before lifting her small suitcase and heading for the corridor.

She'd written Alexander a note and she intended to put it on his bed. But as she approached his suite, she heard voices, and she hesitated outside the door to his living room, not wanting to interrupt.

But one of the voices grew louder, the tone menacing. "You think because your father is gone I won't tell the Parliament what you've done? You think I'm going to protect you when you're a violent, unpredictable man, not fit to lead this country or wear the crown?"

Josephine shivered a little, recognizing the voice as belonging to Damian. But that's not why she shivered. She shivered because she was remembering the yacht and the voices she'd heard the night she'd saved him.

It was the same voice. The same anger. The same delivery, the same inflection.

It was Damian who'd fought with Alexander. Damian who'd struck him.

Fear swamped her, not fear for herself but fear for Alexander, and just like that night on the beach, she couldn't move. She couldn't leave him.

She slowly twisted the doorknob and opened the door just enough to get a look inside. Alexander was sitting in a chair, calm and composed, while Damian paced back and forth.

"I will tell them everything," Damian said. "I will destroy you. I will make sure everyone knows who you really are, and when I'm finished, you will be finished because no one will believe you or trust you, not when they find out you have mental problems and lapses in your memory—"

"Whatever are you talking about?" Josephine interrupted, pushing the door open and entering with a faint smile. "You sound almost…crazy, Damian. I'm surprised because you gave the most moving tribute to King Bruno earlier. Was it all an act? Or is this an act now?"

Alexander was immediately on his feet. "Josephine," he said, a warning in his voice.

She walked toward Damian. "Please explain something," she said, still smiling. "Why do you think people will believe you? What makes you think they won't believe him?"

"Because he's brain damaged. He's lost his memory—"

"Yes, he lost it. But it's back. He's told me everything. I know everything. Shall I fill you in?"

"Josephine," Alexander growled.

She ignored him again, her arms crossed over her chest. "You despise him because he's the heir and you're not. During your trip, you were seething with jealousy because Alexander would soon be king. Not you. Never you. Not as long as he lived. And so you provoked him, hurting Claudia, knowing Alexander would go to her aid. Once Alexander was where you wanted him, you took a lantern—very handy, I might add—and bashed him over the head, and then while he was reeling, you pushed him overboard."

She stood now just in front of him and she practically

vibrated with fury. "You thought you'd gotten away with it, too," she added. "You thought you were going to be Aargau's next king. But then Alexander returned, and you lost your big opportunity. You must have been devastated. I can only imagine your pain. I almost—*almost*—feel sorry for you."

Damian stared down at her for long moments before he stepped back and barked a laugh. "That was good. I almost believed you. But you have no proof, he doesn't remember—"

"But he does. He told me everything. How else do you think I know?"

Damian stopped laughing. He glanced from her to Alexander and back. "If he knew, why hasn't he said something? Done something? It's because he's still brain damaged—"

"I'm not brain damaged," Alexander said mildly. "I object to that. But Josephine is right. I told her everything, and she has told her staff everything, and they in turn told security." He walked to Josephine's side and slipped his arm around her waist, holding her tight. "The palace guard has been instructed to arrest you should they find you anywhere near the palace or any member of the royal family again."

"You're lying. You're bluffing," Damian choked, furious. "You can't arrest me because you had no proof, and you'll never have any—"

"The palace guard is here, Your Highness," a voice said from the doorway.

They all turned as Gerard entered with the palace security. "We've heard everything and there is more than enough evidence to convict you," Gerard said shortly.

"But I did nothing! This is all hearsay!" Damian cried.

Gerard shrugged. "I was able to recover the missing security footage. It's all on camera. Every word Josephine said was true."

"But there was no security camera," Damian protested.
"I know. I checked her room and balcony carefully."

Silence followed. Gerard gestured for the guards to take
him. Panicked, Damien put his hands out. "Wait. I'll leave.
I'll leave Roche. I won't come back. I promise—"

"Not just Roche, but Aargau," Alexander said flatly.
"You're not welcome here, and should you be found trying to enter Aargau, you will be arrested and charged with
crimes against the state. Understood?"

It had been a very long, difficult day, but Alexander was
finally alone with Josephine in his bedroom, which was
just where he wanted her.

"You saved me twice," he said, sitting down in a chair
near the bed and then pulling her onto his lap.

He noticed she'd allowed him to draw her down, but
her posture remained ramrod straight. She was still upset.
He didn't blame her, but he was also beyond proud of her,
and in awe. She was a marvel, a heroine, and she was his.

His hand skimmed over her hair, stroking from the top
down. "How am I to live without you?" He didn't give her
a chance to answer. "I'm afraid it's impossible, which is
why I can't let you go."

Her chin tipped, nose lifting. "You can't make me stay.
I'm done being ordered about."

He checked his smile. "Well, then, I'll just have to lock
you back in the tower."

She turned her head sharply and glared at him. "Have
you learned nothing these past few weeks?"

He lifted one of her long silky curls. "I did. I just told
you. You weren't listening. I can't live without you."

"You'll be fine. You're not in danger anymore."

He stroked another curl and then wrapped it around his
finger. "Not true. I'm in danger of losing you and it'll break

my heart, and what kind of king would I be with a damaged brain and a broken heart?"

She smothered a laugh but he felt her back heave and the inelegant snort made him smile. It felt good to smile. It felt good to have her with him like this. He'd missed her so much.

"You'll be fine without me," she said huskily. "You'll find another princess—"

"Never. You're the only princess I want and the only woman I love." He turned her head toward him. "I love you, Josephine, I do, and I know I don't deserve you, but I'm asking for a second chance. Let me make things right. Let me prove to you how much I love you and how sorry I am for hurting you—"

"You did hurt me."

"I know I did. I wasn't sensitive about the miscarriage, and I shouldn't have forced you to marry me. I should have let you go home and grieve and come back when you were ready."

She said nothing and he gave her hair another stroke.

"I'm not being honest," he said after a moment. "I'm sorry for what I did, but the truth is I'd do it all over again if I thought I might lose you. I didn't let you go home because I was afraid you wouldn't come back. I demanded you marry me because I couldn't imagine living without you. From the time I was on Khronos, I wanted you, and not just for a few days but forever. There is no one else for me, *cara*, only you."

He tipped her chin up and kissed her lightly. "Tell me we can make this work. Tell me you'll give me another chance. You don't have to love me. You don't have to forgive me. Just promise you'll give me time to get it right, because that has been the one thing we have never had enough of…time. It's always been against us. It's always running out. I need time with you, Josephine, time to prove to you that I can make you happy, and make you feel safe—"

"You do," she whispered, interrupting him. "And you have." She blinked, chasing away tears. "I love you," she added simply. "I have loved you from the moment I saw you on my beach. I was meant to rescue you, just as I was meant to love you. Sometimes I think the only reason I was put on this earth was to be there when you needed me."

"If that's the case, know now that I will always need you, and I will always love you, and I will always want you at my side. We belong together. You, me, and the children we will have."

Her eyes filled with tears. "Do you think we'll be able to have another baby? I want to start a family with you."

He clasped her face and kissed her fiercely. "We will," he murmured a long time later. "I promise we will. Just as I promise you my love and my heart forever."

CHAPTER ELEVEN

THEY WAITED UNTIL the period of mourning was over to take a much-needed honeymoon, and then after the honeymoon there was the coronation with all the pomp and circumstance the crowning of Aargau's new king required.

But finally, thankfully, the guests were gone, and the fuss was over, and life was settling into a pleasant routine at the palace. Alexander would be busy during the days, but he was all hers at night, and they made love with an unending passion and hunger.

But after two months of palace walls and palace views, Josephine longed for a change, and she mentioned to Alexander that she hoped they could sneak away for a few days, or even a day, and do something adventurous and new just the two of them.

She didn't think he was listening, but the next morning while she was having breakfast he strolled into her room and told her that they'd be leaving within the hour.

"What should I wear?" she asked.

"Something comfortable, and bring a sweater or a jacket just in case it gets cold."

Their driver ferried them to the dock, where a boat was waiting. Josephine glanced nervously at the boat. "Where are we going?"

"It will take us thirty minutes by boat. At this time it's the only way to get there."

"What are the conditions like today?"

"It'll be a little bumpy, but I'll make sure we take it slow."

She nodded and stepped into the speedboat and told herself she wouldn't get seasick and hoped it was true. "Are you going to tell me anything else?" she asked, taking a seat and watching Alexander take one across from her.

"In a bit," he answered. "But for now, just try to relax and enjoy the adventure." He gave her a faint smile. "You like adventures, and freedom. Remember?"

"I do," she agreed cautiously, even as her stomach lurched. She'd been queasier lately, her morning coffee no longer the treat it had once been. And as the speedboat raced across the water, bouncing on some of the bigger waves, sending up a mist of sea spray, she clung to her seat praying she wouldn't throw up.

This was probably not the best adventure when she wasn't feeling well, but Alexander looked so happy that she didn't want to ruin his pleasure.

"Where are we going?" she asked, as the minutes slid by and the boat kept bouncing and she kept swallowing hard.

"There is a bit of rock ahead, nothing too grand. It's barren and remote. But I thought you might like it. I thought you might need a place of your own, a place off the grid with plenty of sun and quiet beaches." His voice had dropped and he gave her a crooked, rather tender smile. "A place where you can be a mermaid and raise our children away from society, noise, and rules and regulations."

Her eyes suddenly stung. Did he know? Did he suspect? She hadn't said anything yet, but she had seen the doctor and he'd confirmed her suspicions. He'd even done an ultrasound and let her watch the tiny, steady, strong heartbeat. "You're describing paradise," she said softly.

"I wouldn't call it paradise, but it is yours, all yours. I'm giving you your very own island."

The speedboat was slowing and yet the wind tangled her hair, and she struggled to push back wild, damp strands from her salt-sticky face. "An island of my own?"

"It's there, ahead of us. Just keep watching the horizon."

She watched and her gaze narrowed as she waited for

something to appear. He told her a little more about the island that lay off the coast of Aargau. It was rocky and barren and good for nothing, but it did have a small beach and a tiny little cove, neither of which were used by the public since they had been owned for the past 160 years by the Alberici family.

"So you have been here before?" she asked, leaning forward, thinking she could see a small lump of land in the distance, but not sure.

He shook his head. "I was there once as a boy. My father and Uncle Aldo took Damian and me there for a fishing trip. It wasn't a success, though, and we never returned."

"So you have bad memories of the place?"

"I don't know if they were bad, but they weren't good enough to make me want to return. But it's different now. We're going together."

Yes, it was land ahead of them. It appeared to be a small hill rising from the sea. The island wasn't very big, but then again, it wasn't quite as small as she'd imagined, either. She could see little green from where she sat, and she suspected it was, as he said, nearly all rock.

The motorboat slowed yet again as they approached the shore. The purplish-blue water lightened, turning a shimmering aquamarine as they arrived at the cove, capped by an ivory crescent of sand. The sides of the cove were rocky and relatively high, but the beach was lovely, with its generous swathe of pale ivory sand.

Their boat's driver steered them as close to the shore as he could before turning off the motor. Alexander jumped out of the boat, waded into the surf, and held his arms up to Josephine. "Come, Queen, I'll keep you from getting wet."

"I like the water, remember?"

"Yes, you have gills and fins, I believe."

She laughed as he lifted her from the boat and carried

her through the rushing surf to relatively dry, packed sand. Once there, he put her on her feet and together they faced the boat and the view of the sea.

Open water everywhere.

Gorgeous blue sky, a turquoise sea, pale rocks standing sentry at the mouth of the cove, and nothing and no one else for miles until you reached the mainland.

"It's perfect," she said, nodding. "I love it. Is there any place to pitch a tent? Because this is most definitely off grid."

"I thought of that, too. Let me show you what is here and we can see if you think it has potential."

He took her hand and led her toward the back of the beach where it butted against the rocky cliff, and there at the back was a little path carved from the boulders, which actually tunneled back through the rocks.

Josephine felt like she was on a grand adventure as they walked up the path through the small tunnel. She reached out and touched the wall. It was surprisingly smooth. Her lips quirked, wondering at the feat of nature required to make such a tunnel out of what was most likely volcanic rock, and then they emerged into the light, and they'd come to a protected clearing. But it wasn't a true clearing at all as right in the middle sat a small stone house virtually identical to the one she'd called home on Khronos. Josephine's jaw dropped and she looked from the cottage to Alexander and back again.

Same stone. Same shape. Same placement of windows and doors.

She walked quickly to the house, and as she crossed the threshold she felt a jolt of recognition—rough-hewn beams across the ceiling, a big stone hearth dominating the center room, and two bedrooms, although as she inspected both, she discovered that the master bedroom was the one at the front, where Jo's had been, and the one at the back had been divided into two, with a cradle and bunk beds, as if anticipating quite a brood.

"This is my house," she said, doing a slow circle, trying to take it all in.

"I had it copied as closely as I could," he said, arms folded across his chest, a faint smile curving his lips. "The contractor and builders wanted to add more amenities but I refused. I told them it was meant to be rustic and an escape from civilization as we know it."

"You gave me my home back," she whispered, her voice breaking.

"With all the solar-efficient technology we could find," he said, exiting the house and heading to the back where a pretty trellis concealed a tidy grid of solar panels, tubing, and equipment. "Solar power for heating and electricity. Solar-powered communication. Enough energy to run your own little lab of computers as well, if you should so desire. And last but not least, your own desalination system for as much fresh water as you, and your future garden, desire."

She shook her head, incredibly touched and overwhelmed by the thought and effort that had gone into creating this world for her.

From the beach, this was a deserted island, and yet tucked behind the safety of the rocks was a little house ready for her to come play house. "You make me feel like Marie Antoinette with her little farm."

"The Hameau de la Reine," he said, blue eyes creasing as he smiled. "The thought crossed my mind, too, but it's not quite so extravagant. We left out the farm, the mill, the Temple of Love, the belvedere, and the grotto."

"Tell me you didn't import all those stones for the house."

"No. Thankfully the island has an abundance of stone, and we were able to use all local stone, cutting them here, which made it far easier physically, as well as more affordable."

"And yet this is still extremely costly."

"Can I not give my bride a wedding gift?"

"Will your people want my head?"

"My people are your people, and they will want you and our children happy." He drew her into his arms, kissing her, oh, so slowly and tenderly, and when he raised his head, his blue eyes were bright and warm and filled with conviction and love. "You will have more children, *cara*. It will all work out. It might just take time—"

"I know," she interrupted, standing on tiptoe to kiss him back. "And it will work out, always, as long as you and I are together and we stick together. Friends, lovers, partners." She felt the secret rise in her, the joy overwhelming. "Parents."

"Yes, we will be parents," he agreed firmly, sounding like the man who'd served his country in the Royal Navy.

"In just six months," she said, kissing him again. "And next week, we can find out the sex, if you want. Or we can both go and just look at the ultrasound and watch the baby's lovely little heart."

Alexander's jaw worked and he blinked hard, clearing the sheen gathering there. "A baby."

"Our baby."

"You've seen the doctor?"

She nodded. "I have, and I've seen the ultrasound and everything looks good. There should be no problems. I just can't go racing up and down steep stairs."

He glanced toward the water. "Or riding in bumpy speedboats. Why didn't you tell me?"

"The boat ride was fine. Trust me. And I was going to tell you this weekend. I had a special reveal planned, but this was actually so much better."

"I'm calling for the helicopter to take us home."

"Alexander."

"I'm taking no chances."

"Alexander!" she protested, laughing.

"I'm taking no chances at all. I love you, Josephine. I love you more than you'll ever know."

* * * * *

BOUGHT FOR THE
BILLIONAIRE'S
REVENGE

CLARE CONNELLY

For Dan, my beloved.

PROLOGUE

HIS CAR CHEWED up the miles easily, almost as though the Ferrari sensed his impatience.

He exited the M25, the call he'd received that morning heavy on his mind.

'He's broke, Nik. Not just personally, but his business, too. No more assets to mortgage. Banks are too cautious, anyway. The whole family fortune is going to go down the drain. He's about to lose it all.'

Nikos should have felt overjoyed. There was something about chickens coming home to roost that ought to have brought him amusement. But it hadn't.

Seeing Arthur Kenington suffer had never been his goal.

Using the man's plight to avenge the past, though... *That* idea held infinite appeal.

For six years he'd carried the other man's actions in his chest. Oh, Arthur Kenington wasn't the first elitist snob Nikos had come up against. Being the poorest kid at a prestigious school—'the scholarship boy'—had led to an ever-present sense of being an outsider.

But it had been so much worse with Arthur. After all, the man had paid him to get out of Marnie's life, declaring that Nikos would never be good enough for his precious daughter. Worse, Marnie had listened to her father. She'd dropped him like a hot potato.

Marnie.

Or 'Lady Heiress', as she was known: the beautiful, enigmatic, softly spoken society princess who had, a long time ago, held his heart in her elegant hands. Held it, pummelled it, stabbed it and finally, at her father's behest, rejected it. Thrown it away as though it were an inconsequential item of extremely limited value.

It had hurt like hell at the time, but Nikos had long ago credited it as the fuel that had driven his meteoric rise to the top of the finance world.

A dark smile curved his lips as he navigated the car effortlessly through London's southern boroughs.

The tables had turned; the power was his and he would wield it over Marnie until she realised what a fool she'd been.

He had the power to help her father, to prove his own worth, and finally to hold her heart in his hands and see if he felt like being gentle…or repaying her in kind.

CHAPTER ONE

SHE SHOULDN'T HAVE COME.

The whole way into the city she'd told herself to turn around, go back. It wasn't too late.

But of course it was.

The second Marnie had heard from him the die had been cast. It had fallen into the water of her life, changing stillness to storm within seconds.

Nikos.

Nikos was back.

And he wanted to see her.

The elevator ascended inside the glass building, but it might as well have been plunging her into the depths of hell. A fine bead of perspiration had broken out on her top lip. Marnie didn't wipe it. She hardly even noticed it.

Every cell of her body was focussed on the next half-hour of her life and how she'd get through it.

'I need to see you. It's important.'

His voice hadn't changed at all; his tone still resonated with assuredness. Even at twenty-one, with nothing behind him, Nikos Kyriazis had possessed the same confidence bordering on arrogance that was now his stock in trade. Sure, he had the billions to back it up these days, but even without the dollars in his bank he'd still borne that trademark ability to command.

For the briefest of moments she'd thought of refusing him. So long had passed; what good could come from re-hashing ancient history? Especially when she knew, in the deepest corner of her heart, that she was still so vulnerable to him. So exposed to his appeal.

'It's about your father.'

And the tiny part of Marnie that had wanted to run a mile at the very thought of coming face-to-face with this man again had been silenced instantly.

Her father?

She frowned now, thinking of Arthur Kenington. He'd been different lately. Distracted. He'd lost a little weight, too, and not through any admirable leap into a healthy life-style. She'd become worried, and Nikos's call, completely out of the blue, had underscored those concerns.

The elevator paused, the doors sliding open to allow two men to enter, both dressed in suits. One of them stared at her for a moment too long, in that way people did when they weren't sure exactly where they knew her from. Marnie cleared her throat and looked straight ahead, her wide-set eyes carefully blanked of any emotion. She tried to conceal the embarrassment that always curdled her blood when she realised she'd been recognised.

When the elevator doors swished open to the top floor of the glass and steel monolith at the heart of Canary Wharf, she saw an enormous sign on the wall opposite that pronounced: KYRIAZIS.

Her heart thumped angrily in her chest.

Kyriazis.

Nikos.

'Oh, God,' she whispered under her breath, pausing for a moment to settle her nerves.

The painstakingly developed skill she possessed of hiding her innermost thoughts and feelings from the outside world failed her spectacularly in that moment. Her skin, usually like honey all year round, was pale. Her fingers trembled in a way that wouldn't be stopped.

'Madam? May I help you?'

She blinked, her golden-brown eyes showing turmoil before she suppressed the unwanted emotion. With a smile that sat heavily on her lips, Marnie clicked across the tiled foyer.

More recognition.

'Lady Kenington,' the receptionist said with a small tilt of her head, observing the visitor with undisguised interest from the brown hair with its natural blonde highlights to the symmetrical features set in a dainty face down to the petite frame of this reclusive heiress.

Cold-hearted, the tabloids liked to claim, and to the receptionist there seemed indeed an air of aloofness in the beautiful woman's eyes.

'Yes, hello. I have an appointment with...' There was the smallest hesitation as she steeled herself to say his name aloud to another soul. 'Nikos Kyriazis.'

'Of course.' The receptionist flicked her long red hair over one shoulder and nodded to a banquette of chairs across the room. 'He won't be long. Please, take a seat.'

The anticlimax of the moment might have made Marnie laugh under different circumstances. All morning she'd counted down to this very moment, seeing it as a sort of emotional D-day, and now he was going to keep her waiting?

She moved to the seating area, her lips pursed with disapproval for his lack of punctuality. Behind her there was a spectacular view, framed by a wall of pure glass.

She'd followed his meteoric rise to the top, reading about each success and triumph in the papers alongside the rest of the world. It would have been impossible not to track his astounding emergence onto the world's financial stage. Nikos had built himself into a billionaire with the kind of ease with which most people put on shoes in the morning. Everything he'd touched had turned to gold.

Marnie had contented herself with congratulating him in her dreams. Or reading about him on the internet—except when her heart found it could no longer handle the never-ending assault of images that showed Nikos and *her*. The generic 'Other Woman' he habitually dated. She was always tall, with big breasts, blonde hair and the kind of extroverted confidence that the Marnies of this world could only marvel at.

In a thousand years she'd never be like one of them. Those women with their easy sexuality and relaxed happiness.

As if to emphasise her point, her fingers drifted to the elegant chignon she'd styled her shoulder-length hair into that morning. A few clumps had come loose. She tucked them back into place with care, then replaced her manicured hands in her lap.

Almost twenty minutes later the receptionist crossed the room purposefully. 'Lady Kenington?'

Marnie started, her face lifting expectantly.

'Mr Kyriazis is ready to see you.'

Oh, *was* he? Well, it was about time, she thought crossly as she stood and fell into step behind the other woman.

A pair of frosted glass doors showed a dark, blurred figure that could only be him. The details of his features were not yet visible.

'Lady Kenington, sir,' the receptionist announced.

On the threshold of not just the door but of a moment she'd fantasised about for years, Marnie sucked in a fortifying breath and then, on legs that were trembling lightly, stepped into his palatial office.

Would he be the same?

Would the spark between them still exist?

Or had six years eroded it completely?

'Nikos.'

To her own ears her voice was cool and detached, despite the way her heart was stammering painfully against her ribs. Standing by the windows, he turned to face her at the receptionist's pronouncement, the midafternoon sun casting a pale glow over him that focussed her attention on him as a spotlight might have.

The six years since she'd last seen him had been generous to Nikos. The face she'd loved was much the same, perhaps enhanced by wisdom and the hallmarks of success. Dark eyes, wide-set and rimmed by thick black lashes, a nose that had a bump halfway down from a childhood accident, and a wide mouth set above a chin with a thumbprint-sized cleft. His cheekbones were as pronounced as always, as though the features of his face had been carved from stone at the beginning of time. It was a face that conveyed strength and power—a face that had commanded her love.

He wore his dark hair a little shorter now, but it still brushed his collar at the back and had the luxuriant thickness that had always begged her to run her fingers through it. His dark eyes, so captivating, flashed with an emotion that seemed to Marnie almost mocking.

With pure indolent arrogance he flicked his gaze over her face, then lower, letting it travel slowly across her unimpressive cleavage down to her slim waist. She felt a spike of warmth travel through her abdomen as feelings long ago suppressed slammed against her.

Where his eyes travelled, her skin reacted. She was warm as though he'd touched her, as though he'd glided his fingertips over her body, promising pleasure and satisfaction.

'Marnie.'

Her gut churned. She'd always loved the way he said her name, with the emphasis on the second syllable, like a note from a love song.

The door clicked shut behind her and Marnie had to fight against the instinct to jump like a kitten. Only with the greatest of effort was she able to maintain an impassive expression on her subtly made-up face.

Under normal circumstances Marnie would have done what was expected of her. Even in the most awkward of encounters she could generally muster the basics in small talk. But Nikos was different. *This* was different.

'Well, Nikos?' she said, a tight smile her only concession to social convention. 'You summoned me here. I presume it's not just to stare at me?'

He arched a thick dark brow and her stomach flopped. She'd forgotten just how lethal his looks were in person. And it wasn't just that he was handsome. He was completely vibrant. When he frowned it was as if his whole body echoed the feeling. The same could be said when he smiled or laughed. He was a passionate man who hid nothing. She felt his impatience now, and it burned the little part of her heart that had survived the explosive demise of their relationship.

'Would you like a drink?' His accent was flavoured with cinnamon and pepper: sweet and spicy. Her pulse skittered.

'A drink?' Her lips twisted in an imitation of disapproval. 'At this hour? No. Thank you,' she added as an afterthought.

He shrugged, the bespoke suit straining across his muscled chest. She looked away, heat flashing to the extremities of her limbs. When he began walking towards her, she was powerless to move.

He stopped just a foot or so across the floor, his expression impossible to interpret. His fragrance was an assault on her senses, and the intense masculinity of him was setting her body on fire. Her knees felt as if they might buckle. But although her fingers were fidgeting it was the only betraying gesture of her unease. Her face remained impassive, and her eyes were wide with unspoken challenge.

'You said you needed to speak to me. That it was important.'

'Yes,' he murmured, his gaze once again roaming her face, as though the days, months and years they'd spent separated were a story he could read in it if he looked long enough.

Marnie tried to catalogue the changes that had taken place in her physically in the six years since he'd walked out of Kenington Hall for the last time. Her hair, once long and fair, was shoulder-length and much darker now, with a sort of burnt sugar colour that fell with a fashionable wave to her shoulders. She hadn't worn make-up back then, but now she didn't leave the house without at least a little cosmetic help. That was the wariness she had learned to demonstrate when a scrum of paparazzi was potentially sitting in wait, desperate to capture that next unflattering shot.

'Well?' she asked, her voice a throaty husk.

'What is your rush, *agape mou*?'

She started at the endearment, her fingertips itching as though of their own free will they might slap him. It felt as though a knife had been plunged into her chest.

She flattened the desire to correct him. She needed to stay on point to get through this encounter unscathed. 'You've kept me waiting twenty minutes. I have somewhere else to be after this,' she lied. 'I can't spare much more time. So, whatever you've called me here to say, I suggest you get it over with.'

Again, his brow arched imperiously. His disapproval pleased her in that moment. It eclipsed, all too briefly, other far more seductive thoughts.

'Wherever you've got to be after this, I *suggest* you

cancel it.' He repeated her directive back to her with an insouciant shrug.

'Just as dictatorial as ever,' she said.

His laugh whipped around the room, hitting her hard. 'You used to like that about me, I seem to recall.'

Her heart was racing. She lifted her arms, crossing them over her chest, hoping they might hide the way her body was betraying her. 'I'm definitely not here to walk down memory lane,' she said stiffly.

'You have no idea why you're here.'

She met his gaze, felt flame leaping from one to the other. 'No. You're right. I don't.'

Wishing she'd obeyed her instincts and refused to see him, she began to walk towards the door. Being in the same room as him, feeling the force of his enmity, she knew only that nothing could be important enough to go through this wringer.

Some paths were best unfollowed—their relationship was definitely one of them.

'I don't know why I listened.' She shook her head and her hair loosened a little, dropping a tendril from her temple across her cheek. 'I shouldn't have come.'

He laughed again, following her to the door and pressing the flat of his palm against it. 'Stop.'

She started, and it dawned on him that Marnie was nervous. Her facade was exceptional. Cold, unfeeling, composed. But Marnie was uncertain, too. Her enormous almond-shaped eyes, warm like coffee, flew to his face before she seemed to regain her footing and inject her expression with an air of impatience.

But she *wasn't* impatient. How could she be? The past was claiming her. He was him, and she was her, but they were kids again. Teenagers madly in love, sure of nothing and everything, unable to keep their hands off each other in the passionate way of illicit love affairs.

Sensing her prevarication, he spoke firmly. 'Your father is on the brink of total ruin, and if you don't listen to me he'll be bankrupt within a month.'

She froze, all colour draining from her face. She shook her head slowly from side to side, mumbling something about not being able to believe it, but her mind was shredding through that silly denial. After all, she'd seen for herself the change in him recently. The stress. The anger. The drinking too much. The weight loss. Disturbed sleep. Why hadn't she pushed him harder? Why hadn't she demanded that he or her mother tell her honestly what was going on?

'I have no interest in lying to you,' he said simply. 'Sit down.'

She nodded, her throat thick, as she crossed the room and took a chair at the meeting table. He followed, his eyes not leaving her face as he poured two glasses of water and slid one across the table, before hunkering his large frame into the chair opposite.

His feet brushed hers accidentally beneath the table. The shock of her father's situation had robbed her of her usual control and she jumped at the touch, her whole body resonating before she caught herself in the childish reaction.

And he'd noticed it; the smile of sardonic amusement on his face might have embarrassed her if she hadn't been so completely overcome by concern.

'Dad's…I don't…' She shook her head, resting her hands on the table, trying to make sense of the revelation.

'Your father, like many investors who didn't take adequate precautions, is suffering at the hands of a turbulent market. More fool him.'

He spoke with disrespect and obvious dislike, but Marnie didn't leap to defend Arthur Kenington. At one time she'd been her father's biggest champion, but that, too, had changed over time. Shell shock in the immediate aftermath of Libby's death had translated to the kind of loyalty that didn't allow room for doubt. Her need to keep her family close had made it impossible for her to risk upsetting the only people on earth who understood her grief. She would have done anything to save them further pain, even if that had meant walking away from the man she loved because they'd expressed their bitter disapproval.

Her eyes were cloudy as they settled on his frame. Memories were sharp. She pushed at them angrily, relegating them to the locked box of her mind.

Those memories were of the past. The distant past. She and Nikos were different people now.

'He will lose everything without immediate help. Without money.'

Marnie turned the ring she always wore around her finger—a nervous gesture she'd resorted to without realising. Her face—so beautiful, so ethereally elegant—was crushed, and Nikos felt a hint of pity for her. There was a time when he would have said that causing her pain was anathema to him. A time when he would have leapt in front of a speeding bus to save her life—a time when he had promised to love her for ever, to adore her, to cherish her.

And she'd answered that pledge by telling him he'd never be good enough for her, or words to that effect.

He straightened in the chair, honing in on his resolve.

But Marnie spoke first, her voice quietly insistent. 'Dad has lots of associates. People with money.'

'He needs rather a large sum.'

'He'll find it,' she said with false bravado, unknowingly tilting her gaze down her small ski slope nose.

His smile was almost feral in its confidence. 'A hundred million pounds by the end of the month?'

'A…hundred…' Her feathery lashes closed, muting any visible shock. She was hiding herself from him, wanting to keep her turmoil private and secret.

He didn't challenge her; there was no need.

'And that is just to start,' he confirmed with a small nod. 'But if you want to leave…' He waved a hand towards the door, as though he didn't give a damn what she chose to do.

Marnie toyed with the ring again, her eyes studying its gentle golden crenulations before shifting their focus back to his face. 'So? What's *your* interest in my father's business?'

'His business?' Nikos's laugh was short and sharp. 'I have no interest in that.'

Marnie's eyes knitted together, confusion obvious on her features. Even her hair looked uptight, knotted into that style. Her hands, her nails, her perfectly made-up face: she was the picture of stylish grace, just as her parents had always intended her to be.

'I presume you called me here because you have a plan.' She pinned him with her golden-brown eyes until the sensation overpowered her. 'I wish you'd stop prevaricating and just tell me.'

His smile was not one of happiness. 'You are hardly in a position to issue commands to me.'

Marnie's face lifted to his in surprise. 'That's not what I was doing.' She shook her head timidly from side to side. 'I didn't mean to, anyway. It's just…please. Tell me everything.'

He shrugged. 'Bad decisions. Bad investments. Bad business.' He pressed back further in his chair, the intensity of his fierce gaze sending sharp arrows of awareness and emotion through her blood. 'The why of it doesn't matter.'

'It matters to me.'

He spoke on as though she hadn't. His eyes bored into hers. 'I believe there are not ten people in the world who would find themselves in a financial position to help your father. Even fewer who would have any motivation to do so.'

Marnie bit down on her lower lip, trying desperately to

think of anyone who might have enough liquidity to inject some cash into her father's crumbling empire.

Only one man came to mind, and he was staring at her in a way that was turning her mind to mush.

Unable to sit still for a moment longer, Marnie scraped her chair back and stalked to the window. London vibrated beneath them: a collection of cars and souls all going about their own lives, threading together into one enormous carpet of activity. She felt as if she'd been plucked out of the fibres and placed here instead, in a madhouse.

'Dad's never been your favourite person,' she said softly. 'How do I know you're not making this up for some cruel reason of your own?'

'Your father's demise is not a well-kept secret, *matakia mou*. Anderson told me.'

'Anderson?' The name was like a knife in her gut. She thought of Libby's fiancé with the shock of grief that always accompanied anything to do with her sister. With *Before*.

'We're still in touch,' he said with a shrug, as if that wasn't important.

'He knows about this?' She thought of Anderson Holt's family, the fortune they possessed. Maybe *they* could help? She dismissed the thought instantly. A hundred million pounds—cash—was beyond most people's capabilities. Besides, Arthur Kenington would never let himself be bailed out.

'It is no secret,' Nikos said, misunderstanding her question. 'I imagine the whole city knows the truth of your father's position.'

Her spine stiffened and sorrow for the man who had raised her pushed all thoughts of her late sister's fiancé from her mind. She blinked quickly, denying the sting of tears that was threatening. She was not willing to show such weakness in front of anyone, let alone Nikos.

'He *has* seemed stressed lately,' she conceded awkwardly, keeping her vision focussed on the buzz of activity at street level.

'I can well imagine. The idea of losing his life's work and the legacy of his forebears will be weighing heavily on his conscience. Not to mention his monumental ego.'

She let the barb go by. Her mind was completely absorbed with trying to make sense of this information. 'I don't understand why he wouldn't have said anything.'

'Don't you?' His eyes flashed with anger and resentment as his last conversation with Lord Arthur Kenington came to mind. 'The man prides himself on shielding you from the world. He would do anything to spare you the pain of actually inhabiting reality with the rest of us.'

'You call *this* reality?' she quipped, flicking a disapproving glance around the cavernous glass office decorated with modern art masterpieces and furniture that would have looked at home in a gallery.

A muscle jerked in his cheek and Marnie wished she could pull those words back. Who was *she* to sit in judgement of his success? She didn't know the details, but she knew enough of his childhood to realise that if anyone on earth understood poverty it was Nikos.

'I'm sorry,' she said stiffly, lifting a finger to her temple and rubbing at it. 'None of this is your fault.'

A pang of something a lot like sympathy squeezed in Nikos's gut. Recognising that she could still evoke those emotions in him, he consciously pushed aside any softening towards her.

'No.' He rubbed a hand across his stubbled jaw. 'He stands to lose it all, Marnie. His investments. His reputation. Kenington Hall. He will be a cautionary tale at best, a laughing stock more likely.'

'Don't…' She shivered, thinking of what her parents had already suffered and lost in life. The thought of them enduring yet another tragedy weighed so heavily on her chest she could hardly breathe.

'I would be lying if I said I'm not a little tempted to leave him to his fate. A fate that, as it turns out, is not at all dissimilar to what he predicted for *me*.'

A shiver ran down her spine. 'You're still angry about that?'

His eyes flashed. 'Angry? No. Disgusted? Yes.' He dragged a hand through his hair, as though mentally shaking himself. 'He would spend a lifetime repaying his creditors.'

Nikos was conscious that he was driving a proverbial knife into her. He didn't stop.

'Some of his decisions might even be seen as criminally negligent.'

'Oh, my God, Nikos, *don't*.' She spun to face him; it was like being hit with a sledgehammer.

He ground his teeth, refusing to feel sympathy for her even when her world was shattering. 'It is the truth. Would you prefer I'd said nothing?'

When she spoke her voice was hoarse, momentarily weakened by the strength of her feelings. 'Does this bring you pleasure? Did you bring me here to gloat?'

'To gloat?' His smile was like a wolf's. 'No.'

'Well? Then what *do* you want? Why are you telling me any of this?'

A muscle jerked in his cheek. 'I could alleviate all of your father's problems, you know.'

Hope, a fragile bird, fluttered in her gut. 'Yes?'

'It would not be difficult for me to fix this,' he said with a shrug.

Marnie's head spun at the ease of his declaration. 'Even a hundred million pounds?'

'I am a wealthy man. Do you not read the papers?'

'God, Nikos.' Relief was so palpable that she didn't

even acknowledge the insult. Hope loomed. 'I don't know how to thank you.'

'Delay your gratitude until you have considered the terms.'

'The terms?' Her brows drew together in confusion.

'I have the means to help your father, but not yet the inducement.'

Aware she was parroting, she murmured, 'What inducement?'

The breath burned in her lungs. Her heart was hammering so hard in her chest that she thought it might break free and make a bid for freedom. Tension was a rope, twisting around them. She waited on tenterhooks that seemed to have sharp gnashing teeth.

'You, Marnie.' His dark voice was at its arrogant best. 'As my wife. Marry me and I will help him.'

CHAPTER TWO

SHE'D NEVER UNDERSTOOD how silence could vibrate until that moment. The very air they breathed seemed as if it was alive, crackling and humming around them. His words were little daggers, floating through the atmosphere, jabbing at her heart, her soul, her brain, her mind.

'Marry me and I will help him.'

Only the sound of her heavy breathing perforated the air. For support, she pressed back against the glass window. It was warmed by the sun.

'I don't understand,' she said finally, squeezing her eyes shut. Every fibre of her being instantly rejected the idea.

Or did it?

Briefly, childish fantasies bubbled inside her, spreading the kind of pleasure she'd once revelled in freely.

When she blinked a moment later, Nikos was holding a glass of water just in front of her. She took it and drank gratefully, her throat parched.

'It is not a difficult equation. Marriage to me in exchange for a sum of money that will answer your father's debts.'

'That makes no sense,' she contradicted flatly.

'No?'

'No!'

It seemed like the right reaction. It was an absurd proposal, after all. Wasn't it? She should have felt panicked by the very idea. And perhaps a part of her did. This was the man who had disappeared from her life but never fully from her heart.

But panic and wariness were only tiny components of her emotional tangle. Hope and an intense flare of passionate resonance also filled her.

'Marriage…' Her heart squeezed. Her words were a whisper. 'Marriage…is for people in love. That's not us. How can you be so cavalier about it?'

He took a step closer, curling his fingers around the glass. Instead of taking it from her he kept his hand over hers. Electricity sparked along the length of her arm, shooting blue fire through her body.

'Call it…righting a wrong,' he said darkly, his eyes scanning her face with hard emotion. 'Or repaying a debt.'

Her stomach rolled.

'Your father paid me a considerable sum to get out of your life six years ago.'

Her mouth formed a perfect 'o' and she gasped in surprise. He gathered she hadn't known *that* little piece of information. It didn't make him proud, but he enjoyed seeing her sense of betrayal and outrage before she schooled her features once more. Her mask was excellent, though the more tightly she held on to it the more he wanted to force her to drop it. To shock her, surprise her, make her feel so strongly that she could no longer remain impassive.

He put his thumb-pad over her lower lip, remembering how soft they were to kiss.

'I didn't know.' Her eyes were earnest and it didn't enter his mind to doubt her.

'No.' He shrugged. 'It wasn't necessary, in any event. He obviously didn't realise that you had already conclusively ended things.'

Marnie's heart squeezed. 'I had no choice.'

'Of *course* you had a damned choice.' He controlled his temper with effort. 'You could have told him that you'd fallen in love with me. That no amount of comment about the fact that I didn't live up to his exalted expectations would change how you felt about me. You could have told him to shove his snobbery and his stupidity. You could have fought for what we were—as I would have.'

She sucked in a deep breath. The pain was as fresh in that instant as if it was six years ago. She ached all over. 'You know what we'd been through.' She squeezed her eyes shut. 'What my family had lost. I couldn't hurt him. I had to choose between him and…what I felt for you.'

'And you chose him.' His stare was filled with a startling wave of resentment. 'You switched something in here—' he lifted a finger to her chest, pointing at her heart '—and that was it. It was over.'

She swallowed convulsively. It had been nothing like that. He made it sound easy. As if she'd simply decided to forget Nikos and move on. But she hadn't. She'd agonised over the decision.

She'd tried to explain to her parents that she didn't care that Nikos didn't have money or come from one of the established families they approved of. But arguments had led to the unsupportable—her mother in tears, her father furious and not speaking to Marnie, and the certainty that they just wanted Libby back—perfect Libby—to make good choices and be the daughter they were proud of.

'In any event, the financial…*compensation* for leaving you helped to soften the blow. At first I swore I wouldn't take it. But then…'

He spoke with gravelled inflection, sucking Marnie back to the present.

'I was so angry with you, with him. I took it and I told myself I'd double it—just to prove him wrong. To prove a point.'

Marnie's cheeks were flushed. His hand moved to cup her face. She could have pulled away, but she didn't. 'I think you did more than that.'

His smile was grim. 'Yes.'

So Arthur had given her boyfriend money to get out of her life? A chill ran the length of her spine. It seemed like a step too far. Pressuring her to end it was one thing, but actually forcing Nikos out?

'I'm sorry he got involved like that. It wasn't his place to…to pay you off.'

'Not when you'd already done his bidding,' Nikos responded with a lift of his shoulders. 'Your father forbade you from seeing me and, like a good little Lady Heiress, you jumped when he clicked his fingers.'

'Don't call me that,' she said distractedly, hating the tabloid press's moniker for her.

It wasn't that it was cruelly meant, only that they mistook her natural reserve for something far more grandiose: snobbery. Pretension. Airs and graces. The kind of aristocratic aspirations that Marnie had never fallen in line with despite the value her parents put on them. The values that had been at the root of their disapproval of Nikos.

'So this is revenge?' she murmured, her eyes clashing fiercely with his. Pain lanced through her.

'Yes.'

'A dish best served cold?' She shook her head sadly, dislodging his hand. 'You've waited six years for this.'

'Yes.' He brought his body closer, crushing her with his strong thighs, his broad chest. 'But there will be nothing cold about our marriage.'

Desire lurched through her. The world began to spin wildly off its axis. 'There won't be a marriage,' she said, with a confidence that was completely forged. Already the options were closing in around her. 'And there certainly won't be…what you're…suggesting.'

'What's the matter, *agape mou*? Do you worry that we won't still feel as we did then?'

He ground his hips against her and she groaned as sensations that had long since been relegated to the past flared in her belly. Of their own volition her fingers curled into the fabric of his shirt, the warmth from his chest a balm to her fraught nerves.

'Do you remember how I respected your innocence?' He brought his mouth close to hers, so that his words were a breath on her lips. 'How I told you we should wait until we were married, or at least engaged?'

Shame, desire, misery and despair slid through her like a headless snake, twisting and writhing in her heart. She pulled her lower lip between her teeth and nodded once.

'How, even though I had kissed your body all over, and you had begged me to take you, I insisted that I wanted to wait? Because I thought I loved you and that it mattered.'

He dropped his hands to her hips, holding her still as he pushed against her once more. She tilted her head back as far as she could, the window's glass providing a hard barrier.

'Do you remember how you laughed in my face and told me you'd never marry someone like me?'

Those words! How she'd hated saying them! She'd rehearsed them for days, and when the moment had come only the belief that she was doing the right thing for her family had spurred her on to say them. It was the most difficult thing she'd ever done. Even now, six years later, she wondered at the way she'd been led away from him despite the intensity of her feelings.

'*Do* you?' he demanded, scraping his lips against her neck, sending her pulse rioting out of control.

'Yes!' She groaned as desire and memory weakened her body.

'I have met many people like you in my life—like your father. Snobs who value centuries-old fortune above all else.'

'That isn't me,' she said with quiet determination.

'Of course it is.' He almost laughed. 'You broke up with me because you knew your destiny was to marry someone like you. Somebody that your parents approved of.'

'That's what *they* wanted. I just wanted *you*.'

'Not enough.' He sobered, his mouth a grim slash.

Frustrated, she tried to appeal to the man he'd once been: the man who had known her better than anyone on earth. 'God, Nikos. You *know* what my life was like then. We'd just buried Libby. We were all in mourning. I couldn't upset them like you wanted me to. I *couldn't*. Don't you dare think for a moment it was because I thought you weren't good enough.'

'You thought as your parents wished you to,' he said with coldness, shrugging as though it no longer mattered. 'But they will shortly come to realise there is one thing that carries more sway than birth and breeding. And when you are as broke as your father that is *money*.'

His words fell like bricks against her chest.

'Now you will marry me, and he will have to spend the rest of his life knowing it was *me*—the man he wouldn't have in his house—who was his salvation.'

The sheer fury of his words whipped her like a rope. 'Nikos,' she said, surprised at how calm she could sound in the midst of his stormy declaration. 'He should never have made you feel like that.'

'Your father could have called me every name under the sun for all I cared, *agape*. It was *you* I expected more of.'

She swallowed. Expectations were not new to Marnie. Her parents'. Her sister's. Her own.

'And now you *will* marry me.'

Anticipation formed a cliff's edge and she was tumbling over it, free-falling from a great height. She shook her head, but they both knew it was denial for the sake of it.

'No more waiting,' he intoned darkly, crushing his mouth to hers in a kiss that stole her breath and coloured her soul.

His tongue clashed with hers. It was a kiss of slavish possession, a kiss designed to challenge and disarm. He blew away every defence she had, reminding her that his body had always been able to manipulate hers. A single look had always been enough to make her break out in a cold sweat of need.

'No more waiting.'

'You can't still want me,' she said into his mouth, wrapping her hands around his back. 'You've hardly lived the life of a monk. I would have thought I'd lost all appeal by now.'

'Call it unfinished business,' he responded, breaking the kiss to scrape his lips down her neck, nipping at her shoulder.

She pushed her hips forward, instinctively wanting more. Wanting everything.

Her brain was wrapped in cotton wool, foggy and filled with questions softened by confusion. 'It was six years ago.'

'Yes. And still you're the only woman I have ever believed myself in love with. The only woman I have ever wanted a future with. Once upon a time for love.'

'And now?'

'For...less noble reasons.'

He stepped away, breaking their kiss so easily it made her head spin.

'Your father isn't the only one I intend to prove wrong.'

She narrowed her eyes, her heart racing. 'What does *that* mean?'

His laugh was without humour. 'You said I didn't mean

anything to you. That I had been merely a distraction when you needed to escape grief.'

He brought his face closer to hers once more—so close that she could see the thousands of tiny prisms of light that danced in his eyes.

'You told me you didn't want me.'

'I…' She squeezed her eyes shut. 'I don't remember saying that,' she lied.

'You said it. And I will delight in showing you how wrong you were.'

He stepped away, leaving her cresting a wave of emotion. Striving to sound cool, she said, 'So you've been… what? Pining for me for six years? Give me a break, Nikos. You moved on pretty damned fast, so it's a little disingenuous to be playing the heartbroken ex-lover now.'

'We were never lovers, *agape*.'

Her stomach churned; her cheeks were pink. 'That's not the point I'm making.'

'Whatever point it is you are attempting to make it is irrelevant to me.'

She sucked in an indignant breath but he continued. 'I have not been pining for you. But I *am* an opportunist.' His smile was almost cruel—at least it looked it to Marnie. 'Your father's situation presented me with an opportunity I felt I couldn't resist.'

'Oh, yeah?' she snapped, trying desperately to think of a way out. A way to make him realise how foolhardy this was!

'You will spend every day of our marriage faced with the reality of just how wrong you were.'

Speechless, she fidgeted with her ring, her mind unable to grasp exactly what was going on.

Seemingly he took her silence as a form of agreement. 'A licence can be arranged within fifteen days. I have engaged a wedding planner to oversee the details. Her card is on my desk; take it when you leave.'

She shook her head as the words he was saying tumbled over her. She needed to process what was going on. 'Wait a second. It's too sudden. Too soon.'

He arched a single thick brow. 'Any delay will make it impossible for me to help your father in time.'

'You're saying we have to actually *be* married before you'll help him?'

His lip twisted in a smile of cynical derision. 'It would hardly make sense to prop him up *before* the pleasure of having you… As my wife.'

To Marnie, his slight pause implied that he meant something else altogether. That he wanted to sleep with her before money changed hands. It made her feel instantly dirty, and she shifted away from the window, crossing her arms in an attempt to stem the pain that was perforating her heart.

'Do you think I'd renege on our deal?' she asked, realising only after posing the question that it showed her acquiescence when she hadn't actually intended to agree…*yet*.

'I think you will do whatever pleases you—as you always have done.' His eyes narrowed. 'Forgive me—what is the expression? Having been bitten, I am…?'

'Once bitten, twice shy.' She sucked in an unsteady breath, waiting for relief to calm her lungs. But still they burned painfully. She tried to salvage her pride. 'If I agree to do this, I *will* go through with it.'

'I'm not sure I can put much stock in your assurances,' he said with a shrug. 'I credit you and your father for my scepticism. Were it not for you, perhaps I would have continued to take promises at face value. Now I live and die by contracts.'

'That's fine in business. I'm sure it's wise, in fact. But marriage is different, surely.'

'A *real* marriage,' he conceded, with a tight nod.

'You're saying you don't want ours to be a real marriage?'

His laugh sent a shiver down her spine. 'Oh, in the most important ways it will be.'

'Meaning...?' she challenged—though how could she not understand his intention?

'Meaning, Marnie, that I have no interest in paying a hundred million pounds and tying myself to a woman *purely* for revenge.'

His smile curled her toes.

'There will be other benefits to our marriage.'

Her heart slammed hard in her chest. 'I...' She clamped her mouth shut.

What had she been about to say? That she was still a virgin? That after being so madly in love with him and letting him go she'd found she couldn't feel that same desire for another man? Especially not the men her parents approved of her dating.

'I'm not going to sleep with you just because you appear out of the blue...'

'That is not why you'll sleep with me,' he said.

He spoke with a confidence that infuriated her. But he was right! Despite the passage of time, and the insufferable situation she found herself in, she couldn't deny that the same need was rioting through her now, just as it had in their past.

'This is a deal-breaker,' he said with a shrug. 'These are my terms. Accept them or don't.'

'Wait.' She shook her head and lifted a hand to make him pause for a moment. But she was drowning. Possibilities, questions, wants, needs, doubts were churning around inside her—it was background noise but it was going to suck her under. 'There's so much more to discuss.'

'Such as?' he prompted, crossing his arms over his broad chest.

She tried not to notice the way the fabric strained to reveal his impressive pectoral definition.

'Well, such as...' She darted her tongue out and licked her lower lip. 'Say I went along with this absolutely crazy idea—and I'm not saying I will, because clearly it's madness—where would you see us living?'

'That is also non-negotiable. Greece.'

'*Greece?*' She was in free fall again. 'Greece, as in... You mean Greece?'

He stared at her for a long moment, his eyes mocking her. 'Athens. My home.'

'But I've always lived *here*. I can't move.'

Their eyes locked; it was a battle of wills and yet when he spoke it was with an easy nonchalance she admired.

'I will be spending a considerable fortune to save your father's reputation. You do not think it's fair that *you* should make some concessions?'

'Marrying you is *not* a c-concession,' she stammered in disbelief. 'It's so much more than that. And the same can be said of moving to a different country.'

'You are *so* sheltered,' he murmured. 'What would you suggest? That we live in London? Within arm's reach of your father? A man I will always despise? No.'

'How can I marry you knowing you feel that way about him?'

His expression was rock-hard. 'You will find a way.' He shrugged. 'While it might be difficult for you, it is the only way to spare him—and your mother—from a considerable fall from grace.'

'So this is how it would be? You'd dictate terms and I'd be expected to fall in with them?'

The air was thick between them. He studied her for a

long moment and she wondered if he wasn't going to answer. Finally, though, he sighed.

'I have no intention of being unreasonable. When you make a fair request I will hear you out. But this is not one of those instances. I live in Greece. My business is primarily controlled from Athens. You still live with your parents, who hate me as much as I do them. You have no business to speak of. It is obvious that we should move.'

'Just like that?' she murmured, shaking her head at his high-handed dictatorial manner even when a small part of her brain could see that he was raising a decent rationale for the suggestion.

'These are my terms,' he said again.

'You're unbelievable,' she replied softly, worrying at her fingers.

She spun her ring some more, trying to think of a way to appease him that didn't involve anything so drastic as this ridiculous marriage. But there was nothing. He had the money. And there was no way he'd help unless she made it worth his while.

'Yes.' He shrugged. 'So?'

'I wouldn't want a big wedding.' She was thinking aloud, really, though to her ears it sounded as though she was going along with his proposal. 'If I had my way it would just be us. No fanfare. No fuss.'

'Hmm…' he murmured with a shake of his head. 'And no one need ever know? No. I want the world to see that you are my wife. You—a woman who once felt I was far beneath her. A woman who declared she'd never marry someone like me. I want your father to have to stand beside us, smiling as though I am all his dreams come true, when we three will know that I am the last man on earth he wants his daughter to marry.'

The way he'd been treated by her and her parents was a nauseating truth. She wished—not for the first time—

that she'd been able to stand up to them. That she'd been wise enough to fight for the relationship that had mattered so much to her.

'Nikos…' She furrowed her brows, searching for words. 'You have to understand why I…why I couldn't be with you. You know how my parents were after Libby…after…'

He studied her face, torn between listening and shutting down this hollow explanation.

'I know I never explained it properly at the time. The way I was always in her shadow. The certainty that I was a poor comparison to her. The absolute blinding fact that they wished again and again that I could be more like her.' She swallowed, an image of her sister clouding her eyes and making her heart ring with nostalgic affection. 'They wanted me to marry someone like Anderson—her fiancé. And I wanted their approval so badly I would have done anything they asked.'

He compressed his lips. 'Yes. I presumed as much at the time.'

He brought his face closer to hers, so she could feel the waves of his resentment.

'You walked away from me and what we were to each other as though I was nothing to you. You can blame your sister, or you can blame your parents, but the only one who made the decision was *you*.'

'I'm trying to explain why…'

'And I'm telling you that it does not matter to me.' His eyes flared. 'You were wrong.'

She had been. In the six years since she'd watched Nikos leave for the last time, his shoulders set, his head held high, she'd never met anyone who excited in her even a tenth of the emotions he had. He alone had been her true love. And she'd burned him in a way that he'd apparently never forgive.

He brought the conversation back to the wedding. 'The guest list will be extensive and the press coverage—'

'Nikos!' Marnie interrupted, her voice strained.

Something in the pale set of her features communicated her distress and he was quiet, watchful.

'Please.' Her throat worked overtime as she tried to relieve her aching mouth. 'I can't do that.'

'You do agree to marry me?'

She nodded. 'But not like that. I... You know how I feel about the media. And, more to the point, how they feel about me.' She flashed a look at him from beneath thick dark lashes. 'I'll marry you. I will. But without all the fuss. Please.'

It was tempting to push her out of her comfort zone. To say that it was a big wedding or none at all. She was staring at him with a look of icy aloofness that had no doubt helped earn her the nickname of Lady Heiress. That look of untouchable elegance bordering on disdain that he understood was her tightly held shield in moments of wrenching panic. That same look he was desperate to dislodge as soon as possible, shaking her into showing her real feelings.

'You don't like the press any more than I do,' she said with measured persistence. 'If you insist on a big wedding we'll both know it's simply to be spiteful to me. And you're not that petty—are you, Nikos?'

He felt his resolve slipping and a grudging admiration for her reasoned argument spread through him. Still, he drawled, 'I'm blackmailing you into my bed and you don't think I'm petty?'

Heat flooded her system, warring with the ice that had coated her heart. 'No, I don't. I think you want me to marry you. What does it matter how we do it?'

She had an excellent point. Besides Marnie there was only one other person he really cared about having at the wedding.

'Fine,' he said, with a nonchalant lift of his shoulders. His eyes glittered with determination. 'So long as your father is there the rest does not greatly matter.'

'It's enormous,' she intoned flatly, rubbing her fingertip over the flattened edges of paper.

Nikos's stare was loaded with emotion. 'It needs to be.' His accent seemed thicker, spicier than it had been the night before. Her gaze flicked to his face, then skidded away again immediately. His face was all angles and planes, unforgiving and unrelenting.

Harsh.

She had never comprehended the full extent of that hardness before. Not in the past, anyway. When she'd loved him as much as the ocean loved the shore. She had felt, then, just like that. As if she would spend the rest of her life rolling inexorably towards him, needing to touch him, to wash over him, to feel him beneath her and around her. She had believed them to be as organically dependent as those two bodies—sea and sand. That without him she would have nowhere to go.

Foolishly, she had thought he felt the same.

But Nikos had moved on quickly, despite his protestations of love, and his bed had been such a hot spot it might as well have had its own listing on TripAdvisor.

'Mind if I have my lawyer check this out?'

He shrugged his shoulders. '*Sigoura.* Certainly. But that may cause a delay to proceedings.'

Her eyes narrowed. 'You mean you might not be able to help Dad in time?'

He sat back in his chair, his body taut, his face unreadable. 'I will not apply for the marriage licence until you have signed the pre-nup.'

A frown formed a little line between her eyes. 'Why not?'

His laugh was a sharp sound in the busy café. A woman

at the table beside them angled her head curiously before going back to her book.

Marnie lowered her voice, not wanting to risk being overheard. She was obliged to lean a little closer. 'Does it matter if I don't sign it in the next week or two? So long as you have it before the wedding…?'

'The minute I apply for our certificate there's a high probability the press will pick up on it. Do you *want* the world to know we were hastily engaged and that the wedding was then cancelled?'

Her cheeks flamed. 'As if the journalists of the world have nothing better to do than search the registry for your name, waiting with bated breath until such time as you see fit to hang up your well-worn bachelor belt,' she muttered.

He arched a single brow, his expression making her feel instantly ridiculous. 'If you believe our wedding won't excite media interest then you're more naive than I recall.'

Yes, she definitely felt childish now. She dragged her lower lip between her teeth, then caught the betraying gesture and mentally shook herself. She was Lady Marnie Kenington, and it was not for Nikos to berate and humiliate her.

'Each of us on our own would create a stir of interest. Marrying one another guarantees press interest.'

'I know.' She nodded. There was no point, after all, in arguing the toss. He was absolutely right. 'But we agreed on a quiet wedding.'

'And I will do my best to arrange this,' he promised.

'Okay.' She nodded again quickly.

His first instinct was to feel impressed by her ability to be reasonable in the face of an argument. But he quickly realised that she wasn't reasonable so much as changeable. That she was deferring to him at the first sign of pressure. Was that how it had been with her parents?

His mouth was a grim line in his face. 'There are four pages you need to sign.'

She expelled a heavy breath and tapped the pen against the side of the table.

Memories, visceral and sharp, twisted his gut. How familiar that tiny gesture was! Flashes of her studying for exams, writing lists, pausing midsentence to capture the next, flashed into his mind. When she'd had a particularly large problem to solve she'd chewed on the end of the pen, waiting for clarity to flood to her from its inky heart.

'Nikos…' She lifted her gaze to him. 'Doesn't this all seem a bit crazy?'

He didn't react.

She huffed out a sigh. 'I don't know you any more. And you definitely don't know me.'

He narrowed his eyes almost imperceptibly. 'I know you perhaps as well as ever.'

She bit on the pen again and shook her head. 'I just don't see why we have to rush this.'

'It is your father's financial situation that puts a time limit on matters.'

'But—'

'No.'

He leaned across the table, pressing his hand on hers. Sparks shimmered in her heart. Angered by her body's ongoing betrayal to his proximity, she worked overtime to conceal the explosive desire. Her glare was dripping with ice.

'This is the only way I will help your father. It's not a negotiation.'

Backed against a wall, she wondered why she didn't feel more angry.

She looked down at the thick pile of papers. 'If you expect me to sign this today then you're going to have to explain it to me.'

'Fine.' He flicked a glance at his gold wristwatch.

'Sorry if I'm taking up too much of your time,' she snapped sarcastically, and for the briefest moment he felt the full force of her emotions—emotions she was so good at guarding. Fear, worry, stress, uncertainty.

But he had no intention of softening towards his fiancée. He nodded curtly, his expression rock-hard. 'The first section deals with our assets. Any assets you bring to the marriage will be quarantined against becoming communal.'

'So I get to keep what's mine?' she interpreted.

'Yes. I have no interest in your money.'

The way he said it, with such vile distaste, made Marnie shiver.

'Fine. Just as I have no interest in yours.'

He arched a brow, his face filled with sardonic amusement. 'You mean, I presume, beyond the hundred million pounds I will be giving your father?'

Her cheeks flamed. 'Yes.' She couldn't meet his eyes because she felt the sting of tears in her own.

'Irrespective of that, you will be entitled to a sum for each year we remain married.'

'I don't want it,' she said through clenched teeth.

'Fine. Give it away. It's not my concern.' He reached forward impatiently and turned several pages until he arrived at the end of that section. 'Sign here.'

Pressing her lips together, she scrawled her name, blinking her eyes furiously.

They were still suspiciously moist when she lifted her face to his. 'Next?'

He appeared not to notice how close her emotions were to the surface. 'The next section deals with the moral obligations of our union. Any infidelity will lead to an immediate termination of the marriage. It will also invalidate the financial agreement, and will necessitate your father returning half of the money I have given him to that date.'

She blinked in confusion. 'You think I'm going to cheat on you?'

His lips compressed with a dark emotion, one she couldn't fathom. 'I could not say with certainty.' His smile was wolfish. 'Though I imagine this makes it considerably less likely.'

She ground her teeth together. 'And what if *you* cheat?'

'Me?' He laughed again, this time with real humour.

'Yeah. You're the one who seems to be constantly auditioning lovers. What happens if you get bored in our marriage and end up in another woman's bed?'

'You will just have to make sure I don't get bored.'

Her breath snagged in her throat. The threat weakened her. Her pulse throbbed painfully in her body. 'When did you get so cynical?'

He narrowed his eyes, stunning her with the heat she felt emanating from him. 'When do you think, *agape mou*?'

She shook her head, hating the implication that she'd somehow caused his character transformation. 'Nikos…'

What did she want to say? She'd already tried to explain about Libby, and the burden she'd felt to please her parents—a burden that had increased monumentally after Libby's death. He didn't care. He'd said as much. She clamped her mouth shut and shook her head. It was futile.

'I have a meeting after this.'

She swallowed, shaking her head to clear the tangle of thoughts. 'Fine.'

'The third section deals with children.'

Her eyes startled to his face. 'Children?' Her heart was jackhammering inside her chest.

He turned several pages but Marnie was too shocked to bother trying to read them. He fixed her with a direct stare. 'It stipulates that we won't have a child for at least five years.'

Fire and ice were flashing within her, making speech

difficult. She blinked her enormous caramel eyes, then shook her head, but still it didn't make sense. 'You want children?'

He shrugged. 'Perhaps. One day. It's hard to imagine right now—and with you.'

'Oh, gee, thanks.' She rolled her eyes in an attempt to hide the way his words had wounded her. 'As if I'm just lining up to be your baby-baker.'

'My...*baby-baker*?' Despite himself, he felt a smile tickle the corner of his lips.

'I can't believe you're actually contracting hypothetical children.'

He arched a brow. 'It makes sense.'

'A baby isn't...' She dropped her gaze. 'A baby isn't *Section Three, Subsection Eleven A*. A baby is a little person. A new life! You have no right to...to...make such arbitrary decisions about something that should be magical and wonderful.'

'A baby between us would *never* be magical and wonderful,' he responded, with such ease that she genuinely believed he hadn't intended to be unkind. 'It is the very last thing I would want. As for it being arbitrary...' He shrugged his broad shoulders with an air of unconcern. 'You seemed perfectly fine making such decisions in the past.'

'Not about a child!'

'You just said you don't want to be my...baby-baker. Have you changed your mind suddenly?' he asked cynically, his eyes drifting over her features with genuine interest.

'No.' She bit down on her lip. The lie—and she recognised it as such—hurt. Images of what their children might look like were hard to shake. Instantly she could see a tiny chubby version of Nikos, with his imperious expression and dark eyes, and her heart seemed to soar at the prospect.

'Our marriage is not one of love. I can think of nothing worse than bringing a child into that situation.'

'But in five years?' she heard herself ask, as if from a long way away.

He shrugged insolently. 'In five years we will either have found a way to live together with a degree of harmony, or we will hate one another and have long since divorced. It gives us time to see what's what. No?'

She nodded jerkily. He was right. She knew he was. But as she signed her name on the bottom of the page she felt as if she was strangling a large part of herself.

'Next?' She forced a tight smile to her lips; her tone was cool.

'A simple confidentiality agreement. Our business is our own. The press has a fascination with you, and I have often thought, despite what you say, that you court their interest.'

'You've got to be kidding me!' she interrupted sharply. 'I go out of my way to stay off their radar.'

'Which in and of itself only heightens their attention and speculation.'

'So I flirt with the press by hiding from them?' She crossed her legs beneath the table. 'That's absurd.'

'You are "Lady Heiress". They call you that because of your behaviour—'

'They call me that,' she interrupted testily, 'because I refuse to engage with them. After Libby died they were everywhere. I was only seventeen, and they followed me around for sport.'

She didn't add how horrible their comparisons to the beautiful Libby had made her feel. How Marnie's far less stunning looks had drawn the press's derision. She had refused to court them in order to create the impression that she didn't care, but each article had eroded a piece of her confidence until only the 'Lady Heiress' construct had remained. Being cold and untouchable, a renowned ice queen, was better than being the less beautiful, less popular, less charismatic sister of Lady Elizabeth Kenington.

He shrugged. 'You will not be of such interest in Greece. Here you are a society princess. There you will be only my wife.'

Why did that prospect make everything inside her sing? Not just the prospect of marrying him, but of escaping it all! The intrusions and invasions. Freedom was a gulf before her.

'Your parents are included in this agreement. They are to believe our wedding is a real one.'

'Oh? I would have thought you'd like to throw the terms of our deal in Dad's face, just to see him suffer,' she couldn't help snapping.

'Perhaps one day.' His smile tilted her world off-balance. 'But that is *my* decision. Not yours.'

She furrowed her brow. 'This agreement doesn't apply to you?'

'No. It is a contract for you. So you understand what is expected of you.'

'That definitely isn't fair.'

He laughed. 'Perhaps not. Do you want to walk away, Marnie?'

The sting of tears was back. She lowered her eyes in an attempt to hide them and shook her head. But when she put her signature to the bottom of the page she added something unexpected.

A single teardrop rolled down her cheek and splashed onto the white paper, unconsciously dotting the 'i'. It was the perfect addition to the deal—almost like a blood promise.

She closed the contract and pushed it across the table.

It was done, then, and there was nothing left to do but marry the man. Except, of course, to break the news to her parents.

CHAPTER THREE

'YOU CAN'T BE SERIOUS.' Arthur Kenington's face was a study in apoplexy, from the ruddy cheeks to bloodshot eyes and the spittle forming at the corner of his mouth.

Marnie studied him with a mix of detachment and sadness. Perhaps it was normal to emerge into adulthood with a confusing bundle of feelings towards one's parents. Marnie loved them, of course, but as she sat across from Arthur and Anne in the picture-perfect sunroom of Kenington Hall she couldn't help but feel frustration, too.

She lifted her hand, showing the enormous diamond solitaire that branded her as engaged. Anne's eyes dropped to it; her lips fell at the corners. Just a little. Anne Kenington was far too disciplined with her emotions to react as she wished.

'Since when?' The words were flat. Compressed.

'Be vague on the details.' That had been Nikos's directive when they'd spoken that morning. Had he been checking on her? Worrying she was going to balk at this final hurdle? Did he think the idea of breaking the news to her parents might be too difficult?

'We met up again recently. It all happened very fast.'

'You can certainly say that.' Anne's eyes, so like Libby's had been, except without the warmth and laughter, dropped to Marnie's stomach. 'Is it...?'

'Of course not!' Marnie read between the lines. 'I'm not pregnant. That's not why we're getting married.'

Arthur expelled a loud breath and stood. Despite the fact it was just midday, he moved towards the dumb waiter and loudly removed the top from a decanter of sherry. He poured a stiff measure and cradled it in his long, slim fingers.

'Then why the rush?' Anne pushed, looking from her husband to her daughter and trying desperately to make sense of the announcement that was still hanging in the air.

'Be vague on the details.'

'Why not?' she murmured. 'Neither of us wants a big wedding.' She shrugged her slender shoulders, striving to appear nonchalant even when her heart was pounding at the very idea of marriage to Nikos Kyriazis.

'Darling, it's not how things are *done*,' Anne said with a shake of her head.

Marnie stiffened her spine imperceptibly, squaring her shoulders. 'I appreciate that your preference might be for a big, fancy wedding, but the last thing I want is a couture gown and a photographer from *OK! Magazine* breathing down my back.'

Anne arched one perfectly shaped brow, clasped her hands neatly in her lap. At one time, not that long ago, Marnie might have taken Anne's displeasure as reason enough to abandon her plans. But too much was at stake now. If only her parents knew that the wedding they were so quick to disapprove of was their only hope of avoiding financial ruination!

'You don't like the press. That's fine. But our friends. Your family. Your godmother...!'

'No.' Marnie didn't flinch; her eyes were tethered to her mother's. 'That's not going to happen. Just you and Dad.'

'And Nikos? Which of *his* family will be there?' Anne couldn't quite keep the sneer from her voice.

'As you know, he has no family,' Marnie responded with a quiet dignity. 'Besides me.'

How strange it was to say that, knowing it was the literal truth if not a particularly honest representation of the situation.

'I don't like it,' Arthur interjected, his sherry glass empty now, and his focus on Marnie once more.

Marnie had expected this, and yet still she heard the words with an element of disappointment. 'Why not?' she queried quietly.

'I have never thought he was right for you. I still don't.'

There was nothing inherently offensive in the statement, but it was the reasoning behind it that Marnie took exception to. Six years ago she'd let the implication hang in the air, but now she was older and wiser and significantly less worried about upsetting her parents. 'For what reason, Dad?'

He reached for the sherry once more and Anne Kenington, across from Marnie, stiffened visibly.

'He's just not *right*.'

'That's not a reason.' Marnie's smile was forced.

'Fine. He's different. From you. From us.'

'Because he's Greek?' she asked with an assumption of mock innocence.

'Don't be obtuse,' he snapped.

Anne stood, moving her slender figure across the room towards the large glass doors that opened out onto the rolling green grass of the East Lawn. A large oak broke up the expanse of colour a little way in the distance, casting dark shadows beneath its voluminous branches.

'Is there any point in having this discussion?' she asked wearily.

'Meaning…?' Marnie asked softly.

'Your plans appear to be set in stone,' Anne continued, her pale eyes skimming over the gardens, her face a mask of calm despite the storm Marnie knew to be raging beneath.

Was that the only thing they had in common? Their steadfast commitment to burying any display of emotion? Keeping as much of themselves as possible hidden from prying eyes?

Marnie shifted her gaze back to her father. He looked as if he was about to pop a blood vessel. He was glaring at the sherry decanter, his fingers white around the fine crystal glass.

'One hundred per cent.' Marnie nodded. 'I hope you can put the past behind you and be happy for us.'

Arthur's harsh intake of breath was smothered by Anne's rushed statement. 'You're a grown woman. Who you marry is your choice.' She practically coughed on the statement.

Marnie stood, not sure what else she could add to the conversation. 'Thank you.'

A ridiculous way to end the conversation but, then again, what about the circumstances of this wedding *wasn't* ridiculous?

She slipped from the room, the muted voices of Arthur and Anne chasing her down the long corridors of Kenington Hall. She emerged onto the front steps and breathed in deep. Her cheeks were flushed, her skin warm. She moved deliberately away from the East Lawn, wanting to be far from her parents.

She walked with innate elegance until she reached the edge of the rose gardens. Then she slipped her pumps from her feet and cast one last glance towards the house. She began to move as she'd wanted to since she'd first seen Nikos again. As though the earth had turned to magma and was burning through the soles of her feet. She couldn't stand still; she could no longer be composed and calm.

And so she ran.

She ran as though the ghosts of the past had taken animal form: they were lions and tigers and they were chasing her, making her tremble with fear and terror.

'No daughter of mine is going to throw her life away on a no-hoper like that! You will end it, Marnie, or you will be out of this house faster than you can say inheritance.'

Arthur's hateful declaration was a cheetah, fierce and gnashing its teeth.

'I don't care about money! I love him!'

She sobbed as she remembered her impassioned cry, her belief that if she could only get her parents to understand what a good man Nikos was they would shelve their dislike.

But their dislike hadn't had a lot to do with the man he was so much as the man he *wasn't*.

'He's got no class. He will never make you happy, darling.'

At least Anne had tried to couch her objections gently. But her meaning had been clear. No class. No money. No social prestige.

Even then she'd stood fast. She'd fought for him.

'We've been through enough this year, for God's sake!' Arthur had finally shouted. *'We've already lost one daughter. Are you going to make us lose you, too?'*

Marnie ran until her lungs burned and her eyes stung with the tears the wind held in check. She ran past the lake that she'd fallen into as a child, before she'd learned to love the water and to navigate its murky pull; she ran around the remnants of the tree house where she and Libby had spent several long, sticky summers, pretending they were anywhere but Kenington Hall. She ran to the very edges of the estate, where an apple orchard shielded the property from the curious view of a passer-by.

Finally she came to an abrupt stop beneath a particularly established tree, bracing her palm against the trunk and staring back at the sprawling stone mansion.

Her whole life had been lived within its walls. She'd learned to walk, she'd played hide-and-seek, she'd read book after book, she'd been a princess in a castle. It was her place in the world.

But why hadn't she left when her parents had taken a stand against Nikos? Why hadn't she moved to London like most of her friends?

Because of Libby.

A sob clogged her throat. She swallowed it.

They'd lost Libby. And it had changed them for ever. Maybe they would have been difficult and elitist, anyway. But their grief had made it worse. And it had made Marnie more forgiving.

How could she run away from them and leave them alone after burying one of their daughters?

She groaned now, shaking her head.

So she'd put her life on hold. She'd remained at home, under their roof, managing the gardens, working in her little home office, pretending she didn't resent them for their heavy-handed involvement in a relationship that had been so important to her.

Was this marriage to Nikos a second chance? Might they even fall in love again?

Her heart turned over in her chest as she remembered the exquisite emotions he had evoked in her as a teenager. She had loved him fiercely then—but not enough. Because she'd walked away from him instead of staying and fighting and there was no turning back from that.

Goose bumps danced along her soft skin. 'This is beautiful.'

And it was. The house was nothing like she'd imagined. Set high on a hill on the outskirts of Athens, it was crisp white against a perfect blue sky. Geraniums tumbled out of window boxes, creating the impression that the flowers had sprung to life there and decided to blow happily in the light, balmy breeze. Clumps of lavender stood proud from large ceramic pots and the fragrance of orange blossom and jasmine hung heavy in the air.

'I'll give you a tour tomorrow—introduce you to the household staff.'

'Staff?' That was interesting. 'How many staff?'

He put his hand in the small of her back, propelling her gently towards the front door. 'My housekeeper, Eléni, and her husband, Andréas. Two gardeners...'

'That's good,' she said with a nod.

His laugh was a short, sharp bark. 'Did you think it would be just you and me?'

Of course she had.

He leaned closer, so that she could see the hundred and one colours that danced in his irises.

'Don't worry, *agape mou*.'

The heat of his words fanned her cheek.

'They will give us plenty of space in the beginning. We *are* on our honeymoon, after all.'

Her stomach lurched. Desire was swarming over her body, making her pulse hammer. Moist heat slicked through her. It felt as if she'd been waiting an eternity to be possessed by this man. The time was almost upon them, and anticipation was flicking delicious little sparks over her nerves.

He pushed the front door inwards. A wide tiled corridor led all the way to glass doors that showed the moonlit Aegean Sea in the distance.

'Are you hungry?'

Despite the fact that it was their wedding day, she hadn't eaten more than a piece of wedding cake after the ceremony. A sip of champagne to wash it down and Nikos had whisked her away from the disapprovingly tight smiles of her parents.

Her stomach made a little growl of complaint. 'Apparently,' she said, with an embarrassed smile.

His smile was the closest thing to genuine she'd seen on his face. It instantly offered her a hint of reprieve.

'There is food in the fridge. Come.'

She fell into step behind him, taking in the blur of their surroundings as she walked at his pace. Beautiful modern artwork gave much-needed colour to a palette of all glass and white. The home was obviously new, and it was a testament to minimalist architecture. While beautiful, it was severely lacking in comfortable, homely touches.

The kitchen housed a large stainless steel fridge. He reached in and pulled out a platter overflowing with olives, cheese, bread, tomato and *dolmades*. Another selection of bread was complemented with sliced meats and smoked fish.

'Wine, Mrs Kyriazis?'

The name splintered through her heart. 'I thought I'd keep Kenington,' she said, though in truth she'd barely contemplated the matter.

He poured two glasses of a pale, buttery-coloured wine, his face carefully blank of emotion. 'Did you?'

She shrugged. 'Lots of women do, you know.'

He nodded thoughtfully. 'But you are not "lots of women". You are my wife.'

He said it with such a sense of dark ownership that she was startled. Marnie couldn't have said if it was surprise at being spoken of almost as an object that inspired her sense of caution, or the fact that his passionate statement of intent was flooding her with desire and overarching need. A need that made rational thought completely impossible.

She sipped her wine in an attempt to cool the fire that was ravaging her central nervous system. It didn't work.

She nodded jerkily, at a loss for words.

'I want the world to know it.'

The statement hung between them like a challenge.

Her stare was direct. 'I'm not planning on hiding my identity.'

He reached for a cube of feta and lifted it towards her lips. Surprised, she parted them and he slid the cheese into her mouth, watching with satisfaction as she chewed it.

'No.' His eyes bored into hers, holding her gaze for several long, fraught seconds. 'My wife will bear my name.'

There it was again! That flash of pleasure in her abdomen. A sense of *rightness* at the way he wanted to claim her. To possess her. The desire to subjugate herself completely to his will terrified her. She bucked against it even as she wanted to move to him and offer her submission.

'Will she, now?' she murmured.

'Of course it is not too late to back out of this agreement.' He shrugged. 'Our marriage could be easily dissolved at this point, and I have not yet spoken to your father about his business concerns.'

Something lurched inside her. She stared across at him, needing her wine to banish the kaleidoscope of butterflies that were panicking, beating their wings against the walls of her stomach.

'Are you going to threaten me whenever I don't let you have your way?'

His laugh was without humour. 'That was not a threat, Mrs Kyriazis. It was a summation of our current circumstances.'

'So if I don't take your name you'll divorce me?'

His lips twisted in a wry smile. 'At this point I believe we could simply seek an annulment.'

'You should have put it in that damned pre-nup,' she said with a flick of her lips.

Anger flared inside her and beneath the table she turned the ring on her finger, looking for comfort and relief.

'I would have if I had known you were going to be so irrational about such trivialities.'

'It's not a triviality!' she demurred angrily, tipping more wine into her mouth.

How could she possibly explain her feelings? Explain how essential it was to hold on to at least a part of her identity? How terrified she was that she was married to a man who despised her, who was using her to avenge an ancient rebuff, who was determined not to care for her—a man she had always loved?

'You are my wife.'

'And taking your name is the *only* way to be your wife?' She had to force herself not to yell.

'Not the only way, no.'

His teeth were bared in a smile that sent shivers down her spine. Need spiked in her gut. She wouldn't acknowledge it. She couldn't.

'Fine.' She angled her head away. 'Whatever. I don't care enough to fight about it.'

That bothered him far more than the suggestion she might not take his name. The way she'd rolled over, acquiesced to his wishes at the first sign of conflict. Just like the last time he'd challenged her and she'd almost immediately backed down.

Arthur and Anne had insisted she couldn't be involved with him. Had she argued calmly for a moment and then given up? Given *him* up, and with him their future? Had they invoked her dead sister, knowing that Marnie had never felt she measured up to St Libby? Had they compared him—a poor Greek boy—to Libby's blue-blood fiancé, with his title and his properties? Had she looked from Nikos to Anderson and agreed that, yes, she needed someone like the latter?

'These olives are delicious,' she said quietly, anxious to break the awkward silence that was heavy in the room.

But when she lifted her gaze slowly to his face she saw he was lost in thought, staring out of the kitchen windows at the moonlit garden. It allowed her a moment to study his face and see him properly. He looked tired. No, not *tired*, exactly, she corrected, so much as…what? What *was* the emotion flitting across his face? What did she see in the tightening of his lips and the darkening along his cheekbones? In the knitting of his brow and the small pulsing of that muscle in his jaw?

'Fine.' He blinked and turned to face her. 'I'll show you the house now.'

She nodded out of habit.

It was enormous, and modern throughout. Wide corridors, white walls, beautiful art, elegant lighting…

'It's like a boutique,' she murmured to herself as they finished their tour of the downstairs rooms and took the stairs to the next level.

'This will be our room.' He paused on the threshold, inviting her silently to precede him.

Our room. Did he expect her to argue over their sleeping arrangements? She had no intention of giving him the pleasure.

'It's very nice.' Her almond-shaped eyes skimmed the room, taking in the luxurious appointments almost as an afterthought. King-size bed, bay window with a small seat carved into the nook, plush cream carpet and a door that she imagined led to a wardrobe.

She spun round, surprised to find him standing right behind her. They were so close her arms were brushing his sides.

She stepped back jerkily. 'I'm going to need an office space.'

'An office space?' His laugh was laced with disbelief and it irked her to the extreme.

'Yes. Why do you find that funny?'

'Well, *agape*, offices are generally for *work*.'

'Oh, I see.' She nodded with mocking apology. 'Work like *you* do, I suppose you mean?'

He crossed his arms over his chest, drawing Marnie's attention to the impressive span of musculature.

'Yes, generally.'

Her temper snapped, but she didn't show it. She'd had a lot of practice in keeping her deepest feelings hidden—she could only be grateful for that now.

'I need an office.' She said the words slowly and with crisp enunciation. 'For *my* work.'

'What work?'

Curiosity flared in his gut. Six years had passed and he'd presumed she was still simply Lady Marnie Kenington, daughter of Lord and Lady Kenington, employed only in the swanning about of her estate, the beautifying of herself and the upholding of the family name. It had never occurred to him that she might have done what most people did and found gainful employment. Frankly, he was surprised her parents had approved such a pedestrian pursuit.

'Does it matter? Do you care? Or are you just surprised that I haven't been rocking in a corner over the demise of our relationship since you left?'

Though frustrated by her reticence to speak honestly, he liked seeing the spark that brought colour to her cheeks and impishness to her eyes.

It intrigued him. He far preferred it to the obedient contrition she'd modelled in the kitchen. Instantly he thought of other ways in which he might inspire a similar reaction.

He nodded, concealing his innermost thoughts. 'Fine, have it your way. I do not need to know about your employment if you do not wish to speak of it.' He shrugged, as though the conversation was now boring him. 'I'll have a room made available. Just let my assistant know what you need in terms of infrastructure and he'll see you're set up.'

'*He?* You have a male assistant?'

It was Nikos's turn to act surprised. 'Yes. Bart. He's been with me five years.'

She laughed quietly and shook her head. 'I guess that makes sense. I can imagine you'd run through female secretaries pretty damned fast, given your track record for taking any woman with a pulse to bed.'

'Jealous, *agape*?'

She'd been jealous, all right. For years she'd followed his exploits in the gossip columns. Like watching a train crash, she'd been powerless not to stare at the pictures. They'd come to life in her over-fertile imagination so that she hadn't simply looked at an attractive couple coming out of some hot spot so much as imagined them in bed, or perhaps on the dining table, or the kitchen floor, while *she* lay in her own bed. Alone, untouched, able only to dream of Nikos rather than feel his hands on her body...

'Oh, yes,' she simpered, with an attempt at false sincerity. 'I've spent the last six years *desperately* waiting for you to reappear in my life. I've been missing you and dreaming about you and praying you'd turn up and blackmail me into a loveless marriage. This is pretty much the high point of my life, actually.'

'And we haven't even slept together yet,' he said, in a voice that was honey and dynamite.

Her breath caught in her throat. She spun away from him, her cheeks flushed.

'What is it, *agape*? Suddenly you are shy? It is our wedding night.'

She lifted a hand to her throat and lightly rubbed her skin. 'I... Of course not.' She squared her shoulders.

Hadn't she been dreaming about this for as long as she'd known him?'

'Relax.' His hands on her shoulders were firm. He spun her in the circle of his arms so that they were facing one another, his warmth offering some comfort to her. 'You are shaking like a leaf.'

Tell him the truth!

She fluttered her eyes closed, her lashes dark circles against her pale cheeks.

'You are my wife.' He pressed a finger under her chin, lifting her face to his. His eyes were troubled, tormented. 'Are you…*afraid* of me?'

It was so uncharacteristic of him to show doubt that she raced to reassure him. 'Of course I'm not.' She shook her head, inhaling a deep breath that flooded her system with his spicy scent. 'I'm afraid of *myself*, and of what I want right now.'

He nodded, silently imploring her to continue.

'You hate my father. I think you might even hate me.' She lifted a finger to his lips to stop him from speaking. 'But I don't hate you.' Her eyes were enormous, loaded with fear and desire. 'I don't hate you…'

Her finger, initially placed against his mouth to silence him, dragged slowly across his lower lip. Her eyes followed its progress as if mesmerised.

She knew he was going to kiss her. The intent was in every line of his body. If she'd wanted to she could have stepped away. She could have asked for more time. Instead she lifted herself up on tiptoe, crushing her mouth to his.

In that bittersweet moment all Marnie needed was to right one of the biggest wrongs of her past: she wanted Nikos and, damn it, she was finally going to have him.

To hell with the consequences. They'd be waiting for her afterwards.

CHAPTER FOUR

HER BODY FLASHED like flame when his mouth crushed down on hers with the kind of intensity that spoke of long-held desire. She was powerless to swim against the tide of need: powerless and unwilling.

Her feminine heart was hot and wet, slick with moisture and need. Unfamiliar but instinct-driven urges were controlling her body. Her hands pushed under his shirt, seeking skin and warmth. She traced her fingertips up his hair-roughened chest, splaying her fingers wide. She felt the beating of his heart beneath her touch; it was as frantic as her own.

His body weight pushed her downwards—not to the bed but to the floor, to her knees. He knelt with her, kissing her, his tongue clashing fiercely with hers as his hands pulled through her hair then pushed at her head, holding her against his mouth. She groaned into him, marking their kiss with the desperation that was scrawling a painful tattoo across her being—inking her as his in a way that would never be erased.

He pulled at her as his body pushed at hers until she fell back onto the carpet. His weight on top of her was divine. She curved her hands to his back, digging her nails into his warm skin as she felt the power of his arousal for herself. Hard and firm through their layers of clothing, A bodily ache was spreading through her. She lifted her hips, silently begging him for more. To mark her once and for all.

'Nikos!' She cried his name into the room and he groaned in response. 'Please!' She dug her hands inside his jeans, cupping the naked curve of his arse, pressing him against her and grinding herself intimately against his masculinity.

He laughed throatily. 'You want this, huh?'

He kissed her again—hard, fiercely, possessively—and then roamed his lips lower, encircling one of her erect nipples through the fabric of her dress and her bra. Even with such obstacles in the way the warmth and pressure of his mouth sent sharp arrows of need spiralling within her.

'Yes!' she hissed, arching her back, desperately needing more. 'Please, please…'

'In time.'

He smiled, running his mouth lower, over the fabric of her dress, until he reached the apex of her thighs. He skimmed lower, to the hem of the dress, and finally pushed it upwards, so that only a flimsy scrap of lace stood between him and her most intimate flesh.

Her cheeks were pink, her eyes fevered. Even when he wanted to go quickly he took his time, removing her underpants, sliding them down her soft, smooth legs and discarding them to one side. He let his hands dance patterns along her thighs, revelling in the way she quivered beneath his touch as her body responded instantly to him.

His fingers worshipped at her crease, teasing her, exploring her, aching for her. He was more gentle than he'd known he could be, perhaps afraid that she might regret her decision at any moment. That after years of waiting this was, after all, *not* to be.

Greek words, whispered hoarsely, filled the air. Words that swirled around her, wrapping her in magic and myth.

She didn't have a clue what he was saying, but she loved the sound of his native language.

When he slid a finger into her core she bucked hard, writhing at the intimate touch. Even back then, when they'd been fevered and passionate, he hadn't passed *this* threshold. His invasion was completely, utterly unprecedented.

Sharp, hot barbs of pleasure drove through her body, into her mind, weakening every earthly thought before it could be imagined. He moved slowly, curiously, watching her face as he stroked her sensitive flesh, learning what made her almost incandescent with desire before pulling out of her.

She gasped, the withdrawal of his touch an unbearable pain she could not withstand. But he didn't leave her for long before dropping his lips to her opening. His tongue was warm, but she was more so. Her body was on fire… his mouth seemed to kiss flame into her.

It had been a long time since Marnie had felt anything like this. She was completely unprepared for the insanity that his ministrations would bring. She was digging her nails into the carpet at her sides now, her knees lifted towards the ceiling as her toes curled into the ground and her whole body shook and quivered.

The orgasm was intense. She screamed as it saturated her being in long, luxuriant waves.

Sweat beaded her brow; heat painted her cheeks pink. Her throat, her arms—she was burning up. Her breath was loud in the room as she panted, satiated passion making her lungs work overtime.

Before she could drift down from the clouds that had absorbed her into their heavenly orbit Nikos was straddling her, his arousal pressed against her tingling core.

Marnie stared up at him, and everything in her world was perfect.

He studied her as his hands worked the buttons of his

shirt, and she was powerless to look away. Her tongue darted out, licking her lower lip, moistening it hungrily.

His smile was sexy as sin. She groaned, impatient for more. As he pushed at his shirt her trembling fingers unfastened his belt and pulled it from his jeans. She cast it across the room, wincing apologetically when it hit the wall loudly. He didn't react.

His shirt was unbuttoned, his chest exposed to her greedy eyes, and she stared and she touched and she felt, tracing his muscles, circling his nipples and filling with pride when he sucked in a raspy breath. He rotated his hips, taking back the upper hand, making her weak with the promise of what was to come.

She pushed at his shirt, chasing it down his arms, catching the fingers of one hand as she passed, lifting it to her lips and kissing him. It was a tender moment in the midst of passion. Their eyes locked and the past was all around them, threatening to suck them into the vortex of what had been.

'It might have cost me a small fortune, but finally you are going to be mine.'

His eyes glittered with dark anger, and the moment was swallowed up by cruelty as though it had never been.

Marnie bit down on her lip, trying not to react, trying not to let the pain sour what they were sharing.

She didn't have long to absorb his words, to turn them over in her mind. He shifted his body weight so that he could kick his jeans and boxers off. He was naked. Gloriously, wonderfully naked. She stared at him, her mind disappearing completely at the sight of Nikos Kyriazis. Her husband: the definition of tall, dark and sexy.

She groaned, dropping her hand to her womanhood, her fingers lightly grazing her flesh. His chest heaved as he sucked in a breath, his eyes sparking with hers. He stood over her, incapable of looking anywhere but at her hand and incapable of moving.

Until something snapped—and a desperate need to finally possess her cracked through him.

'You're on the pill.'

It was a statement, not a question. As though it hadn't occurred to him in earnest that she might not be.

Her cheeks flushed pink as she nodded. It had been the first thing she'd done after signing the pre-nuptial agreement. It had been all she could do to prepare for this moment, for him.

'I am safe.'

He straddled her, almost trapping her hand, but she snaked it higher. Tentatively, nervously, as though she had no right, she touched his length. He jerked instantly in her palm. She smiled a feminine, feline smile of innate power.

'You?'

'Me…?' He was long and smooth and so, so hard.

He laughed throatily. 'You've been tested?'

'Oh.' She hadn't been but, having never shared her body with another, she supposed it was the same thing. 'I'm safe, yes.'

He kissed her mouth, squashing her hand, his flesh against her stomach. 'Good. Because I want to feel you, *agape*. *Really* feel you.'

He jerked out of her grip, bringing his tip to her opening, teasing her with his nearness before pulling away. His hands pushed her dress higher, so that he could lift her breasts out of her bra, rub his palms over her flesh. He pushed the dress roughly over her body, the fabric grazing against her over-sensitised skin, pushed it over her face. She shifted upwards so that he could lift it and toss it. Her bra was next.

She opened her mouth, knowing she didn't want to surprise him with her virginity. She had no sexual experience, but even *she* thought it was somehow not good etiquette to spring that on someone.

But his mouth took hers, making speech impossible, driving rational thought from her brain once more. She tried to cling on to her conviction, to the knowledge that she should speak the truth to Nikos, but it was like chasing a piece of shell in eggwhite.

It slipped out of her mind. Only the physical remained.

His hands were insistent on her breasts, his thumb and forefinger teasing her nipples, rolling them, before his mouth dragged down her throat to take a peach areola into his mouth. His tongue lashed it and she groaned, felt pleasure building to another inevitable crescendo.

Her heart hammered against her ribs, so hard and fast she could hear the pounding of it in her ears.

She lifted her legs, wrapping them around his waist, pulling him closer. He groaned, his stubble-roughened chin like sandpaper on her soft flesh as he moved his mouth to her other breast, delighting it with the same treatment. His tongue lashed her, chasing invisible circles around the erect peak until she could bear it no longer.

'Nikos!' she cried out, tightening her grip around his waist. 'Please, please now...'

He laughed, but it was a sound without humour. 'I thought we'd at least get to bed,' he said ruefully, bringing his tip closer.

There was no fear for Marnie. Despite her innocence, and his impressive size, she knew that this coming together was somehow destined. She had waited a long time for him, and she wasn't about to let something as silly as fear or concern take the shine off the moment.

Still... That explanation she owed him...the warning...

'Nikos, I need to tell you—'

'No.' He pinned her with his gaze as he lifted himself

up on his arms so that he could stare into her eyes. 'No more explanations. No more words. Not now.'

'But—'

'This is not the time for conversation.'

She might have argued with him. After all, she had a strong sense that it was an important thing to share. But before she could say another word he parted her legs, pressing them back onto the carpet, splaying them wide, and thrust into her.

Not gently, nor slowly—why would he?

They were at a fever pitch of desire and he had no reason to suspect that everything they were doing was new and therefore held the potential for pain.

Her eyes squeezed shut as he slammed past the invisible barrier of her innocence, discarding it as swiftly and easily as he had her bra. He swore, the harsh sound jarring her nerves, then swapped to Greek and released a litany of words in his own tongue.

The pain, which had been sharp and searing, was quick to vanish. Like a receding shoreline it disappeared, leaving only the surrender to pleasure in its wake. She moaned as her muscles stretched to welcome him, squeezing his length, gripping him at her core.

He swore again and then shifted, moving gently now, slowly, his eyes on her face, watching for any sign of discomfort. There was none. She began to moan as he stoked her fires. His lips claimed hers, his tongue duelling with hers in time with each delicious thrust until she was about to explode. She curled her toes into the carpet and cried out, the sound muffled by his mouth.

She was incapable of controlling the sensation of release. It burst from her through every pore, every nerve ending. It flew from her body like a bubble being released underwater. It burst, spilling her pleasure across the room in an effervescence of cries and hard breathing.

She arched her back in an ancient step in the dance of sensuality. He gripped her hips, holding her there, his fingers digging into her flesh. He pressed his forehead to hers, their sweat mingling.

He didn't let her catch her breath before he was torturing her anew. Nerve endings already vibrating at an almost unbearable frequency began to quake and quiver. She groaned as another orgasm, bigger and scarier, chased the other away. This time, though, when she cried out into the room, he chased after her, his own voice combining with hers as pleasure saturated their surroundings.

It was a perfect moment.

Marnie caught the pearl of memory—the way he felt, smelled, tasted—and wrapped it deep into the recesses of her mind, knowing she would want to visit this feeling again and again and again.

He lifted up from her, and the absence of his weight was a pain she hadn't been prepared for. He pulled away, removing himself from her heart and standing in one swift movement. He paced away, gloriously naked, and for the briefest moment Marnie thought he was actually going to stalk out of the room without a word!

Incensed, she got to her feet, wincing as muscles that had never been tested began to groan in complaint. The sound of running water heaped fuel onto the fire of her anger. He was actually going to shower straight away? Hell, she had no point of reference, but Marnie would have put money on that being an absolutely hurtful thing to do.

The door she had initially thought was a wardrobe must conceal an *en-suite* bathroom.

The shower was running when she stepped into the tiled room, but Nikos was not behind the glass. He stood, naked, his hands braced on the vanity unit, his head bent. She couldn't see his expression in the mirror, but tension seemed to emanate from his strong frame.

It arrested her in her tracks.

Fear that she'd somehow got something wrong swirled through her.

She cleared her throat, uncertain what she wanted him to say but knowing she needed to hear *something*. Some form of reassurance or kindness.

He lifted his head, his eyes spearing hers in the mirror's reflection. His face was strained, his expression otherwise unreadable. He scanned her face, seeming to shake himself out of his own reverie, then turned to look at her.

'Did I hurt you?'

It was so far from what she'd expected him to say that relief whooshed through her. She shook her head wordlessly.

He held a hand out, inviting her to join him. She placed her smaller hand in his palm, feeling as if it was symbolic of so much more, and took a step closer. A small line had formed between his brows; he was scowling. Thinking. Deep in analysis.

'I did not expect...' he said, shaking his head again.

He tugged her lightly, pulling her to his body. His hands ran the length of her back gently, carefully.

'Here.' He swallowed, his Adam's apple bobbing visibly as he tried to gain a perspective on this turn of events. He guided her into the shower without breaking his contact with her.

He had one of those enormous ceiling shower heads; warm water doused her the minute she stepped in and she made a little yelp of surprise. Her dark hair was plastered to her face. But once she became accustomed to it the feeling of warmth on her skin was beautiful.

She watched as Nikos took a soft sponge from the shelf and poured shower gel on it. His eyes clung to hers.

'I do not understand,' he said finally, bringing the sponge to her shoulders and soaping her slowly.

The shower gel frothed against her skin. It smelled of lime and vanilla.

'I'm sorry,' Marnie said, then wished she could take the words of contrition back. She bit down on her lower lip. 'Not that I think I did anything wrong,' she hastened to correct. 'Only that I probably should have warned you.'

'Warned me?' A smile flicked at the corners of his lips. 'You think this is something for which I needed *warning*?'

'Well…' She huffed, crossing her arms over her chest. 'I don't know.'

Her eyes dropped to the tiled floor, where the soapy water was fleeing the scene, racing towards the drain.

'Not warning,' he said firmly. 'Just…explanation. How is this possible?'

Her cheeks were glowing; she could feel them. 'Well, it's not that difficult. I've just abstained from having sex. Hardly rocket science.'

His laugh was thick and throaty. Desire flickered in her abdomen, surprising her into blinking her eyes up at him. The air around them seemed to be supercharged with awareness.

He sponged across her décolletage, then lower, slowly, torturously circling one already over-sensitive breast.

'Was it a decision you made? To remain a virgin?'

She was on a precipice. The question wasn't a simple one to answer. If she responded with the truth it would reveal so much more of her heart than she wished to show him! What if she were to tell him that she'd never met a man who'd made her feel remotely tempted in the way he had?

Instinctively she shied away from handing him such a degree of power. 'Yes. I made a little pre-nup with myself,' she breathed with a hint of sarcasm.

He transferred the sponge to her other breast, his attention focussed on the small orbs and the erect nipples that were straining for his touch.

'You wanted to sleep with me back then.'

She shrugged. Her heart was pounding, though. Why hadn't she realised that he would hone in on that? 'Any chance we can *not* talk about this?'

He opened his mouth to say something, but then he nodded, a muscle jerking in his cheek. 'I was surprised,' he said simply. 'You've had boyfriends?'

'Of course I have,' she said, thinking of the handful of men she'd gone on dates with. The men her father had approved of. Suitable men who had left her stone-cold.

'Then how…?'

'I thought we weren't talking about this?' she reminded him quietly.

He nodded once more, his frustration obvious despite his acquiescence. 'It's just so unusual. You are twenty-three years old.'

She nodded, but speech was becoming difficult as he moved the sponge lower, dragging soapy suds over her stomach and lower still, to the space between her legs.

The warm water was heaven against her body. She moaned as he dropped the sponge to the ground with a splash and let his palm rub against her womanhood instead. After wondering briefly if she should be ashamed of the certainty that she wanted him again, she discarded the thought, pressing herself lower, begging him with her body not to remove his hand.

He watched as a fever of desire stole through her body. 'You must have been tempted. From what I recall you had a healthy sexual appetite when we were together.'

She gasped as he teased a finger at her entrance, incapable of responding.

'I had imagined you to have slept with several men by now.'

How those thoughts had tortured him!

'Yes, well…' She groaned, lowering her hips, begging

him for more. 'We're not all as libidinous as you.' She pushed the words out from between clamped teeth.

'*You* are,' he said simply, marvelling at how her body was clamping around him.

He dragged his lips along her jaw, nipping the flesh just beneath her ear before taking an earlobe into his mouth and flicking it between his teeth.

She writhed against the tiles and he jerked in immediate response.

'I would take you again already if I weren't worried about hurting you.'

'You won't hurt me,' she promised throatily. Her eyes were enormous as they lifted to his. 'I want you. *Now*.'

He arched a brow, moving his mouth to her breasts. The soap had long since been washed away and they were warm and moist between his lips. The feeling of his lips on her flesh made her jerk.

'Nik!' she cried out, digging her nails into his shoulder.

The name jarred. *No.* Out of nowhere, it infuriated him. A white-hot rage slammed against him—completely inappropriate but impossible to ignore.

Just her simple use of that name—as though she was slipping back into the past and forgetting that they were no longer a couple. Yes, they were married, but resentment had led to that. Anger, and even hatred. Referring to him as she had done when they were together wasn't something he welcomed.

Nik she'd called him back then. Never Nikos. And her lips had always curved into a sweet smile, as though his name was an invocation of secrets and hopes.

But that had all been a lie. She hadn't really cared for him then; she'd just made him believe she had. She'd played the part perfectly. And he'd fallen for it hook, line and sinker. Well, not again.

She had married him, but only for the sake of her father.

Just as she'd broken up with him because of her father. This was a business deal, plain and simple, and just as in business he needed to keep his focus. Her virginity, while interesting, did not change a thing about their arrangement.

He lifted her against the tiles and wrapped her legs around his waist, driving into her as though his life depended on taking her, on being one with her. It was just sex, but Nikos didn't want anything else from Marnie, anyway. And, no matter how great the sex was, he couldn't forget that.

It was up to him to remember just who he'd married. She was cold to the core—except in his bed.

CHAPTER FIVE

MARNIE PADDED DOWN the stairs, her eyes straining a little against the brightness of Greece and the whiteness of his home. It was warm, too, though a breeze shifted through the wide corridor, lifting her Donna Karan dress as she reached the ground floor.

The house was quiet, except for a buzzing noise coming from the direction of the kitchen. Curious, she followed the sound, her tummy making a little groan of anticipation.

She'd slept late.

Then again, she'd been up late, too.

Her cheeks flushed as she remembered making love to Nikos in the shower, and then afterwards, when she'd almost drifted off to sleep, she'd felt his mouth teasing her body, drifting over her breasts, down her abdomen, to torment her one last time.

It had been a fantasy. She could almost believe she'd dreamed the whole thing. Except that she felt a little sore and tender in the light of day.

The sight of her husband in the kitchen made her heart skid to a stop. She swallowed, drinking him in hungrily. Awareness flooded her body. He was dressed in a business shirt, the sleeves rolled up to his elbows, exposing those dark, muscled forearms of his. The shirt sat tucked in at the waist, revealing that honed stomach and firm hips. A burst of adrenalin and desire flared through her.

She bit down on her lower lip in an attempt to stall the smile that was threatening to split her mouth apart.

'Morning,' she murmured, her eyes sparkling with re-membered intimacies.

He flicked a gaze to her, then returned his attention to the broadsheet paper that was spread across the bench. 'Coffee?'

Her smile was quick to snap into a small frown. 'Oh… um…yes.'

She wasn't sure he'd heard; he remained perfectly still, his head bent as he read an article. After several long sec-onds he sipped his own coffee, then placed the mug down and moved to the corner of the kitchen. She'd expected to see a machine, but she saw Nikos had one of those stain-less steel coffee pots. He poured a measure for Marnie and she wrinkled her nose, remembering instantly his predi-lection for coffee so thick it was almost like tar.

'Perhaps I'll have tea instead.'

He shrugged. 'I would be surprised if you find tea-bags. I don't drink the stuff.' He left the coffee cup on the bench beside her, then topped up his own mug. 'Speak to Eléni about your requirements. She will see the house has whatever you need.'

'Eléni?' Marnie murmured, her voice soft in response to his emotional distance.

'My housekeeper,' he reminded her.

'Right.' She nodded, sipping her coffee and pulling a face at the liquid, claggy against her tongue.

Her eyes lifted to the window, and beyond it to the view. The beach was shimmering in the distance, invitingly cool given the warmth of the day.

'I'm happy to go shopping.' A frown pulled at her brows. She wasn't sure she wanted to leave a housekeeper to run the house completely. 'I suppose we should talk about that, actually.'

He gave no indication that he'd heard her. Whatever he was reading was apparently engrossing. Or he was avoiding her like the plague. But that didn't make sense. Not after what they'd shared the night before.

'Nik?' she murmured, moving to stand right beside him.

There it was again. The word that he hated hearing from her mouth. *Nik*. The name that had given him such pleasure in the past was now like an accusing dagger in his gut. A reminder of what they'd been contrasted with what they were now, of the pain of their history and the resentment that had fuelled this union—all contained in that small, soft sound. *Nik*.

Harsh emotions straightened his spine. He pressed his finger into the page, marking his spot, then lifted his eyes to her face. He skimmed her features thoughtfully, careful not to betray the emotions that the simple shortening of his name evoked.

'I think we should stick with Nikos, don't you?'

The rebuff stung. No, it *killed*. A part of herself withered like a cut flower deprived of water.

She narrowed her eyes, ignoring the tears she could feel heavy in her throat. 'Are you sure you wouldn't prefer Mr Kyriazis?'

A muscle jerked in his jaw but he returned his gaze to the paper and read on for a few moments before closing the pages and turning around, propping his butt against the edge of the kitchen bench. His eyes locked with hers.

'What did you want to speak to me about, Mrs Kyriazis?'

She swallowed, all desire to act the part of his wife for real evaporating in the face of his coldness. Confusion was swirling through her, biting at her confidence bit by bit.

'The housekeeper,' she said finally, knowing the only thing worse than looking overeager was looking like an idiot who couldn't finish a thought. 'I can do some of her stuff.'

He arched a brow, silently imploring her to continue.

'Well,' she said, bitterly regretting embarking on this path. 'I did my own shopping at home. Most of my cooking, too. I also took over the gardens.'

'You? Who can't tell wisteria from jasmine?' he prompted sceptically.

She squared her shoulders. 'That was a long time ago. I love flowers now. Roses especially.'

She was babbling. What was that pervasive feeling of grief? And how could she stem its tide?

'Do you grow roses here? I suppose not. They're more of an English thing, aren't they? But, anyway, you said you have gardeners. In England I...' She tapered off at his complete lack of responsiveness.

'Eléni has been my housekeeper for a long time,' he said finally, his tone as far from encouraging as it was possible to get. 'I am not willing to offend her. She will not want to share her responsibilities.'

Marnie stared at him with rich disbelief. 'Even with your *wife*?'

His smile was not softened by anything like happiness or pleasure. 'My wife has other responsibilities.'

Marnie reached for her coffee. Thick and gloopy or not, it still had the ability to put some fire in her blood. 'What's got into you?' she asked when she'd drunk almost the whole cup. 'You're treating me like...like...'

He waited for her to continue, but when she didn't speak, letting her sentence trail off into nothingness, he prompted, 'Like what?'

He was impatient now. She felt like a recalcitrant child. 'Like you hate me.'

His nostrils flared as he expelled an angry breath. 'Your

words, *agape*, not mine.' He pushed up off the bench. 'I'll be home for dinner.'

'Where are you going?' She stared at him incredulously.

He laughed. 'Well, Marnie, I have to go to *work*. You see, our so-called marriage is really a business deal. You've upheld your end of the bargain spectacularly well so far—even bringing your virginity to the table. Now it is my turn. My assistant's number is on the fridge, should you need me.'

He walked out of the kitchen without so much as a kiss on the cheek.

She stared at his retreating back, gaping like a fish dragged mercilessly from the water. Hurt flashed inside her, but anger was there, too. How could he be so unkind? They were married, and only hours earlier had been as close as two people could be. That had moved things around for her; it had changed the tone of her heart. She wasn't the same woman she'd been the day before, or the week before, or when they'd made this hateful deal.

But for Nikos apparently nothing had changed. *Nothing.*

And he hadn't even told her to call *him* if she needed anything! She was so far down the pecking order that she was supposed to go through his assistant if she needed her own husband for anything.

Well! She'd show him!

She ground her teeth together and wandered over to the newspaper, simply for something to do. The article he'd been reading was an incredibly dry piece on an Italian bank that was restructuring its sub-prime loans.

She flicked out of the finance section and went to international news. Though she generally liked to keep abreast of world events, she looked at the words that morning without comprehension. The black-and-white letters swam like little bugs in her eyes until she gave up in frustration and slammed the paper shut.

She sipped the coffee again, before remembering how disgusting she found it, and then glided across the kitchen floor, pulling the fridge open. The platters from the night before were there; they'd been put back on their shelves. The flavours were reminiscent of childhood family holidays, when the four of them had travelled by yacht around the Med, stopping off at whichever island had taken their fancy, enjoying the local delicacies.

Libby had loved squid. She'd eaten charcoaled tentacles by the dozen. Whereas Marnie had been one for olives, cheese, bread and *dolmades*. Libby had joked about Marnie's metabolism in a way she'd been too young to understand, though now she knew that she'd been unfairly blessed with the ability to eat what she wanted and not see it in her figure.

It was the one small genetic blessing Marnie had in her favour. The rest had gone to Libby. The shimmering blonde hair that had waved down her back, the enormous bright blue eyes, a curving smile that had seemed to dance like the wind on her face, flicking and freshening with each emotion she felt. And Libby had almost always been happy.

Marnie padded across the tiled floor, drawn to the glass doors that framed the view of the ocean. It sparkled in the distance, and she saw with a little sound of pleasure that there was an infinity pool in the foreground. She toyed with the door handle until it clicked open and then slid the glass aside, stepping out onto the paved terrace as though the breeze had dragged her.

She breathed deeply. Salt and pollution were a heady mix for a girl who'd spent much of her time in the English countryside. She grinned, trying to put her situation with Nikos temporarily out of her mind. An almost childlike curiosity was settling around her, and she slipped across the terrace and stood on the edge of pool. The water was turquoise.

Her toe, almost of its own volition, skimmed the surface before diving beneath, taking her foot with it.

Perfection.

Uncaring that her expensive linen dress might get crumpled or wet, and for once not thinking about photographers or what people might think, safe in the knowledge that she was completely alone, Marnie lifted the dress over her head and left it in a roughly folded heap on the tiles.

In only her bra and underpants she slid into the water, making a little moan of delight as it lapped up to her neck. As a child she'd gone swimming often.

She ducked her head underwater, beyond caring that her artfully applied make-up would smudge, and stroked confidently to the far end of the pool. She propped her chin on the edge, studying the bright blue sky, turquoise ocean and faraway buildings for a moment before duck-diving underwater once more and returning to the house side.

It felt good to swim, and she lost count of how many laps she completed. Eventually, though, as she drew to the edge of the pool, her arms a little wobbly, she paused to gain breath.

'You are fast.'

A woman's accented voice reached her and Marnie started a little, her heart racing at the intrusion.

Not knowing exactly what to expect, she spun in the water until her eyes pinned the source of the voice.

A woman was on the terrace, a mop in one hand, a smile on her lined face. She had long hair, going by the voluminous messy bun that was piled on top of her hair, and it was a grey like lead. She wore a dark blue dress that fell to the knees and sensible sandals.

The housekeeper. What had Nikos said her name was? She wished now she'd paid better attention, rather than focussing her mental skills on just what the hell had happened in the hours since they'd made love.

'You swim like a dolphin, no?' the housekeeper said, and when her smile widened, Marnie saw that she was missing a tooth.

'Thank you,' she said, inwardly wincing at how uptight she sounded. She tried to loosen the effect with a smile of her own. 'I'm Marnie.'

'You Mrs Kyriazis.' The housekeeper nodded. 'I know, I know.'

She was tall and wiry and she moved fast, propping the mop against the side of the house before lifting the lid of a cane basket. 'I always keep towels in here. Mr Kyriazis likes his swim after work.'

Dangerous images of Nikos—bare-chested, water trickling over his muscled chest and honed arms—made her insides squeeze with remembered desire. 'Does he?'

'So the towels always are fresh. I can get you one.'

True to her word, she lifted one from the box and placed it on the edge of the pool, beside Marnie's dress. Her hand ran to the item of clothing, lifting it as if on autopilot and draping it over a chair instead.

Marnie was a little shamefaced at the uncharacteristic way she'd discarded it.

'I'm sorry,' she said, her tone stiff. 'Nikos didn't mention your name,' she fibbed.

'I'm Mrs Adona.' She grinned. 'You can call me Eléni, though, like Mr Kyriazis does.'

'Eléni.' Marnie nodded crisply. *That was it.* Curious, she tilted her head to one side, watching as the older woman returned to fetch the mop. 'It's nice to meet you.'

Eléni cackled quietly in response.

'That's funny?' Marnie prompted with a small smile on her face.

Later, she would be mortified to realise that she had big black circles of smudged mascara beneath each eye.

'Oh, it is nice for me to meet you, I was thinking. Nice for him to settle down. In my day men didn't work as hard as him. They had one woman and a simple job. You'll be good for him,' Eléni said, with an optimism that Marnie was loath to dispel.

So she nodded. 'Perhaps.'

Something occurred to her and, spontaneously, she called the woman nearer to the pool.

'Eléni? Nikos is worried that I'll step on your toes if I do the odd bit of grocery shopping or cooking.'

She watched the other woman carefully for any sign of mortification or offence, and instead saw a broad grin.

Spurred on, she continued, 'The thing is, I quite like to cook. And I don't have a lot to do here yet, and shopping kills time. So…well…I hope you won't be upset if you see that happening?'

'Upset?'

Her laugh was contagious and alarming in equal measure. Loud—so loud it seemed almost amplified—it pealed across the courtyard and out towards the sea. Marnie found herself chuckling in response.

Eléni said something in her own language, then rubbed her angled chin as if searching for the words in English. 'I don't know he can like a woman who cooks.'

The sentence was a little disjointed, and the accent was thick, but the meaning came to Marnie loud and clear.

Nikos didn't bring women who cooked to his home.

They had other talents.

And wasn't that just an unpalatable thought?

Well, Marnie would show him.

By the time he returned that night Marnie and Eléni had moved a table onto the tiled terrace and Eléni had set it beautifully. A crisp white cloth fell to the floor, and in its centre she'd placed orange blossoms and red geraniums to create an artful and fragrant arrangement of blooms.

Marnie was just pulling the scallops Mornay from the grill when he arrived. It was difficult to say who was more surprised. Nikos, by the sight of his wife in a black-and-white apron, kitchen glove on one hand, feet bare but for the red toenail polish that was strangely seductive, or Marnie, who took one look at her husband and felt such a surge of emotions that she had to prop her hip on the bench behind her for support.

He placed a black leather bag on the kitchen floor, then crossed his arms. 'I thought we discussed this,' he said finally.

So much for new beginnings.

'*You* discussed it, as I remember.' Her smile was overly saccharine. 'I listened while you told me that I shouldn't get comfortable in your home.'

Her acerbic remark had caught him unawares—that much was obvious.

Choosing not to tackle the bigger issue of her statement, he said thickly, 'I told you—I don't want you upsetting Eléni .'

'Yes, yes…' She moved to the fridge and pulled a bottle of ice-cold champagne from the door. She placed it in his hand and paused right in front of him. 'You also told me that I should save my energy for other wifely duties.'

He had. And he'd enjoyed, in some small part, seeing the way he'd shocked her. But having her say the words back to him switched everything around. A hint of shame whispered across his features.

'Eléni's very happy that you've married someone who enjoys cooking,' she said, with an exaggerated batting of her long, silky lashes. 'I think she finds me surprisingly traditional compared to your usual…*companions*.'

'You've spoken to her?' he said unnecessarily.

'Yes. So you don't need to worry that I've sent her off to cry into her pillows.'

He curled his fingers around the neck of the bottle and unfurled the foiled top, his eyes lingering on his wife's face. Her honey-brown hair was plaited and little tendrils had escaped, curling around her eyes. Her make-up was impeccable, and beneath the apron he could see that she was wearing a simple dress that he was growing impatient to remove.

'You have a smudge on your cheek,' he lied, lifting his thumb to his mouth to wet it before wiping it across her skin. He was rewarded with the sight of her eyes fluttering closed and her full lips parting as she exhaled softly. The same knot of desire that had sat in his gut all day was inside her, too, then.

'I've been busy,' she said softly, her eyes bouncing open and clashing with his. As if consciously slicing through the web that was thick around them, she stepped backwards. 'You open that—thank you.'

A grudging smile lifted half his mouth. 'Yes, Mrs Kyriazis.'

She turned away before he could see the way the name brought an answering smile to her own features.

He popped the top off the bottle, placed the cork on the bench. He reached for two glasses at the same time she did. Their hands connected and she stepped aside quickly. 'You do it. I'll get our starter.'

'Starter?' he murmured, watching as a pink like the sunset dusted her cheekbones.

'Uh-huh. I told you—I like to cook.'

That was new. 'Since when?'

She began to place the scallops in their fan-like shells on a plate, forming a spiral of sorts. 'Some time after we broke up—' she skidded over the words a little awkwardly

'—I discovered it as a hobby. It turns out I love cooking. I've always loved food.'

She reached for a spoon and ran it around the edge of a shell, coating it in the Mornay sauce. She lifted it to his lips and he widened his mouth to taste the sauce. It was as delicious as it smelled.

'Apparently you excel at it.'

'Thank you.' The compliment was a gift. A beautiful gift to cherish in the midst of the turbulent ocean they were stranded in. She lifted the plate and smiled. 'Shall we?'

He turned, two champagne flute stems trapped between the fingers of one hand, the bottle in his other. He began to retreat from the kitchen, but Marnie stalled him.

'Not the dining room,' she said over her shoulder, weaving through the kitchen towards the patio. It was then that Nikos saw that against the backdrop of the setting sun, and the evening sky that sparkled with tiny little diamonds of stardust, a table glowed with candlelight.

Emotions, warm and fierce, surged in his chest. '*You* did this?'

'Eléni helped,' she said honestly, nudging the door with her shoulder.

The night was blissfully warm. She placed the scallops on the table and then stretched behind her back for the ties of the apron.

'Allow me,' he said throatily, settling the drinks onto the table and reaching for her. His fingers worked deftly at the strings but, once they were untied, he kept his hands on her hips. He spun her in the circle of his arms so that he could stare down at her face. In the softness of dusk she was breathtakingly beautiful. But the fragility he sensed in her terrified him.

He wasn't prepared for Marnie's vulnerability. He had no protection against it.

He dropped his hands to his sides and moved to a chair instead. He pulled it from the table, waiting for her to settle herself in the seat. She pushed the apron over her head, not minding that it roughened her hair. She draped it over the timber back of the chair, keeping her eyes on the spectacular view as she sat down.

He glided the chair inwards a little way, his hands resting on her bare shoulders for a moment before he moved to the other side of the table.

At another time, or for another pair, the moment would have been singing with romance. But Marnie knew they didn't qualify for that. And yet the setting was so magical that for a moment she let herself forget the tension and the blackmail, the resentments and regrets.

'Do you remember when we had that picnic in Brighton?'

His eyes skimmed her face, tracing the features he'd stared at that night. It had been only a few weeks before he'd told her he wanted to marry her one day—before she'd told him that would never happen.

'Yes.' He pressed back in his chair. The past was a sharp course he didn't particularly like to contemplate. 'I remember.'

'The sun was a little like this,' she said, obviously not sensing his tone, or perhaps willfully ignoring it.

She watched the glow of the golden orb as its own weight seemed to catch up with it, making it impossible for day to remain any longer. As the sun dipped gratefully towards the sea the sky seemed to serenade it, whispering peach and purple against its outline.

'This is my favourite thing to watch,' she said softly, a self-conscious smile ghosting across her face as she returned her attention to the table.

'Why?'

She lifted a scallop and placed it on her plate, indicating that he should do likewise. But he was fully focussed on his bride.

'I guess I find it somehow reassuring,' she said with a small shrug of her slender shoulders. 'That no matter what happens in a day there'll always be this.'

He arched a brow, finding the sentiment both beautiful and depressing. 'I am more for mornings,' he said after a moment.

'I remember.' She grinned, trying hard to inject their evening with the normality she'd longed for that morning. 'You wake before the sun.'

'I do not need a lot of sleep.'

'Apparently.'

Her cheeks flushed pink as she remembered the previous night—the way he had commanded her body's full attention even when she had been exhausted. And she'd responded to his invitations willingly, rousing herself to join with him, needing him even from behind the veil of exhaustion.

He ate a scallop, though he wasn't particularly hungry. It was divine. A perfect combination of sweetness and salt. He didn't say anything, though, so Marnie continued to wonder if he'd enjoyed it or was simply being polite when he reached for another.

'How was your day?' she asked, after a moment of prickly silence had passed.

He regarded her for a long moment. 'I spoke with your father, if that is your concern.'

Her face slashed with hurt before she concealed it expertly. 'It wasn't,' she responded, shrugging as though he *hadn't* scratched her with the sharp blade of recrimination. 'I was simply making conversation.'

His eyes glowed with the strength of his feelings. Marnie pressed back in her chair, her own appetite waning. She

thought of the fish she was baking in a salt crust. What a
waste it would be if they couldn't even make it through a
few scallops without breaking into war.

'Let us not pretend, Marnie, when there is no one here
to benefit from the performance.'

CHAPTER SIX

SHE PLACED HER fork down carefully beside the plate, using the distraction to rally her rioting emotions. His mood and manner were on a knife's edge. She felt the shift in him and wanted to protest. She wanted to address it. But the implacable set of his features thwarted any thought of that.

'I'm not pretending,' she said instead, with a direct stare that cost her a great deal of effort.

'Of course you are.' He was bored now, or at least he seemed it.

'Really? Why? Because I asked about your day?'

His eyes narrowed. 'Because you act as though your primary concern in this marriage is not your father.'

Denying that assertion wasn't an option—at least it wasn't if she wanted to protect herself from seeming motivated by other more personal feelings. What would he say if she told him more than money had motivated her into marrying him? Would he run a mile? Or use her confused feelings to keep her exactly where he had her?

'Well, Nikos,' she said, impressed that she sounded almost condescending, 'given that you used my father's debts to blackmail me into this, are you really so surprised?'

'I made no claim of surprise,' he corrected. 'I intended to point out the futility of your charade.'

'Wow.' She blinked and lifted her champagne, drinking

several large gulps despite the pain of the bubbles erupting against her insides. 'That's spectacularly rude,' she said when she'd settled the glass back on the table.

'Perhaps.' He shrugged insouciantly. 'In any event, your father was both grateful and, I believe, resentful of my offer to help.'

She was startled, her enormous eyes flying to his face. 'You're not saying he turned you down?'

'He has agreed to take the bare minimum from me to stave off foreclosure. That will buy him another month at the most.' A frown crossed his features. 'He is a stubborn man.'

'Remind you of anyone?' she snapped tartly, biting into another scallop.

'I would not be so foolish as to turn away a lifeline if I were in his situation.'

'He's very proud,' she said silkily, and though she'd meant it to be a subtle insult to Nikos it was ridiculous. She'd realised as soon as she'd uttered the words. For there was no man on earth with more pride than Nikos. She'd damaged it six years earlier and he'd moved heaven and earth to make her pay now.

'To a fault.'

'Thank you for speaking to him,' she said quietly.

She meant it. Were it not for Nikos, her father would have no hope. At least he knew now that there was an option. An alternative to bleak bankruptcy and failure.

'It was our deal, remember?'

The deal. The damned deal! She wanted to tear her hair out! But why? One day after their wedding, did she *really* think anything would have shifted? Just because they'd slept together, and her body had begun to vibrate at a frequency that only he could answer, it didn't mean that it was the same for him.

'Nonetheless, you didn't have to do this. Any of it. You

could have left him to suffer and watched from the sidelines.'

He braced his elbows on the table, his eyes pinning her to the chair as though his fingers were curled around her shoulders. 'Where would the fun be in that?'

The air crackled and hummed with the intensity of his statement.

'You find this *fun*?'

His smile was pure sensual seduction. Like warmed chocolate being dripped over her flesh.

'Last night was certainly pleasurable.'

Memories seared her soul. She shifted a little in the chair as her insides slicked with pleasurable anticipation. 'I'm glad you think so,' she murmured, her heart racing like a butterfly trapped against a window.

His smile was pure arrogance. It said that he knew she thought so, too. 'You disagree?'

Damn it. The wedge between a rock and hard place was a little constricting. She dropped her gaze, unable and unwilling to duel with him in a battle she'd never win.

But Nikos wasn't going to let it go. 'You seemed to enjoy yourself…' he pushed, one hand flicking lazily across the tablecloth, trapping her fingers beneath his. He turned her palm skywards and began to trace an invisible circle across the soft pad of her hand.

'Now who's acting?' Her question was breathy, infused with the hot air in her lungs.

'When it comes to my desire for you there is no necessity to lie.'

'Thank heavens for small mercies.' The statement was lacking sass; it fell flat. She cleared her throat and pulled her hand away. 'How much money?'

The change in conversation, and the removal of her hand, confused him momentarily. But not for long. Nikos hadn't built an empire from scratch by being slow on the uptake.

'Why does it matter? Do you want to make sure you haven't overpaid your end of our bargain?'

She made a sound of surprise and shook her head.

'You did offer your virginity. Perhaps you feel anything less than a hundred mill isn't quite fair on you.'

'How *dare* you?' Her voice quivered with the force of her hurt. 'How dare you equate what we did with an amount of money?'

He had gone too far. He realised that, but it was out of Nikos's character to apologise. Instead he came back to the original question, speaking as though he *hadn't* just virtually equated their marriage with prostitution.

'I have helped him enough for now,' he said, his words soft to placate the rage he'd breathed into her. 'He will not go broke, Marnie. I will not allow that to happen.'

She pulled her lower lip between her teeth, her feelings jumping awkwardly from one extreme to the other. Hurt was making her body sag, and her throat was thick with tears that she damned well would *not* let fall. But there was relief and gratitude, too. Because she *did* trust Nikos. Despite all this, all that he'd done, she believed that he would keep her father from destitution.

He lifted another scallop and ate it, then another, and Marnie watched, a frown unconsciously etched across her face.

'Are you going to have any more?' he prompted, reaching for the second-last.

She shook her head. 'I'm fine, thanks.'

He placed his fork down and stared at her. 'Your father has asked us to return to England for his birthday.'

Marnie nodded thoughtfully. 'He doesn't like to do much, but Mum generally twists his arm into a small party.'

His expression was guarded. 'Would you like to travel home again so soon?'

Home.

The word was one syllable that throbbed with an enormous weight of meaning. She reached for the last scallop, despite having just given up her claim to it. She needed to distract herself and to hide her face as she unpacked the impact that single word was having.

Home.

Other than here.

Home.

Not here. Not in *his* home.

She blinked and shook her head a tiny bit, pushing the thoughts away. 'I'd like to see them,' she said cautiously. 'But it *is* soon. I didn't really imagine that we'd go to England again yet.'

Her family complicated matters. What hope did Nikos and she have of forming any kind of relationship with her parents and his antipathy towards them in the foreground?

'You want to refuse?'

She toyed with her ring, turning it round her finger. 'I didn't say that.'

'No. You didn't say anything,' he drawled, the words lightly teasing.

But Marnie was not in the mood to be teased.

'God, Nikos, you're impossible.'

He laughed throatily, the sound doing something strange to her fractured nerves.

'I am honestly asking what you would like. It occurred to me that I would have more success persuading your father to be reasonable if we were to meet in person.'

The tears he'd brought to the surface were closer now, and she had to dig her nails into her palms to stop from weakening and letting her eyes become moist.

Out of habit, she hardened her expression, creating an

air of nonchalance when she tilted her face to his. 'You'd do that?'

His eyes glittered in his handsome face. 'You'd be content if I didn't?'

Damn it. She was being careless. Slowly she shook her head from side to side, her eyes not quite meeting his. 'You told me you'd sort it out. It's the only reason I married you, remember?'

'Good. Honesty is so much better than role-play.'

She cleared her throat and focussed her gaze on the view. What she'd just said hadn't been honesty, but she let it slide. 'Fine. We'll go back for a weekend. In a month.'

And in the back of her mind she really did hope that their difficulties might have been resolved by then. There had been a time when they were so comfortable together. Was it so unlikely to believe they might return to that footing?

She looked at the man opposite, her heart turning over in her chest.

So familiar.

So foreign.

She knew him intimately, and yet she didn't.

He was a stranger, and yet her husband.

The dichotomies kept flowing through her mind, thick and fast.

'You are staring, Mrs Kyriazis, in a way that makes me want to peel that dress from your body and claim you here and now.'

She started, her pulse shearing her skin. 'I was just thinking…' Her voice was thick with the desire he could so easily evoke. 'So much has happened in six years. You're my husband, and at one time I would have said I knew you better than anyone. But I don't know you at all now.'

'You know me,' he responded, standing up swiftly and reaching for her plate.

She watched as he cleared the table, her mind overflowing with questions.

'When we were together, you only had aspirations in finance. How did you do all this so fast?'

He sent her a look of impatience. 'When someone tells you that you will never amount to anything, that you are not worth a damn, it *is* rather motivating.'

Her father's words mortified her. 'He shouldn't have said that.'

'No.' His eyes glittered. 'But that is what you people are like. Do you *really* believe that the blood in your veins is of more value than mine simply because you can trace your lineage back thousands of years and I am not able to do so?'

'Don't do that.' She followed him into the kitchen. 'Don't tar me with the same brush.' A frown drew her brows together. 'I don't really understand why my dad spoke like that to you. He's not—'

'Of course he is,' Nikos interrupted. He tamped down on his temper with effort, stacking the plates neatly into the dishwasher.

He worked with a finesse that made her wonder if he did this simple domestic act often. Though incongruous, it made sense. Nikos hadn't been born with a silver spoon in his mouth. He'd grown up poor. He'd presumably shouldered his fair share of domestic duties for most of his life.

'Whatever you're about to say, make no mistake. He *is*.'

'Anyway…' She made an effort to salvage the situation. 'I understand why you might have felt you had to prove something. But *how* did you do this?'

His eyes skimmed her face. 'In the same way I won a scholarship to Eton and then Cambridge. I worked a thousand times harder than anyone else. I always have. I don't sleep much, *agape*, because I work.'

Admiration soared through her. 'I think you've done something very impressive,' she said quietly.

He propped himself against a bench. 'Your turn. Why did *you* do all this?' He gestured around the kitchen.

Because I missed you. Because I couldn't stop thinking about you.

'It's our honeymoon, isn't it?'

His lips lifted in a half-smile. 'If you say so.'

The rejection hurt, but she didn't show it. 'Why don't you sit down? I'll get the main course.'

He crossed the kitchen so that he stood right in front of her, without touching. Goose bumps littered her exposed flesh.

'I have a better idea.'

She lifted her eyes to his face slowly. Breathing was suddenly difficult. He overwhelmed every single sense in her body. 'Oh?'

'Let's have a break between courses.' His smile was tight. 'I do not usually eat so early.'

'Oh…'

He'd upset her. He squashed the urge to apologise. 'It is a…ritual I have. I swim as soon as I return from the office. I find it rids me of the day.' He reached down and linked his fingers. 'Join me.'

A command or a question?

An order or an invitation?

Whatever the case, she found herself nodding. 'Okay. I'll just go and get changed.'

His laugh was throaty. 'Why?'

Her eyes were wide. She watched as he began slowly to unbutton his shirt until the sides were separated. He pushed it off his arms, then stepped out of his trousers. In just his boxers, he reached over and lifted her hand to his lips.

His kiss breathed butterflies into her veins. She stifled a moan and then pulled at her hand. It was a necessary tool. She felt around for her zip, and when she couldn't immediately catch it he reached behind her and loosened it, sliding it slowly, seductively, teasingly down her spine.

She shivered as his fingers lingered, taunting the flesh at the small of her back. She lifted her gaze to his face again, searching for something there. Kindness? Affection? She saw only lust. Pure and simple.

It was better than nothing.

With a small exhalation she stepped backwards. 'I'll just need a minute.' She took another step backwards to underscore her resolve. 'I'll meet you in there.'

He shrugged indolently and strode across the tiles with that almost feral power that seemed to emanate from his frame. She watched him go, greedily waiting to see him dive into the water. His muscles rippled as he speared through the air then beneath its surface. She held her breath unconsciously until he stood at the other end. His dark hair was slicked to his head like an animal's pelt.

She moved quickly up the stairs and into their bedroom. The sight of her face that had confronted her after swimming earlier that day was hauntingly close to the surface. She didn't want to turn into a panda again. She lathered her hands with soap and washed at her face until every hint of make-up was removed, then changed into a swimsuit with a low-cut vee at the front and delicate beading in the fabric. It was elegant and inviting.

He was swimming laps when she emerged, his strong body pulling powerfully through the water, each bronzed arm worthy of its own sculpture. He was naked. His boxers had been discarded and she could see his whole body as he cut through the water.

She swallowed huskily, her eyes tracing his progress from where she stood at the edge of the pool. A warm breeze drifted past, lifting her hair. She tucked it behind her ears and approached the edge. He turned underwater, his stroke not breaking the surface.

With a smile, she dived in, pulling up beside him. Underwater, their faces were illuminated by the green lights embedded in the side of the pool. He turned to her. Their eyes locked and Marnie almost lost her rhythm, so fierce was the tumble of awareness that accosted her body.

But she quickly regained her focus, racing him to the end and touching the rounded edge of the pool just as he did. She laughed when they both lifted onto their feet, the thrill of adrenalin and the rush of endorphins pumping through her body.

He stared at her with a sense of confusion.

Her laugh.

That beautiful laugh.

It was as if she'd burst through the cracks in his memory, slowly infiltrating him with what she'd once meant to him.

It wasn't only the musical sound, it was her face. Wiped of make-up, radiating happiness, with a little bit of honey in her complexion from the day she'd spent outdoors.

He swallowed and turned to the view, his face unyielding in profile.

'I haven't swum like this in years,' she confided easily, blissfully unaware of the hurricane of feelings that was besieging him.

His smile lacked warmth. He pinned her with eyes that she couldn't read. A sense of loss wiped the smile from her own features and she spun away, kicking to the opposite side of the pool and propping herself against it. The coping was still warm from the day's heat, despite the lateness of the hour and the coldness of his look.

The sense that her husband—the man she'd married and had once loved—despised her, made her heart hurt in her chest. She turned slowly to see him walking through the water towards her, his gaze pinned to hers.

He was going to kiss her. The fine pulse at the base of her throat was hammering wildly in expectation, and yet every sensible thread of her mind was telling her to step backwards and talk to him.

What did it mean that she had such a small understanding of everything that made him tick except his desire for her?

'Nikos,' she said softly, her eyes silently imploring him to help her make sense of it all.

He caught her hips underwater, pulling her the final distance to meet him. Their bodies melded as one. She drew her lip between her teeth, ignoring the warning voice in her mind as she wrapped her arms around his neck. Her fingers teased the wet hair at his nape.

'I know.'

Her breath hitched in her throat. She wasn't alone. This maelstrom of need after six long years was as unsettling for him as it was her.

Good.

For now that would have to be enough.

His kiss was a claim. It was a seal of their union. She kissed him back fiercely, her tongue clashing with his, her body wrapping around his beneath the water. The feeling of his arousal between her legs, straining at the fabric of her swimsuit, with the warmth of the pool water surrounding them was almost too much to bear.

Impatience crested inside her, bubbling out of control.

She made a sound into his mouth as she pushed back a little, her fingers toying with the straps of her swimsuit. They were saturated, and stuck to her body like a second skin; it didn't help that her hands were unsteady.

He had no such difficulty.

With total confidence he slid the straps down her arms,

revealing her breasts. The dusk light bathed her, spreading gold and peach over her flesh. He continued to push the fabric away, and Marnie lifted her legs to make it easier.

Naked in the water with him, she had a blinding sense that she might actually die if they didn't make love. If something were to happen to change his mind she wasn't sure she could recover. Her desperation for him would have terrified her if she'd had any mental space left with which to process it.

He pulled her back towards him, settling her legs around his waist. His eyes showed strain as he paused, his hard cock nestled between her legs without yet invading her womanhood.

'You have not been sore today?'

She shook her head.

'You must tell me…'

Groaning, she repositioned herself, startling him by thrusting down on his length and taking him deep inside her core. Relief spread through her body, weakening and strengthening her in yet another contradictory sensation. He held her hips, his fingers digging into her soft flesh, his lips seeking hers. His tongue was harsh in her mouth, echoing the movements of his body as he made her completely his.

Her orgasm burst over her swiftly; there was no time to prepare.

The entire day had been a kind of torturous foreplay for Marnie. Memories of their night together had tormented her, driving her body to fever pitch, so that the tiniest things—such as the feeling of the apron as she'd wrapped it around her over-sensitised nipples—had almost driven her over the edge.

Nikos watched as she crested the wave, her face a thousand little nerve endings vibrating with pleasure. The answering swelling in his heart was not something he wished to acknowledge.

Telling himself it was simply relief that they'd found themselves to be sexually compatible, he pushed deeper into her, drifting his fingers lower to cup the neat softness of her buttocks. He dragged his lips down her throat, flicking his tongue against the pulse-point that was frantically trying to move blood through her body, then lower still to her breasts. They were lapped by the water, and he had to lift her a little to take one into his mouth. The second he did she cried out, tilting her wet head back into the water so that her hair, no longer braided, fell like a dark curtain.

He moved one hand to tangle in its lengths, holding her head there while he plundered her core in an insatiable rhythm.

His own control was slipping. Her muscles, so moist and tight, were squeezing him as her pleasure spiralled, and when he felt her tremble and knew she was about to crest the wave again he went with her, holding her close, mirroring her movements until they were both panting, drenched in sweat and pool water, satisfaction emanating from every pore.

Their coming together had been as intense as it had essential. But it was just a prelude to the slow exploration he had been distracted by thinking of all day. To the myriad ways he wanted to torment and delight her.

Satiated, Marnie slowly relaxed, her body reassuring her that nothing bad could eventuate when such uncontainable desire abounded.

It was only then that she remembered the fish in the oven. It would be burned to a crisp.

Well, if that was the only casualty of this desire then she could live with it.

In the small hours of the morning, their naked limbs tangled with crisp white sheets, bodies sheened in postcoital perspiration and satisfaction, sleep fogging around the edges of their tableau, Marnie shifted a little, tilting her head to observe her husband.

His eyes were shut, his breathing heavy.

'How can you call this a pretence?' she whispered—to herself more than anything.

Without opening his eyes, he said thickly, 'This is just great sex, Marnie. Do not confuse it with anything more substantive or you will be hurt.'

He rolled over, his broad, muscled back turned to her, his heart apparently closed.

CHAPTER SEVEN

A FORTNIGHT HAD passed and his words were still sharp in her brain, like shards of glass that made her weep blood whenever she ran the fingertip of her mind over them.

'This is just great sex... Do not confuse it with anything more substantive...'

Her coffee-coloured eyes were flecked with gold as they drifted over the view from the window. For her office she'd chosen a room far away from the pool, their bedroom and the kitchen—that was to say far from any of the rooms that distracted her with what Nikos and she had shared there.

It was a small room, but she didn't need a lot of space, and it afforded an outlook of the city, rather than the ocean. In the distance she could see the Acropolis, bathed in early-evening light, and the buildings of the city sprawled almost like a child's model.

Though she took solace and inspiration from the outlook, this was not why she'd chosen this particular spot from which to work. From her seat she could see the curve of Nikos's driveway. The second his car thrummed through the gates she knew. And then she had the maximum time to prepare herself for his arrival, to gather the facade she had perfected around her slender shoulders. A facade that was essential when faced with her husband.

They shared meals and polite conversation. They were

unstintingly civil. But there was a torrent of emotions swirling hatefully beneath all their appropriate conversations. Only when they came together at night did she find an outlet for her rampant emotions. Sex. Passionate, all-consuming sex that explained everything. She was addicted to him. To his body and to the way he made her feel.

Marnie clicked out of her spreadsheet, her mind half-absorbed with the call-list she had for the following day. How grateful she was to have her work! Were it not for the distraction of the behind-the-scenes fundraising she did for the Future Trust she might have exploded already in a scene reminiscent of Vesuvius.

She flicked a glance to the clock above the door. He was late, and nerves that had been stretched tight for two days—since he'd told her about this event—were at breaking point.

For the first time since marrying they were going *out*.

Strange how she hadn't even realised that she'd become a virtual recluse, spending her time almost exclusively within the confines of his home except for brief trips to the markets with Eléni.

Now it was time to meet the world. She was Mrs Kyriazis—billionaire's wife.

What a joke.

Their marriage was little more than revenge and sex, and yet tonight she would play the part of doting newlywed to perfection. If only to show him how little she cared.

She heard his car and rose quickly from her desk. It wasn't that she had intended to be secretive about her work, but Nikos never came into her office. As if that conversation on her first afternoon in Greece had flagged something in his mind and he had subsequently delineated her office as her own space. For all he knew she might be running some kind of international drug ring, she thought with a small smile as she pulled the door shut behind her.

Marnie rarely wore heels, but for the kind of evening Nikos had foreshadowed she knew they'd be a requirement. They did bolster her height nicely, and she felt the picture of elegance when she walked gracefully down the stairs.

She'd spent a long time styling her hair, and her make-up was a masterpiece. Anne Kenington might not have played Cubby House with her children, nor had she read them the books that a nanny had had more time for, but she had insisted both her daughters were drilled in the skills necessary to present themselves as Ladies.

When Marnie emerged into the foyer at the same moment that Nikos entered the house she waited with a small smile on her red lips for him to see her. Pleasant anticipation swirled through her as she waited for the light of attraction to bounce between them.

The second his eyes lifted to her she felt a bolt of something. Not desire. Not happiness. Something else. Something far darker.

His eyes undertook a slow and thorough inspection, but his expression showed only shock. Marnie held her breath as he stared at her, waiting, aching, needing. Wanting him to say something to explain the reaction.

'You look…' He wiped a hand across his eyes and shook his head.

'Yes?' She braved a smile, though her heart was plummeting to the floor.

'Nothing. It doesn't matter.'

He dropped his keys onto the side table and turned away. Only the ragged movement of his chest showed that he was still struggling with a dark tangle of emotions.

'I will be ready as soon as I can. Why do you not have a drink while you wait?'

A frown marred her features for the briefest of moments before she remembered. She didn't *do* that! She didn't betray how easily he could upset her.

'Fine,' she agreed, her smile ice-cold, her pulse hammering. 'Don't be long. You said it starts at eight.'

He didn't acknowledge her rejoinder. Marnie watched with consternation as he took the stairs two at a time, then she turned away and wove her way to the kitchen.

It was another stunning evening. The sun was almost completely out of sight, leaving inky streaks in the sky and a sprinkling of sparkling lights that heralded night's arrival. She flicked the kettle on to brew tea and then thought better of it. She had a feeling something stronger was called for.

She poured a glass of champagne and held it in both hands as she moved to the terrace. The pool was beautiful. The surface, undisturbed by their usual evening activity, had a stillness to it, and it reflected not only the evening sky and the glow of his house but Marnie's figure, too.

She stared down at the watery image of herself, allowing her earlier frown to tug her lips downwards now that she was alone. Why did he disapprove? Though she hated this sort of mix-and-mingle affair, she'd been to enough of them to know the drill. Her dress was the latest word in couture, her shoes were perfect—everything about her was just what people would expect the wife of Nikos Kyriazis to be.

She crouched down, careful to keep the hem of her dress out of the water, and ran her manicured fingertips through its surface, slashing her image so that only swirls of colour remained. Satisfied, she stood and turned towards the house, startled when she saw Nikos just inside the door.

He'd showered and changed into a formal tuxedo, and his dark hair was slicked back from his brow, showing the hauteur of his handsome features, the strength of his bone structure and the determination of his jaw.

A kaleidoscope of butterflies was swirling through her insides, filling her veins with flutters of anticipation. As she stepped closer a hint of his fragrance—that unmistak-

ably masculine scent of spice and citrus—carried to her
on the balmy breeze.

The tuxedo was jet-black and might as well have been
stitched to his body; it fitted like a second skin, emphasising the breadth of his shoulders and neatness of his waist.

She waited half a beat, giving him an opportunity to re-
deem the situation. It shouldn't be hard. He simply needed
to offer a smile, or compliment her appearance, or ask
about her day. She wasn't fussy. Any of the small ways a
husband might greet his wife would have sufficed.

But instead Nikos looked at his wristwatch. 'Ready?'

She compressed her lips, the spark of mutiny colouring
her complexion for a minute. 'Do I *look* ready?' she asked
tartly, swishing past him and clipping across the room.

In the kitchen, she took two big sips of her champagne
and then placed the glass down on the marble counter a
little more firmly than she'd intended, so that a loud noise
cracked through the room.

'Yes,' he said finally, closing the distance between them.

He stared down at her, his eyes flicking across the
inches of her face. She didn't back away from him; she
didn't let him see that her heart was being shredded by his
lack of kindness. With her shoulders squared she walked
ahead of him, out of the house and into the warm night air.

He opened the passenger door of the Ferrari for her and
Marnie took her seat, careful not to touch him as she slid
into the luxurious interior. The moment he sat beside her
she was aware of his every single breath and movement.
Unconsciously, she felt herself swaying closer to the window on her side, her eyes trained steadfastly on the view
beyond the vehicle as they cruised away from his home.

At the bottom of the drive he turned left. Though Marnie was still getting her bearings, she'd ventured to the
markets with Eléni enough times to know that he'd turned
the car away from the city.

He drove without speaking, and she was glad of that. She needed the time to regain her composure, though she didn't have long. It was only a short distance to their destination: the ocean—and an enormous boat that was sparkling with the power of the thousands of tiny golden fairy lights that zigzagged across its deck. It was moored just off the coast.

'The party's on a boat?' she murmured, shifting to face him.

His eyes stayed trained on the cruise ship. 'As you see.'

She swallowed and bit back on a tart rejoinder. She'd vowed not to argue with him. Even that would show how she'd come to care too greatly. 'Great,' she snapped with acidity. 'I love boats.'

He was out of the car and rounding the side. Marnie pushed the door open and stepped out before he could reach her. After all, she'd opened her own doors all her life; why did that have to change now?

The ramp that led from the shore to the boat looked to have been specially constructed for the event. Though sturdy, it was obviously temporary. They were the only ones on it—though that was hardly surprising given that they were arriving well after the party had started.

'What is this *for*?' she asked as they stepped onto the polished deck.

'My bank throws it every year.'

'*Your* bank?' she clarified, pausing and turning to face him.

'The bank I work with,' he said distractedly. 'I do not own it.'

'I see.'

But from the second they arrived it became blatantly obvious that Nikos enjoyed an almost god-like status with the high and mighty of the institution.

Drinks were brought, food offered and advice sought.

Much of the conversation was in Greek or Italian, which Marnie understood only passably. She stood beside him listening, catching what she could, but her frustration was growing.

What was going on with him? He was acting as though she'd just knifed the tyres of his car or sold the secrets of their marriage to a tabloid. He was furious with her—and for what possible reason? She had done everything right! The clothes she wore, the hair, the make-up—she had put so much effort into being exactly what he needed of her that night. She was the picture-perfect tycoon's wife. And yet that seemed to have angered him.

When the group of men Nikos was deep in conversation with paused for a moment Marnie squeezed his arm. The smile on her face was broad; only Nikos would be able to detect the dark emotions that powered it.

'Excuse me a moment,' she murmured, pulling her hand away from him.

He bent down and whispered in her ear. 'Do you need something?'

'Yes.' She flashed her eyes at him in frustration, then encompassed his companions in her smile, knowing he wouldn't argue in front of them. 'Excuse me.'

She felt his eyes on her as she walked away, and just knowing that he was watching made her walk as though she hadn't a care in the world. Her feet seemed to glide over the deck, despite the crowds that were thick on the ground.

It was a perfect night. Sultry even though it was late in the summer season, and clear. The breeze was warm and soft, providing comfort rather than chill. She wove her way to the edge of the ship, seeking space and solitude. The polite smile on her face and a faraway look in her eyes discouraged conversation, and when she put her back to the crowds and stared out at the view she was all but absenting herself from the festivities.

She stood like that for a long time, enjoying the privacy of her thoughts, until a hand on her shoulder caught her attention.

Expecting to see Nikos, she masked her features with an expression of bland uninterest and turned slowly.

But the man opposite her caused such a flurry of feeling inside of her that tears welled instantly in her eyes.

'Anderson!' She hugged Libby's fiancé, her mind grappling with the question of why he was there even as she acknowledged how thrilled she was to see him. 'Oh! What a surprise.'

'I was hoping you'd be here.' He grinned. 'Nik wasn't sure you'd want to come.'

A frown briefly flashed in her face as she remembered that these two men were still close friends. Anderson was the one who had told Nikos about her father's dire situation, after all.

'Congratulations on the wedding.' He kissed her cheek, then grabbed two glasses of champagne from a passing waiter. 'To happily-ever-after, huh?' He clinked his glass to hers, earning a smile from Marnie.

'Indeed.' She drank the champagne, watching the man who would have become her brother-in-law over the rim of her glass.

'I wish I had been able to come to the wedding,' he said, nudging his hip against the railing and effectively screening them from the other guests.

Marnie studied him thoughtfully. Did he know what a farce their marriage was? 'I would have liked that,' she said finally, earning a laugh from Anderson.

'You sure? You sound ambivalent.'

She laughed, too. 'Sorry. I'm just surprised to see you. I somehow forgot that you and Nikos were close.'

His smile was warm. 'He's my oldest friend.'

Her heart turned over in her chest. She changed the

subject. 'I haven't seen you in a long time. You've been staying away from our house?'

He grimaced. 'I've been meaning to visit. But…'

'But?' she prompted, a smile belying any accusation.

'You know…I feel bad sometimes. Your parents look at me and see only Libby.' His smile was thin. 'I expect you know exactly what *that's* like.'

She sipped her champagne again, and her voice was carefully wiped of feeling when she spoke. 'It's not the same. They look at me and see only my failings as compared to Libby.'

Anderson rubbed a hand over his chin. 'They're wrong to compare the two of you. There's too many differences for it to make sense.'

Colour flashed in Marnie's cheeks. 'Thanks,' she said, with a hint of sarcasm.

'I wasn't being offensive,' he clarified quickly. 'Libby used to laugh and say that you and she were chalk and cheese. But that you were her favourite of all the cheeses in the world.'

Marnie's smile was nostalgic. 'I used to tell her that *she* was cheese and I was chalk. Doesn't that make more sense? She was sweet and more-ish and fair, and I'm a little…thin and brittle.' Her laugh covered a lifetime of insecurity.

'Don't *do* that,' Anderson said with frustration. 'She wouldn't want you to do that. She wasn't vain and she wasn't self-interested and she adored you. I know Arthur and Anne have always made you feel wanting, but that's not a true reflection. You owe it to Libby not to perpetuate that silliness.'

Marnie bit back the comments that were filling her mind. It was all too easy to justify her sense of inferiority, but with Anderson she didn't want to argue. 'I'm glad to see you,' she said finally.

'And I'm thrilled you and Nikos worked everything out. I know he never got over you.'

Marnie's eyes flew to Anderson's, confusion obvious in her features. Was it possible that even Anderson didn't know the true reason for their hasty wedding?

'Don't look so surprised,' Anderson said, sipping his drink. 'He might have played the part of bachelor to perfection but it was always you, Marnie. You're why he did all this.'

She shook her head in silent rejection of the idea, but Anderson continued unchecked. 'One night, not long after you guys broke up, he had far too much of my father's Scotch and told me that he'd earn his fortune and then win you back.'

'I can't imagine Nikos saying that.' But her heart was soaking in the words, buoying itself up with the hope that perhaps he *did* love her; that he *had* missed her.

'Oh, he talked about you all night. How you would only ever be serious about a guy like me. A guy with land and a title. He was determined to prove himself to you before he came back and won you over.' He laughed. 'If you ask me, he went a little far. I mean…a million would have done, right?'

Her smile was lacking warmth. She focussed her gaze on the gentle undulations of the water beneath the boat, her mind absorbing this information. 'It was never about money,' she said gently.

'Oh, I know that. I told him that a thousand times. But he didn't get it.' Anderson drained his champagne. 'Until you see first-hand the uniquely messed-up way Arthur and Anne made you girls feel you can't really understand a thing about you. Right?'

Startled, she spun to face him. Her breath was burning in her lungs and she wasn't sure what to say.

'You think you're the only one who had them in your

head? Libby almost didn't agree to marry me because she knew how *happy* it would make them. She was so sick of living up to their expectations that she said she wanted desperately to do the *wrong* thing—just once.'

'I can't believe it,' Marnie whispered, squeezing her eyes shut as she thought of Libby. 'She was the golden girl, and I never thought that bothered her.'

'It was a big mantle to wear,' he said simply.

Marnie expelled a soft breath and looked away. The breeze drifted some of her hair loose and she absentmindedly reached for it, tucking it back in place. 'I miss her so much,' she said finally.

Anderson was quiet for so long that Marnie wasn't sure he'd even heard her, or that she'd said the words aloud. Then, finally, he nodded and his voice cracked. 'Me, too.'

She wrapped her arms around him spontaneously, knowing that he understood her grief. That even years after losing Libby he stood before her a man as bereft now as he had been then.

From a distance they looked like a couple, he thought. The perfect blue-blooded pair. She with her couture gown and her swan-like neck angled towards Anderson's cheek. Her manicured hand resting on his hip, her flawless arm around his back.

His wife was beautiful, but in this environment, surrounded by Europe's financial elite, she was showcased to perfection—because she was at home. She was completely comfortable, whereas he felt the prestige like a knife in his side.

'If I did not trust you with my life I would be jealous of this little scene.'

Nikos's accented voice sent shivers of sensual awareness down Marnie's spine. She lifted away from Anderson, her eyes suspiciously moist. It caught Nikos's attention instantly. He looked from his wife to his friend, a frown on his face and a chasm in his chest.

'You are upset?'

She rolled her eyes. 'No. This is my happy face.'

He sent her a warning look that was somewhat softened when he reached into his pocket and removed a cloth handkerchief. She took it with genuine surprise at the sweetness of the gesture, dabbing at the corners of her eyes so as not to ruin her eye make-up.

'We were just reminiscing,' Anderson said simply.

Though he was subdued, he appeared to have largely regained control of his emotions.

'Your father was asking for you,' Nikos said to his friend.

'Bertram is here?' Marnie asked, a smile shifting her lips as she thought of the elder statesman. It transformed her face in an expression of such delicate beauty that Nikos had to stifle a sharp intake of breath.

'Yeah.' Anderson extended a hand and shook Nikos's. 'But I suspect your groom just doesn't want me monopolising you any longer.'

He winked at Marnie, obviously intending to make a swift departure.

She put a hand on his forearm to forestall him. 'Are you in Greece much longer? Will you come for dinner?'

'I'd love that,' Anderson said honestly. 'But we fly out tomorrow.'

Marnie's smile was wistful. 'Another time?'

'Sure.' He leaned forward and kissed her cheek, then winked at Nikos.

Alone with her husband, and the hundreds of other partygoers, Marnie felt her air of relaxation disappear. She reached for the railing, gripping it until her knuckles turned white. 'Are you having a good time?' she asked stiffly, her eyes seeking a fixed point on which to focus.

'It is good business for me to be here,' he said, lifting his broad shoulders carelessly.

'I wouldn't have thought your business required this sort of schmoozing.'

'That is true,' he said simply. 'But I do not intend to grow complacent in light of my success.'

She nodded, adding that little soundbite to the dossier of information she'd been building on him: *Nikos: V 2.0.*

This Nikos was determined to prove himself to the world—or was Anderson right? Was it that he wanted to prove himself to *her*? To prove that he deserved her?

No, that couldn't be it.

Had it not been for Arthur's financial ruin, Nikos would never have reappeared in her life.

'He might have played the part of a bachelor to perfection...' Anderson had said, and it had been an enormous understatement. Nikos had dedicated himself to the single life with aplomb. She'd lost count of the number of women he'd been reputed to be dating. And even 'dating' was over-egging it somewhat.

The women never lasted long, but that didn't matter. Each of those women had shared a part of Nikos that Marnie had been denied—a part that she'd denied herself.

Her eyes narrowed as she turned to study her husband. He'd followed her gaze and his eyes were trained on the mainland, giving her a moment to drink in his autocratic profile, the swarthy complexion and beautiful cheekbones that might well have been slashed from stone.

'Do you see that light over there?'

She followed the direction he was pointing in, squinting into the distance. There was a small glow visible in the cliffs near the sea. 'The hut?' she asked.

'Yes. It *is* a hut.' His sneer was not aimed at her; it showed agreement. He pinned her with his gaze; it was hard like gravel. 'That is where I spent the first eight years of my life.'

'Oh!' She resettled her attention on him, curiosity swelling in her chest, for Nikos had never opened up about his childhood even when they'd been madly in love. 'Is it?' She strained to pick out any details, but it was too far away. 'What's it like? Is it part of a town?'

'A town? No. There were four huts when I was growing up.' He gripped the railing tight. 'Two rooms only.'

She didn't want to say anything that might cause him to stop speaking. 'Did you like it?'

'*Like* it?' He lifted his lips in a humourless smile. 'It was a very free childhood.'

'Oh?'

'My father had a trawler. He came out here every day.'

'Squid?'

He nodded. 'Scampi, too.'

'You said you lived there until you were eight. What happened?'

He tilted his head to face her, his expression derisive. 'There was a storm. He died.'

'Nikos!' Sympathy softened her expression, but she saw immediately how unwelcome it was.

He shifted a little, indicating his desire to end the conversation.

'I should have told you he'd be here,' Nikos said only a moment later, surprising her with the lightning-fast change in conversation.

For a moment she didn't comprehend who he was talking about.

'It did not occur to me that Anderson would upset you.'

She drew her brows together in confusion. 'He didn't.'

'The tears in your eyes would suggest otherwise.'

She opened her mouth in an expression of her bemusement. 'This from the man who seems to live to insult me?' The words escaped before she could catch them.

Nikos nodded slowly, as if accepting her charge even

as his words sought to contradict it. 'Hurting you... That is not intentional. It is not what I want.'

She blinked and spun away, turning her body to face the railing. 'I can believe that.' And that hurt so much more! Knowing he could inflict pain without even trying, without even being conscious of her feelings, simply demonstrated how little he thought of her feelings at all.

'Do we have to stay long?' she asked, doing her best to sound unconcerned when emotions were zipping through her.

'No. Let's go. *Now*.'

He trapped her hand in his much bigger palm and led her from the party. Several times people moved to grab his attention, but Nikos apparently had a one-track mind, and it involved getting them off the boat.

At his Ferrari, with the moon cresting high in the sky and the strains of the party muffled by distance, Nikos put his hands on her shoulders and spun her to face him. His eyes seemed to tunnel into the heart of her soul.

'What is it I have done that's insulted you?'

She knew she couldn't deny it; after all, she'd just laid the charge at his feet. She shook her head, yet the words wouldn't climb to her tongue.

'Tell me, *agape*...'

'Nothing. It's fine.' Her eyes didn't meet his.

'Liar!' He groaned, crushing his mouth to hers.

His hands lifted, pulling at the pins that kept her hair in its chignon until they had all dropped to the ground in near-silent protest. He dragged his fingers through her hair, pulling at it and levering her face away.

His eyes bored into hers. 'I was angry with you tonight. I was rude.'

A sob was filling her chest. She wouldn't give in to it. '*Why?* What in the world could you have had to be angry about?'

Was that really her voice? With the exception of a slight tremor, she sounded so cool and in command! How was that possible when her knees were shaking and her heart was pounding?

'This. *You.*' He stepped backwards, as if to shake himself out of the hurricane of feelings. He pulled the door open and stared at her.

Marnie stared back. She wasn't going to let this go just because he appeared to have decided the conversation was at an end.

'What?' she demanded, lifting a hand and splaying her fingers against his broad chest. 'What *about* me? What did I do?'

'Do?' His head snapped back as if in silent revulsion. 'You did nothing. You cannot help that this is who you are.'

Her heart was pounding so hard now that it was paining her. 'I don't understand,' she said, with a soft determination that almost completely hid her wounds.

'No? Allow me to clarify. You are Lady Marnie Kenington and you always will be. You are this dress. This party. This perfect face. You are cold and you are exquisitely untouchable. The girl I thought I loved all those years ago never existed, did she?'

CHAPTER EIGHT

FOR THE FIRST time since her arrival in Greece the early morning was drenched by storm. The sky was leaden with weighty clouds, the ocean a turbulent, raging gradient of steel. White caps frothed all the way to the horizon, and the trees that marked the shore arched in the distance, folded almost completely in half.

Marnie, her knees bent under her chin, her eyes focussed on the ravaged horizon, took a measure of consolation from the destruction. Her mind, numb from the exhausting activity of trying to join the dots of what had happened the night before, looked for some kind of comparison in the wasted outlook.

The storm was trashing everything, and yet in time—perhaps even later that day—the clouds would disperse, the sun would shine, and all would look as it once had. Better, perhaps, for the rain had a spectacular way of cleaning things up, didn't it?

Could the same be said for her and Nikos?

Were they in the midst of a storm that would one day clear? Argument by argument, would they wash away their hurts?

She shook her head sadly from side to side, the question that had plagued her at length tormenting her anew.

Why had he married her?

*'You are Lady Marnie Kenington and you always will
be. The girl I fell in love with all those years ago never
existed, did she?'*

Had she?

He was right. Marnie had changed so much since then.
He seemed to attribute it to her upbringing, to her parents' snobbery. Wasn't it more likely that she'd simply
grown up?

She glanced down at her manicured fingernails and
the enormous diamond that sparkled on her ring finger.

They were husband and wife, but outside of that, they
were strangers. A lump formed in her throat; futility hollowed out her core.

He hadn't come to bed last night. She'd showered and
waited for him—hoping, knowing, that their being together
would make sense of everything. That when they made
love the truth of their hearts was most obvious.

But she had no experience in the matter. Was it as he
said? Just great sex? Or was it love? Or memories of love,
like fragments of a dream, too hard to catch now in the
bright light of reality and daytime?

She scraped her chair back impatiently. The pool was
dark today, too, reflecting the sorrow of the skies. Had it
been a stormy day like this when Nikos had lost his father? When the ocean had swallowed him up, perhaps as
retribution for the fish he'd stolen out of its belly?

He had been silent and brooding on the car trip home,
and Marnie had been too absorbed by his statement to try
to break through that mood, to get to the heart of what he
had meant.

Perhaps this morning they could talk.

She moved towards the kitchen, the thought of a cup
of tea offering unparalleled temptation. And froze when
she saw him.

It was like a flashback to the morning after they'd first

arrived. Impeccably dressed in a high-end business suit, he had his head bent over the newspaper and a cup to his left, which she knew would be filled with that thick coffee he loved.

'Good morning,' she murmured, her voice croaky from disuse.

He flicked a gaze to her face, studying her for one heart-stopping moment before smiling tightly and returning his attention to the paper.

So that was how it was going to be.

Marnie squared her shoulders and tipped up her chin defiantly. 'Did you sleep well?' She walked to the bench, standing directly opposite him.

Without looking up, he responded, 'Fine. And you?'

It was a lie. He hadn't got more than ten minutes altogether.

'Not really,' she said honestly.

He turned the page of the newspaper. Did she imagine that it was with force and irritation? The admission had cost her. It was an offer of peace—an acceptance of their relationship, faults and all.

'Where did you sleep?' she pushed, determined to crack through the facade he'd erected.

'In a guest room.' Still he read the damned newspaper.

Marnie, trying her hardest to forge past the storm, reached down and put her hand over the article. 'Nikos, we need to talk.'

He expelled a sigh and glanced at his watch. 'Do we?'

'You know we do.' She lifted her hand and moved it to his, lacing his fingers with her own. 'This isn't right.'

He moved his hand so that he could lift his coffee cup and drink from it. 'Talk quickly. I have a meeting.'

Hurt lashed her as a whip. 'That's not fair,' she said, with soft steel to her voice. 'You can't keep doing that.'

'Doing what?'

'Making yourself unavailable as soon as things get tough.'

'I relish obstacles. I relish difficult opportunities. But I cannot see the point in discussing anything with you right now.'

'So what you said last night isn't important enough to talk about?'

'What *did* I say?' he asked softly, his eyes roaming her face.

'Don't be fatuous,' she snapped. 'You made it sound like we didn't love each other. Like we didn't know each other.'

His look was one of confusion. 'But we *don't*.'

Denial! The sharpness of it plunged into her heart.

'I meant back then…' She limped the conversation along even when she felt as if she was dying a little.

'I said that the girl I thought I loved never existed,' he said with a shrug. 'That girl would have stood up for what we were. Would have fought to be with me. But you were never that. Seeing you last night, in that dress, you looked so perfect.' Derision lined his face. 'You've become exactly what your parents wanted.'

'You keep *doing* that! You keep making me out to be some kind of construct of theirs.'

'*Aren't* you?'

'Aren't we all?' she challenged. '*You* are a product of your life just as I am of mine. But if you hate me so much why the hell did you insist I marry you? It *has* to be more than revenge against my father'

He closed the paper and drained his coffee cup before placing it neatly on the edge of the sink. The seconds ticked by loudly in the background.

'Why do you think?'

A thousand possibilities clouded her mind, some of them dangling hope and others promising despair. 'I don't know,' she said finally, warily, shaking her head.

'To prove that I could have you.'

She had to brace her hands on the edge of the bench for support.

Her face flashed with such a depth of hurt that Nikos instantly wanted to call the words back. To defuse the situation and make her smile again. To make her laugh in that beautiful, inimitable way she had.

Laughter was a long way from Marnie's mind, though. 'You're serious?' She pressed her lips together, her mind reeling. 'This was just ego? As a seventeen-year-old I rejected you, and you couldn't handle that, could you? And now you've bullied me into this marriage so—what? So you can make me feel like this? So you can berate me and humiliate me...'

He held up a hand to silence her. 'I told you last night— I do not mean to hurt you. I never did.'

'Yeah, *right*.' She swallowed, her throat moving convulsively as she attempted to breathe normally. 'It didn't occur to you that this whole idea would hurt me?'

A muscle jerked in his cheek. 'Are you having regrets?'

'How can I *not* be? You put me in an impossible situation.' She spun away from him, looking out at the storm. She was at a crossroads. She could tell him the truth—that it was impossible to be married to him knowing he would never love her. Or she could remember that she *had* married him. A thousand and one reasons had driven her to it, and they were all still there.

Worse, Marnie stared down the barrel of her future and imagined it without Nikos and she was instantly bereft. Even this shell of a relationship, knowing he would share only a small part of himself with her, was better than nothing.

She'd faced life without him and it had been a sort of half-life. She'd poured all her energy into her work, and she'd dated men that she'd known her parents would approve of, but she hadn't felt truly alive until she'd seen Nikos once more.

Was it better to feel alive and permanently in pain or to be alone and feel nothing?

She turned to face him slowly, her face unknowingly stoic. 'I didn't hope for much from you, Nikos, but I expected at least that you would respect me. And do you know why? Because of who *you* are. Last night you said that the girl you fell in love with never existed. Maybe you feel that—maybe you don't. I don't know. But I have no doubt that I knew *you*. Who you were then. I think I know who you are now, too. And the contempt you are meeting me with is completely unwarranted.'

Her eyes sparked as she spoke the declaration.

'You say you married me to prove that you could have me. Well, I only married *you* to save my father. Did you honestly expect me to do anything less?'

'Not at all.' His voice was gravelly. 'You are excellent at taking direction.'

She sucked in a breath at the cruel remark. 'My parents were right to tell me to break it off with you. Not because you had no money or family prestige, but because you're a jerk.'

It wasn't funny but he laughed—a short, sharp sound of disbelief.

'I'm serious,' she said stiffly. 'I *am* Lady Marnie Kenington. I am the same woman I've always been. You forced me into this marriage and now you're angry with me just for being who I am. *You're* the one who's trying to make me something I'm not.'

Her words were little shards of glass, all the more potent for she was right. He couldn't fault her behaviour as his wife. She'd done and been everything he'd required of her. She hadn't shifted the goalposts—he had.

The realisation only worsened his mood. How could he

explain to her that he never enjoyed being at events like the party they'd attended the night before? That he hated most of the people in attendance, despised their grandiose displays of wealth and their desire to outdo one another. That he hated that entire scene and she was the very epitome of it? That seeing her amongst her own people—people who'd been born to wealth and prestige—made him realise that they'd never see the world the same way?

'You make an excellent point. I knew what I was getting when I suggested this marriage.' He looked at his wife long and hard. She was a woman who projected an image of being cool and untouchable—except with him. A gnawing sense of frustration engulfed him. 'Now, I really *am* late.'

He stalked towards the door, then turned back to face her. She was staring straight ahead with such an attempt at strength and resolve that something inside him twisted painfully.

'Marnie...' *What?* What could he offer her? 'We can make this work. The way we are in bed—'

'Is just great sex,' she reminded him, hating the words even as she spoke them.

But it was more than that. In bed, in his arms, Marnie was as he wanted her to be. Genuine, overflowing with desire and feeling: a real flesh-and-blood woman. Not the fancy ice queen she showed the world.

'Yes. And many marriages are built on less.'

'Great.' She appeared calm and in control, but her strength was crumbling. 'Don't you have a meeting to go to?'

He walked out of the door with a heavy pain in his gut that stayed with him all day.

His mind was shot. He lost concentration, he sent emails to the wrong people, he inverted figures on his spreadsheets.

He gave up on work in the early afternoon.

When he arrived home the place was deserted. He wandered from room to room, pretending he wasn't looking for Marnie, until he heard her voice drifting from the small space she'd claimed as her office.

By silent but mutual agreement he didn't intrude on her there. She generally only utilised it when he was at work, anyway. But curiosity drove him towards the door now, and he lingered for a moment on the threshold.

'We're in stage three of some very promising trials. Yes...'

She paused, and he could imagine the way she'd have that little line between her brows that showed deep concentration.

'That's true. Human trials are still a way off. But every day brings us closer.' Another pause. 'You're a gem, Mrs Finley-Johns. That's really very generous. Thank you.'

Silence filled the room for long enough that Nikos presumed she'd hung up the phone. He pushed the door inwards silently.

Marnie—his wife—was sitting at her desk, her honeyed hair piled into a messy bun, her head bent over a page as she handwrote something. He watched her for a moment and then stepped into the room.

That feeling in his gut didn't dissipate. He'd thought seeing her might do it. That just the sight of her might make everything slide back into place. It didn't.

When she realised she was no longer alone and lifted her gaze to his face he waited impatiently for a smile to burst sunshine through the room and relax his chest. It didn't. If anything, she was impatient, lifting her eyes to the clock above the door.

'Nikos? Is everything okay?' She reached for her phone, rotating it in her hands.

'Why do you ask?'

'It's so early,' she said with a look of confusion. 'You're usually not home for hours.'

He felt as if the ground was slipping beneath him. 'My afternoon was freed up,' he said with a shrug. 'You wanted to speak this morning and I rushed you. I thought we could go out for dinner and talk properly.'

The suggestion had come out of nowhere but as soon as he'd issued the invitation he'd known it was right.

'We did speak this morning.'

Their conversation had chased its way through her mind all day. Like a maze, it had twists and turns, but no matter which path she chased down they all finished in a dead end of despair.

'Not properly.' The words were gruff. He dragged a hand through his hair. 'Let's have dinner and try to be civilised.'

She arched a brow, genuine surprise obvious. 'I'm working.' She bit down on her lip. 'And I don't think anything's served by going out, do you?'

She sounded prim, and inwardly she winced. *You'll always be Lady Marnie Kenington...*

He crossed his arms over his chest, staring down at her. Marnie felt the imbalance in their arrangement and fought an urge to stand, to right it. That would just be symbolic; the true imbalance would remain.

'What is it you are doing? For work?' His smile was an attempt to relax her. To elicit a similar reaction in her. It failed. 'Or is it still a secret?'

'It's not a secret.' She shook her head. 'It never has been. I do behind-the-scenes fundraising for a cancer charity. Specifically leukaemia research.'

It wasn't what he'd expected and that was obvious. He rubbed a hand over his stubbled chin, propping his hip against the doorframe. He was settling in. Marnie swallowed. Her insides were clenching with desire, her mind was sore from trying to figure out what the hell they were doing, and all she could think as she looked at him was how much she wanted him. To hell with everything else.

'Why behind the scenes?'

She blinked, passing her phone from one hand to the other. 'It's more my thing.'

'I would have thought your profile would garner donations…'

'My name does that, too.' She shrugged, placing the phone down on the desk and clasping her hands together in her lap. 'And my contacts.'

He took a step into the office, looking at the computer screen. It had a list of names with donations beside them, tracking various contributions for the last few years.

'You are apparently very effective at this,' he murmured, leaning forward and scrolling down the page.

His body framed hers, trapping her within the circle of his arms. She thought of telling him to stop looking, saying that her work was confidential. But why? Nikos Kyriazis was hardly likely to be indiscreet with the information, and most of her donors released details of their charitable contributions as a way of attracting good publicity.

'Thanks,' she said, allowing herself to extract a small kernel of pleasure from his praise. 'I suppose it's because I feel passionately about it.'

'Yes…' He straightened, but stayed where he was, so that his legs straddled hers. 'How come you have not asked *me* to donate?'

Her smile was a twist of her pink lips. 'You don't think you've donated enough to my cause already?'

That feeling in his gut intensified in a burst of pain. 'This is different.'

She shook her head. 'Not really.' She ran a fingernail over the hem of her skirt, drawing his attention to her smooth, tanned legs.

'Why don't we go for dinner and you can tell me about this? Your charity. Pretend I am a donor you want to win over.'

'But you're not,' she said with a shake of her head. 'And I don't want to ask you to put money into this.'

'It matters so much to you, though,' he pointed out logically. 'Surely you wouldn't turn me down?'

She shrugged, perfecting an air of impatient unconcern. 'If you want to donate, you can. That's your business.'

'Tell me more about it first.'

Marnie bit down on her lip, her eyes drifting to his face. The time she'd spent in an attempt to make sense of their situation had all been a waste, for here was yet another facet of Nikos Kyriazis that wholly renewed the riddle. His ability to set aside their contretemps and the harsh words he'd issued made her head spin.

She nodded finally, expelling a soft sigh. 'Fine. We'll talk at dinner.'

Nikos had dismissed enough people enough times in his life to know that he was being dismissed from her office. Feeling that somewhere in their conversation he'd scored a minor victory, he didn't push it.

CHAPTER NINE

In England, Marnie was used to being recognised. She hated the sensation but she'd come to expect it, so she had long ago given up the idea of eating in glamorous high-profile restaurants without expecting to be photographed and approached by all and sundry.

In Athens it was Nikos who drew the long, speculative glances. Nikos whose name opened doors and inspired attention and curiosity.

Marnie was actually enjoying being an outsider to the sense of celebrity. She'd never craved it, and watching him being fawned over by waitresses and even the manager at the exclusive Athens hot spot from the moment they arrived brought a small smile to her lips now.

He saw it immediately. Of their own volition his eyes dropped to the curve of her pink mouth and fire warmed her belly.

'Yes, Marnie?' he prompted, leaning forward so that a hint of his masculine fragrance teased her nostrils, making her gut clench with unmistakable desire. She tried to ignore it.

She crossed her legs beneath the table and shrugged. 'I was just thinking how nice it is that I'm unknown here.'

'Not unknown,' he said, with a small shake of his head.

'Well, *lesser* known,' she corrected. 'Less relevant. And you're…'

'Yes?' He broke off the query when a waitress appeared with a bottle of ice-cold champagne.

'Compliments of the owner.' She smiled at Nikos, her cleavage exposed as she leaned forward to pour some of the liquid into a long, tapered flute.

'Thank you,' he murmured dismissively. 'You were saying…?'

Marnie waited for the waitress to finish pouring. 'You're who everyone wants to see.' She grinned. 'I'm anonymous and you're hot property.'

His laugh surprised her. It was rich and warm, and reminded her of how long it had been since she'd heard the sound.

'Hot property?' He shook his head. 'I'm glad to hear you think so.'

'You know what I mean.' Colour bloomed in her cheeks. She focussed on the menu. 'What's good here? What do you recommend?'

'It is all excellent.' He shrugged.

She scanned the menu but she was far from hungry. Butterflies had taken up residence in her stomach and their beating wings made it impossible for her to imagine accommodating food into their kaleidoscope.

'What do you suggest?'

His eyes narrowed. 'I can order for you, if you'd like?'

'That won't be necessary.' She shut down his perfectly normal offer, knowing how dire it would be to keep conceding to him.

'As you wish.' He pushed the menu away, his mind apparently made up.

She continued to skim her eyes over the words on the page but they were puddles and blurs.

'How long have you done this work?'

She started, despite the fact his suggestion of dinner had been hung on a desire to learn more about the trust.

'About four years,' she said, reaching for the stem of her champagne flute simply for something to do.

'You didn't go to university?'

She shook her head. 'The timing wasn't right.'

A frown smudged his handsome face. 'In what way?'

Marnie pulled her lower lip between her teeth and Nikos surprised her by reaching over and abruptly swiping his thumb across her mouth, disturbing the gesture.

'Don't think.' He spoke commandingly, his words gravelled. 'You do this too often.'

Her expression was blank. 'I wasn't aware thinking was a crime.'

'It is when you are selecting which words to use to your husband. Just answer my questions directly.'

Marnie gaped, her mouth parted on an exhalation of surprise. 'That hardly seems fair.'

'Why was the timing not right?' He returned to his original question, impatient for an answer.

He was right. She *had* been prevaricating, unconsciously trying to select words that wouldn't apportion blame or imply resentment.

'I wasn't ready to leave home,' she said quietly.

But he understood what she hadn't been willing to say. 'You mean your parents didn't want you to go?' His disapproval was marked, despite the way he spoke quietly.

The waitress reappeared, her smile bright. Was it also inviting? Or was Marnie being paranoid?

She flicked her gaze back to the menu, intent on seeming not to notice the way the waitress lingered a little too close to Nikos as she spoke.

Nikos didn't appreciate the interruption, and his annoyance brought a childish kernel of pleasure to Marnie. She hesitated over ordering for far longer than was necessary, finally selecting scampi followed by chicken, having changed her mind several times.

Nikos glared at her and spoke in Greek, quickly dispensing with the waitress.

'They forbade you from attending university?'

She started, shaking her head softly so that her hair flew around her cheeks. 'Not at all.'

'You wanted to study law. You were passionate about it.'

'Not really.'

He ignored the rejoinder. After all, they'd spent a long time talking about their hopes and dreams. He had not misunderstood her desire to go into law. Nor did he doubt she would have achieved the requisite grades.

'But instead you stayed at home, living with your parents, working for a charity that revolves around your sister's illness,' he murmured, with a directness she hadn't expected.

'Do you think there's something wrong with that?'

'Yes.' He leaned forward and put his hand on hers. 'You are a person, too, Marnie. You are not simply Libby's sister. Nor your parents' daughter. You have your own life to live.'

She compressed her lips and pulled her hand down to her lap. 'You say that even after blackmailing me into this marriage?'

She sipped her champagne but it was too sweet. She didn't want it. She was definitely not in the mood to celebrate. She ran her finger around the rim, staring at the hypnotic, frantic movement of the bubbles as her mind spun over the situation they found themselves in.

'It's not as if I can't move on,' she said quietly, her eyes refusing to meet his. 'But without funds research into leukaemia is slow. It occurred to me that the people most likely to succeed at raising money are probably those who have every reason to passionately pursue it. In ten years— who knows? Maybe girls like Libby won't get sick.'

Finally, she forced herself to lance him with her eyes; they were softened by sorrow.

'It's idealistic, but…'

He surprised her by murmuring, 'Not at all. You are right. Progress does not always happen as you expect it to. Sometimes it is hard-fought, and other times it is overnight, as though a cascade of discoveries slides into place. But without funds neither is likely.'

She nodded, distracted enough by the subject matter to speak naturally. 'I thought I'd do it for a year. As a way of giving back to the trust that was so supportive to us. But it turns out I sort of have a knack for it.'

'I can imagine,' he said. 'Do you regret not studying law?'

It was on the tip of her tongue to deny it, but the truth came to her first. 'Yeah. Sometimes. But that would have been about helping people, too. I'm just helping different people now.'

He let the words sink in and shied away from the intrinsic guilt they evoked. After all, her propensity to help others was what had made it impossible for her to walk away from his marriage proposal.

'And staying at home instead of finding your own place…?'

Her smile was enigmatic. 'You know… Kenington Hall is enormous. I have my own wing. It's much like living on my own.'

'And your parents are your neighbours?' he murmured, his voice ringing with disbelief.

'Yes.' She nodded. 'But apparently I'm a pretty inattentive neighbour,' she said with regret. 'I had no idea about Dad's troubles.'

His desire to comfort her displeased him. 'I imagine he was adept at concealing the truth.'

'Not really.' She shook her head wistfully.

The waitress appeared with their starters, placing them on the table and then disappearing without a word. Marnie wondered if Nikos had commanded her to stop making conversation when he'd switched to speaking Greek earlier.

Nikos watched as Marnie lifted her fork and speared a single scampi. She put it down again almost instantly, and when she looked at him he felt a wave of guilt emanating from her.

'I should have seen the signs.'

'What signs?' he prompted.

'He's been stressed. Angry. He's just not himself.'

Nikos found it hard to find any genuine sympathy for the man, but he realised he didn't like seeing Marnie suffer. *At all.* 'Tell me something…'

She nodded, toying with her fork.

'After your father paid me off, were you angry with him?'

Marnie's eyes flashed with emotion. 'I didn't know about that, remember?'

He waved a hand dismissively through the air. 'Fine. After I left, were you angry with him? With your mother?'

'I…' She shuttered her eyes closed, her dark lashes fanning over her translucent cheek.

'Do not *think*!' He repeated his earlier directive and she grimaced.

'I was furious,' she said, so quietly he had to lean forward to catch the words. 'But they're my parents, and they'd been through so much.' She swallowed. 'My father threatened…' She closed her mouth on the threat she'd been about to repeat. 'My father was devastated by losing Libby.'

'And he threatened you?' Nikos prompted, with a smoothness that spoke of determination.

She thought about lying. But wasn't there so much water under the bridge now?

'They made me choose.'

The anticlimax brought about in him an intense sense

of disappointment. Right when he'd thought he might finally be going to understand just what had led to Marnie pushing him far, far away, she'd gone back to the old lines.

'I mean they *literally* told me they'd disown me if I didn't break it off with you,' she added with a look of grief on her beautiful features.

She was back in the past, her mind far from him in that moment.

'I didn't care when they said they'd disinherit me.' She looked at him—and through him. 'Money meant nothing to me. But they were my link to Libby, and they said they wouldn't have me in their lives so long as I was with you. That I would never be allowed to return to Kenington Hall.' Marnie's voice cracked. 'The house was—is—all I have left of her…'

Marnie woke with a start as the plane pitched a little in one direction. She'd dozed off, despite the fact their flight had been a morning one. She stifled a yawn with the back of her hand, her groggy eyes drifting to her husband's bent head.

He was working.

A smile flicked to her lips with ease, though her stomach churned with a mix of anxiety and an emotion that was so much more confusing.

She didn't have time to attempt to understand it before the plane shuddered and Marnie's panic overtook everything. She dug her fingernails into the armrests, her expression showing distress.

Nikos, attuned to her every move, looked up instantly. 'There is thick cloud-cover over London, that's all.'

She nodded, but her childhood fear of flying was ricocheting through her. Marnie stared out of the window, trying to distract herself with thoughts of her father's birthday weekend—anything to curtail the clear picture she had in her mind of the aeroplane spearing nose-first towards the earth.

Their trip had come round quickly—for Marnie, almost too quickly.

After that one night in Athens when they'd shared dinner she felt as if a new understanding had settled between her and her husband and she wanted to hold on to that, to strengthen the understanding that was building between them. Would a trip back to her parents' unsettle the bridge they'd been building?

They were not a normal couple.

There was no shared love between them—at least not on Nikos's part. Perhaps not on Marnie's part either.

She had spent a great deal of her energy trying to decipher and separate her feelings of lust from love; her feelings of past love from present infatuation. Some days she convinced herself that she'd fallen in love with only the *idea* of Nikos—an idea that bore only a passing resemblance to the ruthless, determined businessman he'd become.

But then he would do something sweet—like bringing her tea in bed when she'd slept late, or calling in the middle of the day to remind her of something small they'd discussed the night before—and her heart would flutter and her soul would know she loved him. Not in a sensible, rational way, but in the way that love sometimes bloomed even when it was not watered or fed.

They barely argued. By tacit agreement each tried to respect the other's limitations. Marnie accepted the dark streak that ran through Nikos—the side of him that was so hell-bent on making her father see how wrong he was to have passed Nikos off as a failure that he'd blackmailed her into marriage. If she thought about it too much it made her queasy, so she pushed it to the recesses of her mind and clung to a sort of blind hope. Maybe one day he wouldn't feel that aching resentment so forcefully?

Their truce was underpinned by a sex life that made her toes curl. He had been right about that. Even if it was all they had to go on it would make their marriage worth staying in. Wouldn't it?

But uncertainty lurked just beyond her acceptance. For they had travelled stormy waters, and weren't there always eyes in storms? The calm that gave a moment's respite before the intensity of the cyclone returned with twice its strength?

Was she in the eye of a storm?

Or was this a lasting peace?

Only time would tell, and Marnie had a lifetime to wait and see.

CHAPTER TEN

THE APPLE WAS as sweetly sun-warmed as those she remembered from childhood. Despite the fact the day was cool, the morning had offered just enough heat to darken the flesh of this one more than the others.

Though it wasn't yet midday, she was tired. They'd been travelling since dawn and the return to Kenington with Nikos by her side had brought with it a sledge-load of emotions.

Juice dribbled down one side of her mouth and she lifted a finger to catch it.

Nikos watched, transfixed.

'I used to love coming down here to the apple orchard…'

'I remember.'

Memories. They were his problem. They were thick in the air around them. Memories of how it had felt then. When he'd been young and in love. He would have plucked a matching apple from another branch and enjoyed its fruity flesh alongside Marnie.

She stopped walking and turned around, her back to the heavily adorned fruit trees. 'I always think this is the best aspect of the house.' She lifted her free hand and framed the building between her forefinger and thumb. Her smile was born of whimsy. 'Until I go to the rose garden or Libby's garden. Then I think *that* view is preferable.'

She crunched into the apple once more.

'Perhaps it is the same from all viewpoints,' he suggested, with a hint of cynicism that was out of place and sounded, even to his own ears, forced.

'Maybe.' She shrugged and began to walk back towards the house.

He resisted the urge to ask her to stay with him where they were a little longer.

'Thank you for coming with me this weekend.'

His laugh was short. 'I presumed my attendance wasn't optional.'

She lifted her face to his. 'I would think almost *everything* is optional for you.'

His smile was without humour—a relic of his twisted laugh. 'Not this.'

She didn't pretend to misunderstand. 'When are you seeing him?'

'We're meeting after lunch.'

Marnie stopped walking, reaching for Nikos's hand. Her fingers curled around his as though they belonged. Familiarity and comfort knotted through her, momentarily putting aside the nausea and anxiety that had besieged her since they'd arrived in London.

'What is it, *agape*?'

A husky question. A promise, too, laced with so many emotions she couldn't translate.

'You know how stubborn he is?'

Nikos's lips curled. 'Yes.'

'I just don't know if he'll let you help. And I'm… I'm scared.'

His eyes held hers, probing her, trying to read her soul. 'Tell me something, Marnie. Why do you care?'

She started, scanning his face. But Nikos wasn't backing off. In fact, he moved closer, welding his body to hers, linking his arms behind her back. His nearness was seductive and distracting.

'Besides the fact he's my father?'

'Blood isn't everything. Your parents don't seem too concerned with your happiness. You're not close to them.'

'Of course I am,' she said with a shake of her head.

He laughed, dismissing her assertion easily. 'You don't speak to them. You don't speak *of* them—except with a sense of obligation and guilt because you survived and Libby died.'

She was startled at his perceptiveness.

'You married a man who saw you only as a means of revenge in order to stave off the financial fate that they deserve.'

'They're my *parents*,' she mumbled, her eyes flicking closed. The pain of his words was washing through her. 'And I'm very grateful to you.'

'Grateful?' He stepped backwards, shaking his head. '*Thee mou*. You offer me *gratitude*? I tell you I see you as a means of revenge and you say thank you?'

She frowned. 'You know what I mean.'

'No, I don't. You have been pushed around by your parents, and by me, and yet you seem to treat us all with civility and thankfulness. I cannot comprehend this.'

She swallowed. 'Do you need to?'

He shook his head. 'No.' He lifted a hand to her cheek and stroked it. 'And I suppose the same could be said for you.'

She pressed a hand to his chest, perhaps intending to put some distance between them, but the warmth of him, the beating of his heart, was mesmerising.

'Do you really believe our marriage comes down to revenge and sex?'

'Our marriage—' He began to speak, the words thick with meaning. He stared into her eyes; he was drowning in them. They were the depths to her soul; the truth to her questions. They mirrored his past, his heart and all his hopes.

They were beautiful eyes. How could people mistake her for being cold-hearted? In her eyes there was always a twisting of emotion and thought, of kindness and concern. Yet he had missed it. He had believed her unfeeling and incapable of true emotion at one point. He'd clung to that; he'd enjoyed believing it of her.

'Yes?'

It was a husk. An invitation for him to say something that would smooth away the pain of their predicament. A contradiction of the fact that he had bought her out of a need to avenge past wrongs.

But they were wrongs he'd carried with him for a long time. Was he willing to let them go? And, if so, what did that mean?

'Marnie?'

The voice was shrill and imperious, cutting across the lawn and breaking through the growing understanding that had been forming between them. He was unwilling to close their conversation, but a cloud instantly seemed to spread across Marnie and she stepped back.

The woman who had pulled a sweet apple from a frothy tree and crunched into it hungrily was gone. Lady Heiress was his companion now—only her eyes showed that Marnie was still in there.

'It doesn't matter,' she said quietly, shifting her gaze to the manor house in the background. 'I'm glad you're going to help him. Only be gentle, Nikos. And…' She turned to face him, hurrying now as Anne Kenington approached them. 'I know you said *you* would decide if you wanted to tell him the truth about our arrangement but…'

It seemed like an age ago that they'd had that conversation, but it had only been a month! Something strange lodged in her mind—a recollection she couldn't quite grab so she pushed it aside.

'But could you not? Not this weekend? I know you hate him, and that it's tempting to throw it in his face. But not now. Please?'

He stared at her without speaking and Marnie continued anxiously.

'I don't think I could forgive that. It would be... It really would be the end of what we used to mean to one another.'

Nikos was perplexed—and something else. Something he couldn't analyse or comprehend. So he spoke honestly. 'I have no intention of telling your father you married me to clear his debts.'

'Don't say that!'

She was visibly stricken, but Anne was almost upon them. Like a consummate professional Marnie blinked and slid her mask into place.

It annoyed him, and he wanted to prise it off again—just for a moment. He was sick and tired of masks and pretence.

'It's the truth,' he replied softly, clinging to that fact for her sake as much as his own.

Did he want her to contradict him? Did he want her to redefine their marriage? How could he expect that of her? A challenge? A gauntlet? One he knew she'd never answer.

'Isn't it?'

Their conversation had left Nikos in a foul mood. The lack of resolution, the constant chasing one another in circles, had given him the feeling that as soon as he began to comprehend a facet of his wife she morphed into something else and slipped out of his grip and downstream from him completely.

Worse was the sense that he was losing his own convictions in the face of hers. To lose one's sister would be hard enough, but to have your parents threaten to cut you completely from their life and support... Even Marnie, who had always seemed to have certainty and strength to her, must have been terrified of what that would mean.

How *dared* they? How had they dared to speak to their own child with such cold disregard?

It was not the ideal mind-set to bring to his meeting with Arthur Kenington. Nor was it the ideal backdrop. This study of Arthur's was familiar, yet different. Since they'd stood here six years earlier many changes had taken place—not least between the two men.

The walls were filled with a collection of books, impressive volumes that had never been thumbed—perhaps carefully selected by an interior designer who had chosen the titles because they would add *gravitas* to a man who was otherwise lacking in it—there was an elegant liquor tray that looked to be well-used, and a family photograph that was framed above Arthur's desk.

Arthur and Anne had barely aged, though Libby and Marnie looked much younger, so the picture must have been taken at least a decade earlier.

Arthur caught Nikos's gaze and grimaced. 'Our last family photo. We used to get them done every year until... we lost her.' He coughed, his slight paunch wobbling a little with the involuntary spasm. 'It didn't make much sense after that.'

Nikos didn't respond. Marnie and Libby stood at the foreground of the photo, Libby's arm wrapped around her sister's shoulders. There was an air of genuine affection between the girls: a sign of true camaraderie. Perhaps it had developed as a result of this environment?

'She was such an angel,' Arthur continued, perhaps misunderstanding Nikos's interest. 'Not a girl in the world like her.'

Nikos felt a possessive protective instinct flash in his gut. Yes, Libby had been lovely. And beautiful in a way that was ordinary and common. Unlike Marnie, with her steely, watchful gaze and determined little chin. Her reserve that made it difficult for her to speak to people unless she really, truly admired them.

'We need to discuss your business,' Nikos said sharply, not wishing to wander down Arthur's Libby-paved Memory Lane a moment longer. 'My information on your situation has me...concerned.'

'And what information is that?'

Nikos leaned forward, bracing his elbows on his thighs. 'It is no secret. You are out of immediate danger, but that is only temporary.'

'I don't believe that.'

'Then you are a fool.' Nikos spoke sharply.

Six years had passed since their last private conversation, and in that time Nikos had become used to having the world obey him. Deference generally met his commands—not dithering indecision.

'Do you want to lose it all, Arthur?'

'Of course I don't. But it won't come to that. Mark my words, there'll be—'

'Nothing.' Nikos eased back in his chair. 'You are overcommitted. There are no more assets left to shore your interests up and the market continues to fluctuate wildly. I am your only chance.'

The silence sparked between them. It was electrified by resentment.

'You're enjoying this, aren't you?'

Nikos didn't pretend to misunderstand; his smile was thin and unknowingly filled with disparagement. 'How I feel isn't relevant,' he said finally.

Strangely, he wasn't enjoying it. He had spent a long time imagining a situation like this. How good it would feel to throw his own success in Arthur Kenington's face. A man who had told him he would never amount to anything! He'd fantasised about it, and he'd done everything he could—even sacrificing his conscience—to achieve this moment.

And he felt nothing. Except, perhaps, a pervasive pity for this man who had let vanity and arrogance get in the way of financial security. His voice was softer when he spoke again, conciliatory.

'You cannot lose your business. Nor this house. It would devastate Marnie.'

'Marnie?' A scoff of surprise. 'She'd recover. This place never meant to her what it did to Libby.'

Nikos's fingers flexed into a fist on his lap, but he kept his face impassive. How was it possible that her own father understood her so little? Did he not see what she didn't say? Didn't he understand that her reticence to express emotions didn't mean that she lacked them?

'It is for Marnie's sake that I offer my assistance, so do not disdain her feelings.'

The statement held a barely contained warning. Nikos, though, knew he had no option *but* to help. It was a promise he had made to Marnie and he would never break it.

Arthur dragged a hand through his hair, his eyes skidding about the room. 'There has to be a way…'

'Yes. There is. *I'm* it. You know I have the money. A single phone call would remove this worry from your life.'

'You have the money?' Arthur spat, his eyes glistening with dark rage. '*You.* A boy I all but dismissed as—' He had the wisdom to cut the sentence off.

'Yes?' Nikos demanded through bared teeth.

'Worthless.' Arthur spat the word with satisfaction.

Nikos stood, his powerful stride taking him to the window. He looked down on Libby's garden and imagined Marnie there. His will strengthened. The papers he'd had couriered to him that morning were heavy in his pocket, begging for attention.

'You were wrong.' He turned, his eyes pinning Arthur where he sat. 'Do you want my help or not?'

A long silence clouded them. Nikos studied his opponent—there was no mistaking the adversarial nature of their relationship in that moment. With no one else to witness their interaction both men had dropped their masks of civility.

'I offer it to you with only one condition.'

Arthur snorted. 'I knew it was too good to be true.'

'Perhaps.' Nikos nodded, knowing for certain now the only way he could make sure Marnie was well-looked-after for the rest of her life. 'But it is your only chance to salvage something of your pride, so I suggest you listen.'

'The gloves are off, eh?' Arthur snapped, but there was weariness in his defiance.

'If the gloves were off you would know about it,' Nikos contradicted. 'The terms of my helping you are to stay between us. Marnie need never know what we have discussed here. Understood?'

Was it any wonder that, hours later, surrounded by formally dressed party guests, Arthur Kenington stayed as far from Nikos as possible? His concessions that afternoon had been hard-fought and potentially confidence-destroying. Evidently he found the idea of celebrating his birthday with his son-in-law impossible to contemplate.

Nikos didn't mind. In fact he barely noticed. Making Arthur eat crow had offered him no satisfaction, and yet he'd thought about the moment for years. How odd that once he'd had the chance to make the man beg for help he'd skated over it and provided assistance on a silver platter instead.

He considered the matter with Arthur closed. He didn't intend to think of it again save for one salient point that would require delicate handling. Would Marnie be angry when she discovered the exact nature of his help? Would she resent what he'd done?

His entire focus shifted to her. He watched her speaking to her parents' friends with the effortless grace that had first captivated his attention. Holding a glass of Scotch cradled in the palm of his hand, he felt the full force of that long-ago afternoon swarm through him.

He had come to Kenington Hall reluctantly. Spending time with Anderson and Libby had tended to leave him feeling like a third wheel, and yet Anderson had been so welcoming to him. He had been the one guy at school who *hadn't* seen Nikos as an outsider, and Nikos had repaid his friendship with unswerving loyalty. So when Anderson had asked Nikos to tag along he'd put aside his own reticence and travelled to the estate of one of England's noble families.

And he'd met Marnie.

She'd been seventeen and utterly breathtaking.

'Don't go near the horses. They're in a foul mood today!'

She had laughed as she'd torn past him, her long hair flowing behind her, the horse moving too quickly to catch more than a passing glimpse. Yet she'd reminded him of a sort of young Boadicea. Beautiful and strong, striking and confident, full of life and vitality.

Had he loved her from that moment? He'd certainly been fascinated.

'Hi.'

Her voice came to him now as if from a long way away. He lifted his head, capturing her in his gaze. But that moment was still around him and before he could question the wisdom of it he smiled at her as though they were back in that time, just Nikos and Marnie, without all the subsequent heartbreak.

She felt the purity of his look and it rang through her,

but she'd been worrying all afternoon and the habit was hard to break. 'Did you speak to him?'

He nodded, his stubborn smile still on his features.

Her hair had caught the sunshine as she'd gone past him that day. It had been like gold. He reached for it now and flicked the ends, bringing his body close to hers. She smelled good. Like apples and desire.

'And…?' Her eyes skimmed his, but her breath was coming fast and hard, making her breasts lift and fall.

'And what?' he prompted, wrapping his arms around her waist.

The band was playing a slow jazz song, the singer crooning gently into the elegant space. The formal dining room was large, and it had been converted into a ballroom for the purpose of tonight. Enormous flower arrangements punctuated the walls at regular intervals.

'Did you…?' She looked around, conscious of their surroundings.

'Yes?' he drawled, though he knew where she was going.

'Did you fix it?'

'Well, I couldn't transfer a hundred million pounds to your father in one afternoon,' he murmured sardonically, 'but, yes, *agape*. He has agreed to accept my help.'

She let out a whoosh of relief and he studied her features thoughtfully.

'You thought he might refuse? Even now?'

She shrugged, her shoulders slim and pale. 'I don't know. Like I said, he's stubborn.'

'You don't need to worry about it any more,' he said gently.

'I know.' She smiled up at him. 'Am I allowed to thank you now?'

'No.' He drew her closer, so that she could feel the strength of his body.

'Why not?'

'My helping him was entirely self-serving. You don't owe me thanks.'

She rested her cheek against his chest, listening to the beating of his strong heart. 'Was he grateful?' she asked instead, changing tack slightly.

His laugh was quiet but she felt it rumble through him. 'He was incensed.'

She grimaced. 'It wouldn't have been easy for him to face you, knowing what a mess his interests are in.'

'No,' Nikos conceded, without feeling the need to point out that Arthur only had himself to blame.

'I don't care.' She looked up at him. 'I'm going to thank you, anyway. How can I not?'

He stared down at her familiar face and the past blurred with the present. 'Fine. Then I can tell you how I wish you to express your gratitude.'

'Yes?' she murmured, her stomach swirling.

'For this night let's not speak about your family. Nor our past. We have spent a month retracing it and I wonder if we'll ever understand one another. Tonight I just want to dance with my wife. To kiss her. To feel her body. To be here with her and not think about the reasons we married. Deal?'

Hope blew open inside her. Surely that spoke of wanting a fresh start—of believing they were worthy of one. She looked at him for a long moment and knew exactly what it was that danced with hope.

Love.

Love for *him*.

Despite everything he'd done to get her into his life, she felt fierce love burst through her. It was not born of gratitude. Nor circumstances. It was the same love she'd always felt for him, only stronger—because it had been scorched by life, loss and disappointment and still it was there.

She stood up on tiptoe and pressed her lips lightly to his. 'Deal.'

The next song was another indistinct jazz tune. The singer's voice was low and husky and they danced slowly, in the middle of the crowd but aware only of each other. Marnie breathed in time with him, her eyes whispering shut, every fibre of her being in sync with her husband. So that when he stopped dancing and dropped his arms to his sides, capturing one of her hands in the process, and began to move towards the large glass doors, Marnie went with him without question.

'Do you know what I was thinking about today?' he asked as they emerged to see the moon casting a silver string from the inky sky above.

'Other than the significant hit your finances are about to take?' she offered with a teasing smile.

'Other than that.' He guided her along the terrace towards a small courtyard he'd seen earlier that day.

'What?'

'I was remembering the first time I met you.'

Marnie's heart was thunder; Nikos was lightning.

'Yes…?' Her voice was a husk.

He moved towards a balustrade, reclining against it with an expression that Marnie couldn't fathom.

'Being back here with you makes it feel like yesterday.'

And yet it wasn't. It was far in the past, with no way of recapturing that time. They could only exist in the moment. What they were now had to sustain them. The past would never be enough.

'I thought we weren't going to talk about our history,' she said with an uncertain smile.

'You're right.'

Marnie closed the distance between them as though a magnetic field was drawing her to him. She stood in front of him, the moon dancing across her face, a small smile on her lips.

'So let's talk about now.' She dared herself to be brave. To look at him with all her hope and want. 'Do you still think that we're just about sex?'

'And revenge,' he murmured, but an answering smile was playing about his lips and it surged her sense of hope higher.

'Of course.' She copied his expression, her look droll. 'Well, if it's meaningless sex you're after, that's fine by me.'

His laugh was warm butter on her frazzled nerves. 'I'm glad to hear it, Mrs Kyriazis.'

His fingers traced the bare skin of her arms and she shivered involuntarily. Anticipation trembled inside her. He caught her hand in his and together they walked. Was he leading her? Or the other way around? Marnie couldn't have said.

They went to the room that had been hers as a child. In the distance, the sounds of merriment could be heard. Wine glasses chinking, music, conversation. But it was all far away from where they were. Their world was their own, their breathing and needs the only noise.

She slipped into the room ahead of him, turning around in time to see him click the door shut and press the ancient lock down. His hands were lifting to his tie, loosening it in one movement so that it hung around his neck, a stunning black contrast to the sharp whiteness of his shirt.

Marnie reached for the zip on her dress, tucked under her arm, but a simple shake of Nikos's head stilled her.

'Let me,' he murmured, stalking towards her with a look she couldn't quite understand.

His face was set in a mask of *something*, and that something made her heart hammer in her chest.

'Let me,' he repeated, though she'd offered no opposition. Was he asking for something else? The air felt heavy with unuttered words, but perhaps they were all inside her.

She swallowed, the fragile column of her neck shifting with the movement. His fingers at her side were gentle, pulling at the zip so that she felt the slow whisper of cool air against her flesh. Goose bumps rioted across her and she drew in a sharp breath as he lowered the dress with a reverence she hadn't imagined possible. Standing before him in just a flimsy pair of knickers and heels, she was trembling—almost as though they were about to make love for the first time.

It was ridiculous. She forced a laugh to break the mood; it didn't work.

'Something amusing?' he queried, sliding his hands beneath the elastic of her underpants and cupping her rear.

It jolted her into a state of hyperawareness. She shook her head but his lips were on hers, stalling any further movement.

It was a slow kiss—a kiss that deepened as his hands roamed her body, a kiss he didn't break even as he removed his hands to strip his own clothes away. He stepped out of his shoes, guiding Marnie towards the bed, all small movements, urgent movements, designed to bring them together as quickly as possible.

They'd kissed in her room before, but they had been different people then. He full of hope and certainty and she so willing to surrender herself to the feelings they shared.

He pushed the past away. It had haunted him long enough.

He was making love to his *wife*—not a figment of his memories. She was a red-blooded woman and she wanted him *now*.

His hands glided over her body, feeling every square inch, paving a way for his mouth to follow. His fingers pulled at her nipples while his lips teased the delicate flesh beneath her breasts, breathing warm air and making her back arch with desperate need. He dragged his mouth higher, running his teeth over her décolletage and then meeting her mouth once more.

There was so much he didn't understand about them—about himself. So much he would say if he knew how to find the words. Instead he kissed her with all the confusion he had become, the contradictions that now filled him.

'Nikos…' She groaned.

Did she understand?

Was this her way of telling him that she, too, was ready to let the past go? To lay those ghosts to rest once and for all?

'Please…'

A soft whisper. A sound of need that he would meet again and again for the rest of his life if he had the opportunity.

He entered her gently but she lifted herself higher, taking him deep and groaning as their bodies were unified once more.

Transfixed, he watched as she rode her first wave, her body quickly adjusting to his possession and welcoming him with giddy delight. He watched her fly high into the peaks of pleasure, so beautiful against this bed from her childhood.

And then he was joining her, his body meeting her questions, taking them, answering them, and cresting with her. Her fingers sought his and laced through them. He lifted their arms above her head, kissing away the pleasure-soaked moans that were becoming louder and more insistent. He absorbed them, but he was an echo chamber for them, for those same cries were deep inside him, too.

He felt her slowly quieten, and her body gradually stopped its fevered trembling so that only the sound of her husky breathing was left. He rolled onto the bed, bringing her with him, cradling her head against his chest. And he stayed like that, holding her, not wanting to speak—finding that he had nothing to say in any event—until her continued silence caused him to realise that she had fallen asleep.

He shifted a little so that he could look at her.

And guilt shot a hole in his heart.

It was Marnie—the Marnie he'd once loved and the Marnie he'd married. How could he think the past didn't matter? The past was a part of them. Her rejection had turned him into who he was. It had happened, but it was over with.

She was *his* Marnie.

His wife, his lover. Just Marnie.

Understanding was chased by bitter recrimination, as though he was waking from the depths of a nightmare.

His eyes slammed shut as acid filled his mouth. Because he'd *forced* her to marry him. He'd taken away any choice in the matter, skilfully applying just the right pressure to ensure she had no way of saying no.

And she'd risen to the challenge. She'd done what he'd asked of her. For her father? Or had there been a part of her that had wanted to see whatever it was they had been through to the bitter end?

The end.

He hadn't thought that far ahead. He lifted his finger and traced a line down her arm. In her sleep she smiled. It was a beautiful smile but it might as well have been a spoken accusation.

What the hell had he done? And why?

He lay there for hours, his mind spinning over the past, his body refusing to move from the closeness of hers. But eventually, somewhere after midnight, he gave up on sleep and shifted from the bed, taking care not to wake her. He dressed in a pair of boxers and a loose shirt before stepping quietly from the bedroom.

The house was in darkness, save for a few lamps placed through the hallway.

In the kitchen, midway through making coffee, he heard a noise and looked towards the door.

Whether Nikos or Anne Kenington was more surprised would have been difficult to say with certainty. Nikos flicked a glance at his wristwatch. Despite the lateness of the hour Anne was still wearing the same dress she'd been in at the party.

'Late night?' he murmured, inserting a pod into the machine.

Anne's smile was tight. 'And for you?'

He shrugged. 'I couldn't sleep.'

Anne expelled a sigh that could only be described as disapproving and moved farther into the kitchen. Closer, Nikos caught the smell of alcohol on her breath and realised her eyes were a little unfocussed.

'You're leaving tomorrow?' she asked.

He nodded. A shorter visit had seemed like a good idea, and nothing he'd seen since arriving had changed his mind. Except Marnie's smile. Out of nowhere he saw her as she'd been in the apple orchard, the sun glinting on her hair, a trickle of sugary fruit juice dribbling down her face, and his gut kicked. If anything, it served as vindication for how he'd handled Arthur's affairs. Her happiness here was no reason to remain longer.

'Such a short trip,' Anne murmured as she walked to the fridge and pulled out a bottle of wine.

Nikos watched as she reached into the cupboard and frowned, running her hands over an empty shelf before reaching lower and pulling out a Royal Doulton teacup. She sloshed Chardonnay into it, then placed the bottle on the bench.

'I'd thought you might be here a few days at least.'

His gaze was narrowed. 'Would you have liked us to stay longer?'

Her eyes met his and for a very brief moment he felt a surge of recognition. He'd adored Libby. She had been different from Marnie, but a beautiful person, and she'd faced her illness with such strength and humour. He saw that same resilience in Anne's eyes—and it surprised him to realise that they must have other similarities, too.

'I suppose not.' She laughed—a brittle sound that made him sad for her.

'Why?' he prompted, pulling his coffee cup from the machine and holding it in one hand.

'You're bad for my husband's blood pressure.'

Nikos laughed with true mirth. 'Am I?'

'He was in quite a mood this afternoon. Some birthday present…'

Curious, Nikos nodded. 'Did he tell you what we discussed?'

Anne's face was pinched. 'He gave me an indication,' she responded with cold civility. 'I suppose you think I should thank you?'

Another moment he'd thought he would relish. He shook his head, though, brushing her words away. 'It was no hardship for me to intervene.'

'I'm surprised you bothered,' she said quietly, imbibing more of her wine.

He shrugged. 'For Marnie…'

He let the rest of the sentence hang in the air, knowing he couldn't speak the bald-faced lie now. After all, it had all been for his own selfish gratification. None of this was really for his wife, was it?

'She loves you,' Anne said, her body so still she might have been carved from stone. 'She always has.'

He heard the words without allowing them to find any

credibility within him. 'She loved me six years ago, when you forced her to end it.'

Anne didn't visibly react. It was as though the past was a ribbon, pulling her backwards. 'She was miserable afterwards. I doubt she ever forgave us.'

It was a strange sense; he was both hot and cold. He didn't want to think of how Marnie had felt. He'd been so furious with her, so concerned with his own hurts, he'd never really given her situation any thought. She'd told him she'd been angry, though. Furious, she'd said. Had her fury matched his? It couldn't have or she would have held their course.

'She moved on,' he said quietly. 'Until recently.'

'But she didn't.'

Anne's eyes were darkened by guilt. She pushed up from the bench and strode a little way across the kitchen, then froze once more—a statue in the room.

'She continued to live and breathe, but that's not the same as moving on. She thought I didn't notice her reading about you in the papers. That I didn't catch her looking at photos of you.' She flicked her head over her shoulder, pinning him with a glance that spoke of true concern. 'She was so careful, but I saw the way she missed you. The way she seemed to wither for a long time. It was almost like losing two daughters.'

Disgust, anger and guilt at the way they had all failed Marnie gnawed through him.

Anne sipped her wine and moved back to her original spot, opposite Nikos. 'We introduced her to some lovely young men—'

'*Suitable* men?' he interjected, with a cynical strength to his words. But Anne's statement was slicing through him. The idea of Marnie having pined for him was one he couldn't contemplate.

'Yes, suitable men. Nice men.' She closed her eyes.

'She never mentioned your name, but I always knew you to be the reason it didn't work out. She never got over you.'

Nikos sipped his coffee but his mind was spinning back over their conversation in his office, when he'd first suggested they marry. She'd been so arctic. So cold!

But wasn't that Marnie's defence mechanism? Wasn't that how she behaved when her emotions were rioting all over the place? And her being a virgin? Was that simply because she'd never found someone who made her body tremble as it did for him? Had she chosen not to get serious with another guy because she still wanted *him*?

'I believed we were doing the right thing.' Anne's smile was tight. 'After Libby, we just wanted Marnie to be safe.'

'You thought I was somehow *unsafe*?' he barked, anger and frustration and impotence to change the past ravaging his temper.

'You *aren't* safe,' she responded sharply. 'The way she feels about you is a recipe for disaster.'

Marnie didn't still love him, did she? How could she after what he'd put her through? She might have loved him a year ago…even two months ago. But the way he'd burst back into her life had been the one thing that must have ruined any love between them.

He closed his eyes briefly.

Anne continued speaking, but she wasn't particularly focussed on her son-in-law. 'You must hate us. I know Marnie did for a long time. But I *love* her, Nikos. Everything I've done has been because I love her.'

'Yet you sought to control her life? You told her you would disinherit her if she didn't leave me?'

Anne winced as though he'd slapped her. 'Yes. Well, Arthur did…' A whisper. A hollow, tormented, grief-soaked admission. 'At the time I told myself that she must have known we were right. She broke up with you. And Marnie knew her own head and heart. If she'd *really* loved you, I told myself, she would have fought harder.'

Nikos felt a familiar sentiment echo within him.

'But she couldn't. We were holding on by a thread and Marnie knew that.'

'And what about Marnie?' he asked with dark anger, though he couldn't have said if it was directed at Anne, Arthur or himself.

'She was *Marnie*,' Anne said finally, drinking more wine with a small shrug. 'Determined to act as though everything was fine even if it was almost killing her.'

Nikos angled his head away, his dark eyes resting on their reflections in the window. Anne appeared smaller there, shrunken. Surprised, he looked at her and realised that the changes had taken place in real time—he just hadn't noticed them. She was smaller, wizened, stressed.

'How could you let her go through this?' he muttered, but his blame and recriminations were focussed on himself.

Anne pinned him with eyes that reminded him once more of Libby. 'Libby was such an easy child—so like me. I just understood her. But with Marnie… She's a puzzle I can't fathom.'

Nikos rubbed a hand across his jaw. 'Marnie is all that is good in the world,' he said finally. 'Often to her own detriment. She wants the best for those she loves, even when it means sacrificing her own happiness.'

Guilt over their marriage was a knife, deep in his gut.

'Yes!' Anne expelled an angry sigh. 'I love that girl, Nikos, but I don't always know *how* to love her. I suppose that sounds tremendously strange to you—she's my child, after all.'

His smile was thin. For Anne's words had lodged deep in his mind and begun to unravel with condemnation and acceptance. He had loved Marnie once, too, but never in the way she'd needed to be loved. His faults were on a par with Anne and Arthur Kenington's.

CHAPTER ELEVEN

MARNIE STOOD UNSTEADILY as the plane pitched yet again, rolled mercilessly by the thick cotton wool clouds that had clogged the entire journey from London to Athens.

Nikos, in the middle of a newspaper article, lifted his gaze curiously. He had been distracted for the entire flight, and he seemed almost to be rousing himself from a long way away now.

'Travel sickness,' she explained, moving quickly away from him towards the back of the plane.

She burst into the toilet, relieved to have made it just a second before losing the entire contents of her stomach. Her brow broke out in sweat and still she heaved, her whole body quivering with the exertion.

She moaned as the taste of metal filled her mouth and finally, spent, straightened. The mirror showed how unwell she'd been: the face that stared back at her was bright red, sweaty, and her eyes were slightly bloodshot in the corners.

She flushed the toilet and ran the cold water, washing her hands and splashing water over her face, enjoying the relief of the ice-cold liquid.

As a child she'd been prone to travel sickness. Even a short journey had brought on a spell of nausea. But it had been a long time since she'd felt it. Years. In fact the last time she'd been sick she'd been ten or eleven.

But what else could it be?

Marnie froze midway through patting her cheeks with a plush hand towel. Mentally she counted back the days to their wedding, her mind moving with an alacrity she wouldn't have thought it capable of a moment ago, while doubled over an aeroplane toilet.

They'd been married just over a month and they'd made love on their wedding night. And since that time a certain something had been glaringly absent.

She'd started the pill in plenty of time for it to have been effective. So what did that mean? Had going on birth control simply changed her normal cycle? Was that it? Or was she pregnant with Nikos's baby? Because what she was feeling felt altogether different, and a little terrifying.

The idea was a tiny seed she couldn't shake. It put roots down through her mind, so that by the time she returned to her seat, looking much more like her normal self, she was almost certain that she was indeed pregnant.

She'd need to do a test to be sure, but there was no room in her mind for doubt.

She barely spoke for the rest of the flight, and she was too caught up in her own imaginings to notice that Nikos was similarly silent. Brooding, even.

Athens was cool but humid when they landed; the clouds that had made their flight so bumpy were thick in the air, making the ground steam.

'I have some business to take care of,' Nikos murmured once they'd disembarked. His Ferrari was waiting on the Tarmac. 'I will need to go straight to my office once we're home.'

Marnie, secretly glad for this reprieve, time to ascertain whether or not she was in fact pregnant, nodded. 'Okay.'

It was all Marnie could do not to tell him of her suspicions as he drove the now familiar roads to his mansion.

But she wouldn't do that. Not until she knew for sure that there was a baby.

It would be a surprise—a shock, really.

But it didn't necessarily follow that it would be a nightmare, did it?

'A baby between us would never be magical and wonderful. It is the very last thing I would want.'

The words circled her mind.

She waited until he'd left, and then for Eléni to arrive, and somehow was casually able to ask for a ride to the markets to pick up some groceries.

The whole way there, making halting chitchat with Eléni, Marnie wondered what it would mean if she was actually, truly pregnant.

She paid for the groceries, stuffing the pregnancy test into her handbag rather than stowing it with the other shopping, and listened to Eléni the whole way home.

Finally she removed herself to her room to find out, once and for all, if her suspicions were right.

The test showed exactly what she had known it would.

Two bright blue lines.

She was pregnant.

With Nikos's baby.

Elation danced deep in her being. She felt its unmistakable warmth zing through her and she treasured it—because she knew that it would not last long. Complications would surely arise soon enough and take away the pleasure she felt.

For it was an incontrovertible truth that no matter what she chose to do she would be a part of Nikos's life for ever. And he of hers.

Where was her despair at that prospect? Her concern?

She looked into her heart and saw nothing—just joy.

Tears ran down her cheeks and for the first time in her

life they were happy tears. Tears that warmed her and blessed her and made her feel as if she wanted to shout her euphoria from the rooftops. It was not a simple joy—there would be complications—but they paled in comparison to the happiness that shone before her.

She needed to tell him—but not on the phone. She would wait until he returned and leave him in no doubt as to how pleased she was with this turn of events. Even though she knew they had broken his cardinal rule…

The minutes of the day seemed to gang up on her, deciding that they'd like to drag their way mutinously towards the hour of Nikos's arrival gleefully slowly rather than with the alacrity she craved.

Just wondering when you'll be home?

She sent the message, her impatience burning through her, fear threatening to take hold of her.

Not for a while. N.

Well, he'd be home eventually, and then she'd just have to put her hope in his hands and pray he didn't crush it.

The first sign that there was a problem was that Nikos didn't drive himself home. A luxurious limousine pulled up out at the front and Marnie, hovering in her office with its view of the driveway, wondered briefly if they had unexpected company.

When Nikos emerged from the back his large frame seemed different. Slightly unsteady. He stood for a moment, a hand braced on the roof of the car, his eyes scanning the front of his house. Why did he look so grim? Had something happened?

Concerned, she moved quickly through the house, reaching the front door at the same time he did. She heard his keys drop to the ground outside and pulled the door inwards, her expression perplexed.

Until she smelled the Scotch and realised that her husband—the father of her tiny, tiny baby—had obviously been drinking. Heavily.

'Nik…?' she said with disbelief, holding the door wide and letting him in.

Marnie had never seen him anything other than in complete control. She was struggling to make sense of what might have happened in the hours since they'd returned from London to lead him to be in this state.

'My wife,' he said, as though it brought him little pleasure.

Confusion thick in her mind, she waited for him to move deeper into the house so she could close the door. 'Have you been out?'

'No,' he muttered. 'I have been in my office.'

Unconsciously, she moved a hand to her stomach. 'Drinking?'

He expelled an angry breath. 'Apparently.'

Marnie nodded, but he still wasn't making sense. The uncharacteristic act jarred with everything she knew about this man. He was a disciplined control freak.

Out of nowhere old jealousies and suspicions erupted. 'Alone?'

His eyes narrowed, but he nodded.

'Why?' she asked finally, putting a hand on his elbow in order to guide him towards the kitchen.

But he pulled away, walking determinedly ahead of her, his physical ability apparently not as affected as she'd first thought.

She walked behind him, and once in the kitchen moved to the fridge. As if on autopilot, she pulled out the ingredients for a toasted cheese sandwich, her eyes flicking to him every few moments. And he stared at her. He stared at her with an intensity that filled her body with fire and flame even as she was laced with confusion and anxiety.

So telling him about the baby wasn't going to happen, she admitted to herself. At least not until the following day, when he might be in a headspace to comprehend what she was saying.

'*Why*, Marnie?' He repeated her question in a tone that was so like the way he'd spoken in the past it made her chest heavy; his words seemed to ring with disdain and dislike.

She tried not to let it fill her heart but it was there. Doubt. Hurt. Aching sadness.

'What's wrong?' she said finally. 'Has something happened?'

He reached into his pocket and pulled out an envelope. 'Your mother believes you've spent the last six years pining for me. That you have loved me this whole time.'

Marnie started, her eyes flying to his involuntarily. Her mouth was dry. 'I…I don't understand why that matters. What my mother says…how I felt. What difference does it make right now to this marriage?'

He spoke slowly, his tone emphatic. 'Did you stay single and celibate because you love me?'

Marnie's heart dropped.

She spun away from him but Nikos raised his voice.

'Damn it, Marnie. You broke up with me. You walked away from us.'

'I know,' she whispered, tears springing to her eyes. The happiness of the last twenty-four hours was being swallowed by old hurts. 'I thought we agreed we wouldn't talk about the past any more?'

He slammed his palm against the benchtop. 'Why didn't you come back? Why didn't you call me when you realised you were still in love with me?'

'You'd moved on,' she said simply. 'And nothing had changed for me.'

'You were so emphatic when you ended it. You convinced me you didn't care for me, that you had never been serious. You completely echoed your father's feelings about me and men of my *upbringing*.' He spat the word like a curse.

She recoiled as though he'd slapped her. 'I *had* to do that! You wouldn't have accepted it unless I made sure you truly believed it was over.' She shook her head and no longer bothered to check the tears that stung her eyes. 'I hated saying those things to you when it was the opposite of how I felt.'

He was not his usual self, but even on a bad day and after a fair measure of Scotch Nikos was better than anyone at debating and reasoning.

He honed his thoughts quickly back to the point at hand. 'You admit you've loved me this whole time?'

Marnie froze, her only movement the rapid rise and fall of her chest as she tried to draw breath into her lungs. She felt that she'd been caught—not in a lie so much as in the truth.

'I would never have done this if I'd known,' he said after a beat of silence had passed—one he took for her acquiescence.

'Done what?' She didn't look at him. Her voice was a whisper into the room.

'This marriage…'

Her heart fell as if from a great height. It was pulverised at her feet, a tangling mass of heaving hopes.

'It was the worst kind of wrong to use you like this.'

She couldn't stifle her sob. 'Is that what you were doing?' She forced herself to look at him—and then wished she hadn't when the intensity of his expression left her short of breath.

He spoke with a cold detachment that was so much worse than the heat of an argument. 'I forced you to marry me. Just as your parents forced you to leave me. I am no better than them. Hell, I consider my crimes to be considerably greater.'

He pushed the back of the envelope open and lifted a piece of paper out. One page. When he handed it to her it was still warm from having been nestled close to his chest all afternoon.

'But at least I can atone for my sins.'

'What's this?' she asked, even as her eyes dropped to the page.

'*Petition for Divorce*' was typed neatly across the top, and as she skimmed lower she saw her name written beside Nikos's. He'd already signed his name. A masculine scrawl of hard intent.

Marnie was still. So still. Briefly she wondered if she might pass out. She felt hot and cold, as she'd done on the flight. She dropped the page and moved backwards until her bottom connected with the bench. She stayed there, glad for the support. Her head was spinning.

'Divorce?'

'I was wrong.' The words were saturated with bleak despair. He was begging her to understand. 'I regret everything I said to you that day in my office. I heard your father was going bankrupt and this idea came to me. I acted on it before I could realise what a stupid mistake it was. I need to undo it.'

She stared at him in shock. 'You can't simply *undo* a marriage. You can't undo what we are!'

'This piece of paper would suggest otherwise,' he said, with a factual determination that left her cold.

'Nikos!' His name was a plea. She looked at the paper. 'Do you want me to leave?'

'I don't want you to stay,' he said thickly. 'Not like this.'

Marnie dropped her head forward. Tears splashed out of her eyes.

'I've had the pre-nuptial agreement voided,' he murmured. 'And you need never worry that your father's finances will be in trouble—'

He thought of the other provisions he'd had enabled, but dismissed the need to discuss them at that point. Actually, he doubted he had the mental wherewithal in that moment to do justice to any of the financial arrangements he'd put in place.

'Listen to me,' she interrupted, her voice unsteady, her tone showing urgency. 'My father has nothing to do with this.'

'He *is* why we married.'

But it was almost a question, a demand for information.

His eyes locked to hers in a way that stole Marnie's breath. It was time to tell him the truth. She didn't believe she'd married for love necessarily, and yet hadn't it always been there? Even when she was furious, wasn't it because she loved him so much and felt so hurt by his actions?

But at that moment her courage was thin on the ground. She tried a different approach, desperately needing to understand what was going on.

'Why don't you tell me what's happened? Last night was fine. Last night was amazing. We danced and spoke as though…as though…we were making progress,' she finished lamely. 'We made love,' she said—an anguished reminder of the beautiful way he'd taken her. It *had* been making love—not just sex, but perfect, intimate love.

'You need to leave me,' he said quietly, taking a step backwards. 'Let me be as clear tonight as you were six years ago, when you ended things the first time. For both our sakes, please leave. Our marriage was a mistake. I should have known better than to even contemplate it.

Now you must go. It is over between us and you should be grateful for that.'

She watched as he strode out of the kitchen in what she considered to be the middle of their argument, and was torn between chasing after him and doing just as he'd said. How easy it would be to numbly pack a suitcase and go— to leave this minefield for the peace of solitude.

Only what followed wouldn't be easy. Leaving him once had hurt like hell and she'd never recovered. And the way she'd felt then was a fraction of what she felt now. She'd lived with him, and beyond that she'd committed her full self to this man and their marriage.

But could she keep trying to make their marriage work if he didn't even *want* the marriage any more? She stared at the piece of paper, anger building brick by brick inside her.

When had her mother and her husband had this *tête-à-tête*? And if Anne knew how badly Marnie had longed for Nikos why hadn't she talked to Marnie about it? Why hadn't she taken back the edict that had led to Marnie ruining her relationship with the only man she'd ever loved?

She caught a scream in her mouth; just a muted sound of frustration erupted into the silent kitchen. She had been pulled in a thousand directions by those she most cared about and now fury was building within her.

She stormed across the room, her feet planted heavily on the tiles, until she reached the sliding glass doors. She pushed them open and went outside. At the pool, she ripped her dress over her head, then leapt in. The water was a balm to her fraught senses and it absorbed the stinging, angry tears that were running freely down her cheeks.

Divorce?

After a month?

When she was pregnant with his baby?

And completely in love with him?

And he loved *her*, didn't he? She was almost sure of it. So why tell her to leave, then? None of it made sense.

But she wasn't going to let history repeat itself. She loved him more than ever before, and that meant staying to fight—not running away.

When Nikos awoke the next morning it was still dark and he was alone in his bed. He sat up, intent on going for his usual run, but a blinding headache shattered his temples.

And then it all came flooding back to him.

His conversation with Anne Kenington... *'I love her. I just don't know* how *to love her.'*

The divorce papers that had seemed like such an inspired idea at his lowest ebb.

Marnie's face as she'd stared at him, tears on her lashes, her slender body shaking as she comprehended his words. 'I want you to go. It is over between us.'

He squeezed his eyes shut, but that only enabled him to remember more clearly. The pain had slammed into her like a wall. Her harsh reaction to his simple solution. His belief that by divorcing her he could erase the barbarism of his behaviour.

He swore loudly and stood, ignoring the blinding pain that spiked in his brain. *Marnie.* Where was she? Had she left?

A cursory inspection of their room showed that her clothes were all in their usual spot. Relief was brief. She hadn't gone anywhere. *Had she?* He moved into their *en-suite* bathroom intent on making himself look slightly more civilised before facing the music.

It smelled of her. Lavender, violets...feminine and sweet. His gut clenched and he swore again.

He showered quickly and wrapped a towel around his waist while brushing his teeth. The toothpaste tube was empty and he tossed it carelessly in the rubbish bin. It missed. When he crouched down to retrieve it, his head complaining the whole time, something unusual caught his eye. A box.

He lifted it out and stared at it in confusion.

A pregnancy test?

That didn't make any sense.

Marnie was on the pill. But it sure as hell wasn't Eléni's. Which meant that somehow, for some reason, Marnie had had reason to believe she might be pregnant. He opened the box but it was empty. Nor was there a test in the trash.

With renewed urgency he pulled on a pair of shorts and shirt and practically ran out of the room and through the house. There were several guest rooms but they were all empty. Fear was building.

What if she *was* pregnant? Would he still be strong enough to let her go? If she chose to divorce him—hell, she might have already signed the damned papers—would he let the divorce proceed?

And what if she stayed with him because of the baby? Could he live with her knowing he'd trapped her—twice—into marriage?

He checked her office. It was empty, neat.

Then his own office—empty.

Finally, he went to the kitchen.

And there she was.

Marnie.

Sitting on the sofa, staring out at the lifting sun, her face pale, her eyes a terrifying maelstrom of feelings and fears.

What could he say to her? What right did he have to explain?

He walked quietly and then crouched in front of her, directly in Marnie's line of sight.

'Have you slept?'

She blinked her eyes at him and then looked away, over

his shoulder, focussing on the colours smudged across the sky. 'I didn't leave.'

A muscle jerked at his temple. 'I'm glad.'

Her eyes flew to his again. Confusion. Hurt. 'Why?'

She reminded him of a wounded animal. He swore under his breath and dragged a hand through his hair. He needed to reassure her. To explain. She deserved at least that much. But his own questions were burning through him.

For a man like Nikos, not knowing what to say or how to negotiate on the terms of his marriage brought with it great frustration. He was used to commanding a room. He had not doubted his ability to bring people to his way of thinking for a very long time.

Business, though, was predictable—easy for a man like Nikos. He would discover what motivated a person and exploit that to gain his own success.

Marnie was motivated by love.

Loyalty.

Affection and faithfulness.

And he didn't want her to be with him for any of those reasons but one.

'You gave me divorce papers last night.' Her eyes had an unexpected strength in them. 'Why?'

He expelled a breath. 'Isn't that obvious?'

'You don't want to be married to me,' she whispered, the words a ghost of sentiment in the large room.

'I don't want you to feel *forced* to stay married to me,' he clarified.

She nodded, her gaze refusing to meet his. If only he *had* pushed her away! She'd ended up falling as much in love with him as ever, and now it was so much worse—for she'd tasted the mind-blowing bliss that came from sharing his bed and his life.

'You were happy to give me an ultimatum at one time. What's changed?'

Did he detect the note of challenge in her voice?

His smile was lacking any true happiness. 'We are married, but you are not my wife.' He stood, his back straight, his shoulders square. 'It turns out you can't really force someone into a marriage.'

'Isn't that what's happened here?'

He shook his head. 'I believed that having you as my wife would make you mine. It doesn't work like that, though.' His expression was bleak for a moment, before hard certainty crossed it. 'You will never be able to forget the way I propositioned you, and nor will I. I look at you and see the man I have become. A man I despise.'

'You have helped my father,' she said quietly. 'I could never hate you after what you've done for him.'

'You have to release us both from this. I can't live with how I've hurt you.'

She nodded, her throat raw from unshed tears. 'You *have* hurt me,' she whispered. 'Just as I hurt you. Does that make us even now?'

He stood up, moving angrily towards the glass doors and staring out. 'You were a teenager. A *grieving* teenager. You hurt my pride and my ego and I left. I should have stayed. It takes courage to stay and fight for what you want. But I didn't like how it felt to be rejected, so I went off like a sulking child.' He thrust his hands in his pockets. 'I didn't deserve you.'

She lifted her feet onto the sofa so she could rest her chin against her knees. 'Fighting would have been pointless. You would have only upset me more than I already was. I truly believed I had no choice but to end it.'

He nodded, thinking of the pregnancy test box he'd discovered. He turned slowly, but pain was a fresh wave crashing over him. She was a contradiction of fragility and strength. Broken but resolved. Determined and disappointed.

He strode to her, a guttural sound of angst tearing from his chest. '*I* have broken whatever we used to be—not you. If you are pregnant I will support you. I will make sure you have everything you and the baby need. But I will not let you use that as a reason to stay with me.'

Shock flashed over Marnie and her skin paled to paperwhite. 'The...baby?' She swallowed. 'How did you know?' What was the point in denying it?

'I found the box in our bathroom,' he responded, so close he could touch her, but not allowing himself to do so.

She hadn't bothered to hide it because she'd thought they would have a perfect dinner together, over which she would share with him the happy news. *Happy news!* Well, at least there was still some truth in that. Thoughts of the baby filled her shattered heart with a slight antiseptic against the pain.

'Is it true?' he asked, his words anguished.

Slowly she nodded, pulling her lower lip between her teeth. 'Yes...'

'Thee mou!' He groaned, standing and running a hand over his eyes. He seemed to stand there for ever, a heaving man, his whole body showing instant rejection of the idea of their child. Just as he'd said he would.

What had she expected? That he would welcome this news?

'I am so sorry.' He groaned again, dropping his hand and pinning her with the full force of his shocked gaze.

'Sorry?' she repeated, feeling numbed now, so fresh pain wasn't capable of sinking in.

'First I trapped you with blackmail and now you must feel trapped by our baby. But you can leave. You *must* leave. A baby is no reason to continue this farce.'

She sobbed and nodded. 'I know that.'

Neither spoke for a long time. Marnie was trying to imagine a life without Nikos and all she saw was the bleakness that had been her bedfellow for these past six years.

'If I could fix this, I would,' he said.

She nodded again, resting her cheek on her knees. She had chosen to stay and fight, but so far she had done a lot of listening and no actual fighting. She tried to find the strength in her heart, but it was in ruins.

'There is something else you should know.' He spoke with a grim finality to his words. 'I could not find the words to explain last night.'

'Explain what?' she whispered, wondering at the pain in her throat.

'I have bought Kenington Hall and put it in your name.'

She lifted her head sharply, almost giving herself whiplash in the process. Everything else disappeared from her mind. 'You've *what*?'

He expelled a sigh and crouched down on his haunches so that their eyes were level. 'You love the property, and I wanted you to know it to be safe. That no matter what happened to your father, or to our marriage, you would have the security of your family home.'

She let that statement sink in. 'When did you do this?'

'When I met with your father.'

She nodded, but nothing was making sense. 'Were you planning to divorce me even then? Was it to be my consolation prize?' Grief lanced her. 'What did I do wrong? I thought we were making this work…'

'You did nothing wrong, Marnie, except fall in love with an arrogant, selfish bastard like me.' He dropped his head into his hands. 'I didn't buy the house because I wanted to leave you. I bought it because I wanted you to understand that you have options. That you and your family are safe. Even before speaking with your mother I knew I had to give you back your freedom before I could even hope to make amends.'

'I have never considered myself to lack freedom,' she inserted seriously, her eyes sparkling, her mind moving quickly. 'So you *did* want to make this marriage a real one?'

A muscle jerked in his jaw. 'I cannot say if I ever thought of it in those terms.'

He dared to lift a hand and touch her soft hair. Fear at what he was on the brink of losing was all around him—a pit of despair he knew would swallow him if he didn't explain himself better than he was doing now.

'I knew only that I wanted you to look at me with the love you once felt. That I wanted to be able to smile at you with the love that is in *here*.' He tapped his hand against his chest.

Marnie made a sound of disbelief.

'You *should* leave me. You can go and it will not change how I feel about you. Your father is out of debt. Kenington Hall is safe in your hands. And I will be as involved as you allow me to be in our child's life. You must decide what will make you happy.'

Happy? That felt so far away.

She stood up, something snapping inside her. She could no longer sit still as though this were a normal discussion. Her temper flared. She spun round, her hands on her hips, her face showing the full extent of her rage. There was nothing remotely cold about her now. She was all feelings and flame.

'You're such an *idiot*!' she shouted at the top of her lungs. 'I have *always* loved you! Always! Even when I thought I was over you, how could I be? I married you! And—newsflash!—I didn't *have* to! Even to save my father's financial situation. I would only ever have married one man on earth. *You*. Only you.'

She wrapped her arms around herself.

'You were right before, when you said that you should have stayed and fought for what we were. I don't think it would have made a difference, but it's what you *do* when you're in love with someone. You don't bloody walk away. I'm not going to walk away now, because I love you—even when you're almost impossible to comprehend.'

He stared at her, but his expression was blank, as though her words were a problem he had to decode.

'I was furious with you when we got married. *Livid.* What a stupid thing you did, blackmailing me like this! But I still loved you. Every night of this marriage has been like slowly unwrapping a present, piece by piece, getting to find my way back to you—'

'I have pushed you away,' he interrupted, arguing the sense of her statement.

'Yes, you have—but you've also pulled me close. So close that I've been inside your soul. You've let me in. And you *dare* turn up with divorce papers, as though our marriage is a simple contract you can dissolve? You *dare* relegate our love to an agreement that you alone can end?'

Startled by her anger, he stood, wishing to placate her. He put an arm on her shoulder but she jerked away.

'No!' she snapped. 'I'm not finished yet.'

Her eyes held a warning and, fascinated, he was silent.

'You have been hitting me over the head with the fact that I flicked a switch and walked away from you six years ago. I didn't. I didn't flick a switch. I made the worst mistake of my life when I left you, and I'm not going to do it again.' She straightened her shoulders. 'If you want to divorce me—if you don't want me any more—then tell me that. You can make that decision. But don't tell me that leaving you is in my best interests—because I know what life is like without you and there is no life on earth that I want more than *this* life, here—right here with you.'

His breath was ragged, torn from his lungs. 'How can you feel that?' he murmured with a growing sense of wonderment. 'I have been—'

'You have been Nikos.' She cut across him, but softly, kindly, with the compassion that was always so close to her surface. 'Determined, arrogant and good.' She moved closer. 'Do you think either of us really understood what we were doing and why? You wanted to help my family. I believe that was at the heart of everything you did.'

He made a sound and shook his head, but she lifted a finger to his lips.

'Whatever motivated you to blackmail me into this marriage, I will never resent you for it. How can I? I've missed you and now I have you.' She paused, her eyes scanning his. 'I *do* have you, don't I?'

He wrapped his arms around her waist, crushing her to him. 'You have all of me, for all time.' The words were a promise against her cheek. '*All* of me. And you are the best of me.'

She shut her eyes and listened to the pounding of his heart. Her lips twitched in a smile that shone with true happiness.

Gradually Nikos pulled backwards, dropping a hand to her flat stomach. 'A baby was not on our agenda,' he said, as if just comprehending the reality of their situation.

'Apparently the baby had other ideas. I dare say it has a lot of your determination.'

He laughed. 'Let us hope that is balanced by your warmth and kindness.'

'Well, I guess we'll find out in about eight months.'

'And you are truly happy?'

'Nikos!' She laughed shakily. 'When I found out I was pregnant I wanted to shout it from the rooftops. I know it wasn't meant to be part of the plan, but it felt so *right*.'

He frowned, wondering how long she'd shouldered this secret. 'When did you first suspect?'

She smiled. 'Not until we were on the plane back to Greece.'

'And then I told you to leave me.' His face paled with remembered regrets. 'It was for *you*, Marnie. I didn't *want* you to go. You know this to be true?'

She nodded. 'I've never seen you like that.'

His smile was grim. 'I have only ever drunk to excess one other time in my life—the night your father paid me off and I took his money. Then, too, I felt like a shadow of the man I wanted to be.'

'Don't say that,' she murmured, resting her head against his chest. She stood there quietly for a moment. 'My father wouldn't have liked selling you the house...'

He breathed in her sweet fragrance and a sense of deep gratitude filled him. To think that he'd almost pushed her away for good! He would never make that mistake again. Not in his life.

'He...understood the necessity of it,' Nikos said after a moment. '*Agape mou*, I thought I would relish that moment. I had fantasised about seeing your father a broken man. I had dreamed of being in a position to throw my own success and wealth in his face and see him suffer. But at the first opportunity to do so I saw only you. I saw you and discovered that loving you meant loving *all* of you. Even your family. If you married me because you love me then you must understand that I have helped Arthur because I love you. It was not a payment for your marrying me.'

The words filled her with love and certainty—certainty that they were right where they should be. Together.

But she pulled a face of mock consideration. 'Well, it seems to me, then, that you haven't upheld your end of the deal.'

Sensing the amusement in her words, he answered in

kind. 'I suppose you're right. Is there something else I can offer instead?'

She pressed a finger to her chin and pretended to consider it. 'I can think of a few things…'

He surprised her by scooping her up and laying her down on the sofa. His mouth sought hers and he tasted her giddy delight there and answered it.

'Starting with right now?'

'I will expect the payment terms to be over a very long time,' she said, pushing at his shorts.

'Would the rest of our lives do?'

She sighed, her body firing with insatiable need for her husband. 'It just might.'

EPILOGUE

One year later

IT WAS THE ice sculpture that was the final straw.

She shook her head, torn between feeling cross and amused as she tore through the villa in search of her husband.

She found him by the pool, hands on hips, eyes staring out at the ocean. They'd been married for almost a year, and still the sight of him could stop her in her tracks. Her heart hammered roughly against her ribs, beating wildly as she approached him.

'A *swan*?' she said from just behind his shoulder, her expression one of utter disbelief. 'Seriously?'

His grin as he turned around skittled any discontent she had felt over his lavish decorations.

'It's summer,' she pointed out with a shake of her head, but her grumble was somewhat faint-hearted.

'Almost autumn.'

'Almost,' she responded archly. 'And it's as hot as Hades today. That thing's going to be iced water before anyone gets here.'

'So we will drink it!' He laughed. 'How many times does our daughter get christened?' he said, with such impeccable logic that all her objections were silenced.

'You're right.' Marnie smiled up at him, giving in to

temptation and wrapping her arms around his waist. 'And now I have another bone to pick with you.'

'Oh?' he murmured, his lips still pressed to hers.

She straightened, trying to be businesslike. 'The trust just called me to report that a rather sizeable donation has been made in Lulu's name.'

His smile lit the world on fire—starting with Marnie's heart. She was scorched with happiness.

'What else can I give you and our daughter on her christening? You will not let me buy you jewels or clothes... you insist she has all she needs. But this, I think, you *will* let me do.'

Marnie nodded, tears of happiness clogging her throat. 'But it's so much...'

'For a cause that means the world to you—and therefore to me. I still remember what you said to me, *agape mou*. That one day, through your efforts and the efforts of people like you, young girls like Libby might not get sick any more.'

He pressed a finger beneath Marnie's chin, lifting her eyes to meet his. She felt the love and commitment that underscored every decision he made.

'We have our own little girl now. How can you doubt my desire to work with you on this?'

Love coiled inside her. 'Thank you.' Her voice was husky. Emotions were too strong to contain. She lifted up on tiptoe and pressed a kiss to his lips. 'Why did we invite all these people over?'

He kissed her hungrily, his tongue exploring her mouth, his hands holding her tight against his body.

But for only a moment.

Then he lifted himself away, grinning as if he *hadn't* been shaken to the core by their molten hot connection.

'To see my ice sculpture,' he said, and laughed.

She rolled her eyes, but her mind was drifting. 'If only we had an extra hour…'

He grimaced, looking past her shoulder. 'If only we had an extra ten minutes…'

He saw their guests through the glass doors and kissed the top of her head.

'I will make you a promise,' he said in an undertone.

Marnie nodded. 'Oh, yes? I'm all ears, Mr Kyriazis.'

'Not from where I am standing.' He grinned at her, his handsome face a collection of lines and shapes that formed an inimitable image of masculinity.

Playfully, Marnie punched his upper arm. 'I believe you were making me a promise?'

'Soon we will be alone in our home again, and then I will show you just what that dress and you are making me want.'

Her pulse was lurching out of control. She lifted herself up on tiptoe again and kissed his lips, smiling as familiar sensations rocked her to her core.

'You'd better,' she said simply.

He wrapped an arm around her shoulder, pulling her to his side and knowing how right it was that they should be together. Everything in his world seemed to shine with the perfection that Marnie brought to his life.

'Your parents are here,' he murmured, looking down into the villa as Anne and Arthur Kenington made their way through the house.

Marnie took a moment to observe them, staying right where she was. Anne was her usual self—elegant and perfectly neat, despite the fact they'd come straight from the airport. Although a flight in Nikos's jet was hardly an arduous ordeal. Arthur Kenington showed the greatest change. He was dressed casually in a pale polo shirt and a pair of beige chinos. His hair was a little longer, and there were more lines on his face now—lines Marnie chose to believe were formed by happiness.

'Darling, there's a puddle forming in the foyer,' Anne said with pursed lips as she swept onto the terrace.

A breeze lifted past them, drawing with it the tang of the ocean and the sweetness of Libby's rose garden. Marnie inhaled, drawing strength from this reminder of her sister before steeling herself to enjoy the next few hours. Her parents were not perfect, but they were still her parents. And, fortunately for Marnie, despite their meddling and strong opinions she and Nikos had found their way together in the end.

'That would be the ice sculpture.' Marnie winked up at her husband, then moved towards her mother, kissing her cheek. She hugged her dad before returning to Nikos's side. 'Thanks for coming.'

'Of course.' Anne nodded. 'Where is our granddaughter?'

'She's with her uncle.' Marnie grinned. 'Her honorary uncle.'

Anderson emerged at that moment, their chubby dark-haired little girl propped on one hip.

'Nothing honourable about *him*,' Nikos teased, with a genuine smile reserved for their closest friend. 'Unlike you, Lady Heiress.'

She shook her head, her hands extended for the baby Elizabeth. But Lulu only had eyes for her father.

Marnie laughed. 'I see!' She shook her head. 'That's the way it's going to be, huh?'

'It is because I am not often here when she is awake.'

'Sure it is,' Marnie said with another laugh. 'And also because you spoil her silly. That's okay—I'm not offended.'

And she wasn't. How could she be? She had everything she'd ever wanted in life.

It was a beautiful afternoon, filled with happiness and

joy. Finally, though, after the last of the guests had left and Lulu was fast asleep, Marnie went in search of her husband.

She found him on the terrace, his eyes focussed contemplatively on the shimmering moon. It was a cool night now, and Marnie wrapped her arms around herself for warmth.

Nikos noticed—as he did everything about his wife—and shrugged out of his jacket, placing it around her slender shoulders on instinct.

'Here, *agape mou*,' he said, pulling her closer to his warmth.

'Thank you,' she murmured, inhaling his intoxicatingly masculine scent. 'Have I ever told you there was a time when I hated you calling me that?' she asked softly.

'Did you?'

'It just reminded me of what I wanted from you. What I doubted you'd ever feel for me.'

Her eyes pierced his, and for a second those thoughts and feelings were right there before her. Such pain and heartbreak! How had that ever been their story when there was now such love between them? Such joy and trust?

She blinked to clear those dark vestiges of the past.

'Did you doubt, Mrs Kyriazis? Did you really doubt?'

His eyes held hers, and in them she saw the truth that perhaps she'd always held deep in her heart. The incontrovertibility of who they were to one another.

His soft sigh breathed warmth across her temple. 'I called you that, even when we were at odds, because I needed to believe we could be that to one another again. I wanted to feel that I had the right...'

Her smile shifted her features, taking his breath away completely.

'It sounds a little like *you* were the one who doubted we'd find our way here.'

He put an arm around her waist, his fingers feathering

over her hip. 'Not for a second.' His voice was gravelly. 'I could never accept a world without you in it.'

'Even if that meant blackmailing me?' she teased, finding it almost impossible to credit the start of their marriage with the state of it now.

'Even then.' He dropped a kiss against her hair. 'Will you ever forgive me for that?'

'Forgive you? Hmm…' She pretended to think, her eyes full of love and amusement. 'I can think of one way you could make it up to me.'

He smiled softly. 'Your wish is my command. Although in this case I think it is my wish also.'

The stars shone overhead and the rose garden was bathed with magical milky moonlight. Nikos Kyriazis kissed his wife, carrying her into their now quiet home.

And it *was* a home. Not simply a house, as it had been for so long.

Now it was a collection of walls that contained their family's life, that was filled with pictures and love and the kind of warmth he had only ever dreamed possible. It was a home he shared with Marnie and Lulu, just as he shared his heart and his being with them.

A man who had never known love was now overflowing with it, and always would be.

* * * * *

THE GREEK'S FORBIDDEN PRINCESS

ANNIE WEST

For Karen, who's there through thick and thin.

Thanks, mate!

And a big thank-you to Efthalia for advising
on the Greek.

CHAPTER ONE

'*THEN KATALEVENO.*' I don't understand. Amelie paused and tried again, working to keep her teeth from chattering as the temperature dropped another degree or six. '*Kyrios Evangelos, parakalo.*' Mr Evangelos, please.

The intercom squawked into a burst of machine-gun-fast Greek. Amelie hadn't a hope of understanding. She'd already used up her handful of phrases.

Clearly the woman inside the house had no patience for foreigners. Or language skills other than Greek. Amelie had already tried French, English, German and finally even Spanish and Russian.

But why should the housekeeper, if that was who she was, speak anything other than Greek? This estate was high in the mountain spine of northern Greece. Tourists headed for the beaches of the Aegean Sea or the ancient ruins. Amelie guessed only the most adventurous foreigners headed to this isolated, beautiful region.

Adventurous or desperate.

Amelie had never had a chance to be adventurous. But a twist of fate had turned her staid, predictable world on its head. Desperate was too mild a description for her situation.

'Please. *Parakalo,*' she began, hunching her shoulders against the icy wind, but the line went dead.

Amelie stared, disbelieving, into the security camera perched above the gates. The woman had hung up! She must have seen Amelie shivering in the unseasonable icy blast.

Amelie blinked, torn between indignation and curiosity. This was a first. Never before had she been ignored—no, not ignored...rejected.

Yet even as she thought it, she knew that was wrong.

She'd been rejected by the very man she'd come here to see. Once, when it had been just her happiness in question, she'd taken his rebuff with all the grace she'd spent a lifetime learning. This time, when it was Seb's happiness, his *future* in question, Amelie refused to accept 'no'.

Her mouth settled in a way her father had called obstinate. But her father had never been pleased, no matter how she tried, or how many of the family burdens she shouldered. Besides, he was dead and gone. Like Michel, her brother, and his wife, Irini.

A giant hand gripped her insides and twisted them till they burned. The ache welled high, clogging her chest, her throat, her whole being.

But Amelie wouldn't let it conquer her. She blinked, refusing to let tears come. There'd been no time for tears since the accident for, of course, everyone relied on her to be strong. The burden might have broken her if she hadn't spent years as the anchor for her family and everyone else. For as if grief wasn't enough, the repercussions from Michel's death were…complicated.

Amelie breathed deep, determined to focus on the positive. She still had Seb.

Her glance strayed to the nondescript hire car pulled over in front of the massive gates. There was no movement inside. Seb must still be asleep. Their journey from St Galla had exhausted him.

It had exhausted her. Amelie almost lifted a hand to her aching head—too much stress and too little sleep— but she was conscious of the security camera. She was watched from inside the house she couldn't even see down its long drive.

A lifetime's training in never revealing weakness kept her arm by her side and her chin up. If Lambis Evangelos and his lackeys thought she'd meekly run away…

Her lips turned up in a mirthless smile. They had no idea what despair could do. What *she* could do.

Slowly, shoulders back and hands swinging at her sides, she strolled to the car. She didn't even flinch when the first snowflakes spattered her face.

It needed only that to put the seal on this horrible journey. The secretive trip to Athens on a friend's boat in order to avoid the paparazzi. The press had mobbed her in St Galla and they'd been forced to slip out in the dead of night. The long journey, the crowds and bustle of Athens, then the stonewalling when she'd arrived at the Evangelos Enterprises office. Then the long, exhausting drive north.

She'd come this far. She refused to return home, defeated. There was too much at stake.

Opening the back door of the car, she slid in beside Seb. Sure enough, he was sleeping, a lock of blond hair flopping over his too-pale face. He looked vulnerable, curled up with his teddy under his chin.

Amelie's heart turned over and love, fierce and fortifying, slammed into her. She shrugged out of her long coat and scooted over against him, draping it over the pair of them. He shifted, frowning in his sleep, opening his mouth as if to protest, but then subsided without so much as a whimper. Under the cashmere, Amelie wrapped her arm around him and hugged him close.

They'd hit a dead end and she was out of alternatives. She'd have to come up with another plan, but for now, she'd allow herself a tiny respite. Ten minutes' rest before she revised her plan of action. With a sigh of exhaustion she closed her eyes.

Ten minutes…

A knocking woke her. She had that awful cotton wool taste in her mouth that told her she'd actually fallen asleep in broad daylight.

Except it wasn't daylight. It was murky twilight and so chilly it was a wonder she'd slept.

Again that knocking, harder this time, and Amelie swung her head round. Through the side window she saw a dark shadow loom like a giant mountain bear. Her heart skidded against her ribs. Adrenaline pumped too hard, too fast, and she had to force down a moment's primitive, instinctive fear.

Then she woke properly, remembering their predicament. If only it was merely wildlife she had to worry about!

She slid along the back seat, carefully tucking her coat around Seb, who, remarkably, still slept. The poor kid truly was running on empty.

As she put her hand on the handle, the massive form outside retreated, allowing her to open the door.

Instantly a blast of frigid air struck. Amelie gasped then forced herself out, shutting the door quickly to keep in the relative warmth. Fat snowflakes tickled her face. She sucked in a draught of oxygen that froze her throat and made all the tiny hairs on her body rise.

Except she suspected it wasn't the cold air alone that did that. More likely it was reaction to the great, shaggy bear of a man standing just a pace away.

At least those profoundly broad shoulders blocked some of the wind. They were a perfect frame for a wickedly bold, dark face—straight black eyebrows, strong, too strong nose, high-cut cheekbones and a jaw that reminded her of the Acropolis's uncompromising angles. It didn't matter that his mouth was finely chiselled and full, for he didn't smile. His mouth was grim, a perfect match for eyes as grey and dour as the mountain looming beyond him.

No welcome. No offer of assistance.

Amelie lifted her chin, the better to see him, refusing to be intimidated by that beetling brow or the aggressive bunch of his huge hands.

Or by the unwanted punch of pure feminine response to his aura of potent masculinity.

By sheer force of will she kept her arms at her sides instead of wrapping them around her freezing body. She'd stood firm against the worst St Galla could throw at her, not least her own father. She wasn't about to fall in a heap because of a scowl.

No matter how much she wanted to turn tail and find some cosy hotel where she could curl up and be alone.

This isn't about you, Amelie.

The reminder gave her strength. Her life had always been about others. Her forays into seeking personal happiness had been disastrous.

'Kalimera.' Good day.

He didn't reply. Not by so much as a muscle twitch did his expression change, yet she had the impression that anger coiled tight within that imposing frame.

The only thing about him that moved was his hair, overlong and tousled by the whipping wind, jet black like his eyebrows, and if his expression was any indication, his heart.

How could a man so stern and unyielding make her pulse quicken and her knees go weak with excitement?

'You're blocking the gates.'

Biting back a retort she knew would win her no friends, Amelie smiled. It was the small public smile she sometimes felt she'd perfected before she could walk. The sort that wore well, no matter how tough the circumstances or how much she wished she was anywhere else.

'So I am.' Because parking here had been the only way to guarantee attention. Lambis Evangelos and his employees couldn't drive in or out with her car parked across the entrance. 'If you open the gates I'll remedy that.'

He didn't even bother to shake his head or, being Greek, to lift his chin in that supremely dismissive reverse nod that signified *no*.

Tiredness dragged at Amelie, and a building fury that she'd travelled so far, hiding from the press all the way, fearing someone would recognise them and destroy their anonymity, to be met by *this*. The blank annoyance of a man who didn't give a damn.

Perhaps this last-ditch effort was doomed to fail.

Acid swirled through her insides and the metallic taste of defeat was bitter on her tongue. Amelie felt a tremor of despair begin deep in the pit of her belly and widened her stance, staking her right to be here.

At the movement something flickered in those deep-set eyes, but he said nothing.

So be it. He might be rugged up in a massive coat but Amelie wasn't dressed for this unseasonably early snow-storm. Her clothes were chic rather than warm. The weather on the Mediterranean island of St Galla had been summery. The cool weather wouldn't begin there for another couple of months and snow was rare.

Amelie turned to open the rear car door.

'What are you doing?' His voice was deep and reso-nant. She felt it circle her ribs then burrow low, making her insides soften.

Suddenly, gloriously, anger welled, burning bright in veins turned sluggish with cold and the prospect of defeat. She would not let this man with a voice like hot whisky, so at odds with those glacial eyes, turn her inside out.

'Since a civil greeting is out of the question, I'm get-ting back in the car, where at least there's some warmth.'

'Stop.' He stretched out one arm, his big, square hand just a hairsbreadth from hers. Then, abruptly, rejecting the idea of physical contact, he let it drop.

Somehow, more than anything, that hurt.

She didn't *want* him to touch her. But that infinitesimal rejection felt like a tipping point. Amelie assured herself this foolishness was just the aftermath of a hellish time, of stress and trauma and worry.

'Why? Do you have something to say that I want to hear?' Her chin hiked up and to her amazement she caught sight of a tiny twist at the corner of that stern mouth. It was nothing like a smile, nothing so human. But it was *something*.

'You shouldn't be here.'

'This is public property. I've every right to park here while I wait to be let in.'

Those long fingers twitched at his sides and Amelie wondered on a snared breath of icy air whether he fought the impulse to shake her or move her bodily.

'There's nothing for you here.' He said it slowly, enunciating each word with a precise perfection that reminded her English wasn't his native language.

'I didn't come for myself.' Amelie kept her voice even, betraying none of the pain she repressed. She was a master at hiding emotion in public. She did it so well she wondered what it would be like to let go—to cry and complain and rail against the cruelty of fate. But that wasn't her way. She didn't know how.

One sleek eyebrow cocked high in silent interrogation.

'I've brought my nephew.'

Silence. More of that absolute, unnerving stillness. Had he trained in being impenetrable? Or just in being unfeeling?

Surely even this dour man, who'd already made it clear she wasn't welcome, had some kernel of softness for a little boy.

Slowly, as if not trusting her to dash past him and scale the huge gates, he bent and peered into the car. When he straightened his face was unchanged. Clearly little Seb's presence made no difference. They could stay here in what appeared to be a full-scale snowstorm and there'd be no offer of shelter.

Amelie bit the inside of her cheek to prevent the indignant outburst jammed in her mouth.

The sensible thing would be to admit defeat, start the car and drive back to the nearest village, looking for accommodation. She'd do that. Soon.

But her hands shook too much to drive down that winding, slick road. Infuriated, with him and herself, she hauled open the rear door and moved to get in.

Instantly a vice clamped on her shoulder. A hot vice with fingers that dug into her flesh through her thin sweater. His heat after the stinging cold surely explained the rush of energy raying out from the spot.

Amelie turned, meeting that gunmetal stare head-on.

'Don't touch me.'

'Or?' This time both jet-black eyebrows rose.

'Or I'll bring a case of assault so fast your head will spin. And, in case you think I'm bluffing, let me warn you I've reached my limit.'

'Even if it means inviting media attention?'

Because he knew—how could he not?—that she'd only made it this far by avoiding the media.

Carefully Amelie closed the door and turned fully to face him. He was so close he ate up her personal space. He was so big she'd feel crowded and intimidated if she weren't past caring.

'That's one thing about reaching the end of your options. I don't give a damn.' She smiled and this time actually felt pleasure, for she saw the shadow of doubt in his stern face. He'd thought she'd be easier to bully.

'I could call a reporter now. By nightfall we'd have a posse of them here, eager for developments.' Amelie rested her hands on her hips, enjoying the fleeting sense of power that flooded her freezing body.

Yet still he didn't take the bait.

She waited as the seconds ticked into a full minute and more. Still he didn't move or give in.

Even if she followed through and made a formal complaint, or brought in the press, she'd be the one to lose. She and Seb.

They had lost.

She'd gambled against the odds with Seb's future and failed. Now time was running out.

The enormity of it was a body slam, jarring her from head to toe. She had to stiffen her knees to stop from crumpling as she unravelled inside. All her hopes shattered and little Seb... No, she couldn't think about it now, with this man watching her like a bird of prey spying on a mouse. She needed privacy when she finally crashed.

Whiplash fast, she shoved his hand off her shoulder and moved towards the driver's door.

'Where are you going?'

Amelie didn't answer. This was probably the first time in her life she'd ignored a direct question. It should have felt liberating, but all she registered was choking misery.

She ripped open the driver's door. They couldn't stay here. If she was to get them safely back down the mountain they had to go now.

The sound of swearing stopped her. Low and soft, his rich voice turned even the tumble of foreign swear words into a stream of velvet heat.

'Just tell me what you want, Princess.'

Amelie didn't let herself flinch at his bitter use of her title. He said it as if they were strangers. Nor did she turn.

She didn't want to see the steely face of Lambis Evangelos, the man who'd shattered her dreams and now held her hopes for little Seb in his brutally hard palm.

'You.' Her throat closed so it came out as a whisper. She swallowed and tried again. 'I want you.'

CHAPTER TWO

I WANT YOU.

Hell and damnation.

Her words shouldn't have any effect.

They *didn't*. She'd just taken him by surprise. How had she managed it? Where was her retinue of officials and paparazzi?

More important—*why* did she want him?

There was nothing here for her. He'd made that plain three years ago. Besides, Amelie had pride; she wouldn't come after him again.

Lambis scowled. The past was a place he refused to visit.

'You'll need to be more specific. What do you want me for?'

Lambis stared down at her slim form as she slowly turned, her hand white-knuckled on the door, her upswept blonde hair and stunning green eyes the only colour in the scene before him. Her whole body trembled from the wintry blast she refused to acknowledge. She wore pale trousers and a matching sweater that clung elegantly and expensively to her lithe frame but did nothing to keep out the cold.

His instinct on seeing her had been to tear off his coat and wrap it around her slender shoulders. But he'd resisted. Better to kill her hopes so she left immediately than let her believe she had a chance of staying.

'Seb needs you. As you'd know if you bothered to check my messages.'

Messages he'd left unopened. Returning to St Galla for the funeral had been tougher than even he had imagined. He didn't want reminders of the tragedy and his own guilt. Or of her.

'Seb?' How could the boy possibly need him?

Amelie's mouth flattened. Her eyes had lost their brilliance. They looked opaque with pain, even though her body language was almost aggressive as she leaned into his space. That in itself was remarkable. Amelie was always poised, graceful and polite, the least aggressive person he knew.

Lambis was horrified to realise her eyes looked even more lifeless than on the day they'd buried her brother and sister-in-law. He hated that blankness.

'You haven't forgotten your godson, surely?'

As if on cue Lambis registered movement in the car. A hand palmed the rear window. A pale, tiny hand. Beside it was a sombre young face, golden hair tufted from sleep.

There was no smile of recognition. It was the numbed look of someone who didn't expect a welcome and it cut like a blade to Lambis's belly.

He hunkered beside the door, putting his face on a level with the boy's. Those big eyes regarded him, unblinking. They looked even more desolate than his aunt's, as if they'd never glowed with mischief or delight.

No four-year-old should look that way. But in the circumstances maybe it was inevitable.

Lambis forced his stiff lips into something like a smile. 'Hey, Sébastien. How are you?'

Haunted eyes stared back through the glass. Sébastien said nothing. Nor did his face register emotion. Just that terrible blankness that stirred the frigid waters of Lambis's soul.

Looking at Amelie, and now at Seb, reminded him suddenly of another snowy day on this mountain. The day all the warmth inside him had been snuffed out in a catastrophic blast of icy reality.

Lambis reached for the door, urgently needing to see that little face smile in recognition.

'Don't!' Amelie's voice was sharp as the crack of doom as she inserted herself between Lambis and the car. He found himself staring at a narrow waist and full breasts, her nipples budded enticingly beneath thin wool.

Lambis's breath stalled as heat ignited in his gut. Unseen parts of him might have long since shrivelled and died, but he was still a man, and it had been too long since he'd had a woman.

Through the frosty scent of the thickening snow, he inhaled the gardenia perfume that always made him think of Amelie and sunny St Galla. He remembered how tempting they'd both been. How tough it had been to leave her.

'Why not?' His gaze strayed lower, over the feminine shape revealed by her fitted trousers, and a pulse quickened in his groin. Instantly he rose, shoving his hands in his pockets.

Amelie looked petite and far too fragile, despite the way her chin swung up as if daring him to test her.

'Because I was wrong. I thought you'd help, but the last thing he needs is some fleeting pretend friendly contact with a man who'd bar his door to us. Especially in this.' The tilt of her head indicated the falling snow.

A flake settled on her cheek, melting, but she didn't seem to notice.

'If you'll step away from the car, we'll be on our way.' She folded her arms and her breasts rose, plump and inviting. Lambis yanked his gaze higher.

She wasn't bluffing.

He should be relieved. He didn't have the time or inclination to deal with their problems. He had a multinational business to run, people relying on him. He didn't want Amelie here, stirring emotions, interrupting the smooth running of his life.

Yet he didn't move.

Whatever the problem, Lambis wasn't the man to solve

it. He knew his limitations. In his profession it was vital to know your strengths and weaknesses, and those of others. Yet the anxiety he'd felt, seeing Sébastien's staring face, made him hesitate.

She seemed ridiculously dainty to try facing him down. Dainty and shattered, though she tried to hide it.

Snow crunched under his boots as he turned. The gates were high, designed to keep the world out. Yet they swung open at the click of his electronic key.

'You go first. I'll follow you in my vehicle.'

Amelie gripped the wheel too hard as she drove slowly through the dusting of snow.

'Isn't this exciting, Seb? Snow!' Her voice wobbled but she doubted her nephew noticed.

In the rear-view mirror she saw he was at least staring at the view, his expression unreadable. Was he even a tiny bit excited to see snow for the first time? To see Lambis, the man he used to follow like a puppy?

Amelie wrenched her mind to the private road winding around a spur of the mountain.

She couldn't quite believe Lambis had let them enter. If it had been her alone she'd be driving back down to the village now. Lambis didn't want her near. He never had.

Pride smarted at asking for his help. And something else, some tiny part of her that had wondered, even when all hope had fled.

Amelie's breath caught when she saw the house. She'd expected something sleek, hard and impersonal, like Lambis. Instead she discovered a charming traditional mountain house. From the size she guessed it had been significantly extended, but it looked as if the mansion had always sat here, cupped by the mountain on three sides.

The ground floor rose organically from the mountain, its walls of stone. Above that rose another couple of floors, white-finished, and decorated with out-thrust balcony rooms overhanging the walls on wooden struts. They were decorated with intricate wooden carvings. Even the white plasterwork was beautifully decorated with what she guessed were traditional designs. The windows were large and the terracotta roof looked welcoming against the falling snow.

Amelie stopped the car, feeling as if she'd turned a wrong corner. This was the home of mega-wealthy Lambis Evangelos? The self-contained man who shunned sentiment?

She was staring when her door opened. There he was, his face stern. The wind stirred a glossy black curl at his collar and Amelie wondered what he was like when he relaxed. Once, long ago, she'd seen another side to him, when he was with her sister-in-law, Irini, for the two had been like brother and sister. Occasionally some of that tenderness he kept for Irini had rubbed off and he'd been enough to steal any woman's breath. Especially one who'd been lonely so long.

Amelie blinked and stiffened. She hadn't slept in forty-eight hours. That was why her mind drifted.

'Do you need help?'

She shook her head. 'Seb and I are fine, aren't we, Seb?' She looked in the rear-view mirror and met familiar green eyes. Was he excited? Scared?

Emotion swept through her and she shuddered.

'Amelie?' Lambis's voice was like soft suede on raw skin. It still had the ability to make her *feel*. To *want*.

She felt it now, the buzz of energy in her lower body, the trip of her pulse. Damn! She was past this. She'd moved on, determined not to wallow in regret.

This had to be exhaustion creating phantom emotions.

'Perhaps you could carry the luggage?' She gave him

one of her polite smiles, the sort she employed with boring diplomats or boorish industrialists.

For a second that cool stare locked with hers, making her wonder how much he read in her face. Then, with a curt nod, he was gone.

It took no time to bundle up Seb in warm clothes and usher him from the car to the house. Even the crunch of fresh snow beneath his feet barely made him pause and Amelie's heart would have cracked if it weren't already riven. Where was the little boy she'd loved for almost five years? A year ago he'd have been whooping with glee, investigating the unfamiliar icy white.

Now he let her hold his hand. He was wide-eyed but so self-contained it would have scared her if it hadn't become almost normal. She had to find a way to help him.

A sturdy woman with iron-grey hair held the door open, expression inquisitive. This must be the woman who'd cut Amelie off as she'd pleaded to be let in. But, instead of disapproval, Amelie caught shock on the woman's face as she appraised them, then a wide smile of welcome as she scooped Seb in out of the cold and Amelie with him.

'This is Anna, my housekeeper.' Lambis launched into a flurry of Greek that had the woman nodding and smiling. Amelie heard the name Sébastien and her own, then something that made the housekeeper's head jerk up even as she dropped into a curtsey.

'No, please.' Amelie put out her hand in protest. 'Tell her that's not necessary.'

Then the implications of Lambis identifying her sank in. She swung around to find herself facing a massive black-clad chest. She froze, refusing to back up and reveal how daunting it was to be so close to all that brawny strength. His evocative scent, so earthy and male, curled around her.

'There was no need to tell her who I am.'

His eyebrows lifted. 'I respect Anna too much to lie.'

'It's not about lying. It's about revealing only what needs to be revealed.' The memory of the press pack outside the palace gates in St Galla, telephoto lenses trained on the windows and gardens, slammed into her. Bile rose. They'd been eager to snap the grieving Princess or 'the tragic little King', as they dubbed Seb. They'd even tried to bribe the palace employees.

Amelie, who'd lived all her life at the centre of public attention, had never felt so degraded. As if she and Seb weren't real people but sideshow freaks that existed purely for the titillation of the viewing public.

'Can you guarantee your staff won't tell anyone we're here?'

Lambis stiffened. His hard face became unforgiving granite, as if she'd questioned *his* integrity, not raised a valid concern.

'You were the one who arrived uninvited and demanded entry. You'll have to live with the consequences.'

Would Lambis really sell them out to the press? She didn't want to believe it. Once she'd thought she knew him well enough to trust him with her life. But this was Seb's life in question.

'Answer the question, please.'

Lambis folded his arms across that massive chest, like some disapproving god of old passing judgement. It wouldn't surprise her if he suddenly pitched a thunderbolt at her.

'You've had my answer.'

Behind her Anna asked a question and Lambis responded, his tone so brusque and dismissive Seb edged up against Amelie, his teddy squeezed to his chest. Amelie put her hand on his shoulder.

It was the reminder she needed. It didn't matter that she'd once thought Lambis Evangelos had a softer side, or that Irini, her sister-in-law, had said he was the best man alive, apart from her dear Michel. Nor did it matter that he had a reputation for integrity.

Amelie couldn't take risks with her nephew. Despite what she'd threatened outside, Seb needed quiet, not paparazzi camped on the doorstep.

She'd thought they'd be safe with Lambis. He was the CEO of the world's most successful international security firm. His private premises would be more secure, she suspected, even than the St Gallan royal palace. But the consequences if she and Seb had to run the gauntlet of the press whenever they stirred weren't to be borne.

Amelie stroked her nephew's soft hair, bending down as she spoke. 'I'm sorry, *mon lapin*. I made a mistake coming—'

'Don't be absurd! You're not up to driving back down the mountain tonight.' The words were soft but the growl in that bass baritone was unmistakable.

Seb flinched and pressed his face into Amelie's skirt, his arms wrapping round her thighs.

She stood unmoving, shocked by his first overt show of emotion in weeks. Something broke inside her as pity and protectiveness vied with a tiny pulse of hope. Heart welling, Amelie gathered him in. 'It's all right, *mon lapin*. Truly. Everything's going to be fine.'

'Sébastien?' Lambis hunkered in front of the boy but didn't touch. 'I'm sorry. I didn't mean to scare you. I'm not angry, truly. You and your aunt are welcome here.'

Liar. He was furious. But Amelie had no sympathy to spare for the man staring at the little boy with all the wariness of someone facing a man-eating beast.

If the situation weren't so dire she'd almost laugh. As if big, bad Lambis Evangelos, the man who organised protection for the world's most eminent VIPs in some of the most dangerous places in the world, was scared of a child.

'Seb?' Amelie knelt and wrapped him close, inhaling the

fresh scents of clean little boy and melted snow. 'Don't be afraid, darling. Everything will be all right. Lambis won't hurt us. In fact—' she lifted her head and glared at the man who hadn't taken his eyes off Seb '—he's sworn to protect you. Did you know that?'

Of course Seb said nothing and Amelie snuggled him tighter, rubbing her hands up and down his thin back.

'Soon we're going to have something to eat and then I think it will be time for Monsieur Bernhard—'

'Monsieur Bernhard?' Lambis's eyes locked on hers, questioning. She didn't bother to respond. If he couldn't work out that Bernhard was a teddy bear, tough.

'I think he's getting sleepy. It's almost his bedtime. Come on, *mon lapin*, come with Aunt Lili.'

She lifted him in her arms and rose, ignoring Lambis when he made to take Seb.

Did he think she wasn't capable of caring for her nephew? Who did he think had been there through the long nights and lonely days since Michel and Irini died?

Anger threaded the aching grief inside her. Grief for her darling nephew, orphaned so young, and grief for herself.

She saw Lambis move deliberately to block the front door. The obstinate set of his jaw told her it would take a bulldozer to move him.

He didn't want them here. Now he'd decided they couldn't go. She wished he'd make up his mind!

Amelie would walk on hot coals if it would bring back the little boy she adored from the well of shock that had swallowed him. But she was fast running out of strength. Her head was reeling and there was a throb behind her eyes as she fought to stand tall.

Then she felt a touch on her elbow. It was the housekeeper, Anna, her expression concerned. Gently she raised her hand and stroked Seb's golden hair as he pressed his face into Amelie's collarbone.

'*Ela. Parakalo, ela.*' Come, please come. That much Greek Amelie understood.

She wavered for barely a second. Pride held no place here. She looked at the work-hardened fingers caressing Seb so tenderly and felt the fight drain out of her.

Amelie nodded. '*Efharisto.*' Thank you.

For good or ill they were staying, at least for tonight.

Whether they'd found the safe haven, and the help they needed, only time would tell.

CHAPTER THREE

AMELIE STARED AT the darkness of the swirling night.

She'd got through the last couple of hours like an automaton. At last Seb was tucked up in bed, asleep.

It seemed disloyal to think it—for who could want to see a child in pain?—but surely the way he'd turned to her when they'd arrived, and again when he'd clung to her as she read to him, signified a change? Some lessening of the dreadful nothingness that gripped him?

Rubbing her forehead with weary fingers, Amelie tried to order her fogged thoughts.

She should sleep. She'd eaten the delicious soup and fresh bread Anna had provided, and taken a hot shower in the luxurious bathroom, feeling chilled bones warm.

But she was wired. There was too much to sort out.

Which meant facing Lambis Evangelos.

Sighing, she turned to her suitcase. She wanted to tug on a comfy sleep shirt and pretend she didn't have to face the big, bad wolf tonight. But sleep would elude her till she did.

Ten minutes later, in trousers and a silky shirt of deep green that matched her eyes and boosted her flagging confidence, she checked that her subtle makeup hid the shadows of fatigue. With a few deft movements she twisted her long hair into a knot. Her earrings were simple pearl studs and she added a fine gold pendant of antique pearls, the only piece of jewellery her mother had given her.

Amelie closed her hand around the pendant, remembering her mother hugging her close, against all royal decorum, and whispering that now Amelie was twelve she was old enough to wear jewellery.

It was a talisman she wore when times got tough. Like when her mother died just months after that twelfth birthday.

Her mother had had the sweetest smile. A smile Michel and his son Seb had inherited. For a moment the ancient image wavered, replaced by Michel's face, the glint in his eyes as he showed off his new speedboat, the charming smile as he invited Irini aboard for a quick spin.

Amelie slammed a steel door on the memory. She snapped open her eyes and deliberately set about cataloguing the beautiful room she'd been given. There was a chance, a slim one, that the place might give a clue to what made Lambis tick, for this was his retreat from the world.

Turning, she saw plain white walls, for the most part bare. Except for a tiny jewel of an icon that glowed richly on the far wall. Amelie wasn't an expert but she recognised it was an original and very, very beautiful. Despite the stiff style of the traditional painting, the serenity and love on Mary's face as she looked down at her baby stole Amelie's breath. Here was love and a joy that made something swell hard in Amelie's chest.

Swiftly she turned away, feeling raw, for she responded to the painting at a visceral level. It tugged at her own secret yearning.

But the important issue was why Lambis secreted this gorgeous piece in a guest room. Why not have it in his room where he'd see it often?

Amelie prowled the space, surveying the high timber ceiling with its ancient beams, the cosiness of intricately woven local rugs on the polished floor and a particularly exquisite one on another wall.

The bed was massive with crisp cotton sheets and a luxurious silk spread. In addition to a huge decorative cupboard was a vast modern walk-in wardrobe. An ancient timber chest carved with mermaids and some mythical beasts she didn't recognise sat under one window, but in a discreet niche was a large screen that swung out to allow guests to watch television from the bed.

The room was an eclectic mix of charming old pieces and sleek functionality. The common thread was money. No expense had been spared to make a guest comfortable.

Which told her what? Lambis valued tradition but demanded modern convenience? He wanted guests to feel at home?

His reception told her he was more likely to bar the door to guests.

Or perhaps it was just she who was unwelcome.

The idea lodged hard and sharp in her chest. Surely he wasn't so brutal with everyone?

Did he really believe she'd swallowed her pride and come here uninvited because she was needy for *him*?

Nausea snaked through her insides. Of course he had.

And when she'd told him Seb needed him?

He'd still wanted them to leave.

Despite what she'd once thought, the man had no heart. It was as simple as that.

Amelie found him in a sitting room, high-ceilinged and huge. Yet instead of being cold, that signature mix of old beauty and luxurious modern functionality made it feel comfortable.

Until Lambis turned and she read his aloof expression. There'd been no thawing. Had she really expected it?

Because Anna had fussed over Amelie and little Seb like a hen with a couple of chicks didn't mean the master of the house had changed his mind. Anna's kindness contrasted starkly with Lambis's brooding stare.

He said not a word as Amelie walked the length of the room, to the huge stone-lintelled fireplace with its bright flames and the dark man beside it.

His bold, handsome face was half-shadowed yet unreasonably, appallingly attractive. If you liked remote, harsh beauty. Amelie didn't. Not any more.

Yet her heart skipped as some part that was all instinct and longing, not logic, stirred to life again.

How could he do that to her even now? Anxiety rippled through her. Amelie couldn't let that happen again.

She stopped within the circle of warmth, feeling cold to the bone. The faint scent of fine brandy reached her nostrils and she spied a rounded glass on the mantelpiece. But Lambis didn't think to offer her a drink. Presumably that was too much to expect.

The thought drove thoughts of a conciliatory approach from Amelie's head. If she read him right, she and Seb would be on their way as soon as the snow eased. That would be soon. It was far too early for winter.

Amelie chose a chair by the fire and sank down onto it. She'd fight every step of the way but she was so worn out she'd do it from a position of comfort.

The silence lengthened from seconds to minutes but for once Amelie didn't move to fill it. All her life she'd been the one to charm and please, to smooth ruffled feathers, to be diplomatic and gracious.

She was here to fight for her nephew's future. She wouldn't make small talk, pretending everything was okay.

'Are you going to explain?' he asked finally.

Amelie refused to flinch at that adamantine tone. 'Have you checked the messages I left?'

'I have, but they didn't help. All I know is that this is to do with your nephew.'

Sébastien, she wanted to scream at him. Or *Seb. You've called him both in your time.* Since when had Lambis thought of him only as someone else's nephew?

What had happened to the man who, however reluctantly, had been kind to a little boy who'd shadowed his every move when he stayed at the St Gallan palace? A little boy whose own father was often too busy with affairs of state for a little one to tag along.

'I didn't want to say more until I saw you.' She lifted her chin and met his eyes. In the shadow beyond the fireplace it was hard to read them but they looked shuttered. As if he was determined not to let anyone in. 'It's confidential.'

He lifted one arm in a gesture that encompassed the building. 'There's no one else here but us.'

It was the invitation Amelie needed and yet the words jammed in her throat. She'd hoped for some speck of interest or concern. Was that too much to ask? Instead it was like talking to a stranger.

Surely even a stranger would be more receptive?

Amelie crossed her ankles and folded her hands in her lap, refusing to show hurt. Surely they'd parted friends?

'Seb is adjusting to the loss of his parents.' Not by so much as a tremor did she betray how she too struggled with that tragedy.

Lambis said nothing.

'You saw how he was at the memorial service.' She'd known something was wrong then but it was only since that the enormity of Seb's condition had unfolded.

'He seemed very controlled.'

She shook her head. 'It looked like that. The press *loved* the photos of the brave little Prince saluting his parents' coffins.' Amelie dragged in a hasty breath as pain jabbed her breastbone. The rampant voyeurism of the press had been expected but still it rankled. 'That wasn't control; it was grief.'

Amelie had strenuously opposed taking a four-year-old to the funeral, but though she was now the most senior member of the family she'd been overruled. She wasn't Regent yet, and might never be, if the Prime Minister had his way. St Gallan law still favoured male over female and until Seb was officially proclaimed heir to the throne, and she his Regent, she had no right to make decisions for him.

In fact, she'd broken a slew of laws taking him out of the country. Right now, that was immaterial. The important thing was Seb.

'It hasn't been long since they died.'

Amelie looked into that stern face and saw not a flicker of emotion. Even for Queen Irini, the woman who'd been like a sister to Lambis.

But then, wasn't Amelie too suppressing a riot of pain? It was comforting to think that maybe, somewhere deep behind that inhumanly blank face, Lambis mourned too.

'I know, but…it's more than that.' She paused as a chill of remembrance feathered her spine. No one had expected the King and Queen of St Galla, both in their mid-twenties and full of life, to die in a freak accident. Everyone had been numbed by it. Even now Amelie still woke every morning to that awful reality slamming into her seconds, sometimes whole minutes after she woke.

Amelie held Lambis's gaze. 'Seb saw it happen. He was going to get in the boat too.' She paused and swallowed, the movement scratching a throat suddenly lined with sandpaper. 'But Irini didn't want him too excited before his nap. She handed him to me.' One more deep breath and she went on. 'Michel promised he'd take him for a ride the next day.'

Except there'd been no next day for Michel and his wife.

'I know.' Lambis's deep voice resonated around her, tugging at something sharp and raw inside.

Of course he knew. She'd told him when he'd flown across for the funeral. Why was she going over it again?

Amelie blinked and looked at the fire. It was easier staring at the golden flames than holding his sombre gaze.

'The point is, Seb's reaction to their deaths is…worrying.' She slanted a look at that chiselled face. Still no hint of understanding. 'He hasn't cried. He hasn't spoken. Not since the accident.'

That had Lambis's attention. He stiffened, his brows furrowing down in a V of concentration, or could it be concern?

'Hasn't spoken at all?'

'Not a word. Not to anyone.'

It had been uncanny, the way little Seb had stayed silent through those first days. It had worried her then but there'd been so much to attend to, so many legal matters and royal duties, meetings and consultations, she'd let herself hope she was wrong and it would resolve itself.

'He doesn't talk or smile or cry. He doesn't *react*.' Just saying it sent a quiver through her. She'd never felt so helpless.

'You've sought advice?'

'Of course. The consensus is that he needs time, though no one knows how much. Time and to feel safe and loved.' Her voice caught on the last word but she refused to look away. She wasn't ashamed of her feelings for Seb.

It was only what she'd once felt for Lambis that embarrassed her.

'Then give him time. Give him love. Be patient.'

It was what the experts had said, each of them studiously ignoring the flaw in that simple approach.

'I can't.'

'What do you mean, you can't?' Lambis had never thought to hear such words from Amelie. They shocked him more than if she'd begun unbuttoning that slinky shirt and invited him to make free with that delectable body.

He scowled furiously.

He didn't want her here.

He didn't want to get involved.

The fact his mind couldn't stop conjuring images of a

sexy, pouting princess, eager for his touch, was flame to the last shreds of his patience.

'Of course you can. It's what you *do*!'

Despite her regal posture and renowned diplomatic skills, the woman was a walking advertisement for all those soft, feminine emotions. She'd raised her younger sibling after her mother's death, since their father, more concerned with power and his own pleasure, had no interest in family life. She'd been the stable, loving centre of their family.

She'd warmly welcomed Irini, married at twenty and feeling out of her depth in royal red tape and a new country.

Lambis still had the letters full of Irini's eager confidences. About how caring Amelie was. How easy to talk to. When others counselled against a royal marriage simply for the sake of an unborn child, Amelie had taken the young lovers' cause and won the day.

For that alone he owed Amelie a debt.

He watched her stiffen, her spine so straight you could use it as a ruler. 'It may be what I *do*, as you so dismissively put it, but I can't this time.'

Lambis opened his mouth to explain he wasn't being dismissive, then caught himself. Never explain. Never discuss emotions. From a safe distance he might admire Amelie's loving nature and the way she shared herself with her family as well as her nation, but it wasn't his way.

Not any more.

Now her hackles were up. He watched, fascinated and, yes, relieved, as colour tinted her too-pale face. Princess Amelie of St Galla was a stunning woman. The warmth of her personality had a way of insidiously wrapping itself around your insides till you could almost believe…

'You can't? Why not?' His voice sounded as if it scraped over ground glass. Not surprising when his throat felt coated with shards.

'It means, much as I want to, I won't have a chance. Time's running out for Sébastien and we can't afford to wait for time to heal him. Besides—' she averted her eyes to stare into the fire '—the palace is no place for him to recuperate. Everywhere he turns there are memories of his parents. He only has to look from his window to see the bay where they died.'

He heard it now, the faintest tremor in her voice. Behind the faultless display of calm, Amelie was hurting.

Once Lambis would have gone to her and—

What? Put his hand on her shoulder? Cuddled her close? Assured her everything would be okay?

He couldn't do it. Not least because he knew touching this woman would be the biggest mistake of the decade. There was no knowing where he'd stop once he started.

More importantly, Lambis no longer believed in happy endings.

He couldn't lie to her. He'd never been able to do that, though for a while he'd been tempted. When, years before, she'd looked at him with those beautiful, luminous eyes and suggested he might spend more time in St Galla, not for Irini's sake, but for hers. He'd been tempted to let her believe he could be the man she wanted, just to bask in her adoration.

'Then take him somewhere quiet. Somewhere he can rest.'

Her eyes met his and fire flashed in his blood. 'Easier said than done. Everywhere we go are reporters.'

'Yet I didn't see the paparazzi outside my gates.' The more he thought about it, the more remarkable it was. He, with his experience as a bodyguard and later, running the best of the best in close personal protection, knew how difficult it was for non-professionals to evade a determined press. Yet Amelie had brought her nephew from St Galla,

an island near the coast of France and Italy, all the way to
Greece without being followed.

How had she managed it? He wouldn't have thought
it possible for a woman who'd led a sheltered life behind
palace walls.

'For now.' Her tone, like her face, was stony. 'You know
I can't evade them long-term. We need somewhere safe
and secure.'

Somewhere like this.

'This is my home, not a safe haven.' Not for anyone but
himself.

'You promised to protect Seb. I heard you tell Irini when
she asked you to be his godfather.'

The mention of Irini was a lead weight dragging at his
guilty conscience. Another life he'd failed to protect.

'I'll find you both a place you can hide away from the
press till you return to St Galla. Somewhere suitable.'

Somewhere not here.

Amelie regarded him coolly. She didn't raise an eyebrow
or twitch a muscle, yet she made it clear his answer wasn't
enough. For the first time in their personal interactions she
turned into Princess Amelie. A woman who held her own
with heads of state and tough negotiators. A woman with
generations of blue blood in her veins. A woman prepared
to take him on in his own territory.

No one did that. For years now Lambis had given orders
and they'd been obeyed. His advice was highly sought, his
presence ditto.

Yet Amelie's cool regard told him she expected more.

'So you'll find your godson a bolt-hole then wash your
hands of him?'

Her words pierced his conscience. Or maybe it was what
remained of his heart.

'It's for the best.'

She shook her head. 'I truly believed you cared. I thought you a man of honour.'

She rose. His trained eye noticed the slight wobble in her legs. She fought emotion or exhaustion or both, determined not to let him see.

She was so valiant his respect for her soared. Even as he wished her and her demands to the very devil. For she was wrong. He wasn't the man to help. He wasn't the man she believed.

She spun on one heel, walking away.

It was what he wanted. Yet his gut hollowed.

'You said time's running out.' The words jerked out before he was conscious of forming them. 'What did you mean?'

'Why ask when clearly you don't care?' She didn't even turn to face him. Only the rigidity of her slim frame and the hands clenched at her sides revealed her tension.

Lambis didn't answer. To say he cared would be tantamount to inviting them to stay, and that he couldn't do. Yet nor could he see her tension and not respond.

Damn the woman! She'd got under his skin once. He couldn't let her do it again.

Suddenly she spun round and the change in her was a punch to the solar plexus. Gone was the touch-me-not Princess, the haughty aristocrat. Everything about Amelie spoke of heat and passion. From her flashing eyes to the heightened colour accentuating those high cheekbones and the sweet bow of her mouth, deliciously plump as if she'd been biting it.

The effect was instant and incendiary—a symphony of want turned his body to hot, brazen metal. He'd wanted her before, too many times to count, but not like this—as if he'd incinerate if he didn't reach out and touch her, taste those kissable lips and possess that poised, perfect body.

Her chin tilted as if she read his lust and was disgusted

by it. Yet when she spoke Lambis realised she'd noticed nothing but the worries tormenting her.

'Because he's underage, Seb can't be crowned King. Instead he'll be officially proclaimed heir and a regent will be confirmed. The date for the proclamation ceremony has been set for his fifth birthday next month. Since he's no longer an infant, on that day he must personally accept his new status.'

'And?'

'And he's required to speak. To accept his future role and swear an oath. If he doesn't—' Amelie paused and the colour faded from her cheeks '—if he can't say the words, another heir will be found.'

'But in the circumstances—?'

Amelie's mouth thinned. 'The law of succession is specific. He must make the oath himself or be barred from the throne for ever.'

Lambis felt his brow furrow. 'But he's Michel and Irini's only son.'

'And the throne is his birthright. But that doesn't matter. What matters under St Gallan law is establishing the next ruler as soon as possible. If it's not Seb then I'm informed it will be a distant cousin, a man currently being investigated for fraud.'

Her words fell like blows. Irini's son disinherited? It didn't seem possible.

'Couldn't the law be changed?'

'Not quickly enough for Seb.'

'What about you?' When she simply stared he continued. 'Why not make you Queen if the next legitimate heir is so distant?' After all, she'd carried much of the royal burden, both for her father, then later for her younger brother as he'd adapted to the role of King.

'Women don't inherit the St Gallan throne. That's a male privilege.' Her tone was dispassionate, but Lambis wondered what it was like, eldest child of a monarch, forced to make a career out of diplomacy and public service, knowing you were barred from taking the throne for ever.

'I need to help Seb find his voice again, because that will mean he's recovering. *And* because without it he'll be denied what should rightfully be his.' She wrapped her arms around herself and something clenched in Lambis's chest. It was so rare for Amelie to reveal vulnerability. 'I couldn't live with myself knowing I'd failed Michel and Irini's trust in me.'

Lambis reached for the brandy he'd nursed before she arrived. One swallow and it shot a heated trail through his chest and down to his belly.

Amelie's talk of trust evoked the harsh remembrance of his responsibility to Irini. Lambis had failed his friend once, with dire consequences. If he failed her son…

'Why bring him here? I'm not a psychologist or speech therapist.'

Her face changed at his words. The grimness turning down her mouth at the corners eased, as if she sensed him weakening.

'He's fascinated by you. You know how he followed you around every time you came to visit. He thinks the world of you.'

Her shoulders lifted in the smallest of shrugs as if she couldn't fathom her nephew's taste. Nor could Lambis.

'I couldn't think of anyone else he cared about so much that they might help him through this.'

Lambis shook his head so vehemently he felt the tickle of his hair on his neck and jaw.

'I wouldn't have the first idea how to help him.'

But that wasn't what made Lambis's chest ice over. It was the idea of anyone, especially that small boy, depending on him to save them.

What a fraud he was! Every day he managed arrangements to protect strangers, some of them in the most fraught environments, but he couldn't protect those closest to him.

It was a cosmic joke. And the tragedy of it was it was no joke. It was all too real.

The consequences haunted him every day.

He looked back to find her eyes fixed on him as if trying to see into his soul. He wished her luck with that. He was pretty sure he no longer possessed one.

Carefully he put the empty glass on the mantelpiece. 'I can't do what you want.'

'You won't try?' Her fine features paled, pared back by tension and disappointment.

'I'm not the man to help Seb. I'm sorry.'

He thought her mouth would crumple, and pain, swift and sharp as a javelin, lanced his chest.

'Then God help him.' She swung around and strode away, heels clicking on the polished floor.

'I'll find a retreat for you both. Somewhere the press can't bother you.' It was the best he could do. His pride and his conscience howled that it was far too little. But he refused to raise false hope. He was no miracle worker. Better for Seb to spend quiet time with his aunt. Surely that was all the miracle he needed. 'It will be sorted by tomorrow.'

Amelie didn't even pause on her way out of the door.

CHAPTER FOUR

LAMBIS TURNED FROM his computer, catching sight of figures outside.

Amelie and Sébastien, out so early that the snowy peak rising behind them glowed pink and orange.

Intrigued, he shoved his chair from the desk and moved to the window. They were an unlikely pair. The Princess wore waterproof boots that were too big for her and a bulky waterproof jacket he guessed was Anna's. Seb's clothes fitted better but the jacket was too long. Where had Anna found the gear?

Amelie led the boy across the pristine white of last night's fall. Maybe they were out early because she knew the snow wouldn't last. By this afternoon it would have disappeared. The forecast was for a return to warm weather. Not that they'd be here then.

He needed to get back to his messages. But he stayed where he was, watching.

Amelie talked, waving her arm enthusiastically. Seb said nothing and, though he walked beside her, his shoulders were slumped and his head drooped. He didn't act like a kid enjoying the first snow of the season. No bounding across the white to leave footprints. He didn't even bend to make a snowball, much less attempt a snowman.

As if reading Lambis's thoughts, Amelie dropped to her knees and began scooping the white stuff together in a mound. Her face, pink with cold, was breath-stealingly beautiful. She smiled, talking as she worked, but there was a quality about her smile that spoke of strain.

She gestured, inviting the boy to join in, but he simply stood and watched.

The Princess's expression froze for a second before she ducked her head, ostensibly concentrating on her task. When she looked up again her smile was as bright as ever.

Yet Lambis *felt* her pain. His chest clenched around the hurt. She was so stoic, so determined to persevere, even against what looked like hopeless odds.

Her words last evening had kept him awake all night, trying to fathom a way to help them. To help Irini's child. To ensure Seb wasn't deprived of his inheritance.

Lambis didn't have what it took to get through to the boy. All he could do was lavish money on the problem and bring in the best specialists. But she'd already done that.

Which left him helpless and useless.

Lambis folded his arms across his chest, feeling the thunderous crash of his heart against his ribs. Frustration rose.

But that had always been his problem, hadn't it?

He could look out for himself, he could keep total strangers safe but when it came to those close to him...

A shuddering breath seared his lungs as he fought the gathering blackness.

Outside in the bright light Amelie hid her fear behind that glorious smile.

As Lambis watched, something twisted and broke inside. His breath expelled in a huge rush and he found himself striding for the door.

'When we're done we'll ask Anna if we can have a carrot for his nose. What do you think?'

Of course, Seb said nothing and Amelie was left to pretend she was having the time of her life, kneeling in the snow while her heart broke a little more.

She'd spent her life hiding feelings behind a charming smile but this was harder than anything she'd ever done. Each day, each hour, was more difficult than the last. She feared soon she wouldn't be able to do it any more. But if she couldn't be strong and reassuring for Seb, who would?

Movement caught her eye. It was Lambis, immensely tall and broad-shouldered, rounding the corner of the house. He wore boots, a black pullover and black jeans. With the golden light catching his bold, unsmiling features, he could have been the god of the mountain, marching down to see who'd invaded his territory.

Amelie's heart gave a little leap and she looked away, concentrating on getting more snow for her rather pathetic snowman.

One day she wouldn't feel this automatic spark of attraction, the infinitesimal catch to her breath when she saw him. *That day couldn't come soon enough.*

When she looked up Lambis had stopped. His attention wasn't on her, but on Seb, and there was something about that hard, handsome face that made her still.

It wasn't brooding anger or disapproval. It looked like desolation.

Amelie recognised it because it was how she'd felt when her mother died, and again after losing Michel and Irini. And this morning, waking to the knowledge there was no one to help her help Seb. That the chance of bringing him back from wherever he was, in time for the royal proclamation ceremony, was almost nil.

She looked at Lambis's still face and fought to make sense of what she saw. He looked…haunted, his mouth a twist that tugged at something deep within.

Instinct urged her to go to him and find out what had triggered his anguish. To comfort him. But the memory of his words last night stopped her.

It's what you do! That was what he'd said.

It was true. She was a nurturer, a carer, yet he'd made it sound like a terrible weakness.

She'd do anything for the people she loved. She'd supported her family and her people all her life. She believed in love. Yet the only times she'd reached out for love, she'd been rejected. Years ago the man she'd wanted to marry had abandoned her, frightened off by her father. The second time it had been this man, Lambis Evangelos, telling her he wanted nothing to do with her.

Well, he could whistle for sympathy. She was *not* wasting her emotions on him!

'A snowman, eh? Not a bad effort considering there's very little snow.' His voice startled her. It held a hint of warmth that reminded her of the man she'd once believed she'd known, years ago in St Galla.

Amelie sucked in a breath of frigid air and let it out as Lambis hunkered beside her and added a clump of snow to her lopsided construction.

'You're out of practice, Princess. Obviously you don't get enough snow on St Galla.' He glanced at Seb, drawing him silently into the conversation, but didn't wait for a response. Instead he reached out his long arms and gathered more snow in one scoop than she'd managed in four, adding it to the now rotund snowman.

And just like that the pent-up fury inside Amelie dissipated.

She couldn't forgive Lambis his refusal to help. But for this moment he was an ally. For a few precious moments, she felt a weight lift from her shoulders as Lambis talked about the deep snows of winter. Lambis, the man who could be taciturn to the point of absolute silence.

Amelie sank back on her heels, brushing back a stray strand of hair with a horribly shaky hand. This morning she'd felt alarmingly close to breaking point, her emotions too near the surface. For weeks there'd been no one to share her worries about Seb except Enide, the elderly cousin who'd moved into the palace to support them when Michel and Irini died.

Dear Enide. She was the only one Amelie had trusted with the truth about this trip, though Enide didn't know exactly where Amelie was so she didn't have to lie if questioned. She was back in St Galla holding the fort, presiding over the few minor royal events that couldn't be cancelled while Amelie and Seb took their 'private holiday'. The major event, a gala celebration with the King of Bengaria, was being rescheduled to next month.

'There, that's better.'

Amelie watched in amazement as Lambis plucked two pebbles from the ground, uncovered by their scrapings, and pressed them into the snowman's face, creating eyes.

Was this the same man who'd rejected her and Seb last night?

'Very fetching,' she murmured.

She glanced at her nephew. His attention was on the little, icy man they'd made. But there was no glow of appreciation or even interest in his expression. Just that blankness that terrified her.

Beside her Lambis rose to his vast, imposing height in one quick movement and Seb started. He didn't precisely shrink back, but he stiffened. So did Lambis. Amelie felt the tension in his big frame, felt it in his utter stillness. Seb was nervous of Lambis, but Lambis was just as wary of him.

What had she expected? That Lambis would bond with the boy over a game in the snow and change his mind about helping?

Grumpy with herself because that was exactly what she'd hoped, Amelie got to her feet and shepherded Seb towards the house.

'Come on, Seb. It's breakfast time. I'm sure Anna's got something nice for us to eat.'

Lambis's voice followed them. 'Then you can pack. I've

organised a place for you to stay where you'll be comfortable and private. Somewhere less wintry.'

He couldn't wait to be rid of them, could he?

Amelie halted, hackles rising despite her attempt to stay calm. But it seemed she'd shed that ability last night.

What was it about Lambis Evangelos that made her feel so *different*? Unlike the controlled, careful woman she'd been for twenty-nine years? Every fine hair on her arms and the back of her neck prickled.

The man was immovable. She should walk away, not let him see how his rejection hurt.

Instead, Amelie discovered she really *had* reached breaking point. There was no other explanation for the instinct that made her, quick as thought, bend and scoop up a handful of snow. She packed it into a hard ball, then spun round and lobbed it straight at the tall figure behind her.

For the first time she could recall, Amelie had no thought for good manners or appropriate royal behaviour—things that had been drummed into her from birth. Only for the need to wipe the satisfaction off her tormentor's face.

Snow exploded on his chin, showering him in white.

For a second, not quite believing she'd done it, Amelie stared, her eyes widening. Then, as he spat out snow, she couldn't prevent the laugh that bubbled up and escaped her frozen lips. A laugh of shock and delight. If she'd aimed properly she couldn't have done better. He looked as astonished as her.

Amazing how good that felt!

To act recklessly. To attack instead of taking her disappointment like a proper princess, always gracious and polite.

Amelie felt a rogue ripple of power through her chest and right down her spine. After the tension and worry of the last weeks it was marvellous.

She was still smiling when Lambis bent, shovelling up a massive handful of snow, shaping and throwing it all in one fluid movement.

It thudded into her arm, raised protectively in front of her face. Without stopping to consider where this would lead, Amelie scrabbled up another handful of snow, compacting it. She pitched it just as another massive snowball hit her shoulder, disintegrating in a starburst of white that blurred her vision.

Amelie couldn't catch her breath. It came in choppy little gasps of searing cold as she bent and reached for more snow. It took a second to realise it was laughter choking her airways, a hoarse chuckle that melded amusement with the rush of pent-up emotions, suddenly let loose. Her pulse was hectic, out of control, and satisfaction sung in her veins as she got Lambis square on the chest, white slamming into his black pullover.

Then his lob caught her full on the face.

The shock of it made her wobble in her borrowed boots, breathing in snow crystals.

When she swiped her face clear it was to see Lambis, arrested in mid movement, watching to see if she'd faint or curse or run away. As if!

Amelie dived for the snow, using two hands to make a massive snowball. 'You may be quick, Evangelos, but you're a much bigger target.' This time her aim was off, catching him on the elbow as he moved, but the joy of a hit urged her on. Ignoring the pelt of snow on her shoulders and chest, she took her time with the next, catching him on the neck as he twisted away.

The woman was utterly glorious.

Gone was the pale, serious Princess who'd twisted his conscience and his belly in knots last night. Instead Amelie glowed. From her bright blonde hair, escaping in loose tendrils around her face, to her incandescent smile and the vivid green of her eyes. Even with snow dripping down one cheek and wetting her hair, she was more beautiful, more vibrant than anyone he'd ever seen.

Lambis wanted to reach out and capture the essence of her.

He wanted to turn his back and run from her.

And keep running.

Because no good could come from this.

Damn. She turned him inside out! Every time he pushed her away she sneaked under his guard. And she didn't have a clue she did it. She brimmed with a joy that was artless and contagious. He could almost feel his lips twitch in response and—

Ice exploded on his face. Lambis brushed it off and shook his head, shaking snow crystals from his hair. That was when he noticed Sébastien, tucked up against the corner of the house, watching. His features were as blank and unsmiling as before. But Lambis saw his eyes looked different...engaged.

Memory stirred, of that same little boy skipping along beside him in St Galla, chattering about everything and nothing, asking so many questions his head spun, laughing at some absurd rhyming game he'd made up.

Heat stabbed. Lambis had tried in the past to avoid Sébastien but it hadn't worked. In the end he'd almost become accustomed to having the kid as his shadow. Now, seeing that glimmer of animation in his eyes brought memories flooding. Memories he'd repressed.

Amelie caught him staring and turned too. She stilled then swallowed hard, her gaze on her nephew. Yet she didn't go to the boy. Instead she quickly turned back, scooping up more snow as if she hadn't noticed the change in Sébastien. But she had. It was there in her too tight mouth and the sudden, rapid blink of her eyes.

She was scared, he realised. Distress clawed his vitals. Scared that by going to Sébastien, by making a fuss, the child would retreat again into complete blankness.

That was the moment, as her next missile hit him full on the chest, Lambis decided, against every instinct for self-preservation, he'd travel with them to the refuge he'd organised.

He raised both hands in surrender. 'Enough. We need to get dry and you two need to eat. You've got a long trip.'

Immediately Amelie stilled. Though she kept her chin up and her shoulders straight, he sensed strain behind her calm façade. Because he'd already glimpsed her pain?

Lambis discovered he preferred her defiance, even the contempt she'd shown last night, than this careful nothingness that uncannily resembled her nephew's expression.

'I hope you like flying, Sébastien.' It was the first time he'd addressed the child directly since they'd arrived, but it was easier now than addressing his aunt. 'I'm taking you in a helicopter and the view from up there is terrific. You can see all the villages and the winding mountain roads. It's almost like looking at a map.'

'*You're* taking us?' Amelie's brow wrinkled.

'Don't worry. I'm a qualified pilot. It's the fastest option, and the least public.' He watched her digest that. 'I'll have someone return your hire car.'

If he'd expected thanks he'd have been disappointed. Amelie merely nodded and took Sébastien's hand, drawing him towards the house.

Lambis took his time following. His plan had been to have someone else escort them to his island villa in the Ionian Sea to the west of the mainland. It was a simple arrangement and it had the beauty of removing his unwanted guests as soon as possible.

Yet he'd changed his plans. All because of the jagged

hurt when he saw Irini's little boy bereft and Amelie so heartbreakingly stoic.

Which was inexplicable since Lambis no longer had a heart to break.

CHAPTER FIVE

AMELIE HAD SEEN a lot of beautiful things. From the royal heirloom jewellery she'd inherited, to the view from the palace of St Galla across the Mediterranean. From ballrooms and exquisite finery to the joy on her sister-in-law Irini's face the day Seb was born.

Yet she caught her breath as Lambis brought the helicopter towards a small island ringed by azure and turquoise water. Pale cliffs cupped sheltered, secret coves and elsewhere the rocky, wooded slopes eased down to beaches so white they could have been spun from sugar.

Winter was a lifetime away from this place, basking in bright sunlight. In the distance she spied a small village curved around a tiny natural harbour, but her attention focused on the house that stood alone on this side of the island. A rambling house that seemed to grow from the rocks and flow down the hill towards its private, pristine beach.

'Your place?' she asked through the microphone on her headset. How else could he arrange so quickly a hideaway for them, safe from the prying press?

'Yes.' He paused then added, 'It's only just finished.'

Amelie swung round to watch Lambis as he brought the chopper down onto a helipad tucked behind the house. It was a tiny thing but the added information about the house being new was unnecessary. Last night, when they'd arrived at his mountain home, there had been no unnecessary words from him.

Did this signify a softening? Like the way he'd been in the snow this morning? Or was she seeking signs of a thaw because she so desperately wanted them?

She turned back to Seb. 'Do you see the pretty colour of

the water and the white beaches? It's probably still warm enough to swim here.'

'It is.' Again that bass baritone filled her ears. 'The snow in the mountains was unseasonably early. Winter won't reach here for months.'

Amelie smiled at Seb, helping him with his seat belt, trying to still the hope clamouring inside. Lambis had decided to help Seb recover after all. She couldn't stop the optimistic quickening of her heart.

'The staff here will look after you both. Anything you want, just ask them.' He didn't even look at her, instead concentrating on the control panel as the rotors slowed. 'The place is yours for as long as you need it and there will be no press intrusion.'

What thanks she might have offered dried and crumbled in her throat. So, they were to be left with the staff, not their host. Amelie firmed her mouth and helped Seb out of his headphones, hanging them up then taking hers off. Of course she was grateful Lambis was providing a refuge but she'd actually believed he'd changed his mind.

Appalling how much it hurt to realise she'd been wrong. How many more times would she let this man hurt her?

The door opened and Lambis was there already, holding it open, eager for them to go. She lifted Seb out, not trusting herself to look at Lambis. But his tall, intimidating presence made every sense prickle. Her reaction was pure disapproval, like a spitting cat's fur standing on end. It could *not* be sexual awareness. That would be the ultimate self-betrayal.

A woman on the edge of the helipad smiled and approached, introducing herself as the housekeeper, welcoming them.

It was so civilised, so *easy*. Lambis would remove them from his presence with as little fuss as if he'd ordered a meal.

Fury, hurt, grief, and all the despair she'd battled for so

long rose like a column of fire, filling her till Amelie felt as if she were about to explode.

She smiled at the housekeeper, though it hurt her frozen facial muscles, and asked her to take Seb ahead while she, Amelie, had a quick word with Lambis. The fact Seb went with the woman, without hesitation or a backward look, simply compounded her incendiary emotions.

Once he'd have either skipped ahead, eager to explore, or, if tired, hung back, clutching her hand. Every day the change in him tore at her heart, and her sense of helplessness grew.

She watched them head to the house, all the while aware of Lambis standing like an enormous, encompassing shadow behind her. She never needed to see him to know where he was. Right from the first time he'd come to St Galla for Michel and Irini's wedding, Amelie had been able to pinpoint his location with unerring accuracy. There was a little buzz of awareness whenever he was around, a preternatural sense that never failed.

How shaming that even after he'd rejected her she was still attuned to him!

She swung round. He was too close. She had to lift her head to meet his eyes.

'What sort of man are you?'

His brows drew together in a frown, yet even that didn't detract from the powerful attractiveness of those bold features. Amelie's heart rapped hard and fast and she knew it was only partly from anger.

Her green eyes sparked and Lambis felt an answering flare deep in his belly. The Amelie he'd known was charming, attractive, delightful, but never confrontational. Not till she'd arrived at his Greek home. Perversely, he found her vibrancy, the raw energy of her emotions, arousing.

'Have you no heart?' Her finger jammed into his breastbone, right where his heart pumped too hard, too fast. He tried to tell himself it was because no one else would dare speak to him like this, but he knew it was from the effort of not sweeping her into his arms and kissing her into silence.

It had been there inside him ever since she'd turned up on his doorstep—the clawing hunger that grew more voracious each time they met. That sense he could cheerfully lose himself in this woman and never surface again.

It was outrageous and horrifying, for she could never be for him. He'd taken pains to sever his links with her.

Yet he'd spent untold nights sleepless, wondering how Amelie's lips tasted. How it would feel to meld his body with hers. Seeing her in the snow this morning, so outwardly cheerful, yet, he sensed, so close to the brink of emotional collapse, had punched a hole through the wall he'd built around himself. A hole he couldn't mend, no matter how often he reminded himself he was no saviour, either for the boy or her.

'Did you hear me?' She looked outraged and delectable.

'I heard, Princess.' He captured that jabbing hand, encircling it with his, drawing it down to their side. She was warm and smooth, her flesh soft against his calluses. Even that simple touch seemed erotically charged. At least to him.

Clearly she didn't notice.

'And you have nothing to say?' Indignation coloured her tone. 'You really are some piece of work.' She shook her head. 'To think Irini loved you. She said you were the brother she'd never had. She said she'd trust you with her life.'

A great tremor of pain started somewhere in Lambis's belly and rose, spreading everywhere. Irini had trusted him and he'd let her down.

'What's wrong?' Amelie's words were machine gun fire,

aimed at his heart. 'You don't like to be reminded that Irini would expect you to do more for Seb than fob him off?'

'I'm not fobbing him off.' The words ground from him. Hadn't he brought them here? Wasn't he doing his best to protect them?

'You're deserting him. Because you can't be bothered to give up your precious time.' The words peppered him. 'Or...' she tilted her head to survey him '...because you're afraid.'

Lambis stiffened, stunned. How did she know? He hadn't even admitted it to himself. But she was right, he realised in shock. He was scared at a bone-deep level he couldn't explain to anyone, especially this bright, brave woman who stared at him with such contempt.

'I can't imagine what your problem is, Lambis. I don't want to know. But you're not the man I thought. Or the man Irini believed you. I don't know how you can live with yourself.'

Lambis didn't respond as the missile words slammed into him. They weren't anything he hadn't told himself. Yet, hearing them from Amelie, he felt himself dredge a new low.

But it was nothing to the ragged, raw pain that seared him when he saw her eyes turn over-bright with unshed tears.

'Don't, Amelie!' With one urgent movement he tugged her to him so hard he heard the soft huff of her breath as she landed on his chest. He wrapped his arms around her, pinioning her so she couldn't move, pressing her face into the place where his heart thudded like an out of control piston.

His breath sawed through cramped lungs. The whole of him hurt, except where he touched Amelie. For they fitted together perfectly, her head tucked under his chin, her feminine softness balm to his rigid body. It was all he could do not to stroke her, soften his hold and explore that lithe body.

Did she feel it too? The rising need? She didn't struggle to pull back.

Who was he kidding? She despised him. Whatever feelings she'd once had for him were dead and buried, and who could blame her?

How he'd had the willpower three years ago to resist her overtures and draw back from her he didn't know. But then he'd never held her in his arms, had he? He'd had that much honour at least, even though the temptation to hold her, to have her, had been almost impossible to resist.

Just as the need to lift her chin now and taste her lips was a compulsion he needed all his strength to fight.

With a mighty effort he lifted one hand, intending to let her go. Instead he watched his fingers stroke the wheaten ripeness of her hair. His breath shuddered at how soft it was, so at odds with the severely simple way she'd styled it high on her head.

Lambis drew in a deep breath that brought with it the scent of gardenias. He bent his head, burying his face in her hair. It was like diving into silken sunshine richly perfumed with flowers. For a second longer he stood, indulging the craving he'd managed to withstand for so long.

Then he dropped his hands and stepped back.

Amelie's eyes were enormous, the irises wide as if she'd just woken. Her trembling fury was gone. Instead she looked stunned, just as he felt. But of course that was his imagination working overtime. Amelie hated him. She no longer cared for him. He should be glad. He didn't want her to care, did he? He'd gone to great lengths to ensure she didn't.

'You're wrong, Amelie. I'm not the one Sébastien needs. I can't help him talk again.' He wished he could. It would be some small salve to his conscience. 'But I'll stay.' For her sake. Because it scared him to see this poised, generous woman distraught.

'You'll stay?' Her whisper skated across his senses. Even now, seeing her distressed, he had to fight his baser male instinct to haul her in and kiss her into oblivion. Or preferably into his bed.

Lambis raked a hand through his hair. This was a mistake; he knew it with every fibre of his being. With the sixth sense he'd honed in years of protection work. But he couldn't walk away.

'I'll stay. But don't expect a miracle. The boy's scared of me, if anything.' The way Sébastien had cringed last night when Lambis had growled his displeasure haunted his conscience. 'And I have a business to run. I'll be in my office most of the time.'

But Amelie was nodding, her mouth turning up into a tentative smile of hope that caught him in the chest.

'Thank you, Lambis. I…' She shook her head as if speaking was too hard and again he felt that terrible plummeting sensation. She wasn't listening. She was building hopes that were doomed to be smashed. 'This means so much.'

He couldn't bear the gratitude in her voice or the hope in her eyes. He turned towards the house. 'Just put it down to my one act of generosity for the decade.'

Next morning the sun shone bright and clear, sparkling off the vast infinity pool that encircled the front of the house, and the turquoise waters of the sea beyond.

Amelie felt the heat on her arms as she stood, enraptured. In St Galla the palace sat high on its headland, looking across gardens and forest to its private cove. She'd always loved the view. But this was something else. They were right down near the shore, as if the house were part of the landscape itself.

Had Lambis designed it? She couldn't link the airy, welcoming spaces she'd seen, all capturing exquisite views, with the brooding, closed off man he'd become. Only the attention to detail, the insistence on quality in everything, gelled with the man she'd once believed she knew.

She lifted her head to the sun, shutting her eyes as she inhaled the scent of sea and wild herbs. The only time she'd been to Greece before had been on an official visit to Athens with her father. There'd been banquets and photo opportunities and the usual endless meet and greets. The closest she'd come to experiencing the magic of Greece had been attending an evening outdoor play performed in an ancient theatre in the shadow of the Acropolis.

But this place had a magic of its own. It was impossible to stop the bubble of hope and optimism welling inside.

Which gave her the confidence she needed to beard Lambis in his den. He'd been absent last night, excusing himself on the grounds of outstanding work. She'd seen Seb to bed early then dined alone in a charming outdoor alcove overlooking the sea and the pool.

She hadn't missed Lambis, not one scrap! But now she found herself reluctant to face him. Stupid to feel self-conscious because she'd told him what she thought of him yesterday, calling him on his selfishness and his obligations. He'd deserved every word.

Yet a lifetime of pouring oil on troubled waters, being gracious and diplomatic and always shutting her feelings away, had left their mark. That was why she felt…edgy at the idea of meeting him. It wasn't attraction.

It had been indignation she'd felt yesterday when he'd hauled her against him. Nothing more.

Yet through the long, restless night she'd found herself remembering the rich, intriguing scent of him as she'd stood with her nostrils buried in his shirt, her palms against the moulded, hot steel of that powerful torso.

Amelie swallowed and forced herself to face the truth. There'd been something about being held in his arms. A spike of…need, of desire.

Firmly she told herself it was an echo of the past. For though she'd once believed herself falling in love with him, they'd never embraced, never kissed. She'd once wanted that so badly; of course she was curious about how his touch would feel.

Now she knew. She could put it behind her, couldn't she?

She spun on her foot, ready to seek him out, only to find the man himself standing in the shadow of the broad roof, watching her. He looked imposing and implacable in faded jeans and a black short-sleeved shirt that revealed bronzed, powerful arms. His glossy dark hair was tousled as if he'd run his hands through it and immediately Amelie wondered how it would feel against her fingers. Soft and silky or thick and springy?

Her heart sped to a lopsided gallop and she clasped her hands before her as if to stop herself reaching out.

How long had he been there?

What was going on behind that impenetrable expression?

'Lambis,' she faltered, thrown by the little thrill of excitement that whispered through her as she said his name. 'I was just about to look for you.'

'The boy is all right?' Was that concern in his voice? Maybe he did care after all.

'He's fine. Still sleeping, in fact.'

Lambis nodded but said nothing. Not even a polite enquiry about how she'd slept. Which was as well as she'd found it hard to settle, even with the sound of the sea as a lullaby.

What had she expected? Smiles and casual conversation? There'd never been anything casual about Lambis. He'd always been intense, controlled. But once, surely, there'd been kindness and moments of tenderness. She remembered the rare sound of his laughter wrapping around her, captivating and enticing.

Amelie blinked and dragged her mind back to the present.

'I have a favour to ask.'

One dark eyebrow rose.

She repressed a huff of annoyance. 'Nothing too difficult. I need to get some clothes.'

A second eyebrow rose. 'There's no need to dress to impress.'

Amelie shook her head. 'I'm not interested in impressing anyone here.' She stared straight into those hooded eyes. 'We left in rather a hurry. I wasn't sure what to pack and—'

Lambis shoved his hands into the pockets of his jeans. The movement tugged at the dark cotton of his shirt as his shoulders and biceps bunched. 'Whatever you wear is fine. There are no fashion police here.'

She clung to her patience with an effort. Did he really think she cared so much about her appearance? True, she always took care to look neat and stylish in public, but surely he didn't think she was hung up on clothes? Hadn't he seen her yesterday in Anna's oversized jacket and boots, bundled up like a bag lady?

'What I'm trying to explain is that neither Seb nor I have swimsuits or broad-brimmed hats or anything for the beach. Seb loves swimming, or he used to. Spending time in the water might help him.' She tilted her jaw in challenge. 'We could, of course, swim in our underwear but it would be more comfortable and convenient if I could buy a few things. Unless you have spare beachwear?'

The house was beautifully furnished, with every small detail attended to, right down to fresh flowers and deliciously aromatic bath oils. It wouldn't surprise her if there was a room full of beach gear for guests.

'I'm not in the habit of keeping women's swimsuits.'

Which meant he was ruthless about ensuring his lovers' belongings were cleared out when each affair ended.

Or perhaps they had no need for clothes while they were with him.

A little shimmy of...*something* raced through Amelie and heat spilled low in her abdomen.

Or maybe he just didn't invite women to his home. That was more likely. She couldn't believe a man as virile as Lambis, with that air of leashed power, would ever be short of female company. But it would always be on his terms.

'In that case, is there somewhere I can buy clothes? The town on the other side of the island, perhaps?'

He shook his head. 'Too small. You'd need to go to the mainland or one of the larger islands.' He paused and Amelie felt the weight of his assessing gaze. 'I suppose you'd like to fly out to shop?'

'No, thank you.' She repressed a shiver at the idea of facing a crowd of tourists with cameras. Just one stray snap, one person who identified her as Princess Amelie, and the paparazzi would be searching the area for her and Seb. 'I don't want to risk being seen.'

He nodded. 'If you're after something simple and don't mind someone else buying for you, my housekeeper could put in an order. Our seafood is caught here on the island and most of the vegetables are grown locally but we get supplies by boat too. I can't guarantee the clothes would be up to your usual standard but—'

'That sounds perfect, thank you. It doesn't need to be haute couture. We just need something simple we can use at the beach. I'll go and talk to her about it now.'

Late that afternoon Lambis stood on the terrace watching the pair on the beach. The quiet little boy and the svelte, glorious naiad chatting as she built a sandcastle.

It was a quiet, charming scene, but there was nothing quiet or soothing about its impact. Apart from the fact Sébastien was as animated as a doll, there was Amelie.

Not haute couture, she'd said. Something simple. Yet she looked a million dollars in that swimsuit, like a sexy mermaid out to entice some poor, foolish mortal.

Reason told him she hadn't chosen the outfit herself. He'd bet half his fortune it had been chosen by Costa, the guy who brought their supplies. It was definitely a man's choice. That bright lime bikini, outrageously brief and with side ties at the hip, made a man fantasise about tugging it undone and watching it fall.

Heat sparked in Lambis's belly and his groin tightened. He'd known Amelie for years, meeting her on his visits to Irini in St Galla. In that time he'd seen Amelie in ball gowns and designer dresses, in sedate suits and in mourning. He'd never seen her like this.

He leaned back against the wall of the villa, the effort of supporting himself too much.

All the world knew she was beautiful. He'd long ago realised she was too desirable for his peace of mind. She didn't wear revealing clothes but there'd been no mistaking her slim, womanly shape. Yet the sight of all that pale gold flesh, of those curves and hollows, of her breasts just on the verge of spilling from their confinement. And that waist, so narrow Lambis's hands itched at the thought he could probably span it.

He sucked oxygen into lungs so cramped it felt as if someone had tightened a lasso around them. His pulse thudded at his temple and his groin.

All day he'd locked himself away in the office, burying himself in work till his dormant conscience woke and urged him to spend time with his guests.

Not that he believed that would make a difference to Sébastien, but if it made Amelie feel better he'd do it.

Except nothing could make him go down there now. Not with an arousal the size of Mount Parnassus making every step painful. He might have managed to convince Amelie all those years ago that he wasn't interested in her, but the woman had eyes in her head. She'd take one look and *know* he wanted her.

Then where would they be?

She'd probably run a mile. Or if, miracle of miracles, she was willing to forgive his boorish behaviour, and the electric attraction he felt wasn't one-sided…

No. He couldn't even think it. A liaison with Amelie would be disastrous. He could never give her what she wanted. And he feared what being with her might do to his own carefully controlled and compartmentalised life.

He turned and walked slowly inside, the familiar bitter tang of regret on his tongue.

CHAPTER SIX

THE DAYS FELL into a routine. Every morning as dawn broke, like now, Lambis headed to the sea for a vigorous swim to clear the cobwebs of a night with too little sleep. By the time Amelie and Sébastien appeared he was always in his office. Evangelos Enterprises handled everything from close personal protection of VIPs to security for major events—international conferences to rock concerts and most things in between.

Business was booming, and demanding, yet it didn't hold his full attention.

Each day he'd emerge to lunch with his guests. It was his one gesture towards placating Amelie and her demand that he help her nephew.

Lambis knew there was nothing he could do for Sébastien, and it was confirmed daily when the boy avoided his gaze. There was no more tagging behind Lambis as he'd once done, leaving Lambis torn between relief and familiar guilt that he'd failed the child.

The rest of the day and evening was devoted to work and trying to avoid thinking about Amelie. With little success. The woman sneaked into his thoughts time and again, even though she'd given up demanding he do more for the boy.

Even now, as he powered through the clear waters of the bay, his head was filled with her, not his business. Not the trip he should be taking to LA soon, or the opportunities opening up in Asia, or any of the other issues demanding attention.

Lambis stopped, treading water, and flicked moisture from his hair. It was late, the sun already high as the silvery sheen of early morning gave way to the bright blue glare of another perfect day.

Amelie and Sébastien would be up and about soon.

On that thought he swam for the shore, cleaving easily through the crystal water. Nevertheless, he made a mental note to head to his gym for a long workout this afternoon. He'd spent too much time cooped up. No wonder he felt fractious. He'd always been a physical kind of guy, happiest when active, which was why following in his father's footsteps to become a bodyguard working for Irini's billionaire father had suited him down to the ground.

Hiding behind his desk wasn't his style.

Hiding. Had it come to that?

He hit the shallows and put his feet down, striding up onto the white sand beach. He drew in a breath, feeling the satisfied buzz he always got from exercise, the sun on his back and the scent of fresh salt air in his lungs.

He was actually smiling, till he saw the small figure curled up on the sand.

His heart knocked hard at his ribs and he faltered.

Sébastien sat with his knees up to his chin and his arms wrapped around his legs, right beside the towel Lambis had brought from the house.

The boy didn't meet his eyes but looked at a point just past him.

Only once recently had Sébastien met his gaze, when Lambis had a face full of snow. Then there'd been a tickle of…something behind the pale, blank face. His eyes had looked alive again. Now there was nothing.

That memory, and the urge to reach out and help the kid, ate at him. For once Lambis ignored the clamouring voice that urged him to turn and leave the boy where he was, alone but safe.

'Hello, Seb.' He cleared his throat and even so his voice came out rough. 'You're up early.'

Lambis picked up the towel and made himself stand beside the kid, rubbing his saturated hair.

'You're not going for a swim?' No response. He should be used to it but his heart clenched at the child's complete unresponsiveness. Did he even hear Lambis's words or was he lost completely in a world of grief and shock?

How hard it must be for Amelie to see her nephew like this. Every day, every hour, must take a toll, not just on her patience but on her strength and optimism. How did she keep going?

Lambis had no idea. He'd given up on optimism a long time ago.

He turned to survey the bay as he towelled his shoulders and torso. 'It's the best time of day for swimming. The water is a perfect temperature.'

Who was he kidding? Idle chatter had never been his style. He didn't have the skills to coax a traumatised child from his shell. As for Amelie's belief the kid had connected with him...once maybe. But there was no evidence of it now. Even if Lambis wanted to cultivate a relationship, which he didn't, he hadn't a clue how to go about it.

Once he'd had the knack. The glimmer of that memory was like the slice of a bright blade, slashing to the bone and deeper, right to his heart.

Lambis stood still, not even breathing, as he absorbed the familiar pain. It was long ago and whatever capacity he'd had for human connection, for tenderness, had been lost in the maelstrom of pain that had upended his life.

Losing both wife and child changed a man.

A distant buzz reached his ears and he frowned. Not a plane, and no one on the small island had a powerful speedboat. He turned, surveying the headland to the south. Sure enough, seconds later, a sleek powerboat erupted into the bay, still far enough out not to impinge on their privacy, but an unwelcome intrusion to the pristine morning.

Lambis raised his hand to shadow his eyes as he looked into the sun. The boat didn't veer towards the shore, nor did it slow. Chances were it was simply some holidaymaker from a distant island, out early with their expensive new toy. But he'd take no chances. He'd have it identified and tracked. Nothing, no one, would violate Amelie and Sébastien's privacy here.

He was already planning his first call when something, not a sound but a changed quality in the air, made him tense and turn.

It was Sébastien, no longer sitting curled up, but on his feet. His mouth had dropped open and his eyes stared as he tracked the speedboat. His skinny little body shook and his breathing was harsh.

Asthma attack? Allergic reaction?

Instantly, heart in mouth, Lambis was on his knees beside the boy, fighting back panic and dark memories. 'Sébastien? What is it?' Then, more slowly, forcing a tone of calm, 'Look at me, Seb. Can you catch your breath? Shake your head if you can't.'

In the split second while he waited for confirmation, Lambis was forming a plan. Carry the boy to the house, call the hospital, then onto the chopper and into the air.

Sébastien didn't look to him. His attention was on the boat. His open mouth worked. Not as if he were gasping for air, but almost as if he were speaking.

Lambis leaned closer, feeling for a fever but finding none. There was no sound except that grinding breath, an almost silent groan of air as if the very earth had ripped open. It made the hairs at Lambis's nape stand up.

Then, abruptly it hit him. The over-bright gleam in the little boy's staring eyes. The unspoken word his lips formed.

Mama.

He was remembering his parents. And another speedboat, not red but white and Royal St Gallan green, as befitted a boat belonging to the King.

That boat had sped across another bay, struck a submerged obstacle, veered dangerously and, before the proud new owner could correct its direction, hit rocks. The explosion that ripped the boat apart had been heard right through the capital of St Galla. Sébastien had stood with his aunt on the pier, watching.

Lambis gripped the child's shoulders as the boat disappeared around the next headland.

'It's all right, Seb. It's all right.'

The kid was stiff, every muscle straining, as the tremor grew to a terrible shudder. His breathing grew even more laboured, yet Lambis knew now it was emotional pain tearing at him, not some allergic reaction.

'You're thinking of your mother and father.' He dropped his voice to a low croon, the sort he'd once used for lullabies. A tone he'd have sworn he'd forgotten. 'It's not them, *agori mou*. Truly.' The child's distress engulfed him.

Did Sébastien even understand his parents were gone for ever?

Lambis saw the brimming green eyes, felt the raw, aching gasps racking the small body and gave up wondering about the right approach. Instead he acted on instinct, wrapping his arms around Sébastien's thin frame, lifting him off his feet and into his embrace as he sat down on the sun-warmed sand.

Tears came. Bright streams of grief, pouring silently down those too-pale cheeks.

Such soul-deep loss, such dazed heartbreak was something Lambis could relate to. This wasn't the time for words, but for the physical comfort of being held.

Briefly Lambis wondered if it would have made a difference, years ago, if there'd been anyone to hold him. Then the fleeting thought disintegrated as he put all his energies into comforting Irini's boy.

'It's okay,' he crooned, rocking that thin little body. 'It's okay.' When of course it patently wasn't. 'I'm here and Aunt Amelie is too. Everything's going to be okay.'

The child was fragile in his hold and something deep-seated in Lambis's chest seemed to loosen and tear. Lambis began whispering in Greek, for the words of solace and love came more easily in his mother tongue. And maybe Sébastien understood, for Irini had often spoken to him in Greek.

For the first time in years Lambis didn't guard his speech. He let dammed emotions break free. His only concern was this small scrap of humanity held close in his arms.

It seemed to work. That terrible tension in Sébastien's small frame eased, the shuddering, racking breaths eventually grew quieter, even if the stream of tears flowed ceaselessly.

Then the child did something that gutted him. He snuggled into Lambis's hold, hands curled up against his bony little chin as he turned his head into Lambis's chest.

For a second Lambis stilled, undone by the simple familiarity of the moment. Then, as ever, he shoved memory to the back of his mind and crooned again to the child who needed him.

Amelie stopped a few steps away. She'd been on her way from the house when she heard the boat and saw Seb's reaction. But long before she could reach him Lambis had rescued him.

Now, watching how the big man sheltered the tiny boy, those massive shoulders curved protectively around the child, buried emotions erupted.

She'd thought he hadn't cared, that Lambis was genuinely cold-hearted. How wrong she'd been. His voice, a continual stream of soft sound, was thick with emotion. She couldn't understand the words, but they spoke to the need deep within both Seb and her. The need for love and support. For comfort and sharing.

Lambis gave it all unstintingly, wrapped little Seb close, rocking him like a father would, ensuring he felt safe, even if he couldn't change the terrible tragedy that had orphaned her nephew.

Amelie's heart clenched, her mouth crumpled. Her whole being wobbled.

Even as gratitude welled for what he was doing, other emotions struck. *She* wanted to be held like that. She wanted someone to care for *her* as Lambis did now for Seb.

Not to tell her everything would be okay, for of course it could never be as it was. But to assure her that, just for a little while, she wasn't alone. That she had someone to share her burdens.

She blinked and made a conscious effort to cut loose that yearning. It was made immeasurably more difficult by the sight and sound of the man she'd once begun to love consoling her darling nephew.

In other circumstances—

No! She wasn't going there again.

She was made of stronger stuff.

She stepped forward, her shadow covering Lambis, and he tilted his head back. His eyes met hers, dark as a thunderstorm and cloudy with emotion. That emotion was a punch to her lungs. She'd never seen Lambis so...adrift.

Even as she thought it, he gathered himself. His gaze grew focused. He sat straighter, switching to English, and her fleeting sense of seeing the real man behind all that machismo faded.

'Look who's here, Sébastien. Your Aunt Lili. Didn't I tell you she'd be along soon?'

Seb's lack of response didn't faze him, but Amelie's

blood ran cold as she saw her nephew's face. His skin was awash with tears, his eyes red and swollen.

'Seb. Darling.' She dropped to her knees, leaning in to cup his wet cheek, to smooth her unsteady hand across his bright gilt hair. 'Did the boat scare you?'

He let out a long, shuddering sigh, then, to Amelie's astonishment, nodded.

It was the smallest of movements but unmistakable. Her heart fluttered and long-dormant hope stirred. Her gaze lifted to Lambis's, so close, she realised, that his breath feathered her cheek. The heat of his big body encircled her as she leaned in to Seb.

Everything inside Amelie stilled, slowed. She became conscious of the minutest details. Of the long sooty lashes half lowered over Lambis's eyes, of the fine grain of his dark-toned skin and the shadow of stubble accentuating the hard angles of his jaw.

Sucking in a breath heady with male spice and the sea, she snapped her attention back to Seb. He was blinking, knuckling a hand to his eye, and love clenched her chest.

She'd do anything for her nephew. Whatever it took to secure his future. Even…

Not now. The future could wait. What mattered was making sure he was okay.

'Everything's going to be all right. You're safe here with me and Lambis.' She pinned on a smile. 'How about we go inside for breakfast?' She reached for him, but Lambis shook his head and she froze, abruptly aware that the backs of her hands touched his hot flesh where he encircled Seb. Belatedly she withdrew. Her skin prickled as if singed.

'I'll carry him. Okay, Seb?'

To Amelie's amazement, her nephew tilted his head again. It was what she'd hoped and prayed for. Some sign of life. Yet the reality of it was like a knife cutting too close to the fears she'd hidden since the accident.

It must be relief making her feel…odd. She sank back on her heels, blinking, overwhelmed, almost smothered by rising emotions.

'Amelie? Are you all right?' There it was again, that husky, beautiful cadence. Like a caress.

She cleared her throat. 'Of course.' It was stupid to feel overcome. She should be celebrating.

For too long she'd feared Seb might always live in that grey half world, separated from the rest of them. She'd been strong when he was stricken and silent. She needed to be strong now.

Her legs were stiff as she stood, and her smile felt as if it cracked her face. 'Let's all go inside and eat.' She didn't look at Lambis, confirming his agreement. After this he couldn't, surely, make his excuses and leave.

'That sounds like a fine idea. Swimming always gives me an appetite.' With an easy, athletic grace, Lambis rose to his feet, Seb safe in his arms, and turned towards the house.

Amelie followed, her gaze on his broad-shouldered frame. Every step revealed the clench and release of powerful muscles, of a raw, unvarnished masculinity that wasn't just about size and physical strength. It came from his absolute confidence and self-assurance.

Despite a lifetime's lessons in relying on no one but herself, in being the rock around which everyone else found safe anchor, Amelie found that incredibly attractive.

She paused and drew a deep breath.

No matter how strong, how appealing, Lambis wasn't for her. All that mattered was Seb and his happiness.

Amelie paused in the doorway of Lambis's study. Sunlight streamed in, lighting the vast desk, almost empty but for a computer screen and a phone. Clearly he was a man who preferred organisation to clutter. No doubt he managed his work demands with ruthless efficiency.

Her thoughts strayed to the decisive way he'd squashed her dreams years ago. He'd cut her off quickly, ending her tentative hopes and leaving no lingering doubts. Kinder, she supposed, than letting her wonder if he'd change his mind.

Amelie blinked and tore her gaze from the dark head of unruly hair that made her want to reach out and run her fingers through it.

He had his back to her, talking on the phone in Greek as he surveyed the view. Which gave her time to take in the rest of the room. It was simple, almost spare. Plain white walls and marble floor. Two jewel-toned icons glowed with an inner fire on the wall furthest from the wall of glass that looked over the bay. Beautiful as they were, the paintings didn't compare with the mother and child she'd seen in his mountain home. On another wall was a spectacular photograph of a sheer mountain top, with a tiny figure in bright climbing clothes, clinging to rock. Amelie felt dizzy just looking at it.

She stepped into the room and Lambis stilled. Moments later, his call ended, he swung round.

'I'm sorry to interrupt.' Her voice was too light, almost breathless, and she swallowed, determined to see this through. 'But I need to thank you for this morning.'

Lambis stood and instantly she felt at a disadvantage. Even from beyond the desk he towered over her. Worse was the difficulty she had stopping her gaze from straying over that powerful, muscular body she'd seen in all its glory a few hours before.

How many times had she berated herself for noticing? It was worse now, for she'd seen the tenderness he was capable of and it had evoked long-buried memories of the summer he'd spent in St Galla and the feelings she'd once harboured.

'There's no need for thanks. I did what anyone would have done.' His tone was brusque and his brow furrowed.

Yesterday she wouldn't have looked beyond that. Now she wondered.

'Perhaps. But I'm grateful you were there. Seb was sound asleep, or so I thought, when I went to shower. I know you value your privacy, so I've made sure we wait till you've finished your swim to go outside.'

Lambis's frown became a scowl. 'You kept him indoors for that?'

Amelie shrugged. *He* was the one who'd made it clear he didn't want their company. He saw them only when they shared the brief midday meal. 'It seemed easiest.'

He raised his hand and forked it back through that shaggy mop of sable hair. No one else Amelie knew wore their hair like that. Her acquaintances prided themselves on their appearance, or made an effort to conform when meeting royalty. Lambis looked like he didn't give a damn how it looked or what anyone thought. Yet it suited him. That and his still unshaven chin made him look like a marauder, a pirate. The sort of man who'd dare anything.

'Is that you?' She turned to the breathtaking photo of the climber.

'No. I'm not interested in photos of myself.' Something kindled in his gaze. 'I took the shot from the next peak up.'

So she'd been right. He *was* an adventurer. But not, she guessed, in business. There he was all about risk management, as she knew from the recommendations he'd made for royal security in St Galla.

'Was there anything else?'

Amelie stiffened. Had she really expected this morning would change things?

'I'd hoped to persuade you to share dinner with me so we could talk.' Amelie paused but there was no change in his expression. She hated the feeling she was a supplicant, seeking his favour.

'But that doesn't matter.' Might as well get this off her

chest. Delaying would only make it more difficult. 'Mainly I wanted to apologise.' Amelie stood straight, meeting his gaze with all the outward calm a lifetime's practice could muster.

'You don't owe me an apology.' The scowl became positively thunderous. Yet, contrarily, all that did was emphasise the strong planes of his bold features. Even grumpy, Lambis fascinated her.

'I do.' She stepped forward then stopped. He wouldn't appreciate her invading his space. He was putting out enough *keep away* vibes to power an electric fence. She hadn't missed the way his chin hitched at her approach or the curl of his hands.

Something thudded through her. Did he dislike her so very much? But Amelie was too proud to dwell on that.

'I accused you of not caring. I believed you hadn't loved Irini as she did you, and that Seb meant nothing.' His features were so still they could have been cast in bronze.

Amelie shook her head. 'For that I'm sorry. I was wrong.' She swallowed hard, her throat tight, and made herself continue. 'Your reasons for protecting your privacy are your own, but what I saw on the beach…that wasn't simply *what anyone would have done.* That was *love.*'

She hefted a breath and heard her words echo in the silence. It wasn't a welcoming silence. It vibrated with the tension emanating from the man before her.

'You care about Seb deeply and I apologise for questioning that.' Even if she had to bite her lip from asking what made Lambis try to keep the boy at a distance. 'You helped Seb when it mattered. Everything else is unimportant.'

She met his hard stare, wondering what was going on behind the dour expression. But what was the point? 'I also wanted to ask if Seb could spend a little more time with you.' Asking was difficult but Seb's wellbeing was more important than pride. 'This morning was a huge turning point for him and I don't want—'

'I understand. You're hoping to encourage more change in him.' Lambis saw it in her eyes, blazing with hope.

Her tentative smile tugged at him, made him uncomfortable.

'Don't read too much into what happened this morning.' Lambis felt his frown deepen. 'I'm no miracle cure.'

The idea was laughable. Deliberately his tone was harsh, covering the fact he didn't feel nearly as sure about things now as he had before. Where before there was certainty, now there was confusion.

These last few hours he'd felt emotions, yearnings he'd long ago emptied from his life. The feel of little Sébastien, clinging so needily in his arms. The look on Amelie's face, her gratitude when she'd found him cradling the boy, her touch as she'd burrowed into his embrace to comfort her nephew...

Tangled feelings enmeshed Lambis. Whichever direction he moved, whatever he did, they were waiting to tighten and knot around him. His breathing quickened.

'But you won't back away from him now?' There was real fear in her fine eyes.

Lambis felt the weight of her hope like a yoke across his shoulders. But how could he pull back now? This morning he'd simply been the one on the spot when Sébastien reacted. Yet he hesitated to say that. Stress had worn at Amelie, though she'd tried to conceal it. Pain circled his belly at the idea of her shouldering this burden alone.

He let go a long, slow breath and rolled his shoulders. 'I'll help if I can.' He forced the words through stiff lips.

His word was his bond and now there was no escape.

It was almost worth it to see the blaze of pleasure turn Amelie's face from beautiful to incandescent.

'Thank you, Lambis.' She opened her mouth as if to say more, then instead nodded and left the room.

Lambis watched her go, knowing he was doomed to disappoint her. That was his curse.

He'd inadvertently been responsible for his mother's death in childbirth.

Because of him, his wife and child had died before their time.

Just this year, he'd failed to keep Irini and her husband safe.

He wore guilt like a badge only he could see. Yet Amelie, sweet, caring, indomitable Amelie, believed him a protector, a saviour.

The worst of it was, he didn't have the heart to disabuse her because all his battling had been in vain. Years of self-denial and distance hadn't succeeded in banishing his feelings for her, though he'd tried, for her sake.

He cared for her.

Wanted her.

Desired her.

He feared he didn't have the strength to hold back any longer.

CHAPTER SEVEN

AMELIE SMOOTHED THE fabric of her bronze-green dress with a hand that was a little clammy. She was *not* nervous to be sharing dinner with Lambis now Seb was asleep. It was just that the invitation was…unexpected.

As had been Lambis's arrival at the pool this afternoon. She and Seb had been in the shade of a huge awning, Amelie reading a story out loud and Seb curled against her. When Lambis appeared, striding out of the house in nothing but black swim shorts, her heart had thundered out of control and stayed that way as he sauntered across the flagstones.

His size and overt masculinity were almost daunting. His aura of barely contained power and raw edginess hinted at something wild and untamed beneath all that control.

Watching him stroll, half naked, towards them had been pure sensual delight. It wasn't just Amelie's pulse pounding hard in response. There'd been a throb deep in her womb, a quickening of arousal, and a softening as if her feminine core readied for his possession.

Heat flagged Amelie's cheeks even now, remembering. But Lambis hadn't noticed. His whole focus had been on Seb. Besides, she was a past master at hiding her response to him. He'd never have invited her to his home if he knew the number of nights he'd haunted her most erotic fantasies.

Yet what made Lambis Evangelos more devastating than mere sculpted beauty was the patient way he'd focused on Seb. He'd coaxed the little boy into the pool and, if Seb hadn't actually smiled or spoken, he'd responded, even at one point initiating a new phase of their game.

Amelie had sat back and watched, her heart full.

It had been easier when she detested Lambis for trying to turn them away. Now, as reluctant host, he was making a real difference to Seb, succeeding where she'd failed. All her defences against him, against further hurt, trembled on their foundations.

Pushing back her shoulders, she stepped out onto the wide terrace. This was just a meal. How many times had she sat through meals with complete strangers or people she didn't particularly like and made small talk? Yet a frisson of warning touched her nape as she followed the house-keeper's instructions to the far end of the terrace.

Subtle lighting turned the pool area to an idyllic retreat. But it was the scene at the end of the house that caught her breath.

A private patio extended from what she guessed were Lambis's rooms right to the white sand beach. A pergola draped with bright bougainvillea and other blooms gave the area a sense of intimacy and scented the evening air with flowers.

For a moment she hesitated, unnerved by the romantic scene, till she realised that, in addition to the fat white pillar candles in their glasses, there were lights everywhere. Clearly Lambis didn't want her misunderstanding and thinking this was some romantic rendezvous.

'Amelie.' A shadow moved at the far end of the terrace, prowling closer with that distinctive loose-limbed walk.

Her breath seized. In broad daylight Lambis Evangelos was stunning. In the soft glow of evening, dressed all in black and freshly shaved, Amelie couldn't drag her eyes away.

He stopped before her, his gaze skating over her dress and neat shoes, then back up to linger a second at her collarbone, where her pearl pendant rose with her rapid pulse, then up to meet her eyes.

His eyes looked darker than usual and for a moment

they seemed to glow. She waited for him to say something, strangely disappointed when it was simply, 'Thank you for joining me.'

She inclined her head. 'My pleasure.' Stupidly she felt stiff and slightly breathless, as if her lifetime's experience in handling difficult social occasions had disintegrated.

Lambis, on the other hand, was a perfect host as he invited her to a seat at the table for two, offered wine and explained the aromatic seafood dishes prepared from today's catch on the other side of the island.

The problem was her. She was on edge, gauche as a girl on a first date. But this wasn't a date. This was Lambis being a good host. The change in him over a couple of days was remarkable. Today with Seb she'd again seen that quiet kindness that had drawn her years ago.

'Thank you, Lambis.' She met his eyes and held them despite the sizzle that fired in her veins. 'I know you don't want us here. I know you don't like your privacy invaded. But I *do* appreciate what you're doing for Seb.'

For a pulse beat, then another he was silent. '*Trying* to do. There are no guarantees.' The grooves at the corners of his mouth deepened. 'If anyone will make a difference it will be *you*. You're the one he loves. I'm almost a stranger.'

Amelie shook her head as she helped herself to the platter he held out. 'I haven't made a difference so far.' It took everything she had not to let her voice wobble. She'd failed Seb, and his dead parents.

'Don't underestimate what you've done.' Lambis's voice was gravel and silk, making tiny ripples of delight break out on her bare arms. 'You've always been there for him. He adores you. And I didn't trigger what happened today. It was the shock of the speedboat.'

'Perhaps. But he's responded to you. He's always responded to you.'

As she had. From the first moment Irini had introduced her to the imposing man whose rare, incredibly sexy smiles set her heart pounding.

'I'm a novelty.'

'More than that.' It was the essence of the man before her. A man she'd always believed honourable and strong, genuine when so many around her weren't. Hadn't she believed in him enough to uproot Seb and bring him all the way to Greece?

On the thought Amelie busied herself with her meal. Despite everything she'd told herself, despite him not wanting her, the wanting inside *her* hadn't died at all.

What a terrible time to realise she still had a weakness for the man!

'The fact is…' she squashed the feeling she was being disloyal '… Seb has needed a father figure for a long time. My brother Michel was a doting dad but there was a lot of pressure when he inherited the crown. He wasn't able to be with Seb a lot.' She paused and made herself taste some of the delicious fish before continuing.

'There's been a power struggle since my father's death between progressives wanting to update our constitution and the way St Galla runs, and more conservative elements.' Her mouth tightened as she thought of the current Prime Minister, Monsieur Barthe, who'd stymied Michel whenever he tried to introduce reforms.

'Irini mentioned something about it.'

Of course. Her sister-in-law had counted Lambis as one of her closest friends.

'Michel worked long hours and, because he was young, and people were used to my father's ways, not his, he had to work doubly hard at persuading parliament on key issues.' Her brother's impatience for change hadn't sat well with some of the country's powerbrokers. 'Seb didn't see as much of him, or Irini, as they wanted.'

'So you filled in for them.' He said it as if he already knew how it had been.

'Irini and Michel did the best they could. But it was natural they'd want some time alone together too. It was rare enough, given the demands on their time.'

'And the demands on yours?' Lambis's flinty tone made her look up, catching a spark of something she couldn't read in those deep-set eyes.

Amelie frowned. 'Only the usual.'

'That's not the way I remember it.' His eyes locked with hers and she couldn't look away. 'You were always there, ready with advice for the pair of them when they needed it, seeing to so many of the official royal functions, ready to lend a hand with Sébastien—'

Amelie's cutlery clattered onto her plate. 'Are you saying I interfered?' She'd done her best to step back from her previous role as royal hostess when her father died and Michel inherited. She'd *wanted* the younger couple to take their rightful places.

'No. I'm saying your own workload was enormous. You took on a lot of Irini's responsibilities as well as your own, plus advised your brother. I saw it for myself. Irini confessed she felt she wasn't pulling her weight.'

Poor Irini. Amelie's heart squeezed. 'It's not an easy thing to become royal. Besides, she was sick through her pregnancy. She did the best she could.'

'I know.' His face was set. 'I just wish she'd learned to say no to your brother more often.'

Pain lanced Amelie and she slid a palm over her ribs, trying to hold it in. He had to be thinking of the day they'd died. Irini had been reluctant to go in the new speedboat but had given in when Michel smiled. He could charm anyone with that smile.

'It was an accident.' She sat straighter in her seat and

reached for her fork. 'Not Michel's fault.' Even the coroner had confirmed it. 'No one could have predicted it.'

Lambis surveyed her from under straight black eyebrows, his expression unreadable. 'As you say. An accident.'

Amelie reached for her glass and searched for an easier topic of conversation. Anything to banish those thoughts of 'if only' that taunted her when she thought of the accident.

'How did you come to build on this island? Is it where you grew up?'

For a moment longer Lambis seemed caught in the past. Then his mouth curled up in a hint of a smile and Amelie felt her insides flutter.

'Actually, it's here because of another accident. Irini's father grew up on this island, before he left to make his fortune.'

'Really? I had no idea. Irini didn't mention it.'

'She lived mostly on the mainland. But the old man built a villa right here on the bay, for holidays.'

'You bought it from him?'

Lambis shook his head then lifted his wine glass to his lips. Amelie watched his throat muscles work as he swallowed, fascinated that something so simple should feel so intimate.

'He gave it to me, along with a loan that allowed me to start my business. It's because of him I've got what I have today.'

'I don't understand. I thought you worked for him.'

'That's right. My father was his head of security and my mother was housekeeper in the Athens house. That's how I knew Irini. We grew up in the same house and were close, despite the age difference.'

Amelie took another forkful of her meal, nodding. 'But why did her father give you this place?'

Lambis turned his attention to his own meal. 'When I

left school I worked for him as a bodyguard. I was here on the island one night when a fire broke out. There was a fault with the fire prevention system which meant the smoke alarms didn't sound and the sprinklers came on late. By the time I got Irini's father and the others out, the damage was irreparable.'

'You got them all out?'

Amelie watched him flex his hand, his gaze on a long scar running up to his wrist that she'd wondered about.

'It was simple enough once they woke. The danger was they'd succumb to the smoke.'

Amelie suspected his role hadn't been quite so simple, especially given that the scar looked like an old burn, but Lambis wasn't the sort to brag.

'Unfortunately the villa burned to the ground.'

'But Irini's father was so grateful he gave you the property?'

'He did. He didn't want to rebuild here, and chose an island closer to Athens for that. But he supported me when I wanted to start out on my own. For that I'm grateful.'

'So you grew up in Athens?' She'd expected to find him in the capital, not in the rugged mountains to the north.

'There and wherever his family moved. But for holidays my parents and I went to the mountains.' He looked up, snaring her gaze. 'They came from a village near the house you stayed in.'

'So you made that your permanent home?'

Emotion rippled across his face so swiftly Amelie couldn't read it, yet she was left feeling she'd missed something. Those eyes, almost warm before, now held emptiness.

'Lambis?'

He lifted his glass, taking his time to sip the fine white wine. 'I live there part-time. I have homes in a number of places.'

Amelie opened her mouth to probe then stopped. Having Lambis share so much of his past was more than she'd expected. The change in him, from the dismissive man she'd met in the mountains to tonight's host, was remarkable.

Was it because of his feelings for Seb? Or was there more to this change?

'Tell me about this proclamation ceremony. Can't someone else speak for Seb? Accept the crown on his behalf?'

No wonder Lambis was phenomenally successful. He always cut straight to the key issue.

'His Regent will do most of the talking but all the experts agree—' and she'd consulted them all '—that Seb has to speak too, proving he understands and accepts.' Was it foolish to believe it might be possible after all? The change in Seb today was dramatic, though he still wasn't talking.

'His Regent? That would be you?'

He *really* did have an uncanny knack for zeroing in on problems!

Amelie took another bite of her meal, chewing slowly before responding. Even now, Monsieur Barthe's position on this infuriated her. Hearing the Prime Minister voice his doubts had been a slap to the face.

'Ideally, yes.'

'But?' She saw his eyes narrow as if sensing her bottled-up anger. Surely she wasn't so easily read? But Lambis was an expert at that. It was an uncanny knack he'd used more than once to protect those in his care, according to Irini.

Amelie tore her gaze away to the straw-coloured wine in her glass.

'I'm the best person for the role and, I'd have thought, the only suitable one.'

'Of course you are. You're his aunt. You have a strong loving bond. Plus you were your father's right hand, and your brother's. You're the expert on what it takes to rule St Galla.'

Silently she nodded and eased back in her seat.

'That's a very enlightened view. Some people seem to think because I'm female I'm just…decorative, merely a hostess.' Despite the fact many of St Galla's recent reforms had been designed by her. Even when her father had been alive it had mainly been Amelie doing the hard work behind the scenes. Her father didn't have the patience.

'Whoever thinks that doesn't know you.'

Something in Lambis's voice yanked her head up. He meant it. She read admiration in those steely eyes.

Amelie blinked, unprepared for the flood of delight that washed through her.

Oh, this isn't good. Not good at all.

She lifted her glass and took a small sip, buying time. Lambis's approval shouldn't matter and yet… She put the glass down, telling herself it was natural to be pleased she had someone on her side, though it made no material difference to the tussle for power back in St Galla.

'Thank you, Lambis.'

'It's the truth.' He paused and she sensed his sharp scrutiny, even though she busied herself with her meal. 'Are you going to tell me what's going on?'

Amelie's instinctive response was to gloss over her troubles. Life as a royal meant keeping them to herself, never looking to others for sympathy. While the St Gallan royal family was extremely popular, Amelie had no illusions. They led lives of privilege, despite the demands placed on them.

'Amelie?' His voice dropped, softening, and she felt something melt inside. Her caution?

What did it matter? There could be no harm in telling Lambis. He was the most circumspect person she knew.

'The Prime Minister, Monsieur Barthe, has made it clear he has concerns about a woman being Seb's Regent, especially a single woman.' She swallowed the knot of fury blocking her throat. 'He believes Seb's Regent should be a man or, failing that, he'd accept a princess of St Galla as Regent on condition she's married to a *suitable* man.'

Amelie's teeth clenched at the memory of his superior attitude and the misogynistic things he'd said, attempting to dictate her future and her nephew's. Then she looked up, startled, as she heard a stream of soft, rapid Greek.

'Sorry? What did you say?'

Lambis shook his head, his dark locks like glossy jet against his golden olive skin. 'Nothing for your ears, Princess.' His solid jaw was clamped as tight as hers felt. 'This man, Barthe, is a fool! He couldn't ask for anyone better for the role.'

Amelie felt the corners of her mouth tickle in a hint of a smile. It was nothing to the gush of heat through her taut body at Lambis's support.

'What's the guy's problem? Does he want to marry you himself?'

She couldn't help it. A choked laugh escaped. 'Hardly. He's sixty if he's a day.'

Lambis's straight eyebrows rose. 'And? It wouldn't be the first time an older man fell for a younger, beautiful woman.'

Amelie had been called beautiful, usually by a gushing press. It didn't mean anything, especially to someone whose father had been quick to point out defects in her demeanour, appearance or behaviour. Yes, she had even features and a healthy body but a lot of what passed for beauty was window dressing—jewellery, expensive clothes, makeup and a level of confidence.

Why did Lambis's casual reference to her as beautiful set the blood zinging in her veins? She even felt it scorch her cheeks!

'Our Prime Minister is already married, to a very quiet, respectable woman, who, I suspect, is a very obedient wife.

Besides—' Amelie's mouth tightened '—he's already suggested he'd be willing to act as Seb's Regent.'

'The devil he did!' Lambis's scowl was ferocious but for once not in the least intimidating, since his anger was on her behalf, and Seb's.

Was she really so lonely that Lambis's support, and his good opinion, made such a difference?

'The man wants power for himself.'

'Absolutely. He's always been a schemer but lately he's interfered in things that don't concern him.' Like pestering her to marry King Alex of Bengaria, even beginning discussions with the Bengarians before consulting her.

That rankled. Amelie had signalled some time ago that she'd agree to *consider* an arranged royal marriage, *if* she and her prospective bridegroom were compatible. She wanted a family and her attempts so far to find true love had been disastrous. A dynastic match might be the answer. But, since her brother's death, the Prime Minister kept pushing her to commit. As if she'd give her word to marry a man she'd never met! What century did they think it was?

'What right has Barthe to dictate the next Regent?' Lambis's words broke into her thoughts. 'Surely he hasn't got the power to move you out of the equation?'

Amelie shrugged and sat back, giving up the pretence of eating. 'That's just it. I can't say for certain. I *can* say that he has a significant majority in parliament and a female Regent would be a first in St Galla. The country's views on the monarchy are still rather old-fashioned.'

'But your people love you! They always have.'

Amelie's mouth curled up at one corner. Strangely, it was reassuring to discover that Lambis, after all, wasn't infallible. She was so used to seeing him as supremely self-contained, competent and successful.

'Yes, I'm popular. But this isn't something the people will decide. There's a royal privy council, primarily politicians, who make the final decision. The majority older men, and a lot of them belong to Barthe's side of politics.'

'So you'll simply let him force your hand?'

'It won't be simple at all. I intend to fight for Seb's right to the throne, and my right to be Regent. The idea of him brought up by Monsieur Barthe or one of his cronies doesn't bear thinking about.'

Suddenly it was all too much. Not just grief for her loss, and fear for Seb's wellbeing, but all the other pressures too.

'Thank you for the meal, Lambis. It was exquisite.' Carefully she folded her napkin and placed it on the table beside her plate. Then she moved her chair back. 'But I'm afraid I've lost my appetite.' Amelie gave him a small polite smile. 'If you'll excuse me, I think it's best if I go to my room now.'

She was on her feet and turning away when she heard the scratch of his chair on the paving.

'Wait, don't go.' A big hand closed around her upper arm.

For a millisecond Amelie's jagged nerves eased at the reassurance of that touch. Till she heard Lambis's hiss of indrawn breath and his hand dropped away.

Amelie stood, blinking at the view of garden lights and the dark bay beyond, telling herself it didn't matter. Truly. She'd had plenty of time to accept he didn't want her.

But that instant reaction told her more. It told her she actually *repelled* him.

What was wrong with her? Twice in her life she'd reached out to a man, believing they shared something special. Twice she'd been pushed away.

She blinked again, horrified by this curious stasis gripping her. She couldn't lift her feet. It was all she could do to repress the wild tumble of emotions churning inside.

'Why, Lambis? What is it about me?'

She hadn't intended the words. Heaven knew she'd worked for years to put on a bland, unconcerned face on the few occasions she and Lambis had met since that fateful summer. Pride dictated she say nothing, just accept she was flawed in some way that made her attractive from a distance, to the adoring crowds and the press, but not up close. Not to a man she cared about.

'What do you mean?'

Amelie counted to five, telling herself to forget this and walk away. She had enough to contend with without opening up this too. Yet how could she fix whatever was wrong with her, if she didn't know the problem? Was she doomed for ever to repel rather than attract?

On a spurt of defiant courage she spun on her heel. He stood close behind her. So close she had to hike up her chin to meet his unreadable gaze.

'Why don't you want to touch me? It's not that you're afraid I'll misinterpret and think you've changed your mind about…us.' She swallowed hard but kept going, determined to have this out. 'What is it about me that's so…' she waved a hand, searching for the word '…wrong?'

'Wrong?' His brow wrinkled. 'There's nothing wrong with you, Amelie.'

Yet she read strain in the tendons of his neck that stood proud. In the flare of his nostrils and the pulse racing at his temple. Amelie looked down and saw his hands bunched into fists.

'Isn't there?' She lifted her hand and lightly touched his cheek. Silky heat and just a touch of abrasiveness met the pads of her fingertips.

She'd wondered how it would feel to touch him.

But his instant step back told her everything she needed to know.

'Actually, don't bother answering.' She'd been wrong. She didn't need to know the answer. Tonight, with so many other insurmountable problems, she didn't have strength to wrestle with another.

She was turning when his arm shot out, barring her way. Again, he didn't touch her, yet it felt as if the air between them snapped and sizzled with electricity. How she deluded herself.

'You want to know why I don't touch you?' His voice sounded different, raw and hard. 'It's because I don't dare.'

Amelie frowned. 'What are you saying, Lambis? I don't understand.'

'No, you don't, do you?' His voice was husky. His hands closed around her shoulders, turning her to face him, pulling her so close she shivered as the heat of his big body encompassed her. 'I've tried to resist you, Amelie. I thought I'd succeeded, but I can't do it any more. Not when you're so close, so…' He shook his head. 'Every time I see you I want to touch you, *more* than touch you.'

Amelie's eyes widened. Her breath caught as he lowered his head. His eyes, the colour of a storm cloud shot with lightning, captured hers.

'There's absolutely nothing wrong with you, Amelie.' His breath feathered her cheeks. 'The problem is me. And the fact I want to do this.'

He hauled her up on her toes, wrapping powerful arms around her, then slanted his mouth over hers.

CHAPTER EIGHT

HIS MOUTH TOUCHED Amelie's, settled hard and demanding, his tongue probing till she—*ah!*

Lambis's thoughts fractured as Amelie's mouth opened under his, sweet and willing. Almost as if she'd been going crazy too, trying to stifle a longing so great it turned him inside out.

But that couldn't be. After his behaviour years before she'd washed her hands of him.

This was wrong, wrong, wrong.

He knew it. His conscience pounded out the word with every frantic beat of his pulse. They'd regret this.

Yet soaring delight undermined any hope of pulling away.

He gathered Amelie in, exulting in her soft femininity against him, the scent of her, heady as spring after eternal winter. The taste of her. Her gasp of surprise and pleasure. He leaned in, delving deeper, senses exploding at the nectar sweetness of her mouth fused with his, her tongue sliding against his, almost as eagerly as he devoured her.

Her hand rested on his chest, right where his heart pounded riotously. Then, in torturous slow motion, her other hand crept up his chest to slide beneath his collar, stoking his temperature to dangerous levels.

He'd known from the first that Amelie was a threat to his resolve This gentle caress of skin on skin proved it. He shuddered with the effort it took to stand there, merely kissing, when he wanted her touch all over him. Wanted to touch her all over and more, far more.

Her fingers slid higher, raking his scalp and the potent eroticism all but undid him.

His knees went weak and great racking shudders ripped through him, cracking what was left of his self-control.

'Amelie. Sweet Amelie.' He cupped the back of her head, holding it still as he bowed her back over his arm, lost in the give and take, the thrust and parry of their voracious kiss.

He could barely breathe, yet for the first time in memory his chest felt lighter, not banded tight by pain and regret.

She did this to him. This wondrous woman. She kissed like an angel and— No, not an angel, but a woman whose blood sang with need like his. Who'd pent up passion too long.

Lambis hauled her higher in his arms, felt her hand go to his shoulder for support as he lifted her off her feet and still it wasn't enough.

She was addictive. He'd always suspected it, from the moment he fell under the spell of her devastating smile and dazzling eyes, her lush body and charming personality with just the tiniest hint of diffidence when she spoke to him.

There was nothing diffident about her now.

Lambis backed her up against one of the columns supporting the arbour. Was that a hum of approval as he propped her up with his body? His massively aroused body. To his delight, she pressed closer, curving her pelvis against him. He shuddered, close to losing all willpower.

He'd dreamed of Amelie, spent hour upon hour torturing himself imagining how it would be to kiss her, touch her, possess her. Yet reality outstripped expectation. This woman was eager, responsive, as sensual as any fantasy lover. More. She was somehow more than he'd ever dared imagine.

The realisation was a blast of lightning to his frigid soul.

His kiss turned slow, inviting her to melt into him. All the while his head swam. She was sunlight and joy. Warmth and life after the dark well of nothing he'd inhabited so long.

Inhabited because that was his destiny, his penance.

The thought filtered slowly into his fogged brain and he almost groaned aloud as it registered. For how could he pull back when Amelie kissed him like this? When her fingers dug into him needily as he pressed his hips to her belly?

Because she deserves better.

That, finally, slashed through desire, through a wanting so great he didn't know how he managed to lift his head from hers.

The rush of oxygen into starved lungs hurt. So did the waft of warm air brushing his lips. He opened his eyes and his heart stilled.

Amelie's head rested back on a column, her throat arched at an abandoned angle, her lips plump and red from his kisses. A flush covered her face and throat and a tiny tic of a pulse shimmered at the base of her neck.

She was utterly glorious. A feast for the senses.

Lambis couldn't resist. He pressed his lips to the corner of her mouth. When she turned towards him offering her lips, she made his poor, crippled heart leap. The temptation to taste Paradise one more time was immense.

He had just enough sense to pull back and kiss his way across her jaw and down her neck, revelling in the little breathy sighs that set his groin hard.

The trouble was, at the base of her throat was more bare skin and from there the slope of her beautiful breasts.

Shaking with effort, not quite believing he'd finally found the strength to do it, Lambis stepped back, lowering Amelie till her feet touched the ground. His hands locked around her hips, securing her till he knew she could stand. Somehow his hands slid up to clasp her waist. He'd been right. Despite her height and gorgeous curving femininity, Amelie was so slim he could almost span her waist with his big hands.

It was that reminder of her vulnerability, of the disparity between them, that finally forced him to end this.

She'd come to him seeking help not sex. She hadn't asked for this, no matter how unwittingly she'd tempted him these past days.

Days? Years it had been. Years of torture as he felt himself under her gentle spell yet knew they could never be together.

'Amelie.' It was a croak, barely intelligible.

Her eyelids fluttered. A tremor passed through her, then those brilliant jewel eyes met his and Lambis felt a heavy punch to the solar plexus. Not just need this time, but pain as he registered the question in her expression.

She swallowed then swiped her lips with her tongue. Did she taste him there? He knew he'd never eradicate the taste of her from his senses. It would torment him for years to come, when he was back in his own sterile world.

'Lambis.' Even the sound of her saying his name tested his resolution to let her go. Her hand moved against his scalp, a slow caress that sent tingles of sensual delight skittering across his flesh.

Amelie frowned, tilting her head to survey him from a different angle.

'Talk to me. Why...push me away then kiss me like that?' Her voice was delightfully uneven, as if she were as thrown by this as he.

She deserved the truth. He'd always been honest with her, just not totally honest.

Some things had been better left unsaid.

'Why did you kiss me?' Her brow twitched and her mouth twisted. 'Because you're bored and I'm convenient?'

'No!' His hands tightened convulsively on her waist. 'You can't believe that. Convenience has nothing to do with it.'

These feelings were anything but convenient.

Amelie's eyes held his for what seemed an age. But she didn't move to break free and, selfish as he was, even knowing he shouldn't, Lambis revelled in the lithe heat of her narrow waist in his hands.

Nor did she remove her hands. One still splayed against his chest, the other clamped on his skull. Because, like him, she couldn't bear to break away? Now there was a bit of wishful thinking!

'You're attracted to me?' Her chin angled and Lambis realised how much her straight talking cost her.

'Attracted?' He shook his head, feeling his features settle into implacable lines. 'I've wanted you from the moment I saw you.'

He couldn't hide it any more.

Amelie flinched, shock widening her eyes. She would have drawn away except he wouldn't let her.

She was going nowhere.

The aching hunger he'd tried to bury rose up, obliterating everything. His brain screamed he needed to release her, but his body acted on a primitive level that overrode conscious thought.

Instinct told him to forget conversation and claim the woman he'd craved for years. Take what, surely, her kiss implied she'd willingly give.

His hands twitched. To pull her close? To push her away? Lambis was on a knife-edge, battling for control.

'I find that hard to believe. You never said or even hinted—'

'I remember that first time we met.' His voice was a growl, hoarse as he recalled the effort it had taken to hold back all this time. 'I was with Irini when you walked in.' He'd been ready for a beautiful woman, but the reality had transfixed him. 'You wore a sleeveless white dress, belted at the waist.' That tiny waist he held now. 'There were green leaves all around the bottom of the skirt and little cut-outs between the leaves. You wore the same pearl pendant.'

The sun had caught her hair, turning it to gold, and she'd glowed with an inner radiance that had beckoned with a terrible, unstoppable power. She'd looked fresh as a spring morning and that smile of hers, the dancing delight in her eyes as she'd chatted so easily about the upcoming royal wedding, had cracked the icy carapace around his soul.

Even in those first moments, before he'd discovered she was as beautiful inside as out, Lambis had realised Amelie had the power to make him hunger and, worse, hope. That, above all, had convinced him she was best avoided.

Her eyes looked huge and when she spoke her voice was hushed. 'You remember that?'

'I do.' He remembered everything.

'I don't understand.' Her beautiful mouth trembled. She looked so lost, as if he'd suddenly proved the earth was flat and the sun circled the moon.

'It's simple,' he murmured. Devastatingly simple. 'I want you, Amelie. I always have.'

Lambis couldn't resist any more. Not when he read such hurt and confusion in her face. He leaned in and gently, so gently he shook with the effort of control, brushed his lips across hers.

Amelie's eyes fluttered closed as his mouth, soft and warm, touched hers. Instantly that tingling rush of heat filled her, that unstoppable longing.

She should pull back, demand answers.

But there was magic in his caress. In this butterfly-light kiss that made her want to lean closer and offer herself.

His hands tightened on her waist and shuddery delight surged. She'd never been held quite like this. Lambis's big hands around her made her feel small and feminine, sexy and...desirable. Amelie wasn't an innocent. She'd had a lover. But Jules's youthful fumblings had never made her feel like *this*.

She slid her hand to the back of Lambis's head and pulled him to her, opening her lips and inviting him in. It was an invitation he accepted without hesitation, invading her mouth, and making her body come alive.

It was a miracle. Lambis and her. She'd wanted him so long. Liked and admired and desired him. Years of putting on a brave face hadn't cauterised her feelings. Even rejection hadn't ended those.

She was straining against him, rising on her toes, eager for more, when belatedly her brain began to work.

Lambis wasn't pulling her close but holding her off him, even as his languorous, impossibly sexy kiss invited her to lose herself completely. It was as if he seduced her, but at a careful distance.

This was the man who'd *rejected* her three years before.

Was she so under his thrall, all he had to do was crook his finger? There'd been no explanation, nothing but the bald statement that he'd always wanted her.

The fact he remembered the day they'd met, as she did, sliced through caution and sent her spinning straight into yearning. Amelie put her hands to his shoulders, trying not to savour their hard strength as she pushed against them, levering herself away.

His mouth lifted, leaving her breathless and shattered, gulping air. Her mouth throbbed and her peaked nipples strained against her bra, still seeking contact with his solid frame.

'Let me go.' Her voice was strangled, raspy, yet he heard. She felt him tense, his fingers digging against her ribs.

Then abruptly he stepped back, leaving her bereft and swaying. She still felt the imprint of his big hands at her waist and the rich taste of him on her tongue.

It had been tough, years ago, accepting his rejection with

her head high. But this, standing so close, knowing he too felt this incredible pulse of attraction, tested her to the limit. His eyes shone with a silver light that promised passion and Amelie wanted it, so badly it shocked her.

She rubbed her hands up her arms.

'What's going on, Lambis?' He owed her an explanation.

His expression didn't alter. He looked down at her with the intensity of a mountain eagle surveying its prey. Did he see the way her flesh prickled on her bare arms? The way her nipples puckered hard and tight?

Amelie suspected Lambis saw that and much more. All those tiny signs of arousal she didn't even recognise, but he, a man with such a powerful sexual aura, must. Despite his air of self-control, of distance, there was no mistaking Lambis Evangelos for anything other than a sexual being, a man of strong passions.

'Tell me!' Long repressed pain vied with recent anger. 'You say you've always wanted me, yet for years you've avoided being alone with me as if I was tainted—'

'No. Not that.'

Her chin hiked up. 'You rejected me. I didn't imagine that!' Oh, he'd been kind, or as kind as you could be when telling a woman you weren't interested. 'Either you lied then or you're lying now. I want to know which.'

He hefted a deep breath and rolled his head as if easing taut muscles. 'I didn't lie, though I was tempted. You have no idea how much I wanted to make love to you.'

Amelie folded her arms at her waist, holding in the trembling excitement his words evoked. 'You're right. I have no idea. You told me it was better if we didn't spend time together. That it would be a mistake to get close.'

She fought to keep the hurt from her voice. The memory of her tentative hopes and how he'd dashed them made her feel sick.

Lambis looked immovable, not lover-like, with his muscles bunched, his jaw set.

'You wanted a long-term relationship. You wanted someone to fall in love with. I couldn't be that man.'

Amelie's throat seized. By the time she'd confronted Lambis, she'd already been a fair way towards falling in love with him. Had he known?

'Let me get this right. You were attracted but—'

'I *am* attracted.' The timbre of his voice wove, deep and seductive, around her bones. 'That never changed. I've always wanted you, Amelie.' The searing intensity of his stare scored her flesh and made her heart hammer. 'But I can't give you what you want. I couldn't promise hearts and flowers and a lifetime together.'

'Hold on!' Amelie raised her palm, cutting off his words. 'I never asked for a lifetime together. I told you I was attracted and asked you to stay on in St Galla so we could get to know each other.' It had taken courage to reveal her feelings to the enigmatic man who was her sister-in-law's friend.

'You're saying you wanted a quick lay? A one-night stand?'

'No!' Why twist her words?

'Exactly.' He nodded as if she'd proved his point. 'You're not that sort of woman. You want a family, someone to build your life around.' Something flickered in his eyes as he uncrossed his arms and dropped them. 'You didn't talk about a permanent relationship but that's where you hoped it would lead.'

He was right. She *had* hoped.

As for a family—was that so wrong? At twenty-nine her body clock ticked louder. She'd long ago realised that what she craved most wasn't pomp and glitter, or even the love of her people, though she treasured that. It was to love and be loved for herself, as a wife and mother, not a royal princess.

'So you rejected me because...?'

'Because I'm not the man you want. I can't give you that and I won't lie and pretend I can.'

Amelie frowned, resenting that he'd withheld vital information from her, apparently for her own good, like some paternalistic...

'You can't know that. You haven't even tried.'

As Amelie watched there was a change in the man before her. She couldn't put her finger on it but it was as sure as a shadow blocking out sunlight. There was a flicker in his eyes and he stared down at her with none of the heat that just seconds before had made her blood sizzle. It was as if a light had gone out inside.

'I did. Once. It didn't work.' Lambis's voice rang hollow. It sounded so empty a shudder raced across her nape. 'I can't promise any woman love. It would have been criminal to let you believe I could.'

Questions tumbled in Amelie's head. But the stark, bereft look in those piercing eyes stopped her tongue.

Suddenly she remembered Irini talking about her childhood friend, saying he deserved his business success, not simply because of his drive to succeed, but because he needed something good in his life. When Amelie had queried her, she'd clammed up, saying only that Lambis had faced private problems but preferred not to talk about them. Irini being Irini, she hadn't betrayed his trust and gossiped.

Which left Amelie where?

'You don't want love? A family?'

'That's not for me. It can never be.'

This time, fleeting as it was, she recognised the emotion that slashed across his face like jagged lightning. Pain. No, anguish. Her chest cramped in sympathy. No matter the persona he presented, Lambis was a man who felt deeply rather than not enough.

She wanted to touch him, soothe him.

As if reading her sympathy, Lambis spoke again, his voice cool. 'I can't offer love or happy ever afters. He paused, making sure she had time to process his words.

'But there's something I *can* offer.' His eyes held hers and Amelie couldn't look away. 'Passion. An affair that would bring us both pleasure.'

'Sex without strings?' Amelie heard herself saying. 'It's not my style.'

She'd had but one lover, a man she'd once believed she'd spend her life with, until he'd betrayed her love and walked away, eventually marrying someone else.

Was that why Lambis's outrageous suggestion tempted? Because she'd never been lucky in love?

Or because she'd never got over Lambis?

'Why not?' His dark eyes held hers. 'We both feel this desire. We both…want.'

As he spoke Amelie felt heat flare low in her pelvis and a heavy, needy pulse begin deep inside.

'We wouldn't be hurting anyone. Why not find pleasure in each other's arms?'

His was the voice of temptation, Amelie decided as it rumbled through her, its echo eddying deep and low. She stifled a gasp at the way her body responded, softening, eager. Even after all that had gone before, Lambis had only to mention sex and she was excited, hungry.

Amelie blinked, fighting back emotions too mixed, too strong, to contain. 'I've heard enough. I'm going to bed.' Pivoting on her foot she turned away.

She was almost around the corner of the house when his voice feathered the night. 'Think about it, Amelie.'

CHAPTER NINE

THINK ABOUT IT?

She did nothing but think about it!

All through the long, sultry night Amelie couldn't wrest her mind from Lambis's proposition. Even this morning, busy with Seb, her thoughts kept straying to the idea of an affair. A hot, passionate, purely physical affair.

Her body said *Yes*. All but screamed it, as that betraying heat settled tight and low in her pelvis and a throb of anticipation started up at the apex of her thighs.

Yet her heart and her head warned of danger. From the first she'd felt drawn to Lambis, sexually and emotionally. Till she'd had to smother those feelings.

When, last night, he'd revealed he'd tried love and it hadn't worked, regret had pounded hard in her blood. Regret for his pain. Surely that was dangerous?

Yet the idea of an affair with Lambis was alluring.

Her thoughts circled as she tried to use logic and failed dismally. She *wanted* to take a risk on transitory, utterly selfish pleasure.

She'd spent her life being dependable, responsible and, in her youth, obedient. Her one act of rebellion had been when she was a university student. Even then she hadn't managed to escape the demands of duty or, more specifically, her father, by leaving St Galla to study. He'd insisted she stay close and act as his hostess so she'd studied locally, never quite accepted by the other students since, between lectures, she regularly appeared at official events in diamonds and jewels.

Only Jules had treated her like anyone else. Jules, the quiet medical student who'd wooed and won her. His lovemaking had been tender rather than ardent but she'd been so in love, so wrapped up in thoughts of their future together, she hadn't minded.

Not till her father stepped in, declaring it impossible a royal princess should marry a commoner. Amelie had defied her father, only to discover Jules had backed off, cowed by her father's bluster and, she realised later, a hefty payout to help him set up his medical practice. He'd dropped her unceremoniously, telling her he'd been wrong; clearly people from such different backgrounds couldn't make a marriage work.

So much for love.

Since then she'd guarded her heart. Until Lambis strode into the palace and she felt herself spin out of control, losing the battle not to fall for him.

The second time she'd put herself on the line, shoving aside pride. She hadn't waited in the hope *he* might declare an interest, but had made the first move. Only to be rejected.

Love clearly wasn't for her. The way Lambis had turned from her had been the final straw. After that she'd begun to think seriously on the Prime Minister's suggestion, more frequent in the last couple of years, that she accept an arranged marriage. It was why she'd consented to meet King Alex of Bengaria. Now, with the pressure to marry before being made Regent, an arranged marriage was more than ever desirable.

If she could stomach a loveless marriage. Surely it wouldn't be as difficult as her parents' marriage? King Alex was supposed to be a fine man, an honest man, not a philanderer.

'Is something wrong?' Lambis's voice interrupted her circling thoughts and she stiffened. Heat washed her cheeks.

'Nothing at all.' She didn't meet his look but turned to

Seb, beside her on the back seat of the large rowing boat. 'Have you seen any fish yet, *mon lapin*?'

Seb shook his head, then, a second later, reached out and tugged her hand, pointing down into the miraculously clear blue-green depths.

Instantly Amelie forgot her problems, excitement rising. Seb was a changed boy since he'd cried in Lambis's arms. He didn't speak, but he was responsive as he hadn't been before.

'I see them. Aren't they quick? See how the sun catches them when they turn?'

The rhythmic lap of the oars ceased and Lambis leaned towards the side too. 'Well spotted, Sébastien. Do you like fishing?'

The small golden head turned as Seb looked up at the big man who took up most of the space in the boat.

'I don't think you've ever been fishing, have you, Seb?' While Amelie had tried to ensure her nephew lived a life as close to ordinary as possible, she'd never taken him fishing. She doubted his parents had.

The boy shook his head and Amelie felt again that tiny flare of hope. Maybe, after all, with patience he'd get through this. At least now he was interacting. It was a precious start.

'Well, if you'd like to try one day, just let me know. I know a secret spot the local fishermen say is the best.' Without waiting for an answer, Lambis picked up the oars and began pulling on them again, ploughing them easily through the water towards the headland.

It had been an inspired suggestion of his to take out the rowing boat instead of the sleek powerboat in the boathouse. He'd rowed it to the beach so Seb didn't have to see the other boat, so like the one that had scared him, and Seb had actually smiled at the novelty of wading out then being scooped up in Lambis's arms and settled on the back seat.

That smile had pierced Amelie's heart and she'd found herself unaccountably close to tears. Till she'd seen Lambis looking at her and turned away, climbing clumsily into the boat rather than accept his assistance.

The rowing boat had another thing to recommend it. She got to watch Lambis row. No matter how often she told herself not to stare, and kept busy chatting with Seb, her gaze slid back to the big man pulling at the oars. Every stroke emphasised the power in his arms and upper body, pulling his T-shirt across the fascinating play of muscles. His long legs stretched out so she found hers brushing them as she turned. And every time showers of sparks ignited under her skin.

An affair that would bring us both pleasure.

Passion.

Excitement ripped through her as she remembered his words. Was he thinking about it too? Lambis had been particularly unreadable this morning. It drove her crazy, wondering if he regretted his words last night.

He didn't look like he'd paced the floor half the night, as she had. He looked rested, fit, and comfortable in his skin. Sure of himself.

Sure he couldn't offer love.

Again she circled back to that nugget of information, worrying at it like a tongue at a sore tooth. But what was the point? She'd long ago accepted he'd never love her.

'Here we are. Now, keep your hands inside the boat; the entrance is narrow.'

They approached a dark hole in the white cliff of the headland. Seb shifted closer and she put her arm around him.

'It's okay, *mon lapin*. Lambis has promised us a nice surprise. A surprise is worth a little adventure, don't you think?'

Seb nodded against her side, staying close as Lambis

guided the boat gently into the black entrance. The temperature dropped as they floated into the cave, and darkness engulfed them. Seb leaned closer.

'Are you watching?' Lambis's voice floated out of the gloom. 'Any minute now.' He paused. 'There! What do you think?'

Amelie felt her eyes widen as the boat turned a corner and suddenly the darkness retreated. Ahead was a bright blue bowl of water. So bright it seemed iridescent. Above, the roof of the cavern soared high till, where the top of the vast space must once have been, there was only clear Aegean sky.

'It's wonderful,' she breathed, her hand tightening on Seb. 'Spectacular.'

'I thought you'd enjoy it.' For a moment Lambis held her eyes and she felt her breath seize. Then he turned to her nephew. 'All this used to be underground, until one day, hundreds of years ago, part of the roof fell, letting in the light. Now it's a secret place, perfect for private picnics.'

Seb stirred, pulling back from her side and sliding along the seat to take in the magical view. Everything about it felt magical, from the crystal blue depths to the bright dome of sky above, and the sense of being cut off from the world.

The boat bumped gently against the shore and Lambis shipped the oars. Moments later he was ashore, tugging the boat in close and tying it to a rock. Then he lifted Seb out.

Amelie watched as her nephew immediately investigated the shoreline of a tiny beach beneath the overhang. He was on hands and knees, peering into the watery depths, just like any other curious child.

How long since she'd seen him like that?

'Thank you, Lambis,' she murmured as she stood and passed him the picnic basket his housekeeper had provided. She didn't try to hide her delight. 'This was a great idea. Seb loves it.'

A hand, large and callused, closed around hers instead of taking the basket's handle. Instantly longing tugged, hard and tight, from her nipples to her womb. One touch and the hours since he'd held her vanished. It was as if Lambis had kissed her mere moments ago. Her heart skidded against her ribcage and the feel of his breath sluicing down over her mouth made her lips tingle and part in unconscious invitation.

He focused on the movement and the lines bracketing his mouth grew deeper. 'It's not just for Sébastien. Do *you* like it, Amelie?'

She loved it when his voice eddied down to that impossibly deep resonance that scoured her belly. Loved and hated it, because it made her feel on the edge of control. As if she were a creature of instinct, not thought. A woman liable to do something dangerous, like give herself to a man who didn't care for her.

But isn't that what you'd do if you went through with an arranged marriage? At least this way you'd enjoy passion with the only man who's made you feel desirable in years.

'Amelie?'

She nodded and slid her hand from beneath his. 'I've never seen anything like it. It's wonderful. Thank you for bringing us here.'

She waited till he turned to put the basket ashore then moved to alight, but he swung round quickly, catching her about the waist and lifting her out as easily as he had Seb.

Slowly he lowered her to the ground. So slowly she was aware of every plane and angle of his hard-packed body as she passed just a hairsbreadth from it.

It felt as if she'd brushed against him. All of her, from her hard nipples to her quivering thighs and clenched fingers, tingled.

Lambis's eyes held hers. He read her response, knew exactly what he was doing. It was there in the banked heat of his expression and the way those massive hands held her even after she was on her own feet.

'You can let me go.'

She didn't think he was going to respond. His body canted towards her. Then a splash broke the silence. Instantly alert, Amelie wheeled to look for Seb. But he was safe, merely throwing stones into the water, his tongue between his lips and his forehead bunched in concentration.

Amelie sagged in Lambis's hold, then the moment was gone. He released her and moved away, shaking out a blanket. She remained where she was, surveying the scene. The little boy playing his age-old game and the big man, apparently domesticated, setting up a picnic.

For a second, no longer, Amelie let herself remember the dreams she'd had for so long—children of her own, a man who loved her enough to mesh his life with hers. A man who was honest, faithful and caring, who saw her as something other than a princess, a diplomatic helpmeet or a trophy to be won in furthering his political ambitions.

She pursed her lips and shoved aside the yearning for what she'd never possess.

She had no idea if she'd accept an arranged marriage with the King of Bengaria. That could wait till she discovered if they were compatible.

Compatible was a far cry from love.

Who was she to cry for the moon and the stars? She had Seb to look after, to love. She had a responsibility to do what was best for him. That had to be her priority, not pining for the impossible.

Yet, as she smiled and joined him at the water's edge, she couldn't stifle a pang of regret.

Two hours later Amelie lay, head pillowed on her arm, watching Seb and Lambis in the water. Her lack of sleep caught up with her and she felt her eyelids droop. But she didn't want to sleep. Not when she could watch the pair of them, exploring the brilliant blue waters of the cave.

They were on the far side of the cavern now, two sleek, wet heads together, one dark as night and the other glowing old gold in the sunlight. Lambis's bare broad shoulders crested the water as he slowly swam breaststroke across the pool. Seb clung to his back, his small hands clasping dark olive skin.

Emotion crested at the sight of them together.

For all their differences, in size, age and temperament, there was something similar about them. The intensity of their expressions for one. The way Seb nodded in response to something Lambis pointed out.

And more. That almost impenetrable air of reserve.

Amelie frowned. In Seb that was a new characteristic. Before his parents' death he'd been lively and gregarious, a little chatterbox with an insatiable curiosity. In Lambis it seemed ingrained. Maybe it was the nature of his work, but she felt restraint and control, as much as a lack of demonstrativeness, had been part of Lambis for a long, long time.

Inevitably her thoughts worried at his words last night. He had tried love once and it hadn't worked.

Whom had he loved? Had the woman rejected him? Betrayed him?

It was none of her business yet she couldn't leave it alone.

Had Lambis always been so ferociously self-contained or had he once been lively and loving? Had he suffered hurt like her nephew and never recovered?

She remembered his rare, sweet smiles, usually directed at Irini but occasionally at her or Seb. They'd been like shafts of sunlight breaking through dissipating mist and they'd made her yearn.

It wasn't that he was bad-tempered, despite the awful, grumpy reception he'd given her at his mountain home. It was that he was...cut off. Completely self-contained.

The nurturing side of her wanted to break through to the man inside. The man who was doing more for her nephew than all the doctors and do-gooders they'd seen.

But Amelie had learned her lesson. It wasn't up to her to save Lambis, or heal him. He'd made it clear he was content with his life. He didn't want her help.

Just her body.

Heat slammed through her. Even thinking of it in those crude, unvarnished terms—two lonely people sharing sex—his proposition was devastatingly tempting.

She'd all but given up her dream of love, apart from her love for her nephew.

Why not take what Lambis suggested? As he said there was no harm—

'Look! Look!'

Amelie's head jerked up. Seconds later she was on her feet, heart throbbing high in her throat, straining to hear over the racing pulse that thundered in her ears. Eyes wide as saucers, she stared across the cavern to where Lambis trod water and Seb, on his back, sat up high, pointing towards the middle of the pool.

'Aunt Lili, look!'

Amelie swayed as if the very sea had risen to knock her off her feet. She stumbled forward, right to the water's edge, her gaze fixed on the little boy who stared with such rapt attention at the water.

Her hand was at her throat, as if to keep down the hammering heart that had risen there.

'See?' Familiar green eyes met hers from over Lambis's shoulder and it was like electricity jolting through her. 'See?' Seb demanded.

Reluctantly, not wanting to look away, Amelie turned. At first she saw nothing, then, from out of the shadows a dark blob emerged. She leaned forward, frowning. The blob swam closer and suddenly, despite her hammering pulse and the raw blast of shock reverberating through her, she smiled.

'I see! It's a turtle.'

Her gaze darted to Seb but he didn't answer. He was too busy following the animal's progress through the water. Did he realise he'd spoken? Her hand pressed down on her breastbone. She couldn't quite believe it.

'That's right,' Lambis said in a calm, deep voice, as if nothing momentous had happened. 'They come ashore on a nearby island to lay their eggs.'

Seb nodded, but didn't comment.

That didn't matter. He'd spoken! If he could do it once, surely, soon, he could do it again.

Overwhelmed, Amelie sank to the ground, her legs too weak to support her. Shock and relief confounded her and she blinked back tears. She should be happy, exultant even. Instead she felt horribly wobbly. Happy, but wobbly.

She'd spent so long hoping and praying for this day but in her heart of hearts she'd wondered if it would ever come. She scooted her hands up and down her chilled arms, feeling the gooseflesh there.

Her neck was stiff as she raised her head again to peer towards the pair in the water. They were closer now, Lambis's dark eyes unreadable as he stared straight at her.

'Well done, Seb.' Her voice was croaky and uneven. 'You have very sharp eyes. I've never seen a turtle in the wild.'

'I think we ought to head back,' Lambis said. 'Your aunt is tired.'

'Oh, no. Please. Couldn't we stay a little longer?' It was Amelie who spoke, not Seb. She was loath to leave this magical place where miracles clearly happened. Seb was happy and relaxed here. Surely a little bit more of that magic could only help? 'Are you tired, Seb?'

He merely shook his head, his attention on the water,

and Amelie told herself not to expect too much. Small steps were a vast improvement on none at all.

She met Lambis's eyes and found herself smiling.

Lambis stood in the shadows of the wide terrace, watching Amelie. The westering sun gilded her, turning her into an ethereal creature of gold.

She still wore the swimsuit and sarong from their trip to the cave and, as usual, it was all but impossible to drag his eyes away. Technically the filmy fabric covered her from where it was tied, just above her breasts, to just above her knees. Yet it teased and tantalised, giving glimpses of her toned body that meant he'd been forced to spend most of their earlier outing in the water rather than on dry land where his arousal would be obvious.

Deliberately he'd closeted himself in his office this afternoon, catching up on work. Allowing Amelie private time with her nephew. Now Sébastien was in bed and there was nothing to distract Lambis from this constant tug of desire.

Last night, after that kiss, he'd waited, hoping she'd change her mind and come to him. Accept his offer of an affair. For, God help him, it was all he could offer. That and this place as a refuge.

She needed, and deserved, far more. That was why he'd pulled back from her years ago, rather than pursue the intense attraction between them. But now, here they were, both alone, both hungry for each other.

Amelie had given herself away last night. She wanted him with a flagrant, earthy hunger that matched his.

He'd wondered if she'd be too refined to let herself go with a man, too fastidious for absolute passion.

Her response last night, her soft gasps of encouragement and pleasure, the demands of her beautiful body sliding against his, had been a revelation.

She walked the length of the white sand beach, then turned, looking towards the headland they'd visited earlier. Her shoulders hunched and her head dropped as she wrapped her arms around herself. Even from here Lambis recognised her pain. It echoed through him too.

Damn it! He thought she'd be happy after hearing Sébastien speak. Had something else gone wrong? The thought sent fear crashing through him.

Before he could stop to consider, he was striding down the steps to the sand.

He might not be able to offer what she most wanted, but he couldn't leave her alone, hurting. Lambis's mouth turned down in a tight grimace.

Every day this woman taught him something new. He'd believed all the tenderness within him had died years ago with his wife, Delia, and little Dimitri. But here it was again, welling like an enormous tide, terrifying and unstoppable.

It had trickled over him as he'd watched Amelie at his mountain home, so brave in defence of her nephew, proud yet so vulnerable. It had flooded high when Sébastien had broken down, turning to him in his grief. Lambis had discovered anew the powerful, once familiar feelings of affection and protectiveness as he'd held the little boy tight. Then today, watching Amelie's face when Sébastien spoke— Lambis had been swamped by emotion.

'Amelie?' He halted behind her on the sand, so close he smelled the sweet floral perfume of her hair. 'What's happened? What's wrong?'

Her shoulders rose as if to shut him out.

'Nothing. Everything is good.' Yet her voice broke.

Lambis didn't wait for more lies. He stepped around her, then looked down into her face. Amelie's eyes shone huge and bright and her lush mouth tugged down at one corner as if she bit it.

'Tell me.' Distance was impossible.

She shook her head and golden strands of hair feathered her neck where her neat chignon collapsed. 'There's nothing wrong.' She blinked and forced a smile. He could tell it took effort. 'It's silly of me. I tucked Seb into bed and told him I loved him. And he…put his arms around my neck and told me he loved me too.' Her smile turned lopsided. 'That and those few words in the cave are the first time he's spoken since the accident. Isn't it ridiculous? I should be celebrating!'

'Not ridiculous at all. You've carried this burden too long.' She'd been so worried for Sébastien she probably hadn't had time to deal with her own grief.

Lambis paused. The old impulse to protect and care might be back but he was woefully out of practice. Besides, instinct, sharp as a blade to his bones, warned against getting involved. Yet it was too late. He *was* involved.

Sea-green eyes fixed on his and for a moment the impression of water and sky and the warm breeze died, as he lost himself there.

'Hold me for a little? Please?'

Without thought he moved closer, enfolding her in his embrace, pulling her head to his chest and letting his hand slide over the pure silk of her hair.

Lambis's breath faltered as she sank against him, her arms sliding around to hug him tight. He inhaled deeply, drawing in salt air and gardenia perfume, the sea and the rich scent of Amelie's skin. She nestled against him and he was torn between a trembling, poignant joy and the unstoppable, inevitable tension creeping through his body as arousal flared.

It was no good; despite his determination to squash it, desire rose. His body hardened, his erection pressing against her slim, soft form.

Yet Lambis stood unmoving, except for his fingers in

her hair, gently circling and soothing, trying to offer the comfort she needed.

Finally, with a juddering sigh he felt all the way to his core, Amelie lifted her head. She arched her beautiful neck back and captured his gaze. Something deep within jolted and teetered, off balance. His breath stalled with the effort it took *not* to kiss her.

'Is your offer still open?'

'Offer?' It couldn't be what he thought. Life had taught him never to expect joy.

'For a no-strings affair.'

Silently Lambis stared down into her flushed, beautiful face.

Through the years he'd assuaged pain with brief sexual encounters, intense only in their carnality.

With Amelie any liaison would be *more*. Headier, more exciting, more satisfying. His arms tightened and his mouth curved in a hard feral smile of anticipation that ignored the warning voice inside.

Lambis knew happiness was transitory. Seven years ago God, life, fate had stolen everything from him and left him mired in an endless sea of pain and remorse. But not now. Not tonight, with Amelie bright and vital in his arms.

Tonight he wanted to *live*.

For one brief, glorious interlude he could have everything he hadn't permitted himself to dream about.

He didn't answer her question. Instead he swept her up in his arms and marched towards the villa, his stride lengthening to take the steps to the terrace three at a time.

CHAPTER TEN

SHE'D NEVER KNOWN a man like Lambis. The touch of those hard hands, his potent strength as he snatched her off the ground, beckoned to her at a primitive, visceral level. He held her high against his chest, the sturdy beat of his heart against her.

Amelie looked up at the beautiful, utterly male planes and angles of his face, and felt more feminine, more *cherished* than she ever had in her life.

Stupid when he was taking her inside for what she hoped would simply be hot sex that would obliterate her cares for an hour.

But it was true. Despite the fierce light in his eyes and the almost aggressive jut of his starkly defined jaw, she *did* feel cherished. And desired.

It had been ten long years since she'd had a lover. Ten years to lick her wounds and vow never to give herself to a man unless she was sure he loved her as she did him.

She cared for Lambis, cared too much. She was willing to throw over her hard-earned rules for a night in his arms.

She was fed up waiting for love.

Fed up being alone.

She'd take sex and the euphoria it brought. Even if the reason she'd eventually agreed to his proposition was the caring side Lambis usually hid.

Amelie pressed her hand to his chest and his heartbeat quickened. She turned and buried her face against the soft fabric of his shirt and inhaled the intriguing scent of soap, earthy male and base notes of musk that set her trembling with desire.

'I want you,' she murmured. So much easier to say it when she wasn't meeting that piercing stare.

Movement rippled through him, like an earth tremor, and his pace quickened.

She smiled. He was as eager as she.

Then he shouldered open a door to the master suite. Amelie had an impression of white walls, a lofty ceiling and touches of turquoise furnishings before she landed with a soft gasp on a wide mattress.

Lambis stood above her, his shoulders rising and falling with each deep breath. His hooded eyes glittered.

'Take your clothes off.' His lips barely moved. If it weren't for the tension radiating off him, Amelie might have taken offence at his brusqueness.

Her eyes dropped to his hands, clenching and releasing at his sides, and the unmistakable bulge in his trousers. The bulge she'd felt press into her on the beach.

'Why don't you do it for me?' She spread her arms wide, as if casual sex was an everyday occurrence and her throat hadn't dried with excitement and nerves.

She refused to let her relative inexperience matter. Excitement skittered through her at the demands of this new Amelie, who focused, for the first time, on satisfying her own wants.

'Because,' he growled, his voice soft yet taut, 'I don't dare lay hands on you yet. I want to last long enough to give you pleasure.'

Heat seared Amelie's throat, climbing to her cheeks and washing down her breasts. Her nipples turned to hard nubs and she caught her breath as Lambis's eyes zeroed in on them. Her body came alive as if he'd touched her with that hard stare and delicious anticipation quivered the length of her spine.

'Then take off your clothes for me.' She couldn't believe she addressed him so coolly when she was burning up, her body melting in places she hadn't even been conscious of for years.

A muscle worked in his jaw and his nostrils flared, accentuating the proud line of his nose and the ripe fullness of those chiselled lips. Without a word, his hands lifted to his shirt front and yanked it open. Tiny buttons spattered her thigh, ripped off by his violence, and Amelie's pulse quickened.

Lambis shrugged off the torn garment, revealing that broad golden torso she'd spent the morning trying not to stare at.

Lambis was a big man. Tall, well-muscled, built like an athlete. Not a fine-boned long distance runner but the sort of man who could wrestle or toss a javelin or swim. Broad at the shoulders, deep across the chest, his torso was a perfectly sculpted example of male power. Defined pectoral muscles, flat belly and tight abdominals. His flesh glowed golden olive and a light dusting of dark hair covered his chest then thinned to a narrow line that bisected his torso and disappeared into his jeans.

Her gaze dropped to his narrow hips and solid thighs. And that other solidity hidden by straining denim.

Amelie swallowed and found the movement difficult, as if her throat muscles forgot how to work.

He was magnificent, virile and outrageously sexy. And so different from Jules, who'd been young and boyishly skinny. For a second Amelie felt a flicker of trepidation, wondering if she was out of her depth.

Then Lambis tugged open his belt and reached for the zip of his jeans and Amelie was too excited to feel anxious. Slowly, deliberately, he undid his jeans, then peeled his clothes down.

Amelie's pulse hammered out of control and her breath came in little pants as he revealed himself. There was a tingling, melting heat between her legs and she shifted on the bed, pressing her thighs together as if that would ease the ache within.

Lambis saw the movement and his lips tilted at one corner in what might have been a smile if his expression weren't so taut.

Finally he kicked off his clothes and stood before her, utterly, gloriously naked.

The symmetry of his beautiful body made Amelie wish she were an artist, to capture him for posterity. But as she took in those long, heavy thighs, the thatch of black hair above them, and the proud, massive erection pointing towards her, the urgency gripping her had nothing to do with art.

Her fingers fumbled at the tie of her sarong. The knot of it tightened, grew more uncooperative with each attempt, till her hands grew damp with frustration.

She jerked her gaze away from Lambis and focused on the fabric, finally tearing it open and tossing the material off the bed. As she did, he stepped close and her heart beat double-time in anticipation. But, instead of coming to her, he opened a bedside drawer and took out a foil packet.

Amelie averted her eyes. Not from prudishness, but from fear she'd explode from the sheer carnal excitement of watching him sheathe himself. She'd never been so turned on. Her whole body was alive with pinpricks of awareness. Even the brush of bed linen beneath her bikini-clad flesh was too much, and the rub of the material against her nipples…

'Take the bikini off.' His voice had bottomed out to that bass resonance that seeped into her bones and melted any last scrap of doubt.

Reaching back, Amelie tugged at the bikini strap, then, not allowing herself time to think, hauled the swimsuit top up and over her head, feeling the bounce of her freed breasts.

The hiss of his indrawn breath yanked her gaze around. His eyes were molten silver, hot enough to incinerate. His gaze travelled over her nakedness and she felt it as if he'd traced one big callused palm over soft flesh.

'Now the rest.' It wasn't a request but an order. Yet the harsh edge to his voice was a caress.

Amelie kept her eyes on his as she lifted her hips and wriggled free, dropping the scrap of fabric off the bed. He watched every movement with a hawk-like intensity that might have made her nervous if she weren't so eager.

'Come here.' It wasn't her voice. It was the voice of a sultry stranger. Lambis lowered himself to the bed, kneeling astride her, his hands braced wide so his shoulders blocked the dying daylight.

Amelie shook, drawn so tight with arousal she could barely contain it. Just the waft of air across her bare flesh as he moved was like invisible fingers stroking. She smelt heat and musk and that heady, uniquely earthy tang that was Lambis.

She slipped her hands around his neck and felt him shudder. He closed his eyes, soft, incomprehensible words spilling from his lips. Yet she understood. This was both delight and torture.

'Amelie.' She'd never heard her name sound like that. A groan and a prayer. Instead of being awed or nervous about their mismatch in experience and size, it made Amelie feel strong.

'Take me, Lambis. Now.' She shifted, lifting her hips towards him.

His eyes snapped open and it was like watching an electrical storm over the Mediterranean. Searing light and piercing brilliance.

Yet despite the glaze of carnal intent in those stunning eyes, and the pared back determination on his bold face, Lambis didn't settle between her legs. Instead he dipped his head between those incredible shoulders and slowly, deliberately licked her breast from bottom to top.

Amelie gasped, her hands tightening around his neck, tangling in his dark, soft curls.

He did it again, stopping this time to circle her nipple, making her bow up to meet his mouth. The heat between her legs intensified and she wriggled, spreading her thighs till they met his, solid on either side of her.

She tried to pull his head down, clamp him to her breast, but he wouldn't be pushed. Instead he moved lower, nuzzling her ribcage, pressing kisses in a line down to her navel where his tongue took possession in a caress that nearly undid her.

'Lambis!' Amelie had thought she'd known desire but, with each second of his slow caresses, she moved from eager to officially desperate.

Her fingers dug into his slick shoulders and her hips lifted as he forayed further, licking her belly and planting tiny kisses across to her hip bone and back. One big hand feathered her inner thigh, sliding up to stroke her cleft and the wetness there.

Amelie shuddered, her eyelids fluttering shut as her breath snagged. He stroked again, sliding further this time, testing her, then his mouth—

'No! No, don't!' She snapped her eyes open to find him blinking up at her as if *he'd* been the one roused from sensual abandon instead of the one playing her body like a finely tuned instrument.

'You don't like it?' His brow furrowed and for the first time Amelie read something other than confidence and arousal in his features.

'Too much,' she panted. 'Please. I want *you*.' She had no doubt she'd have flown to the moon at the touch of his hand or mouth, or both, but that wasn't what she craved.

His jaw tightened and again she saw the fascinating little tic of pulse betraying his agitation. 'The way you make me feel, I won't last long enough to—'

'Good.' She shuddered. Just talking about it drew her to the brink. Or maybe it was the way his breath feathered her sensitive skin and his thumb circled the slick centre of her. 'I want you *now*.'

The words were barely out when he moved. Lambis nudged her knees wide then lifted her calves in his big hands, stroking then kissing them as he placed her heels on his shoulders. A moment later he rose on his knees, his hands gentle on her legs as they rose with him.

Amelie's breath sawed. His erection lay hard against her and she felt so *open* to him. He could see her stretched out before him and with her feet up in the air, her legs resting on his solid body, for a moment she felt scarily helpless.

'It's okay, *glyka mou*. I just want to see you.'

Lambis pressed forward and Amelie's eyes widened as the hot breadth of him stretched her, slowly, inexorably. Deliciously. Her breath stopped and something caught in her chest at his expression as he watched her. His brow puckered in concentration and his mouth twisted as if with pain. Yet still he pushed further.

Was it because Lambis was such a big man, or was it the angle at which he held her, that made his glacially slow possession so much *more*? Or perhaps it was the heat in his eyes, and his low moan of pleasure that made her heart palpitate and pleasure radiate in rippling waves.

He surged higher, further than she'd thought possible. Her fingers clutched the bedding at how impossibly good that felt. So good her inner muscles grasped him of their own accord and he stilled, sucking in a breath.

For long seconds neither moved, each absorbing the exquisite sensations of their coupling. Then, with a groan, Lambis withdrew.

Amelie reached out and tried to anchor herself, grabbing his thighs, not wanting him to go. Her fingers dug into solid muscle as he retreated then, at the last moment, thrust hard and sure right to her core.

White light flickered on the edge of her vision. Her throat closed as she pushed high, impaling herself on him. Another retreat, another quick, decisive thrust and the flicker became sheet lightning, exploding around her.

Another thrust and another, his pace quickening, his possession so deep she felt melded to him. Amelie had never experienced anything like this. She relished every thrust, every caress, every second. His raw, urgent need and her own savage hunger to possess him. As if she'd waited all her life for this man and this moment.

When his hand dropped between her thighs, feathering that most sensitive spot, a spark detonated the long-banked fire within her. She called his name, needy and grateful, as he pushed her into ecstasy, into a place she'd never been before.

Seconds later he faltered, his fluid rhythm grew uncoordinated and he pulsed, out of control within her. Lambis leaned in, slipping her wobbly legs aside and took her mouth, tongue dancing with hers as their climaxes crashed through them and their bodies jerked and shuddered as one.

Dimly Amelie was aware of her hands lifting to tangle in his hair. Of the brush of chest hair and heavy pectorals against her breasts. Of the restless, almost worshipful stroke of his hand along her trembling body as she eased from ecstasy into a dreamy state of boneless satisfaction.

Lambis lifted his head then drew back but she wrapped her rubbery legs about him and hung on tight, refusing to let go. He didn't go far, just enough to kiss her breast. Instantly fire shot from her womb to her nipple and she arched helplessly against him, her eyes snapping open in astonishment.

Satisfaction flared in those silvery eyes, a tight, knowing smile curved his lips and again his hand slipped low.

His thumb pressed her clitoris, circling, pleasing, and she heard her gasp of pleasure. Lambis leaned down, kissed her nipple then sucked hard at it just as his thumb pressed again and, to her astonishment, another explosion consumed her.

Amelie convulsed around him, heard her own high-pitched cry and felt herself disintegrate into wave upon wave of rapture.

Her only compass point was Lambis, his heat surrounding her, his breath feathering her flesh and his deep voice stroking through her. He whispered words she couldn't translate but knew instinctively were endearments.

Strong arms surrounded her, pulling her to him as he rolled over and clamped her to his chest. Amelie never wanted to move again.

How long she lay in that blissful state, Amelie didn't know. She might even have slept. Finally she became aware of change, of movement. She was in Lambis's arms, her face turned instinctively into that solid wall of hot, honed muscle that was his chest. The steady rhythm of his heart reassured, as did the way he held her, sure and safe as he crossed the room.

Amelie smiled muzzily, still overcome by the glow of wellbeing that had been his gift to her.

Then to her amazement she felt water against her heels. Her eyes shot open. They were in a vast bathroom, softly lit by candles. Lambis had run her a bath while she slept.

'I didn't think you were a candle person.' Her words were slurred. Yet even as she said it she remembered how they'd dined by candlelight.

Lambis huffed and she heard a smile in his voice. 'My housekeeper is. But it seemed right to use them tonight.'

With that he lowered her into the deep, warm bath.

Amelie didn't try to stop the sigh of pleasure as she sank below the surface. Before she could settle, Lambis stepped in behind her, pulling her back against him so she reclined between his long legs, one of his arms wrapped around her waist.

She let her head loll back against his shoulder, concentrating only on this moment, coveting this interlude of peace and…oneness.

No, she wouldn't think about that, how from the moment on the beach she'd felt…connected.

'This is perfect,' she purred. 'How did you know?' She'd been incapable of coherent thought after their urgent, explosive coupling.

She felt him shrug. When he spoke, the sound rumbled up inside him, making her smile. 'I wondered if you might be sore. I'm not a small man and you were…tight.' His voice dropped to that bass note she loved. It sent desire quaking through her.

'Amelie?' Definitely concern in his voice. '*Are* you okay?'

'Yes.' Now he mentioned it, she was achy between the thighs and her muscles felt well-used, as if she'd spent a long session in the gym. But that was nothing to the hum of delight in her pleasure-hazed body. 'Lovely.'

'Truly? I should have been gentler.'

Amelie roused and she slid her arm over his where it circled her waist. 'You didn't hurt me. And I was too hungry for you to care about gentle.' A tiny smile caught her lips. 'My only other experience was so gentle it was almost a non-event.'

Hazily she realised she was letting slip information she'd never shared with anyone. Never even voiced to herself. But in this candlelit room, seduced by the luxury of Lambis's closeness and the sensual heat of the water, that didn't seem important.

'You've only had sex once before?' He stiffened, his voice shocked.

Amelie patted his hand and ran her other hand down

the muscled thigh beside her, intrigued by its shape and the way it twitched beneath her hand.

'No. More than once. But with the same man. Jules. And it was a long time ago.' She frowned, calculating. 'Ten years.'

Lambis said nothing, yet she heard him thinking. His heart rate quickened and the arm holding her curved closer.

'You were celibate for ten years and you suddenly give yourself to *me*?'

Now she heard it, an echo of something that might even have been fear, if she didn't know Lambis was scared of nothing.

'Don't read too much into it, Lambis. I'm not expecting hearts and flowers. I know this is a no-strings arrangement.' Even so, looking around the candlelit room, inhaling the seductive scent of the bath salts he'd thought to use for her, Amelie knew Lambis wasn't as unfeeling as he pretended. He'd taken time to think about how she felt and what would please her.

'I don't regret what we've done.' Far from it. Making love with Lambis—no, having sex—was an experience she wouldn't have missed for anything.

'Who was this Jules?' His voice was gruff.

She shrugged, aware of the way her shoulder blades slid up over his chest and his hand relaxed a little to splay over her stomach. A tiny trickle of awareness stirred within and she shifted in his hold.

Seconds passed. Why not tell him? Lambis was one of the few people she'd trust not to reveal secrets. She'd never had the luxury of a confidante. Irini, lovely as she was, had continually looked to her for support and guidance. Amelie hadn't felt able to unburden her own troubles.

'Jules was a medical student when I was at university in St Galla.'

'He swept you off your feet?' Lambis's breath feathered her scalp. Strange how that tiny sensation made her flesh prickle.

'Not exactly. Jules wasn't one for dramatic gestures. But he was kind and funny and he didn't treat me like a princess.' That didn't come out right. 'I mean, he didn't care about my title or connections. He saw *me*, liked me for who I was.' How appealing that had been. To her father she'd been an asset to be trotted out for official occasions, playing royal hostess after her mother's death and, as time passed, doing more and more of the behind the scenes work he couldn't be bothered with.

'We were engaged.' Amelie blinked, surprised the words slipped out.

'Yet you didn't marry?' Lambis's deep voice wrapped around her like his embrace.

Funny how easy it was to share confidences with him.

'No.' She strove to keep emotion from her voice. 'My father didn't approve. He was of the old school, insisting a princess of St Galla marry another royal, not a commoner. He persuaded Jules to leave.'

Silence. Finally Lambis spoke. 'You felt betrayed. That's why you haven't been with another man?'

Amelie's mouth twisted. 'I couldn't blame Jules. He was a poor student. Who could expect him to stand up against a king?' Yet that didn't stop the flutter of remembered distress, the echo of shattered dreams and the sense of betrayal. She'd stood up to the King. She'd been prepared to walk away from the palace, her title, any financial support, since that was what her father had threatened. She'd have left with only the clothes on her back if she had to, because she'd believed in Jules, believed in *them*.

She drew a shuddery breath and shook her head. 'I was naïve. I thought he loved me and we'd be together no matter what. Instead he said he'd made a mistake. He'd come into a sudden…inheritance and was moving to the far end of St Galla to set up as a GP.' She injected a lighter note into her voice. 'Last I heard he was married, with a brood of children.'

Lambis said nothing, merely lifted her hair from her shoulder and pressed his lips there. Instantly a fine wire of tension pulled taut from the spot straight down to her pelvis. Her head angled back against him.

'He soured you off men.'

Again Amelie shrugged. It was true, but she hated him imagining her as some tragedy queen. 'You'd be surprised how few opportunities I have to be intimate. Everywhere I go the press are watching. Every holiday is just a couple of days tacked on to the end of official engagements. It's hard to get to know men away from my royal responsibilities and I've never been interested in a purely sexual affair, or one conducted under the press spotlight.'

The exception had been Lambis. But he'd shied from her and her desire for a meaningful relationship.

He wasn't shying now. She lowered her hand to his other leg, stroking and delighting in the shifting bunch of his muscles that told her he wasn't immune to her touch. Behind her his erection stirred. Her inner muscles clenched.

'Why now?' He breathed against her shoulder, his breath humid and seductive on her shivery flesh. 'Why me?'

Why Lambis? Because, despite what she'd told herself, it had always been Lambis, from the moment he'd walked into her life. She'd tried to obliterate her feelings but hadn't succeeded. All she could do was accept she still had a weakness for him and hope their affair would cure her of it.

'Because I've given up on love.' Saying the words made her feel strong, despite the pang of distress. 'It's not for me.' If she made it her mantra one day she'd convince herself.

'But you want a husband and children, surely? A family? I see it in you when you're with Sébastien.'

Damn the man for being so perceptive. And for forcing this issue. *He* was the one, with Jules, who'd trampled
her romantic dreams. What did he want? Reassurance she
wasn't hoping he'd change his mind and offer her more
than sex?

Amelie moved to sit straighter and put distance between
them but Lambis tightened his arm around her middle and
for some reason she let him pull her back.

*Face it, you like being held by him! Even when you feel
you shouldn't.*

'Well, I've got Seb to look after, haven't I? And if I want
more I can go the old-fashioned route. Our Prime Minister has already suggested an arranged marriage with another royal.'

'You? In an arranged marriage?' Again that note of
shock. For some reason it pleased Amelie that she'd surprised Lambis. She hated the idea of being an open book
to a man who kept so much of himself hidden.

'Why not?'

His answer, when it came, stunned her. 'Because you
need love. You're the sort of woman who devotes her life to
those she cares about. You deserve someone who'll care for
you too. Someone who will fight for you, no matter what
the odds.' There was a resonance about his words that spoke
of deep feeling, and conviction, and it melted the frost of
indignation forming around her heart.

See? He really is a nice guy.

He does care, even if only from a distance.

*He wants you to be happy, even if he can't be the man
you want.*

Yet it would be a terrible mistake to read more into his
concern. She might still yearn but he couldn't give her what
she needed. Pain squeezed her chest.

She had to live for the moment. Enjoy this liaison to the
full then walk away with her head high.

Deliberately she stroked her fingers up his thighs, trailing higher and higher till he shifted.

'You'd better not do that,' he growled. 'It's difficult enough already just holding you and not doing any more.'

'You mean sex?'

His erection twitched, making Amelie smile.

'I'm trying to restrain myself.' It sounded as if he spoke through gritted teeth and Amelie's smile widened. She loved that he made her feel desirable.

'What if I don't want you restrained?'

CHAPTER ELEVEN

LAMBIS CLENCHED HIS jaw and prayed for control.

Amelie's words threatened to undo him.

All through this conversation he'd struggled against baser instincts that urged him to take her again, *now*, but he'd held back.

The shock in her eyes when he'd positioned her on the bed, the exquisite tightness of her inner muscles, had proved what she'd since revealed, that she was a sexual novice.

'I don't want to hurt you, Amelie.' The words ground from him. That was why he'd tried to keep his distance, right from the start. Yet there was an inevitability about them together that he couldn't deny. There'd always been something about her, a brightness and gentle tenderness, that attracted him.

He hadn't been gentle. He felt guilty about that, but not enough. For she'd surprised him with her eagerness.

'You won't hurt me. I know you won't. Besides, we don't have much time. Seb and I must return to St Galla soon. We can't stay away indefinitely.'

Strange that, instead of satisfaction, her words unsettled him.

'I want to have sex with you again.' Did she know how those words struck home? His already hard groin hardened even further. It was all he could do not to grind himself against her. 'I want to learn more.'

'Learn?' Lambis was so busy trying to control himself.

'Yes.' One of those delicate hands crept round behind her and circled his shaft. Lambis shut his eyes and shuddered. This felt impossibly good. 'Before tonight my sexual experience was very limited.'

The idea of being Amelie's sexual tutor should have delighted him. It did. Except Lambis felt far too close to the edge. Amelie was dainty and inexperienced and he was—

Her fingers tightened, sliding up in a long voluptuous stroke that had him groaning aloud.

On the other hand, she'd welcomed his carnality, with an ardour that stunned and excited. Far from being the fragile creature he'd once imagined, Amelie surprised him again and again with her strength, facing him down, calling him on his behaviour instead of shrinking back.

She stroked him again and he was lost. 'Turn around,' he ordered through gritted teeth, hands rising to her waist, turning her. Water splashed over the side of the bath and limbs tangled.

Then she was kneeling above him, slick and wet, her tip-tilted breasts glowing pink and glossy from the warm water. He traced a line from her breastbone down to her navel, then over her smooth belly to the triangle of dark golden hair just visible above the water.

Amelie shuddered as he stroked her there, her eyes growing heavy-lidded, her hips circling.

Did she have any idea how beautiful she looked, with her long golden hair falling damp around her breasts and her eyes foggy with arousal?

She leaned over, putting her hands on his shoulders and made to lower herself, but he stopped her. Watching her in the bedroom, writhing with the climaxes he'd given her, made him hungry for more.

Holding her hips, he moved forward, exploring that secret cleft with his tongue. She jolted as if an electric current passed through her and his erection throbbed in response. Again he licked, this time parting her folds and finding that tiny, sensitive pearl. Her heat enveloped him, her scent, the tremors of her body as he licked again, harder this time, and her fingers clawed at his shoulders.

'Lambis!' It was a gasp and a cry of tension as that judder came again and she tilted towards him. This time he kissed her, open-mouthed, drawing at her core until the soft cries became a scream and he heard his name echo again and again around the room.

Amelie shook against him, her breath tiny sobs that took his creaky heart and wrung it.

Tenderly, carefully, he drew her down into the warm water and kissed her, absorbing those final shudders of ecstasy, his heart sprinting. Then he rose, reached across and grabbed the condom he'd left near the bath.

When he was sheathed he sat, moving down till her knees were either side of his hips and he nudged against her. One gentle tug and she slid down, enveloping him, drawing him home. He felt heat and wonder and a sense of rightness that was new, yet familiar.

That was when he saw the glitter of tears staining her cheeks and he wrapped his arms around her, his chest turning over.

'Don't cry, *glyka mou*. It's okay. I'll make it okay.'

He hadn't hurt her. He was sure he hadn't. Yet he stilled.

Amelie's eyes opened and he stared into brilliant, overfull pools of green. Her dark lashes were spiked and wet. But she managed a tremulous smile and feathered one shaky hand across his lips in a caress that tugged at long-hoarded emotions in his locked heart.

'It's more than okay, Lambis. I didn't know anything could feel like this.' Her mouth twisted. 'I know it's only sex,' she whispered, 'but you make me feel…' She shook her head, her lips firming, leaving him wondering just how he made her feel.

He didn't wonder long for she leaned in and kissed him, slowly, thoroughly, gratefully, and he felt the most uncommon sensations rise and whirl about him.

Then she was rocking against him, partly drawn by his

insistent hands, but following a rhythm all her own. Lambis bucked up in time with each swing of her hips, rejoicing in the little circling movement she made that prolonged the ecstasy of their joining.

Still she kissed him, her hands cupping his face, her mouth sharing choked little mews of feminine satisfaction that had to be the sweetest, most erotic sound.

Lambis urged her faster, and she complied with that little shimmy of her hips that drove him harder and wilder against her. Till finally he could take no more, despite his determination to please her first. His climax erupted monumentally, throbbing so hard his head whirled at the euphoria of losing himself inside Amelie. He grabbed the back of her head, kissing her with such passion he shook with it. Then he felt the clutch of her orgasm around him and the bliss of it undid him.

Lambis lay on his back watching the first grey-pink light of dawn creep across the room. Amelie lay in his arms, her thick blonde hair draped like silk over his chest and shoulders, her body sprawled across him.

Through the evening and the night that followed they'd been insatiable. One touch, one soft sigh had been all it took for his libido to fire and, to his delight, Amelie had been just as eager.

Was it because neither had had a recent lover?

He found her long celibacy incredible. Despite her demure façade, Amelie was highly sexed, a woman who gave her all to a lover.

She wasn't the woman he'd imagined her. His first impression, apart from instant interest and just as instant lust, was that Amelie was charming but reserved, caring of her family and dutiful. He remembered her sweet diffidence as she'd suggested he stay on in St Galla so they could explore the attraction between them.

Somehow he'd never recognised the fire in her. The Amelie he'd begun to know in Greece was more like a firecracker, gunpowder hidden inside a decorative casing. Her temper, the way she'd refused to take no for an answer about getting him to help her nephew, had surprised. He was used to seeing her easy smile and diplomacy as she helped her brother manage his kingdom. Her love for her family had cemented the idea of her as a nurturer.

Her sexual passion had been a revelation, as had her stark honesty. His mind still reeled with some of the things she'd revealed.

Lambis's mouth tightened when he recalled her tears as they'd made love. It was easy to ascribe them to an excess of passion, to the shock of ecstasy after long celibacy. But it was more. Despite her feisty determination, Amelie was vulnerable. She grieved for her brother and on top of that worried over Sébastien.

Lambis's conscience warned he should back off. He was taking advantage of her when she was needy.

Yet, despite the grate of his conscience, he couldn't pull back. For so long he'd lived in his bleak, lonely world. It was where he deserved to be, of course. But now Amelie had smashed down the wall cutting him off from the world, it was beyond him to rebuild it.

Soon. He'd do it soon. A principled man would pull away from her, knowing she was better off without him. But Lambis had long ago faced the truth that he was brutally flawed. It wasn't right, but he'd take what he could from her, live this bright brief moment of pleasure.

He tugged the sheet up her bare back, lingering at the sweet indentation of her waist. So slender and supple yet strong. Amelie had been a miracle in his arms, reminding him how poignantly beautiful life could be.

He'd forgotten that in the years since he'd lost Delia and Dimitri. Pain and guilt had cast a pall over even his most precious memories. But, spending time with Amelie and Sébastien, Lambis had begun to remember the joy that had once been so intrinsic in his world. How caring and being cared for could transform you.

Lambis looked down at Amelie's head, nestled trustingly on his chest. Dawn light gilded her straight hair, as if reminding him she was beyond his reach, even if for this brief time she shared herself with him.

Amelie deserved better. Far better than Jules, the man who'd seduced then betrayed her. The thought of him made Lambis clench his teeth in thwarted anger. But he was no better. She needed someone who'd stand at her side, supporting, protecting and loving.

Once Lambis might have been that man. But not now. He was a shell of the man he'd believed himself to be.

'Don't stop.' The words were a gentle breath across his bare chest.

'I woke you? I'm sorry. Go back to sleep.' She'd need it after the hours they'd spent awake through the night.

For answer Amelie stretched, arching her back and pressing her breasts against him. Her smooth thigh slid across his legs and inevitably his half erect shaft stirred.

Lambis tried to focus on the stack of work waiting for his attention. The recruitment drive in the US, the potential problem with the big job in Russia—

'But I'm wide awake.' His eyes snapped open as Amelie lifted her head. Something shifted hard inside his chest as her slightly unfocused gaze met his. Something that was more than lust, though that was part of it.

Tenderness, desire and possessiveness surged in a potent mix he hadn't a hope of stopping, though it scared him witless. He hadn't felt anything so profound since—

'Lambis? Are you all right?'

Amelie's hair was a rumpled halo, her lips a sultry pout that was too enticing for a man trying to do the decent thing and rein in his apparently unstoppable libido. She must be sore after last night yet Lambis found himself stroking her supple flanks, letting his touch dip to explore her breasts.

Instantly those bright eyes glazed with a heat that matched the fire stirring in his loins.

'Very all right,' he growled.

And Amelie, the precious Princess he'd once thought as cosseted and delicate as a porcelain figurine, leaned up and whispered in his ear exactly how she'd like to celebrate the new day.

Seconds later she was on her back beneath him, smiling as he settled between her thighs. Ruthlessly Lambis banished his troubled conscience and focused on giving them both what they so desired.

'This was a brilliant idea, Lambis.' Amelie grinned and sat back beneath the vine-covered pergola. Dappled sunlight played across her features, already obscured by the dark glasses she'd insisted on wearing for their excursion into the village. 'I'm glad you persuaded me it was safe to come.'

'I wouldn't have suggested it if I hadn't known you'd be safe from the press.' He shrugged. 'I'm glad you like it. It's very simple.'

'But lovely.' Her gesture took in the plain wooden tables and rush-bottomed chairs in the small outdoor space where they were now the only customers, and the small harbour a few steps away. 'Even the boats are picturesque, and the colour of the water.' She sighed and leaned back, sipping her tiny cup of coffee. 'No wonder you wanted to have your home on the island.'

Ridiculous, but Lambis felt his smile grow at her enthusiasm. To many he knew, the quiet, unspoiled island would be too unsophisticated, too boring.

Amelie seemed to thrive on it. As for excitement, the closest she got were nights in his bed as he devoted himself to her. Nights filled with such potent pleasure he was hooked on the thrill of watching Amelie gasp out her completion in his arms, her beautiful eyes wide with awe. And, of course, to the rapture he himself found with his generous, sensual lover.

Lambis even felt a proprietorial pleasure at the way she'd developed a taste for Greek coffee, strong, short and pungently aromatic. And the way she'd eaten the plain village fare, with an easy relish that endeared her to the few locals who'd nodded their greeting.

He'd always known Amelie was genuine, but previously he'd only seen her in a royal setting, in that fanciful pale pink and white palace surrounded by its perfectly manicured grounds. There she drank from crystal and finest porcelain, surrounded by treasured antiques. Today she'd laughed, licking her fingers as oil dripped from the bread she'd used to mop up her plate.

The woman he'd come to know here was disarmingly frank, genuine and easy to please.

'Lambis!'

He blinked, diverted from thoughts of the many ways he enjoyed pleasing her.

'What is it?'

'Look at Seb.' Her whispered excitement was unmistakable. He whipped his head round to where Seb viewed the small fishing boats drawn up along the harbour. Lambis had been keeping an eye on him until thoughts of Amelie, naked in his bed, distracted him.

His shoulders relaxed as he saw Seb nodding at another boy about the same age who was speaking to him.

'He *talked*,' Amelie murmured. 'To a stranger!'

Lambis was unprepared for the blast of relief and excitement that rocked him as Sébastien smiled and spoke to the other kid. 'Didn't I tell you he'd be okay?' Till now, the boy had spoken rarely and, despite his optimism in front of

Amelie, Lambis had harboured fears about the child's full recovery. 'Those experts were right. He just needs time.'

Slender fingers closed over his, yanking his attention back to Amelie. 'Time and somewhere he feels safe and unpressured. *You've* provided that. Thank you.'

'It was nothing.' He hadn't done anything special. It was *she* who'd fought for her nephew's recovery, not him. 'Here he gets to practice his Greek.'

The kid understood not only his father's native French but his mother's Greek as well as English, which was St Galla's second language. Suddenly it struck Lambis that unless he took a hand, Sébastien would lose the Greek his mother had taught him.

'Perhaps he could come back to Greece occasionally.'

Amelie's smile widened and instantly Lambis's pulse quickened. 'What a wonderful offer. Thank you. I'm sure he'd love visiting your island again.' Her hand squeezed his. 'You two have a special bond and that's strengthened since we came here.' Lambis watched her expression still. 'One day you'll make a wonderful father.'

As quickly as that the bright day dimmed. His stomach hollowed and metallic despair filled his mouth.

Lambis yanked his hand free. He couldn't see Amelie's eyes for the dark glasses but he read her voice—warm and approving.

He shuddered in denial.

The old wellspring of pain erupted, drenching him in icy ripples. 'I'll never be a father!'

Amelie stared as Lambis's face transformed. That hint of an indulgent smile, just turning up the corners of his mouth, vanished as his lips flattened. His skin somehow pared back, leaving his proud features angular and harsh, those black brows angling down in a frown that was nothing short of forbidding.

Fear rose as suddenly as a summer squall and she snapped her gaze around to check Seb. He was fine, sitting a few metres away in the sun, intent on what looked like a game of marbles.

She pressed a palm to her racing heart, trying to quell anxiety.

'Lambis? Are you all right?' Stupid question. Of course he wasn't all right. He looked like he had when she'd turned up unannounced at his mountain home—ruthlessly distant. Except she could read him better now and what she saw spoke of pain.

'I'm sorry. I didn't mean to offend you.' Though how she had she didn't know. 'I don't expect you to act as a surrogate father to Seb.' Though, no matter how hard she tried, she hadn't been able to douse that fantasy of her, Seb and Lambis together. She forced a tentative smile. 'I just meant—'

'You don't need to explain. I'm not offended.'

Yet something had happened. It was there in the way Lambis sat, ramrod straight, where before he'd lounged, relaxed and happy. His stormy eyes avoided hers.

Pain sliced through her. This last week they'd grown closer. She'd thought he trusted her.

She'd imagined that because they shared their bodies…

'Good.' She forced a bright smile as she pushed her cup aside. 'I think it's time Seb and I—'

'Leave the boy. It will do him good being with another kid.' Lambis's voice was gruff. Then his eyes met hers and her shoulders slammed back in her seat at the force of his bleak expression. 'There's nothing wrong. I just…' He shook his head in a tiny, impatient gesture. 'I won't ever have children. Didn't Irini tell you?'

Amelie shook her head. 'Irini never gossiped.' Except to say Lambis had had a difficult past. Amelie had never imagined that referred to an inability to father children.

'Ah.' Lambis nodded and turned his attention to the

boys playing nearby. 'I had a son once,' he said quietly, the words strung taut and low. 'And a wife too. But they died.'

Such simple, straightforward words. But the power of them sucked Amelie dry. She stared into Lambis's lifeless eyes. They stared blindly back and she guessed he didn't see her but the family he'd lost. A great gulf opened up inside her. It was as if an unseen force ripped her apart.

'I'm so very sorry, Lambis.' She leaned towards him, feeling the terrible inadequacy of mere speech, but needing to express her sympathy.

He nodded briefly. 'It was a long time ago.' Yet obviously it haunted him. How could it not?

Amelie ached with the need to touch him, to put her arms around him and draw him close. Not as a prelude to sex, but to offer that most basic comfort, a human touch, a reminder that someone cared.

Now she understood a little that withdrawn look she'd witnessed in the mountains.

To lose both a wife and child—it must have been some terrible accident. Having just lost her brother and sister-in-law so suddenly, she had some concept of what Lambis was going through. But she couldn't begin to understand what it was like to lose a child and a life partner.

Amelie swallowed, the movement convulsive. She had no more words.

His eyes met hers and this time he focused on her, so intently she felt the blood rise in her cheeks. 'I could never go through that again. I'll never marry or have another child.'

Dumbly, Amelie nodded, mind racing. Was that why Lambis had rejected her before? It seemed likely, especially as they'd proved since how compatible they were.

So much made sense—his initial diffidence with Seb, never unfriendly but never actively encouraging the boy, until that day on the beach when he'd seen the extent of Seb's distress. She wondered if it also explained why Lambis had relegated that beautiful, moving icon of mother and child to a guest room where he wouldn't see it. How could he look at it and not remember all he'd lost?

She hadn't thought it was possible to feel more pain than she had recently, but she did. It welled like a high summer tide, washing away her fragile hopes.

But her pain was nothing to Lambis's. Impulsively she shoved her chair back and got up, reaching for his fist, clenched so tight it quivered in her hold.

'Come on, Lambis. Let's walk. You promised to show us the little chapel at the end of the harbour.' Anything, surely, was better than watching him brood over the past.

She couldn't wipe away his hurt but she could at least distract him.

Beyond that, she could only share with him all the tenderness she felt until it was time for her and Seb to leave.

That would be the toughest part, she realised as Lambis got to his feet, his hand still in hers. For as he towered over her, that awful blankness still masking his features, Amelie realised something she'd gone to enormous lengths to avoid thinking about.

She loved Lambis Evangelos.

She'd never stopped loving him.

And while his heart was held by a dead woman there was no chance he'd come to love her.

CHAPTER TWELVE

'YOU'RE SURE THERE'S nothing wrong, Enide?' Amelie stared from Lambis's bedroom to the matchless view of sea and sky and perfect crescent beach. What was it about this conversation with her elderly relative that concerned her? She couldn't put her finger on it.

'Everything's under control. Now go and relax. And give Seb a cuddle for me. I'm so pleased to hear he's speaking again.'

'Not very much though.' Amelie bit her lip, wondering if she should risk returning with him to St Galla yet. Since hearing Lambis's story she couldn't help but suspect being around Seb was too close a reminder of the child he'd lost. 'Perhaps, after all, in his own home—'

'No!' Enide's vehemence surprised her. 'No, stay where you are a little longer. Why risk his recovery when he's doing well in Greece? Give the poor child time to recuperate. You could do with a longer break too.'

Enide's words made sense, yet Amelie couldn't shake the instinct that something was awry. 'Enide, I—'

'I'm sorry, Amelie. I really need to dash or I'll be late for a function. We'll talk later, yes?'

Before Amelie could respond, the line went dead, leaving her pondering. Her elegant, super-organised cousin Enide never dashed. She was never late. She was a stickler for punctuality and protocol, hiding her kind heart behind a cool exterior.

Amelie considered ringing back, but surely, if something was wrong, Enide would tell her. She'd been a brick, her quiet presence steadying Amelie when her whole world shattered.

'Everything okay?' Lambis's low voice encircled her as he entered the room. His arm slid around her waist from behind and instantly she melted against him, her pulse notching faster.

How long could she hide her feelings? It was a wonder he hadn't guessed. Every time they made love her passion held a dimension she knew was reserved solely for him.

Even the knowledge he still loved his wife and could never care for Amelie in that way hadn't changed her feelings. If anything, in the past days her love had strengthened, even as she told herself she needed to pull back.

But how could she when she craved his touch? When he was tender and gentle, passionate and demanding in ways that attuned so perfectly to her own needs? How could she when she understood his hurt and wanted to wrap him in her love, bringing him what solace she could, even knowing she couldn't heal him?

'I think so.'

'You don't sound sure. What can I do to help?'

Amelie turned in his embrace, delighting in this closeness, aware this must end soon. She had to make the break, though it seemed sometimes as if Lambis needed her as much as she needed him. His loving was so intense, so hungry… Which, she realised, was simply wishful thinking.

His grey eyes surveyed her seriously. He *would* help if he could. Without even knowing what that might involve.

What would he say if she admitted she loved him and what she needed was for him to let go of the past and love her?

Amelie sank against his chest, unable to resist temptation, and smiled, a tight, hard little smile as he pulled her close, one sinewy arm wrapped around her back and the other palming her hair in a familiar caress.

'Nothing. Everything's fine, Lambis.'

It scared her how adept she'd become at lying.

* * *

He should be working. Lambis felt the restlessness of a man who habitually devoted all his energies to business, yet who suddenly found himself distracted, neglecting his routine.

Yet, as his managers assured him, business was booming and, because of the structures and excellent staff he'd introduced, his company ran almost autonomously without micromanagement. Which meant he could take time out.

Face it. The business is all but running itself. You're just looking for an excuse not to be here.

Here being the ancient olive grove on the hill behind the villa, watching Amelie, in another of those wispy sarongs, and Sébastien explore the stony ground, intent on some insect they'd discovered.

The restlessness wasn't because Lambis wanted to be at his desk or on the phone. It was because Amelie and Sébastien had become integral to his days. Lambis found himself deciding certain matters he'd always handled could be delegated. He spent more time out of his office and even when he worked his thoughts turned to them—Sébastien, whose reserve was gradually disappearing, and Amelie. Above all, Amelie.

Lambis shifted his shoulders against the wide trunk of an old tree where he sat amongst the debris of their picnic.

His eyes narrowed on the remarkable woman who was as much at home in a filmy blue sarong and bare feet as she was in a full-length gown and tiara. Amelie couldn't be pigeonholed and she continued to surprise him. It had been days since he'd mentioned that he'd had a wife and child but Amelie hadn't once prodded for more details. She'd accepted the information with characteristic compassion but there'd been no interrogation.

Strangely, as the days passed, and the precious nights when Amelie shared herself ardently, making him feel more alive than he had in years, Lambis almost *wished* she'd ask.

He couldn't fathom it. He never talked about Dimitri and Delia. Ever.

Yet with Amelie more than once he'd been on the verge of talking about them. Like now as she stumbled her way through an old Greek rhyme Irini must have taught Sébastien. The boy was teaching Amelie and they giggled over her mistakes.

The rhyme, the laughter, the balmy air of the old orchard, reminded him of a day he'd forgotten till now, of Delia with Dimitri chanting the same rhyme.

Instinctively Lambis braced for the lancing agony that accompanied such memories. Instead, to his surprise, there was poignant sadness but it was swamped by gratitude that he had that memory. Gratitude for the years he'd had with them both.

Lambis's mouth firmed to a hard line. It wasn't right. He didn't deserve *not* to feel pain. It was because of him—

'Lambis.' Amelie's voice broke through his thoughts and he looked up to see her and Sébastien approaching, hand in hand. For a second, looking into the light, he couldn't make out her blonde hair. She could have been another woman, straight dark hair down around her shoulders, and a wide smile filling his heart with joy.

Lambis's breath caught. Then Amelie and Sébastien were standing before him and his vision cleared. Yet his lungs wouldn't work and guilt smote deep in his chest, cleaving right down to his belly.

What was she doing to his memories of Delia?

What was *he* doing to them?

He surged to his feet, heart thundering. It was only as Sébastien stared up in consternation that he realised how abruptly he'd moved. Tentatively he reached down and rumpled the kid's hair. But it was beyond him to force a smile.

'Sorry,' he said, his voice rougher than intended. 'I missed what you said.'

Amelie's smile had a fixed quality that told him he hadn't concealed his turmoil. Deliberately he wiped his face clear, an art he'd perfected not just in his years as a bodyguard, but as a man grieving the loss of everything that had made his life worth living.

'It's not important. It was just a bit of nonsense that can wait.' She glanced down at her nephew then back to him, her fine, arched eyebrows flattening. 'What's important is that Seb and I were talking about keeping up his Greek. I told him you'd help him with that in future. He'll always be able to count on you, like he can count on me. Right?'

Lambis knew what he had to say, what the boy needed to hear. Yet the idea of the lad *counting* on him turned that ache in his belly into a sharp slash of pain that threatened to undo him.

He cleared his throat but the words stuck in his throat. The worst thing the boy could do was count on him. That knowledge ate at Lambis.

He heaved a deep breath and nodded, planting his hand on Sébastien's shoulder. 'Of course you can. I'm your god-father after all.' He gave the bony little shoulder a gentle squeeze then stepped away.

'I'm afraid you'll have to excuse me. There's something I need to attend to.' Not meeting Amelie's eyes, he turned and marched back to the house. All the way his conscience, what was left of it, tormented him. It was dangerous to let the child think Lambis would be around to protect him. But what else could he have done?

He could only hope once Sébastien grew up, under the nurturing care of his aunt, he'd never need Lambis again.

'Do you want to talk about it?'

'Talk about what?' Lambis realised too late he shouldn't have agreed to this moonlit stroll by the sea with Amelie.

All evening she'd watched him, masking her scrutiny

with smiles and light conversation. But he knew he'd worried her today. She'd been trying to allay Sébastien's fears about being left alone by reassuring him that she and Lambis would always support him. Lambis had done a poor job, though he'd done his best.

A spark of gallows humour flared. Since when had his best been good enough?

'About whatever's hurting you.' She didn't look at him, but kept up a steady pace as they walked the curve of the beach. 'Something is wrong. I want to help.'

'There's nothing anyone can do to help.'

He saw her face swing round and realised he'd just confirmed her suspicions.

'Sometimes talking can ease the burden.'

His mouth tightened. Nothing could ease what he felt, nor should it. Yet Amelie deserved to know, for didn't she look to him to support Sébastien? He couldn't let her raise unrealistic expectations.

'You told your nephew he could count on me.' That awful metallic taste was back in his mouth. 'But it's better not to let him think I'll be around to protect him.'

Her steps faltered. 'You're planning on deserting him?'

Lambis shook his head. 'No. But neither of you should rely on me. It's not wise.'

Not wise? It was too late to be wise where Lambis was concerned.

Amelie stopped as he turned to face the moonlit sea. How could she and Seb pull back now? They cared for and, yes, relied on him. Had she done wrong, bringing Seb here?

'I'm not good at protecting people.' A laugh emerged, but it sounded hard, a thing of pain, not humour. 'Ironic, isn't it, for a man who runs a security firm?'

Amelie stood silent, waiting.

'I can organise protection for complete strangers, but

when it's people I care for...' His words trailed off and in the silvery light she saw his jaw tighten. 'I should have been able to protect Irini. I *should* have. I'd just done a security audit for the palace, after all.'

'You couldn't have saved her. You weren't even there.'

Lambis swung round to face her. 'But I'd seen the way your brother drove his previous boat and I knew about the powerful new racing one he'd ordered. He was good, but not that good. It was beyond his capabilities. I warned him that he needed proper training from a professional before using it.'

'I didn't know.' Amelie was stunned. Lambis was right about Michel at the wheel of a boat. He'd loved speed, loved cutting a course fine. 'But he'd never take risks with Irini!'

Lambis seemed not to hear. 'I think he took my advice as an insult. He certainly didn't thank me for it.'

Amelie could imagine that. 'He'd spent all his life being told how to behave by older men. Even when he became King our Prime Minister tried to shackle him.' And Michel had been headstrong, a little impatient. But not reckless.

'I told Irini not to go out with him till he had some instruction. I should have made her promise. I should have made *him* see.' Lambis's voice was taut with regret, making Amelie remember her sister-in-law's hesitation to go out that day. Had she been recalling Lambis's advice?

'No one forced Irini to go with him.' Amelie stepped in front of Lambis. He refused to look at her. 'It was *her* decision. They were two adults and you had no way of stopping them.' She touched his hand, sliding her fingers through his and curling them tight. 'I saw them that day. He was going fast, but not recklessly. It was an accident. It's not your fault.'

Lambis shook his head, his features grim.

Amelie tugged at his hand. 'Michel adored her. He would never endanger Irini. It was an *accident*.'

But her words, instead of soothing, seemed to inflame. His fingers returned her grip with a strength that made hers tingle. His mouth flattened into a harsh slash.

'Lambis?'

Finally his gaze lowered. Even in the moonlight his pain was clear. So clear it jammed her breath tight in her lungs.

'I know what I'm talking about, Amelie. Love is no protection. I loved my wife and son. But they're dead because of me.'

Amelie heard her breath hiss at the self-hatred in his voice, at the bitter twist of his mouth and, above all, the hurt in his eyes.

'I can't believe you did anything to endanger them, Lambis.'

It was true. The man she knew was strong, honourable, with a protective streak a mile wide. That protective instinct had overcome his need for solitude and his aversion to spending time with Seb. An aversion, she now guessed, that had nothing to do with Seb, but with Lambis's grief for his son. The way Lambis and Seb interacted now proved Lambis was a man with a profound capacity for caring. He was generous and gentle, and—

'Believe what you like. But it's true. Those close to me suffer.' His mouth twisted. 'In the old days they'd have said I was bad luck from the first, since my mother died giving birth to me.'

'What utter nonsense!' Amelie clutched both his hands, anger welling. 'That wasn't your fault.'

He shrugged. 'Delia and Dimitri, they were my fault.'

Delia and Dimitri. She hadn't heard their names before. 'What were they like?' she whispered.

Lambis's mouth turned up in a crooked smile. 'I fell in

love with Delia when I was sixteen but we waited to marry until we had some money behind us.' His gaze took on a faraway look but Amelie guessed he wasn't seeing the silvered bay over her shoulder.

'Delia had a laugh that always made those around her smile and she had a kind word for everyone. Dimitri looked just like her—straight black hair, dark, merry eyes and that grin… He'd hare around the place at top speed, so full of energy.'

'He sounds like a lovely little boy.' And so like Seb had been before the accident—full of life and laughter. As for Delia, Amelie felt her heart hammer in sympathy for Lambis. Clearly he'd been head over heels in love with his wife. To Amelie's shame there was also possibly a tinge of jealousy. Because Lambis would never talk of *her* with such love in his voice.

What was it like to be so loved? Not for your position or title but for yourself? Loved by Lambis Evangelos, a man who committed himself totally and unswervingly to whatever he did?

Mentally Amelie gave herself a shake. This wasn't about her; it was about Lambis and the family that had been ripped from him. She squeezed his hands, sliding her thumbs over his, hoping the unspoken contact might ease just a tiny fraction of his grief.

'What happened to them?'

She felt a shudder pass through him, saw his jaw tighten. In the dark he looked like some carved sentinel, forbidding yet so boldly alluring it was impossible to look away from him.

'It was winter and we were staying in the mountains. There was a problem with a big new contract and I took the helicopter to Athens for a meeting.' He shook his head. 'I should never have gone. I had staff who could deal with it but I was so used to taking all the major decisions myself, managing every aspect of the business as it expanded...'

The raspy cadence of his voice tore at Amelie. She felt his desolation with a strength that only someone who'd experienced grief could understand.

'What we didn't know was that Dimitri was severely allergic to nuts. Anna said later that he went into anaphylactic shock. It would take too long for medical help so Delia bundled him into the car while Anna made the emergency calls. But Delia's car was at the mechanic's and there was only mine in the garage. She wasn't used to driving such a powerful vehicle, especially in snow.'

He pulled his hands from Amelie's as if he couldn't bear to be touched and Amelie felt part of her own heart crumble at his distress.

'They went off the side of the mountain road on a bend.' He paused, his breath labouring. 'The authorities said it would have been quick, almost instantaneous.'

'Oh, Lambis!' Amelie reached for him, then stopped herself. Clearly he didn't want to be touched. 'I'm so very sorry. That was such a tragic thing to happen.'

'And avoidable.' His voice reminded her of broken glass. Or maybe it was the tightness in her own throat as she tried to swallow. 'Worse, it was my fault. Persuading Delia to live in such an isolated spot, just because my family had once lived there. Leaving them both alone instead of letting someone else handle the meeting.'

'You weren't to know that. You're not to blame, Lambis. No one knew about your son's allergy.'

He shook his head. 'I should have been there. If I'd been there with the chopper, things would have been different.'

'Everyone feels like that after a tragedy, but you're not to blame. No one could have known what would happen that day.' She paused, but he didn't seem to hear her. Amelie grabbed his arm. 'Don't you think I've thought again and again of how different things would have been if I'd suggested to Michel that he not take the boat out but spend the afternoon ashore instead?'

Lambis didn't respond. 'You can't keep thinking that way, Lambis. You'll go crazy.'

'Don't you see? They were my responsibility and I failed them. Just as I failed Irini.'

His utter implacability scared her. And angered her. 'You're not God, you're not omnipotent! You're just a man, Lambis, and you can't blame yourself for things that are totally out of your control.' She shook his arm, till he looked down at her. 'All you can do is pick up the pieces and move on as best you can. Anyone who loved you, like your wife did, would be horrified to think of you racked with guilt for something that wasn't your responsibility.'

Still no reaction from him. It shredded her heart, seeing him like this and being unable to reach him. She let go her hold and stepped back.

'Wallowing in the past is easier than facing the present or the future. It's self-indulgent, Lambis, especially when there are people who need you *now*.' Like Seb. And her. 'Do you really think Delia would want to see you like this? Anyone who loved life the way you say she did, would expect you to move on and keep living.'

Had she gone too far, invoking his wife's name? Yet Amelie had to try. The sight of Lambis bound in that tight web of guilt, unable to move on, unable to do anything but blame himself, was heart-wrenching.

Finally, when he remained silent, she withdrew her hand, to walk silent and alone to the house.

She had her answers. To why Lambis cut himself off. Why he'd avoided Seb, and rejected her. He had no room in his heart to love again.

Yet surely it was something close to love she'd seen as

he interacted with Seb? Or maybe that was just a shadow of what he'd felt for his son.

As for coming to love her... She had a better chance of flying to the moon than seeing him turn to her with love in his eyes.

'Amelie?' Lambis's voice reached her across the gloom of his bedroom.

She shifted, leaning up on one elbow to watch him stride across the room and plant his feet beside the bed they'd shared for the last couple of weeks.

'I didn't think you'd be here.' She heard something in his tone that made everything in her still. Surprise, hesitance and...hope. It was the last that gave her courage. After all, her first instinct had been to sleep in her guest bedroom. Yet she couldn't bear the thought of leaving him, even though she'd given him solitude on the beach.

She pushed her hair back over her shoulder and tried to read his face. 'You want me to leave?'

'No! No, I'm just surprised.'

'You thought I'd turn my back on you?' Maybe she should have. Tonight had made it clear she had no hope of Lambis ever feeling for her as she did for him. He was a one-woman man, racked with guilt over his family.

'I didn't know. You sounded angry.'

She saw his hands tighten then unclench at his sides as if he were restless, suppressing powerful emotions.

Amelie shrugged, surprised to find he was right. Anger at the pointlessness of it mixed with regret and a deep, abiding sadness. 'I hate to see you torturing yourself this way. You have so much to offer, Lambis. So much to give.' She took a slow, steadying breath. 'One day I hope you find someone who'll help you realise that. Someone worth taking a risk for.'

Though it wouldn't be her, Amelie sincerely hoped one

day the right woman would help Lambis tear free of the miasma that shrouded him.

'I don't want to think about the future.'

He looked so proud and strong standing there, silhouetted by moonlight. As if he were unassailable. Yet Amelie remembered the raw ache in his voice as he spoke of his family, and saw his apparent self-control for what it was—a defence mechanism. Her heart turned over.

Amelie pushed aside the sheet and opened her arms. 'Then let's just concentrate on here and now.'

He wasn't interested in her love, would probably run a mile if he guessed. But she could give him comfort. A comfort she discovered she needed almost as much.

For one tremulous moment she held her breath, wondering if he'd reject her. Then, before she had time to process the thought, he was in her arms, pushing her back onto the bed, his hot breath at her throat, her jaw, her breasts as he pressed hungry kisses to her flesh. Callused, urgent hands scraped her thighs as he tugged her nightdress high, then left her to make short work of his clothes.

Lambis came to her, hard and so needy he trembled with it. So driven there was no time for his usual generous foreplay. Instead, after one purposeful caress that found her wet and eager, he slid his hands beneath her bottom, tilting her up to meet him and thrust home, sure and true as if that was where he belonged.

Amelie blinked back hot tears. That was where he *did* belong. At the heart of her, making them both whole.

She grabbed his shoulders, winding her legs around his hips and feeling him sink even deeper. *Home.*

Then there was no more thought as his mouth took hers and he found the powerful rhythm that bound them tighter and tighter together until, lips still locked and hearts pounding in tandem, they raced to the edge of the precipice and flew off into the stars.

CHAPTER THIRTEEN

SEB'S LAUGHTER RANG out from the pool, followed by the deep burr of Lambis's voice. Ordinarily that would have made Amelie smile, for the pair had forged a bond of affection that grew stronger every hour. Despite occasional tears and clinginess, each day Seb seemed a little more like his old self. And he was talking!

Lambis might berate himself for not protecting his son, yet despite the pain he'd revealed that night on the beach he hadn't withdrawn from Seb. Lambis was too protective, too caring for that. He'd no sooner hurt the little boy than he would intentionally hurt Amelie.

Yet it was too late.

She was already hurt in ways that couldn't be fixed, loving a man who'd locked himself away because, she guessed, he was afraid of caring. Losing his family had all but broken this powerful man. Lambis felt so deeply.

Shutting her eyes, Amelie forced her mind away from Lambis. Back to the calamitous new problem on her hands.

Wearily she pressed her hand to her forehead as she turned back to the computer screen. But there was no mistaking the effusive media piece. King Alex of Bengaria was definitely in St Galla, staying in *her* home, ready to attend the gala celebration that Amelie had cancelled ages ago in a discussion with the Prime Minister. Monsieur Barthe had nodded, saying he understood Seb had to be her priority. He'd promised his staff would make the necessary arrangements to reschedule the event.

Heart hammering, Amelie tried to recall the original date of the event. This week surely? She clicked on another report, this time with photos.

The world stopped.

Amelie blinked, trying to clear her vision, but nothing could shift the photo before her. King Alex outside a scientific research centre in St Galla after an official visit. And at his side, looking just a little distracted, was Princess Amelie of St Galla!

Amelie pressed the heel of her hand to her chest, trying to stop her galloping heart leaping free. She blinked, reading and rereading the caption. But there was no sane explanation. She'd never met Alex. His visit was to be the meeting that would help her decide if she wanted to get to know him better with a view to matrimony.

This wasn't an old photo of her and the handsome Prince.

Which meant she had a lookalike. Another woman who looked like her, pretending to *be* her!

Amelie sank back in her chair, mind racing, her skin clammy as nausea rose.

It should be impossible that anyone could look so much like her. Yet as she stared at the screen it was evident this wasn't just a matter of makeup and a wig. The woman could have been her double. *Was* her double!

It was the weirdest feeling, staring at a photo of herself and realising the woman in the photo wasn't her. Was there some slight difference in the angle of her jaw? Maybe around the eyes? Or was that wishful thinking? An instinctive rejection of the idea anyone could pass as her double? It was hard to tell but the other woman might be just a fraction shorter.

Which was neither here nor there. What mattered was finding out who she was and what she was doing taking Amelie's place.

Amelie had no close relations except Seb and Enide, the elderly second cousin who held the fort while she was away. So where did the unmistakable family resemblance come from?

Too easily her thoughts scrolled back to half-heard rumours about her father's infidelities. She'd been old enough to realise her parents hadn't had a happy marriage but she'd assumed the muted whispers were exaggerated. Now she wondered.

Taking a deep breath, Amelie reached for her phone and rang Enide.

Twenty minutes later, her head was spinning. She could barely believe what Enide had reluctantly admitted.

Far from cancelling King Alex's visit, the Prime Minister, Monsieur Barthe, had encouraged it, even having the temerity to tell Alex's staff she'd already *agreed* to a royal marriage! Barthe was set on her marrying a suitable husband, which in his old-fashioned reckoning meant a man with blood as blue as hers. Amelie ground her teeth, thinking of the lies he'd told. Of how he'd *used* her in his devious games.

Obviously Barthe thought he had her over a barrel with his threat to withhold the regency unless she married. As if she had to be a wife in order to be a mother to Seb!

Well, he had a fight on his hands. She'd always intended to dispute that. Now there was no way she'd bow to such pressure.

Plus he'd brought in a body double for her, a woman called Catherine or Cat Dubois. According to Enide, this Cat wasn't the go-getter she'd expected. Enide had taken a shine to her, which was rare since she was so protective of Amelie. True to form, Barthe had conned Cat as well. He hadn't told her King Alex would visit and she'd have to pretend to be Amelie with the man everyone now assumed Amelie would marry.

Not only that, but the public reception where they'd both appear was tonight! In just a couple of hours.

Amelie had no idea if she could get home by then. How long to fly to St Galla?

Lambis and Seb had disappeared so she'd called the housekeeper on the internal phone but she hadn't been able to tell Amelie if the helicopter would return today from the mainland.

Amelie pressed a hand to her breastbone, trying to still her racing heart. For, as if all that wasn't enough, Enide had other news too. Cat was Amelie's half-sister. She was the daughter of a maid who'd worked at the palace when Amelie's parents were first married.

Amelie swallowed bile at the idea of her father being unfaithful to her mother straight after their honeymoon. Disloyalty was anathema to her but that...

She'd always known her father was lazy and self-indulgent but she hadn't thought he'd stoop so low.

She shot to her feet, her emotions too turbulent to name. Except that deep within the roiling mess was excitement. She had a sister! That fact shone bright and hopeful.

How did you make the acquaintance of a sibling you hadn't known you possessed? A sibling who was doing her best to cover for you in difficult circumstances?

A sister she'd been deprived of all her life.

Amelie had learned it was best to live in the present, for everything could be snatched from you in an instant. She wouldn't give up Seb or put up with Barthe's machinations. She *would* get to know her sister. She might never have the love of the man who'd stolen her heart years ago, but there were other consolations in a life devoted to duty.

The phone rang. It would be Enide calling back as instructed. Amelie's blood ricocheted around her body so fast she reached out and grabbed the back of a chair.

She sank into it and reached for the phone. 'Hello? Enide?'

'Amelie? I can't tell you how sorry I am. I—' Enide sounded distraught.

'It's okay, Enide. This isn't your fault.' No, it was Prime

Minister Barthe's for bullying her elderly relation into keeping quiet about this ludicrous masquerade. Poor Enide had thought she was protecting Amelie and Seb, knowing they needed peace and quiet.

'Is she there?' Funny how Amelie hesitated to speak her sister's name. Enide had said the woman was likeable and engaging yet Amelie felt nerves flutter in her stomach.

'I have her here. Are you absolutely sure—?'

'I'm sure. I'm fine, truly, Enide. Worry instead about Barthe. Keep an eye on him. He's more dangerous than even I realised.'

'Yes, of course. I will. But please, take care of yourself.'

'Of course.'

Amelie heard muffled noise at the other end of the line then a new voice.

'Hello?' It was a woman about her own age, speaking with an American accent. Amelie's pulse sped.

'Ms Dubois?'

'Yes?'

'It's Amelie here. Princess Amelie.' Never had she been more grateful for the years of experience in dealing with challenging situations. Her throat almost closed with nerves and excitement but her voice sounded fine.

'Your Highness.' Cat's voice was husky. With shock? Or was that how she usually sounded?

'Amelie, please.' She paused, slicking her tongue around dry lips. This was so hard over the phone. She wanted to *be* there to meet her sister and sort out this tangled mess. 'May I call you Cat?'

'Of course.'

'Thank you.' Questions hammered her brain. All the things she should ask about King Alex and Barthe and the reception. How had her half-sister, with absolutely no experience of the palace, coped? 'Are you all right, Cat?'

'I'm sorry?'

'I asked if you're okay.' Amelie sighed, drawing the hair back from her face with trembling fingers. How she wished Lambis were here. He'd tell her if she could get to St Galla tonight.

'I've just found out about this scheme for you to take my place at tonight's reception. I had no idea. The event should have been cancelled when I told the Prime Minister I wouldn't be there. I believed it *had* been cancelled.' Her mouth tightened at the prospect of confronting Barthe. He might run the nation but he'd learn he didn't run her!

'I haven't been watching the news, you see, and I haven't been in regular contact with anyone at the palace.' Except Enide, who'd known she was at her wits' end trying help Seb. 'So I didn't know you'd been brought in. Are you all right?'

'I'm fine. I…well, I'm not very good at being a princess, but I'm muddling through.'

Despite her tension, Amelie smiled. She admired how Cat downplayed what must have been a massive challenge. Maybe they did have some things in common. 'Even with King Alex in the palace?'

There was no answer.

'Cat? Are you sure you're all right?' Concern tinged her voice. Crazy to be worried about someone she didn't know existed till now, but there it was.

'I'm fine. And Alex knows the truth. He guessed some time ago.'

'Yet he's still there?' Amelie couldn't hide her astonishment. She'd heard only good things about Alex, which was why she hadn't rejected the marriage idea instantly. But why hadn't he left St Galla when he'd realised he was being duped?

'He knows it's not your doing. He blames Monsieur Barthe. But he's willing to go along with the pretence so there's no public scandal.' Cat paused. 'But there's something else you need to know. He made it clear, even before he found out who I was, that he wasn't interested in marriage.'

Amelie slumped back in her chair. 'Thank God. That's one thing less to worry about.'

'You're pleased?' Cat was confused.

'I agreed to entertain the idea, but my heart wasn't in it.' Amelie's laugh was bitter. Now wasn't the time to dwell on where her heart *was* engaged.

'Are *you* all right? I've been worried you might be in trouble.'

'That's kind of you.' Amelie felt a rush of warmth for this stranger who didn't feel like a stranger. 'Things haven't gone quite as I'd expected but I'm coming home.' She'd put that off too long, hoping to reach Lambis at more than a physical level. As if somehow she could *will* him to love her. How pathetic was that? Amelie straightened. 'I'd like, very much, to meet you. I...' She paused, struck anew by the depth of her emotions. 'I didn't know you existed till Enide told me.'

'I'd like that.' Amelie heard the emotion in Cat's voice too.

'Good. I'm looking forward to it too.' Amelie forced herself to focus on the tangled mess in St Galla. 'Now, about tonight. I'll see if I can get there in time. Transport is a bit limited from here and—'

'It's all right. I can do it. It's only for a couple of hours and with Enide and Alex watching out for me I'll be fine.'

'Alex?' The way Cat said his name intrigued her.

'He's been...helpful.'

'I see.' Amelie paused, frantically trying to calculate the most sensible way forward. Was it better for both of them to be in St Galla tonight, assuming she could get transport? Or safer to stay away till after the reception so there weren't two princesses in the same place? Enide had said Cat was leaving tomorrow. 'Are you absolutely sure? I couldn't guarantee I'd get there exactly on time but—'

'I'm sure. I'll manage. I'm sure you have other things on your mind than tonight's reception.' There was a pause. 'I hope Prince Sébastien is well.'

'He's fine.' Despite everything, Amelie smiled. No matter what scandal they courted with this charade in St Galla, Seb was on the mend. *That* was what mattered. 'Much better than before.'

'Amelie?' Lambis's deep voice made her turn in her seat. He stood, filling the doorway, and inevitably her heart gave that little shimmy of delight.

She pressed her hand to her chest. She *had* to move on. She couldn't continue like this.

Amelie turned away from the door. 'I'm sorry. I have to go. Are you sure about tonight? I can try—'

'Absolutely.' The certainty in her sister's voice convinced her. Amelie sat back, surprised at the relief filling her. She'd have to deal with Monsieur Barthe and King Alex, but not till tomorrow. She was used to being the one who managed, who kept everything running, who took responsibility. It was a novel thing to relinquish control to another.

As she had with Seb, she realised, letting Lambis help shoulder the burden of responsibility and care.

'Thank you, Cat. If you can manage tonight it will give me a little time to…organise things. But we'll talk soon and arrange to meet, either in St Galla or elsewhere.'

Amelie was surprised her hand didn't shake as she put the phone down. When she looked up Lambis stood before her. He was so unnaturally still she sensed his hyper-alertness. What did he read in her face?

She looked away, telling herself it didn't matter what he read, or how he reacted. Lambis had made it clear he had no place in her future, except as an occasional visitor to Seb. It was time to move on.

'What's happened? What's the problem?' His voice was terse, that of a man used to taking charge in difficult situations.

Well, he wouldn't have to deal with this. She'd handle it alone.

It was time to say goodbye.

Pinning on a smile, she met those piercing eyes, ignoring the way her heart fluttered. 'It's time Seb and I went home.'

Home? Shock jerked his body. Lambis had guessed it when his housekeeper relayed the query about the chopper. But hearing Amelie say it…

It was a measure of the change she'd wrought in him that, instead of being relieved at the prospect of solitude, Lambis wanted to wail and gnash his teeth. More, he wanted to wipe that polite smile off her beautiful lips with a kiss that would turn her compliant and eager in his arms. He wanted her to say she wouldn't leave him.

His head reared back.

'Leaving? You can't go yet. Seb's not fully recovered.'

Her smile looked strained but she didn't turn away. 'I suspect that will take a long time, for both of us.'

What was she saying? That he'd taken advantage of her grief?

She was right. Where Amelie was concerned he hadn't any restraint—possibly because he'd been keeping his distance for years. His resistance to her had finally eroded.

'Seb's talking, which is a start. It will be enough for the upcoming ceremony, so his future will be secure. That's what matters.' Her gaze left his and he found himself bereft. Adrift like an unmoored boat.

Had he expected her to say *they* mattered? That together they'd created a bond that couldn't be ignored?

He was the one who'd warned her he couldn't commit.

He sensed he was already losing her. Her thoughts were in St Galla.

For an insane moment Lambis wanted to grab her chin and pull her face round to his, make her look him in the eye and admit they were—

Nothing. They were nothing. She wasn't for him.

Yet the prospect of her leaving hurt more than he'd thought possible.

'Why do you need to go? What's happened?'

She shrugged. 'It's a long story.'

Lambis folded his arms. 'I have time.'

That made her look up. Green eyes met his and he leaned closer, inevitably drawn by the unguarded confusion he read there.

'Amelie—'

'It's all a mess.' She spoke quickly. 'Monsieur Barthe was supposed to cancel an official visit by King Alex of Bengaria. I told him to reschedule it but he hasn't. The King is there now and…' She shook her head. 'It's complicated.'

'Alex of Bengaria?' Lambis's firm had done work in Bengaria. He remembered the King—decisive, approachable and, according to Lambis's female staff, utterly irresistible.

Lambis's gaze narrowed on the woman before him, looking so ill at ease. 'He's the royal they want you to marry?'

She started at his harsh tone, then nodded. 'Yes. But it's unlikely now.'

Lambis barely heard her over the rush of blood filling his head. '*That's* what's so important? You're rushing back to be with *him*?' He grimaced at the bitter taste in his mouth.

'There's no need to look like that. There are complications I need to sort out.' Amelie got to her feet, staring at him as if she'd never seen him. Or perhaps comparing him to the polished, pretty-boy Prince waiting for her in St Galla.

Something dark and feral stirred in Lambis's soul. Something he didn't recognise. It was angry, wanting to lash out, but hurting too. Of course Amelie would choose to be with another blue-blood, instead of a reclusive man with working class roots. He had no right to feel indignant. He'd told her time and again she couldn't rely on him long-term. Alex, on the other hand, was apparently ready for marriage.

He owed it to Amelie to shut up and let her walk away.

'You'd really give yourself to him?' The thought of Amelie in another man's arms, in his bed, all but broke him. He felt as if his ribs were caught in a vice that screwed tighter and tighter.

Amelie frowned and Lambis wanted to kiss her brow smooth, stroke her cheeks, tease her lips till she opened for him.

'I told you, it's unlikely.' Her chin tilted with a hauteur designed to freeze him on the spot, but which instead made the fire in his belly burn even brighter.

'You deserve better than someone who doesn't even *care* for you. You tried that with Jules, and you got hurt.' She'd tried to hide that but she wasn't as adept at concealing emotion as she thought. Besides, Lambis knew her now. He understood that however strong she was, Amelie was a woman with heart. She loved and deserved love in return.

'You need someone who'll fight for you. Not someone who views you as a convenient spouse.' His words spilled out, harsh and overloud.

Lambis could never be the man she wanted. Yet he couldn't stand by while she threw herself away on a man who'd ultimately destroy her. However good his intentions,

Alex's indifference would eventually kill a woman who was clearly designed for love.

'Well.' Her eyes glittered gem-bright, her nostrils flaring as she dragged in air. 'If ever you find such a man, be sure to tell me. I've yet to find one.' Her eyes flashed like daggers. He felt the sharp prick of that look at his heart. Guilt drove into him like a sharpened spike through soft flesh. For, of course, it wasn't just Jules who'd let her down. It was Lambis too.

He couldn't reconcile his no-emotional-entanglements attitude with this urgent need to keep her here and convince her Alex wasn't the man for her.

He couldn't offer what she wanted, yet he didn't want anyone else getting close to her.

'Now, is it possible to use your helicopter? I want to return to St Galla tomorrow. I'll pay, naturally, and—'

'Don't!' What she heard in his voice, Lambis didn't know. He only knew he was closer to doing something utterly reckless than he'd been in all the years since he'd lost Delia and Dimitri. He hefted in a draught of oxygen. 'I'll take you. Leave everything to me.'

Hours later, with every detail of the trip sorted and his schedule cleared, Lambis slowly walked back from the beach. He hadn't seen Amelie since dinner, where their conversation had been stilted, like a couple of chance met strangers, picking their way through neutral topics.

He hated the distance between them. The invisible but real barriers Amelie had erected. Was that how it had felt for her when he'd pushed her away years before?

He shook his head, swearing under his breath. Everything felt wrong. Out of control. Nothing was as it should be. He didn't want Amelie and Sébastien to leave.

He didn't want to be alone.

Lambis slammed to a halt, heart pounding. Since when had solitude been anything but a balm?

Since Amelie and Sébastien had made him feel again.

He grimaced. It sounded so simple. If this were a movie he'd magically forget all the reasons he was a bad risk. Forget how he'd failed those he cared for. But he couldn't do that to Amelie. She deserved far better.

His throat and lungs ached as he drew in another, laboured breath.

He wanted her but couldn't, *mustn't*, have her. What he had to do was let her go.

He stood, swaying, forcing himself to face that unbearable fact.

Finally, his heart, his whole body aching, he followed the path up to the house and the French windows giving directly onto his room.

He'd deliver her to St Galla and he'd make it clear to this Alex that he'd have Lambis to deal with if he let Amelie down. He stepped into the dark room, mind fixed on that interview, when he realised he wasn't alone.

Amelie was in his bed.

His heart stalled as she sat up. The sheet fell away to reveal the sweet, proud jut of her breasts. Her hair cascaded around her shoulders like pale silk. Her eyes were unreadable in the shadows, but there was a vulnerability about the set of her shoulders and the too-high angle of her chin, almost as if she expected him to reject her.

It was all he could do not to sink to his knees in thankfulness.

That ache in his chest honed to a fixed point of sharp pain, a counterpoint to the razor-edge of desire slicing his belly.

Lambis wanted her so badly he could barely contain himself. He wanted her tenderness as well as her body. Her smiles, her...

He shoved aside thought, unable to cope with all he was about to lose when she returned to St Galla. Instead he paced to the bed, eating her up with his eyes.

Steadily she stared back as he tore at his clothes, flinging them aside. There was no doubt in her as she proudly faced him, only a certainty that humbled him.

Lambis pulled the sheet aside. Then he began worshipping her with his body, his heart and soul. He would give them both memories that would last long after she'd gone.

CHAPTER FOURTEEN

THEY ARRIVED THE next afternoon at a private airfield. Lambis had flown them via helicopter to the Greek mainland and organised the private jet and the anonymous car with heavily tinted windows that took them to the St Gallan palace.

He glanced at Amelie, on the other side of the limo's wide back seat. She was tense despite the bright smile she gave her nephew. 'Here we are, *mon lapin*, home again. Tonight you'll sleep in your own bed and before that you can play with all your toys.'

Sébastien nodded and cuddled his teddy bear close. He'd been quiet since they touched down.

'Perhaps you can show me the best place to swim here,' Lambis found himself saying. 'I haven't swum for so long!'

The boy giggled. 'But we swam yesterday.' Lambis saw Amelie's high shoulders relax a little at that giggle. Clearly she'd been worried too how her nephew would cope, returning to the palace with its memories.

'So I did. How silly of me to forget. Will you swim with me?' He kept the boy talking, giving Amelie time to harness her emotions. For despite her almost iron control he could read her now. Her tension had increased steadily all day. Or perhaps it was anger.

Finally, in the early hours, as they lay sated yet wide awake in each other's arms, she'd told him about the Prime Minister's audacious masquerade scheme. About the half-sister she'd yet to meet, and the increasing pressure being brought to bear on Amelie to marry.

At least that was one thing Lambis had been able to do for Amelie, tell her a little about Cat. For it had been Lambis who'd met her years before and recommended her to the St Gallan authorities in case a body double was ever needed for Amelie. He hadn't known they were half-sisters, just that they looked remarkably similar. And Cat had impressed him as honest, talented and likeable. If he'd known the Prime Minister would use his recommendation to deceive everyone in this way… Fury coursed through him.

But it was nothing to the other emotions haunting him.

Holding her in his arms, Lambis had felt a regret so poignant it unnerved him. For he had nothing to give that would keep her with him.

They'd both been conscious it was their last night together. It had been there in each caress and their quiet desperation as they shared themselves. As if neither wanted to face the dawn.

Now, knowing the enormity of what Amelie confronted, Lambis was determined to do whatever he could to help. For the moment that meant keeping Sébastien occupied and happy.

Lambis looked up as the limo turned into a wide gateway and drove sedately towards the fanciful *belle époque* palace. Its soft pink stone was decorated with white marble windows and doors that from a distance looked as delicate as frosting on a cake. Yet there was no mistaking it for anything but a seat of power, set in its own extensive gardens that occupied the whole southern tip of the island.

Minutes later they stood at the palace entrance, the scent of flowers mingling with the rich perfume of pines and the sea. Enide, the elderly relative Lambis knew from previous visits, was whispering to Amelie. The old woman's well-bred, slightly horsey face was creased with anxiety. As she spoke Lambis watched the last vestige of Amelie's animation flicker and die. She didn't frown but the smooth, expressionless mask of calm she adopted was worse.

The warm, sensual woman he knew was being buried beneath her royal burdens.

Lambis's hand tightened on Sébastien's as he fought the impulse to go to her. The urge to wrap his arms around both Amelie and Sébastien grew. He was accustomed to being there for them.

Someone else—a secretary?—joined the small, serious group and Amelie nodded, answering a question about an urgent meeting. Her voice was crisp and businesslike.

He wasn't surprised. Amelie was far more than a pretty face or a devoted aunt. She was capable and efficient.

She'd be fine.

Yet Lambis couldn't dispel the memory of her in his arms before dawn. How she'd trembled with indignation at the devious schemes of her Prime Minister. How her voice had been strained and her touch needy.

How she'd sighed her pleasure and given herself to Lambis utterly, no holding back. He'd felt for that too-brief interlude as if they'd both found peace. As if he'd found the missing part that completed him.

Lambis hunkered down beside Sébastien, asking him about the view from the palace. But as the little kid replied, more than half Lambis's attention was on Amelie. She was in control, no doubt of that, and more than capable. Yet he couldn't quench the emotions that wrenched at him, seeing her so alone, the weight of the kingdom, her nephew's wellbeing and now this fiasco with the Prime Minister on her shoulders.

'Seb? Shall we go in?' Her smile for the boy was the same as always. Only the shadows in her eyes were different. And the way she avoided looking at Lambis. His heart thudded dully in his chest cavity.

Then they were moving into the palace. Staff clustered and welcomed. Enide shook his hand, thanking him for all he'd done, which only made Lambis recall how reluctantly he'd helped. Only after Amelie had forced his hand.

Lambis looked around the grand foyer, built to impress and intimidate. A huge chandelier dripped from the ceiling and the walls were hung with a collection of art that had left more than one connoisseur breathless. The place even smelled different. Rich, luxurious, refined.

This was Amelie's world, her home.

Yet he knew in his deepest self that she'd never been more alone than now. A vast ache pulsed within him.

'Wait!' His voice echoed around the vast space, too strident and peremptory. Faces turned.

Lambis turned to Sébastien. 'How about you go with your Aunt Enide? I'm sure Monsieur Bernhard wants to check out his old bed. Then I'll join you and we can swim together.'

Sébastien regarded him for a moment then looked at Bernhard, his bear. 'Okay. But don't be long.'

More than one person gasped, surprised the little Prince was speaking. But Lambis's attention wasn't on the attendants, it was on Amelie. 'We need to talk.'

'Later. I have to meet—'

'I know.' His eyes locked with hers over Sébastien's head. Lambis ignored the shocked glances that he'd dared interrupt the Princess. 'But first there's something you need to hear.' His heart beat a sharp, accelerating tattoo and his jaw clenched so hard pain radiated down his neck.

Finally she nodded and, with a hug for Sébastien and a couple of murmured words to the others, led the way down a wide hall into a salon.

Lambis closed the door behind them, watching Amelie pace to the window. The afternoon light limned her in gold, accentuating that aura of untouchability she'd donned along with her regal composure. She wore a skirt and jacket he hadn't seen before today, slim-fitting, in a soft green that matched the peridot earrings that swayed as she turned. Her only other jewellery was the familiar pearl and gold pendant but she couldn't be more breathtaking if she wore a whole treasury of royal finery.

His heart clenched then tripped to a quickening rhythm as he crossed the room. He pulled up as she raised her hand.

Gone was this morning's lover. Where before there'd been tenderness, now he read…nothing.

Even knowing this was a necessary tactic for Amelie to concentrate on the onerous tasks before her, Lambis silently railed at this change. He didn't want distance. He didn't want them to be strangers again.

'Marry me.' The words surged out, rough and urgent.

Her eyes widened and he thought she swayed on her delicate heels.

'Marry me, Amelie.' His voice was pure gravel. He swallowed hard, trying to clear the restriction in his throat. 'Let me help you.'

He moved closer though he kept his arms by his sides. If he touched her he wouldn't be able to keep the lid on the bubbling brew of emotions. The strain of keeping his distance reverberated through him, a discordant note.

'Help me?' Her face was pale, her nostrils flared as if she couldn't get enough air. One hand lifted to her pearl pendant then dropped away.

'Yes.' Another step closer, breathing in her entrancing scent, warm flesh and gardenias. His gaze dropped to her mouth with its delicate pink tint then to the little pulse at the base of her throat, tripping so fast. 'There's no need to marry a total stranger, like Alex of Bengaria.'

There's no need to sell yourself for your nephew's sake.

She was going to fight the Prime Minister for the right to be named Sébastien's Regent, but if she was unsuccessful…

The thought of Amelie in a stranger's bed was bad enough. The idea of her with someone who'd married her only for her status and ability to breed an heir left Lambis sick to the stomach.

He couldn't let that happen.

He took a deep breath and felt a sense of absolute rightness creep over him. 'You don't have to do this alone.' His voice was smoother now, the words coming more easily. 'Marry me. I can...' The word *protect* hovered on his tongue but he couldn't lie. 'I can help. Marry me and you'll be made Regent. Sébastien's future will be secure. You deserve to have someone who'll fight for you. Someone who knows and respects you.'

Amelie stared into those hooded grey eyes. She'd seen them dark as storm clouds as Lambis had thundered at her, trying to push her away. She'd seen them bright as summer lightning, their heat searing her as they made love and he lost himself inside her. She'd thought then that nothing could be more intense than that pinnacle of exquisite oneness, that oneness she'd known only with Lambis.

She'd been wrong. Looking into his serious eyes, reading the dreadful tension in his big frame, Amelie felt a pain so sharp it was as if someone had stabbed her through the heart.

Her poor, stupid, still hopeful heart that for one thrilling, heady moment had waited for Lambis to talk of love.

Amelie swallowed. Lambis had given his heart to his wife, Delia, and that was the end of it. It was Amelie's luck to fall head over heels for a one-woman man. A man who was strong, honest, loyal and caring, who was wonderful with Seb and made Amelie feel...

She blinked and shook her head. She didn't know whether to laugh or cry.

How she wanted to say yes. She actually had to bite her tongue to stop the words leaping out. Especially when she saw what this cost Lambis. His hands were clenched into white-knuckled fists and there was a repressed energy about him that she guessed came from the effort to stand there and make the offer he thought she wanted.

But it was so much less than what she needed.

'Thank you, Lambis.' Her voice wasn't her own. She paused, her gaze fixed on his face, though what she really wanted to do was swing away and give in to the hot tears pressing the back of her eyes. 'Thank you, but no.'

His flesh tightened on his bones, emphasising his strong features, as if he'd shrunk before her eyes. But he was still utterly imposing. Tall, powerful, chivalrous. He was trying to protect her even though he'd reasoned himself into believing he could protect no one. He was hardwired that way. He could no sooner ignore her plight than she could ignore the love for him that thrummed in her blood.

But what they couldn't change they could ignore. They had to.

Lambis opened his mouth to speak and Amelie hurried on, not trusting herself not to be swayed.

'It's a kind offer. I appreciate it.' She swallowed hard, tasting the salt tang of distress. 'I'm honoured that you respect me and I know without doubt you'd fight for me and for Seb, but…' One slow breath. Another. She clasped her hands before her, tight enough to hide the way they shook.

'But while I appreciate that, I want more. I don't want sacrifice, I want *love*. You had love once, so you know how important it is. I want…the chance to find that.' Her words petered out to a hoarse whisper. 'So thank you for your concern, and your offer, but I can't accept.' Amelie tugged in a swift, shallow breath, trying to mask crushing hurt. 'You'll always be welcome here. I know Seb loves you.' She halted the words on her tongue about how *she* loved him too. 'And I hope you'll always be part of his life.'

Lambis stared unblinking, as if she'd dealt him a stunning blow. Pain seized her at the hurt she'd inflicted. Until she reasoned it wasn't hurt. Maybe Lambis's pride was bruised at the rejection.

'Now, I'm sorry, but I really must go. I have to meet King Alex and the Prime Minister.'

Amelie bit back a mirthless smile. Facing the bullying Barthe and Alex of Bengaria, the man who'd been shamelessly lied to ever since he'd set foot in her home, had seemed daunting an hour ago. Now that paled to insignificance in the face of rejecting a proposal from the only man she'd ever truly loved.

CHAPTER FIFTEEN

'THANK YOU AGAIN, ALEX. You've been unbelievably understanding.'

The man before her on the terrace shook his head, his deep blue eyes crinkling as he smiled. Truly, if she weren't pining for a man she could never have, Amelie could imagine falling for Alex of Bengaria. He had so many qualities she admired.

He just wasn't Lambis.

Her heart clenched and she had to force herself to breathe. She'd deal with the pain when she had the luxury of being alone.

'It wasn't your fault. You knew nothing about Barthe's machinations and Cat's masquerade.'

They'd spent the afternoon together, dealing with the Prime Minister and ensuring there was no fallout from Cat's masquerade as Amelie. More, between them, they'd made Barthe see he had no future leading the nation. They'd given him a choice—resign or have them expose his double dealing. He'd chosen to resign, and with his departure the opposition to Amelie as Regent lost its drive. Now, with Seb able to talk, the upcoming ceremony should be a mere formality.

It had been a long, exhausting few hours, but the way ahead was brighter. If only Amelie could feel jubilant about it.

'I feel responsible. You'll go away thinking we St Gallans are liars and cheats.'

Alex shook his head. 'On the contrary, I've developed a soft spot for St Galla and its people.'

'And particularly for Cat?' It was none of her business,

but discovering her half-sister Cat and Alex were close, and seeing his concern on learning Cat had already left for New York, she couldn't help wondering.

His smile disintegrated. 'Absolutely. But *she* doesn't think so. I was so busy racing off to confront your Prime Minister to scotch rumours about the pair of us, she left St Galla before I could talk to her. Now she's not answering her phone.'

Amelie reached out and touched his hand. 'Then follow her. Make her listen.' Her voice dropped. 'Love is too important to give up.'

His blue eyes narrowed. 'You understand, don't you?'

Amelie's instinct was to deny it. What was the point? Alex wouldn't tell anyone, and besides, the urge to confide was overwhelming.

'I do.'

She didn't say any more but Alex heard the hurt in her voice, or perhaps read her face. His hand turned to clasp hers. 'It's not something that can be worked out?'

Amelie's mouth tightened as familiar pain welled. 'Sadly, no. He's in love with someone else.'

'Ah. I'm sorry.'

For a moment they stood, unmoving and silent in the rich afternoon light. Then Amelie forced a lighter note. 'Can I persuade you to spend another evening here as my guest, or are you going to hotfoot it after my sister?'

Something flared in Alex's eyes and Amelie told herself Cat was one lucky woman. He was obviously head over heels in love.

'I'm not sure. I want to follow her but I suspect she's furious and won't listen. I may have to think of a better plan.'

Intrigued, Amelie was about to enquire further when she noticed someone coming towards them through the formal garden. A tall, imposing figure who moved with a casual grace that belied the strength in that massive form.

Beside him skipped Seb, golden hair bright in the last rays of sunlight.

She stilled, willing herself not to feel anything and failing miserably.

Alex released her hand and turned to follow her gaze. When he turned back his expression was sympathetic. 'Actually, I think I'll leave now, if you don't mind?'

'Of course not.' She summoned a smile. 'Good luck with Cat. I'm hoping to visit her in New York soon.'

'If I'm successful, you may be visiting her in Bengaria instead.'

Amelie nodded. 'Good luck.' She liked and admired Alex and, though they'd never met, she already had a soft spot for her half-sister, Cat. She couldn't wait to get to know her properly. It would be wonderful if this pair could sort out their differences and find happiness together.

Alex took her hand and raised it to his lips. 'I'll hope to see you soon in Bengaria. No need to see me out. I suspect you have other important matters to deal with.'

Amelie stilled. There was nothing more to sort out. Seb's future was safe and her role as his guardian secure. As for Lambis... No, there was nothing more to be done.

Alex entered the palace and Amelie turned to follow. She didn't want a *tête-à-tête* with Lambis. But the sound of voices stopped her. Enide had approached down one of the gravel paths, meeting Seb and Lambis.

Then, before Amelie could move, Enide and Seb headed off together and Lambis strode directly towards her. His long legs ate up the distance at an alarming rate. In black jeans and a charcoal shirt that matched his eyes, and with his glossy hair falling over his brow, he looked deliciously ruffled and dangerously sexy.

Amelie's pulse fluttered, matching the butterflies in her stomach. Or were they swallows, swooping and dipping in dizzying aerobatics?

She made herself stand firm. Surely, after facing down her Prime Minister and the foreign King who'd been duped and deceived in her own palace, Amelie could face Lambis?

He was probably coming to say he was leaving. There was nothing to keep him now he'd brought her and Seb home. He must be relieved she hadn't clutched at his unwilling proposal.

Pasting on a gracious smile, she swung to face him fully, telling herself she wasn't in the least disconcerted by his aura of restless energy.

He stopped too near. So near instinct screamed she should retreat. Instead she widened her stance. This was her home. She'd be polite, wish him bon voyage and that would be it.

'You and King Alex? You came to an agreement?' Gone were the rich, deep tones she'd become addicted to. The soft burr of sound that had wrapped around her and soothed her into sleep more than once. Instead that bass voice was harsh, rough-edged.

'Sorry?'

'You touched him.'

Lambis stood before her, arms akimbo, those broad shoulders thrust back, accentuating the sheer masculine power of him. But it was the accusation in his tone that confused her.

Till understanding kicked in, then anger. He didn't want love her, but he resented her touching another man?

Amelie folded her arms. 'I fail to see what that's got to do with you.'

'He kissed your hand.' It came out as a growl like the first warning roll of thunder before a violent electrical storm.

Instead of scaring her, that stoked her defiance. 'Again, none of your business.' She tried to freeze him with the haughty glare that had been her father's stock-in-trade.

Lambis ignored it, stepping in so she had to tilt her head back. But Amelie refused to back away. She'd had enough of men trying to tell her how to live her life.

'What if I make it my business?' There was no mistaking that aggressively proprietorial tone. Despite her anger, Amelie felt a thrill of feminine delight. Till she reminded herself this was dog-in-the-manger stuff.

'We've been over this, Lambis.'

Slowly he shook his head, his eyes never leaving hers. That was when the fiercely combative electricity between them changed. When she saw what was in those clouded eyes.

'Lambis?' Her voice cracked.

'Have you agreed to marry him? You let him *kiss* you.'

'Only my hand.' Amelie stared, her brain seizing at what she thought she saw in his face.

'You let him *kiss* you.' Large hands folded around her shoulders. He didn't pull her close, just held her, and to her amazement Amelie felt him shake.

She reached out. To push him away? Instead her hand settled on the solid heat of his chest. His heart pounded urgently beneath her palm. Her mouth dried.

'Don't do this, Amelie. He's not the man for you.'

'He's a fine, decent man.' Where the words came from, Amelie had no idea. Lambis was right—Alex wasn't for her.

'He won't make you happy.' Lambis's hands tightened on her shoulders.

'You can't know that.' How dare he act as if he knew what was best?

'I've never been more certain of anything.' Beneath her hand his massive chest rose with a shuddering sigh. 'You belong with me.'

Instantly Amelie stepped back, or tried to. Lambis stopped her.

This was too much to bear, too tempting for a woman

in love, no matter how many times she'd told herself she deserved more than a convenient marriage for the sake of her nephew.

'Please let go, Lambis.' She swiped her tongue over lips grown suddenly parched, her gaze skittering away. She was deluding herself, imagining he felt—

'Never.'

Amelie's head jerked up in shock. But before she had a chance to speak he bent to her, his mouth settling on hers firmly, possessively, so sweetly she was sure she heard angels sing. His lips moved on hers, coaxing and enticing, so that when his tongue swiped the seam of her mouth it took no pressure at all for him to delve inside.

Lambis's kiss was tender but not tentative. It was the kiss of a lover coming home. A partner sharing pleasure. It undid her utterly.

'Ah, Amelie, *karthia mou*. Don't cry.' Gentle thumbs swiped her cheeks as he pulled back, resting his forehead on hers.

Her shoulders shook on a sobbing breath. She couldn't do this any longer, couldn't pretend.

'Forgive me, *agapi mou*. I can't bear to see you hurt.' One big hand gently stroked the hair back from her face. Then, when she said nothing, Lambis folded her closer, pushing her head against his chest, wrapping his arms around her.

'I was an idiot.' That hypnotic voice welled from deep within, vibrating beneath her ear. 'I didn't see until it was too late.'

'What didn't you see?' Amelie knew she should pull back and stand on her own two feet. She was a princess of St Galla, soon to be Regent, an independent, confident woman. But she couldn't bring herself to leave the shelter of Lambis's arms. It would be the last time he held her, surely, and she wasn't ready to miss a second of it. Later she'd berate herself for being weak and needy but not now.

His hand swept her back in a slow, soothing stroke. 'That I loved you.'

'What?' Her head jerked back and she found herself staring up into dark, serious eyes.

'I love you, Amelie.'

She shook her head, wondering why he'd torment her this way. 'You love your wife.'

'She and Dimitri will always hold a special place in my heart.' He spoke slowly, his tone measured as if to emphasise his meaning. 'But I've loved you for a long time. For years. Even when I rejected you here in St Galla, I loved you.'

Amelie strained back against his hold. 'No. You're saying that because you think it's what I want to hear. I don't need a husband, Lambis. I can get by without. Seb and I will be fine.'

'But I won't.' The words, so grave, so forthright, stopped her mid protest. 'I love you, Amelie, and I need you. I hadn't realised how much till I saw I was losing you.'

Bewildered, Amelie tried to make sense of his words. He looked at her with such openness, as if sharing such feelings was completely natural. Yet this man had deliberately isolated himself, protecting himself from emotions as far as he could.

'There's no need for this. I'm not marrying Alex. I'm not marrying anyone. Now, please, let me go.' She'd reached her limit. Standing in the circle of his arms, encompassed by his heat, feeling his heart beating beneath her hand, was too intimate.

Lambis closed his eyes and said something under his breath in Greek. Amelie couldn't understand a word, but felt his big frame shudder.

Then his eyes snapped open and it was like looking at a

pewter sky, bright with sheet lightning. Slowly his mouth tipped into a wide smile, a grin that, despite her churning emotions, she couldn't help responding to.

'I think I loved you from the first day we met,' he said in that low, mesmerising voice. 'You were beautiful and kind and so utterly unaware of how entrancing you were.'

Amelie shook her head. 'You scowled at me.'

'I was a grouch. I was mired in guilt and regret and right from the start you made me feel things I didn't deserve to feel.'

Amelie's heart rolled over as she read the honesty in his eyes. Her hand slid up to his face, cupping that starkly angled jaw, feeling the erotic sensation of incipient bristles against her palm. 'You know you're not to blame. I hate that you feel like that and I'm sure Delia would hate it too.'

Unwavering, his eyes met hers and this time she read a flicker of assent there.

'You don't have to do this, Lambis. I'm really not going to marry Alex.'

'You think I'm lying?' His brow furrowed into a scowl that should have made him look forbidding yet only made her melt. 'I've been many things, Amelie, but no liar. I was brutally cruel when you came to me in Greece. I reneged on my duty to Sébastien because I was scared.' His deep breath pushed their chests together. 'I was scared of what you made me feel. Scared I'd be unfaithful to Delia's memory.'

Amelie nodded, trying and not quite succeeding in quashing a flare of jealousy.

'I didn't understand then.' Lambis brushed back a stray strand of hair from her face. 'Delia was my past. You're my present, Amelie, and my future. If you'll have me.' His voice shook. 'I love you, sweetheart. Would you consider marrying me?'

Yes. Say yes.

She tasted the word in her mouth.

'You only decided you cared when you saw me with Alex.' Pushing the words out took all Amelie's willpower. 'Because you thought I'd marry him.' She had to be sure.

Lambis shook his head. 'You're wrong. I knew when I made that appalling proposal a few hours ago. As soon as I blurted the words I realised it was what I wanted, but not for the reasons I told myself. It wasn't about protecting the pair of you. It wasn't about duty.'

His voice dropped to a rumbling bass pitch that reached her very core. 'I want to marry you for utterly selfish reasons. Because I love you. I need you. You turn my darkness into light. You give me a reason to wake each day. A reason to smile.' He lifted his hand and wiped the moisture that spilled down her cheek. 'You give me life, Amelie.'

She stared into that strong face, now vivid with hope and, could it be, love?

'At least give me a chance to show you how it can be between us. Given time you might come to love me too.'

There was such yearning in his voice, such intensity in those glittering grey eyes, Amelie felt the last of her defences crumble. 'I do love you, Lambis. I've loved you so long.'

She barely got the words out before his mouth was on hers, his arms crushing her to him. She felt the fine tremors racking his body, the hard, quickened pulse of his heart and dared, for the first time, to believe.

His kiss was a wonder. Not urgent like his embrace, but tender, so tender awe rose within her.

To be so loved, and by such a man. Was it possible?

When he lifted his mouth, he pressed kisses over her face and she caught a broken stream of Greek that, despite the language difference, made her heart swell. For they were unmistakably words of love.

Amelie cupped her hands around his face and drew it

up so she could meet his eyes. They shone over-bright, in a way she'd never seen. 'I love you, Lambis Evangelos.'

'And I love you.' He paused, frowning. 'I don't even know your surname! Do royals even have surnames?'

Amelie stifled a laugh. 'They do. But I have a fancy to change mine.'

Instantly his hold tightened so much she had trouble drawing breath. But she didn't complain because the look on Lambis's face was one she'd never tire of.

'Could you bear to marry a commoner? A foreigner?'

'There's absolutely nothing common about you, my love. You're the light of my life.'

For long still moments they gazed into each other's eyes. 'Amelie Evangelos has a ring to it,' he said finally. 'If you're sure?'

'I've never been more sure of anything in my life.'

EPILOGUE

IT WAS A small wedding by royal standards, since Amelie and Lambis hadn't wanted to wait. Their eagerness had nothing to do with that last, unguarded morning in Greece when neither had thought about protection. Though more and more Lambis found himself speculating with excitement about the way his betrothed glowed.

Surveying today's crowd, he wondered how much more pomp and splendour a large royal wedding would manage.

The St Gallans had pulled out all stops for their beloved Princess. From the VIPs filling the great cathedral to the thousands gathered in the square outside, everyone wore finery, silks and jewels, dazzling uniforms or bright traditional cottons.

Flowers were everywhere. In huge arrangements and pinned to dresses and shirts, or carried ready to toss before the bride and groom as they left the cathedral.

Lambis swallowed, overcome by the familiar feeling that he didn't deserve this, didn't deserve Amelie. That he'd wake up and discover it a dream.

'Don't be scared, Lambis. I'll help you.' Beside him Sébastien's face was grave but his eyes sparkled. 'I know about important ceremonies.'

He did. Only a week ago he'd given his formal acceptance speech before parliament, on the same day Amelie had been made Regent.

'Thank you, Your Highness. I'm lucky to have you as my best man.'

The boy frowned. 'It's only Highness in public. *You* know that.' A small hand slipped into his. 'If you're scared, I'll hold your hand.'

Emotion blindsided Lambis as he looked down into those eyes so like his beloved Amelie's. It wasn't only Amelie he loved. The three of them were already a family. 'Thank you, Seb. I'd like that.'

A trumpet fanfare sounded high above and Lambis's heart quickened. Slowly he turned.

In the front row, with the new Prime Minister and other dignitaries, was Cat Dubois, eye-catching in green and almost as pretty as her half-sister. She smiled and winked. Beside her, King Alex of Bengaria looked ridiculously handsome in his dress uniform but his eyes were only for Cat, so Lambis had come to like his almost brother-in-law. Lambis's own friends were scattered in the front rows, either grinning at him or craning for a view of the bride.

The music changed to something softer yet jubilant and there was movement in the great arched doorway. Out of the light stepped two figures. One, upright despite her years, was Lady Enide, beaming as Lambis had never seen her.

Holding her arm was Amelie. Gorgeous Amelie, who regularly stole his breath with just a smile. Now, wearing a long traditional gown, she was stunning. The fitted bodice of heirloom lace accentuated her slim yet lush femininity. The spreading skirt and the glimpse he caught of a delicate train made her look like something out of a fairy story. She wore no veil, but had been persuaded to wear a tiara of brilliant diamonds, trembling and glittering as she moved. She'd joked that wearing it might lessen their height difference at the altar.

All that Lambis took in with one sweeping glance before his eyes locked on hers. Heat pounded through him, and pride. The Princess Regent of St Galla was utterly magnificent, and she was his. He grinned and watched her mouth twitch into an answering smile.

Then she was before him and everything else faded.

'No second thoughts?' He held her gaze.

'Never,' she whispered.

'Good.' Against all protocol he bent and nuzzled her ear. 'Because I'm never letting you go.' He grazed her cheek with his lips and straightened, satisfied now her eyes shone brighter than her diamonds.

Then he closed his left hand around hers, his right hand still grasping Sébastien's, and turned the three of them towards the waiting archbishop.

His love. His family. For ever.

* * * * *

LET'S TALK
Romance

For exclusive extracts, competitions
and special offers, find us online:

- **f**   facebook.com/millsandboon
- **🐦**   @MillsandBoon
- **📷**   @MillsandBoonUK

Get in touch on 01413 063232

For all the latest titles coming soon, visit
millsandboon.co.uk/nextmonth